Julie Anne Lindsey is a ... torn between the love ... toe-curling romance and chew-your-nails suspense. Now she gets to write both for Mills & Boon Heroes. When she's not creating new worlds, Julie can be found carpooling her three kids around northeastern Ohio and plotting with her shamelessly enabling friends. Winner of the Daphne du Maurier Award for Excellence in Mystery/Suspense, Julie is a member of International Thriller Writers, Romance Writers of America and Sisters in Crime. Learn more about Julie and her books at julieannelindsey.com

New York Times and *USA Today* bestselling, award-winning author **Lisa Childs** has written more than eighty-five novels. Published in twenty countries, she's also appeared on the Publishers Weekly, Barnes & Noble and Nielsen Top 100 bestseller lists. Lisa writes contemporary romance, romantic suspense, paranormal and women's fiction. She's a wife, mum, bonus mum, avid reader and less avid runner. Readers can reach her through Facebook or her website, lisachilds.com

Also by Julie Anne Lindsey

Beaumont Brothers Justice
Closing In On Clues

Heartland Heroes
SVU Surveillance
Protecting His Witness
Kentucky Crime Ring
Stay Hidden
Accidental Witness
To Catch a Killer

Also by Lisa Childs

Hotshot Heroes
Hotshot Hero Under Fire
Hotshot Hero on the Edge
Hotshot Heroes Under Threat
Hotshot Hero in Disguise

The Coltons of New York
Protecting Colton's Secret Daughters

Bachelor Bodyguards
Nanny Bodyguard
Single Mum's Bodyguard

Discover more at millsandboon.co.uk

ALWAYS WATCHING

JULIE ANNE LINDSEY

HOTSHOT HERO FOR THE HOLIDAYS

LISA CHILDS

MILLS & BOON

First Published in Great Britain 2023
by Mills & Boon, an imprint of HarperCollins*Publishers* Ltd
1 London Bridge Street, London, SE1 9GF

www.harpercollins.co.uk

HarperCollins*Publishers*
Macken House, 39/40 Mayor Street Upper,
Dublin 1, D01 C9W8, Ireland

Always Watching © 2023 Julie Anne Lindsey
Hotshot Hero for the Holidays © 2023 Lisa Childs

ISBN: 978-0-263-30750-4

1123

This book is produced from independently certified FSC™ paper to ensure responsible forest management.

For more information visit: www.harpercollins.co.uk/green

Printed and Bound in the UK using 100% Renewable Electricity at CPI Group (UK) Ltd, Croydon, CR0 4YY

ALWAYS WATCHING

JULIE ANNE LINDSEY

Chapter One

Scarlet Wills paced the empty living room of the moderately priced two-story home on Wentworth Drive, hands clutched before her, heart rate on the rise. Thanks to a recent overhaul of the outdated Coulter Realty website, house hunters could now request a walk-through of any available property by completing an online request form. Scarlet had assumed this new feature would lead to an increase in appointments, showings, clients and sales. She hadn't, however, considered the lack of personal interaction meant never really knowing who was on the other side of the requests.

The contact form required only a name, phone number or email address, and the home a buyer wanted to see. Half the time, Scarlet didn't know who she was meeting until they'd arrived. Other times, like this one, no one arrived at all.

She rolled her tight shoulders and leaned her head side to side, hoping to alleviate the painful tension gathered there. This was beginning to look like Scarlet's third no-show in the five weeks since Coulter Realty's website changes went live.

And, like the other times, she felt distinctly as if she was being watched.

She'd breathed easier when she'd first arrived, glad to see another agent already at the home with a couple of potential

buyers. Evan's familiar face and ready smile had been a welcome surprise. He'd even complimented her short-sleeved
navy blouse and the way she'd worn her pale blond hair in
a tight chignon. But now, he and his clients were leaving,
and she would be alone.

According to her watch, it was nearing six o'clock. Hardly
late, but the sky was already dark when she'd pulled her
compact SUV into the long driveway. Autumn in her small
coastal town of Marshal's Bluff, North Carolina, meant eating dinner after dark for more than a few months of the
year. And Wentworth Drive was heavily lined with trees,
the homes cloaked in shadows.

Ideally, Scarlet's potential client would've shown up before Evan left, but that, apparently, wasn't meant to be.

Now, she paced alone inside the eerily quiet structure,
watching helplessly as gooseflesh climbed the exposed skin
of her arms and Evan said goodbye to his clients on the lawn
outside the dining room's bay window.

He waved a hand as his clients drove away, and Scarlet willed him to return inside. But he dropped into his car
without another look in her, or the home's, direction.

A heavy, shuddered sigh escaped her as she checked her
watch again. Pat Cranston, the contact who'd reached out
to her, was officially more than fifteen minutes late, and
her nerves were beginning to fray.

She refocused on the scene outside the window. October
was once her favorite month of the year. The beauty that
came with changing leaves and blooming mums was un-
paralleled. And her small coastal town thrived on harvest
festivals, pumpkins patches and gratuitous, multicolored
gourds on every doorstep.

Currently, however, it was hard to see past the early sunsets and shorter days. There was too much darkness and there were too many shadows.

Too much paranoia, she thought, chastising herself for the continued fixation on something unseen. Something that likely wasn't even real.

Moving to Marshal's Bluff four years ago had been an easy decision. She'd grown up in a neighboring county, where her mother, Trina, was a successful real estate agent. And in small-town North Carolina, one Wills woman selling homes was enough. In Marshal's Bluff, she didn't have to compete with her mother for home sales, and no one referred to her as Trina's daughter. Two big bonuses of setting up shop an hour away.

She stared at her SUV for long minutes, debating on when she could reasonably call it a night.

Soon the grandfather clock in the foyer gonged, and Scarlet's green eyes widened in the reflection of the glass. It was definitely time to give up and head home. Pat hadn't responded to any of Scarlet's texts attempting to confirm the appointment, and twenty minutes was more than enough grace time on Scarlet's part. Besides, she had a bottle of merlot, an excellent book and set of new satin pajamas just waiting for her at home.

She began the process of shutting off lights at the back of the home and moving forward, careful not to leave any unnecessarily on, extra grateful Evan had turned off the upstairs and basement lights before he'd left. Scarlet double-checked the locks on all exterior doors, then paused to collect her business cards and flyers she'd printed with details on the home and local market.

It really was a pretty home. Only three years old and full of modern charm. High ceilings. White woodwork and trim. Fancy, geometric-shaped light fixtures and marble everywhere marble was acceptable. Not her style, but lovely nonetheless.

The rooms, though flawlessly designed, were mostly empty now, thanks to a relocation that had taken the family to another state more than a week prior. Another similarity, she realized, in the homes where she'd been stood up. The appointments were always made online. Always for a home with limited neighbors and a family no longer in the area.

Her phone buzzed, and she flinched before rolling her eyes belatedly at the overreaction. The name of another client living out of state appeared on her caller ID.

"Good evening, Mr. Perez," she said sweetly, thankful for the bit of normal in her current situation. "How are you tonight?"

"Not good," he griped. "You assured me you could sell my house in a week, and it's been a month."

Scarlet headed into the foyer, tugging her purse onto one shoulder. "No, Mr. Perez," she corrected pleasantly. "I said I could sell your house in a week at the listing price I suggested. I told you I would do my best to sell your home at the price you insisted upon."

"I don't see the difference."

She highly doubted that. He was a businessman after all. And she'd explained the difference to him more than once. *Still*, she reasoned, *it would be nice to keep him on the phone a little longer.* "Your price is significantly higher than I recommended, which limits the number of prospective buyers. That's not to say the property won't sell at your price. I'm confident you can get the amount you're asking, but it won't happen as quickly. We're going to have to wait for the right buyer."

She stepped into the night and locked the door behind her. A cool breeze whipped the fabric of her blouse, sending a sharp chill down her spine. "If you can be patient a little longer, I'll brainstorm new ideas for spreading the word on a larger scale."

He grunted. Not happy, but not angry. With Mr. Perez, she'd call that a win.

Scarlet stilled as motion caught her eyes in the reaching shadows along the roadside. She stared and squinted into the darkness, begging the vague, sweeping movement to grow into something recognizable and harmless. A neighbor walking a dog, or a few wandering deer.

"I don't have forever on this," Mr. Perez complained. "My family's move was expensive, and we can't afford to pay two mortgages long term."

Scarlet made a break for her little SUV, racing down the steps and across the black asphalt driveway toward her vehicle. The lights flashed when she pressed the unlock button on her key fob. "Give me two more weeks to find a buyer at this price," she suggested. "Then we can revisit the subject of pricing."

"All right," he agreed reluctantly. "Two more weeks. But I want it sold. At my price."

"Understood."

She slid behind the wheel and dropped the phone into her cup holder, enjoying the satisfying snap of her power locks as the door closed. A few frantic heartbeats later, she reversed carefully away from the dark, empty home.

She queued up an audiobook at the nearest intersection, obeying a stop sign. A pair of headlights flashed on behind her, pulling her attention to the blinding reflection in her rearview mirror. Unfounded tension coiled through her limbs. "It's just a car," she whispered, pressing the gas pedal once more.

It didn't make any sense to assume the car was intentionally following her, so she motored on, shaking away the nonsensical thoughts. For good measure, she pressed the gas pedal with purpose, putting extra space between the vehicles.

Her company's online request form for house showings popped back into her mind. As did her three no-shows. Was it ridiculous to wonder if those requests had been made by the same person? Even if the names and contact numbers were different?

Above her an abundance of stars twinkled in an inky sky. Behind her, the glow of headlights grew until she had to look away. The other vehicle erased the distance she'd gained then crept uncomfortably closer before matching her speed.

Scarlet's grip on the wheel tightened, and she worked a little harder to convince herself the car wasn't following her and the driver wasn't trying to unsettle her. Whoever was back there probably always drove like a jerk, too close and too fast. It had nothing to do with her. She accelerated anyway, reaching nearly sixty miles per hour in the stretch of road marked forty-five. She'd cheerfully accept the speeding ticket if it meant seeing a cop anytime soon. At least then the car behind her would be gone, and if she played her cards right, the officer might willingly follow her home for good measure.

She decided to drive into town to be safe instead of heading straight home. As the downtown lights came into view on the horizon, she made a mental plan. She'd drive into the busiest parking lot and call a friend. If the car followed, she'd call the police. If the car went away, she'd wait five minutes, then take a roundabout and convoluted path home to be sure no one else was behind her when she arrived.

Paranoid? Maybe. But at least she had a plan.

She pulled her phone into her lap for good measure. If

anything else happened, if the car hit her or the driver got out at the upcoming stoplight and moved in her direction, she would dial 911.

Her attention fixed on the rearview mirror as she slowed. The car picked up speed, and she braced for impact, until it suddenly peeled away, taking the exit ramp for the highway instead of stopping at the light.

Breath whooshed from her lungs, and a ragged laugh burst from her trembling lips. "Good grief," she whispered. "I'm losing it."

The other driver had simply been a jerk in a hurry to get somewhere, and she'd been prepared to call emergency services. For what? Tailgating? Clearly she needed a good night's sleep more than she'd thought.

When the light turned green, she drove straight home.

SCARLET SLID INTO bed that night with a glass of red wine and her favorite novel. A long, hot shower had washed the fear from her mind. "Just one chapter," she vowed. "Then it's bedtime."

She lifted the glass to her lips, and her cell phone vibrated, announcing an incoming message before she'd taken a single sip.

She didn't recognize the name, but that wasn't unusual. She'd printed her cell phone number on her business cards and shared it on the company website. Also, the new contact form pushed requests for home showings to their assigned agents via text.

She set her wine aside and raised the device reluctantly, hoping it was someone interested in the Perez property and willing to pay his asking price. She accessed the message with a swipe of her thumb.

Unknown: Nice seeing you again tonight

 Not an offer on the Perez place, but at least it was a wrong number.
 The phone buzzed a second time before she could return it to the nightstand.
 Scarlet stilled, eyes fixed on the four little words.

Unknown: Thanks for the showing

 Breath caught in her throat. Was it possible this too was a coincidence? A message meant for another agent? A confused buyer texting the wrong number from the website?
 Or was this the point where she could no longer tell herself there wasn't anything to worry about?
 A final text made her decision clear.

Unknown: CU soon

Chapter Two

Austin Beaumont leaned against the darkly tinted window at the front of his office, watching morning traffic creep along outside. His simple T-shirt and jeans reflected in the glass, as did the mug of coffee in his hands.

Every shop on the street had dragged out their autumn decor, complete with piles of pumpkins on hay bales and scarecrows with goofy grins. Even the private detective firm he owned with his older brother Dean had a bundle of cornstalks outside the door and a wreath of multicolored leaves with a Welcome sign. Not exactly the intimidating, highly serious, let us take your case vibe he imagined for his business, but there wasn't any use saying no to their mother. She insisted on making everyone comfortable.

She'd arrived with decor and a dinner invitation three weeks back. He'd declined the former and accepted the latter, but received both instead. The upside to his loss, he supposed, was the likelihood of making potential clients feel less on edge and more welcome. In his experience, when someone contacted a private investigator, they'd already made up their mind about getting help. He'd prefer his firm got the job.

A small SUV appeared in the curb lane, slowing by a fraction, then bouncing gently ahead. The warped brick streets of downtown Marshal's Bluff weren't built to handle the recent influx of vehicles. But a tax reduction for businesses had drawn the attention of several companies with ties to national corporations, which meant the town's population was experiencing a boom.

"What are you looking at?" Dean asked. The sounds of his brother's fingers on his keyboard underscored the words.

Austin peered over his shoulder at Dean's amused expression, and his partner stilled.

"What is it?"

"A dark SUV has passed here twice. It slows outside, then continues each time."

"What are you thinking?" Dean asked. "Lost commuter or possible trouble?"

Austin shrugged, maintaining the carefully disinterested facade he preferred to the tightly wound, barely suppressed, ball of tension he was. He'd perfected the act in the military and found it worked wonders in civilian life as well. People who looked cool and confident bred trust and put others at ease, exactly what a businessman wanted and what a calculating investigator needed. Being underestimated, or even overlooked, was often a golden ticket in his work.

He sipped his cooling coffee, which had become more of a prop than it had been when he'd poured it. Then flashed his brother a smug half smile. "Given the amount of criminals and cheating spouses we help bust every month, I'm hoping it's not the latter."

"That makes both of us," Dean said, doubling down on whatever he was up to on the computer.

The click-clacking of keys only lasted another minute before the office phone rang, and Dean's voice rose again. "Beaumont Investigations."

Austin returned the mug to his desk and grabbed a black ball cap from his bottom drawer.

The office was wide and rectangular, with two desks out front, bookshelves, chairs and other homey touches their mother had insisted upon. Two small conference rooms lined a corridor leading to the private employee section, where they kept a well-stocked kitchenette for long hours at the office and stakeouts.

Austin tugged the hat over his shaggy, sandy brown hair, reminding himself again to get a trim, and adjusted the bill low on his forehead. Then he strolled out the front door. He walked along the sidewalk to the end of the block and around the corner.

Brisk morning air swept along the streets between historic brick buildings, stirring up fallen leaves and setting a discarded plastic bag into flight.

He leaned casually against the wall at his back. The position of the building compared to the morning sun created a long shadow where he was likely to go unnoticed. He lowered his head, as if enraptured by his cell phone, just in case he caught a passerby's eye.

As predicted, the SUV reappeared, making its turn onto the street before him. And in a stroke of luck, the light at the corner turned red. Unfortunately, the same sun that had helped him blend into the shade, cast a bright glint off the vehicle's windshield, making it impossible to get a good look at the driver.

Austin murmured a curse and revised his plan. Better to know what he was dealing with than to be unprepared. He pushed away from the wall and strode into traffic, crossing the single narrow lane of moving cars with ease. He stopped on the yellow lines at the road's center and rapped his knuckles against the lightly tinted driver's-side window.

Clouds passed over the brilliant North Carolina sun, removing the glare from the glass and enabling him to get his first look at the driver, just as she screamed.

His hands flipped up in innocence, and he took in the shock and horror on the woman's beautiful face. Her pale green eyes flashed with fear, then red-hot anger.

"I'm calling the police!" she yelled, turning her phone to face him as if snapping a picture.

Austin reared back, stunned and a little amused, but earning a honk from an oncoming car. He raised a hand in apology to the vehicle, then returned to the double yellow lines.

When his eyes met hers again, the woman pointed pepper spray at her closed window, cell phone at her ear.

A hearty laugh rumbled unexpectedly from his chest, opening his lips into a wide smile. The light changed, and the SUV rolled away. He waited for a break in traffic then jogged back to the sidewalk at his first opportunity.

He took a minute to remove his hat and run a hand through his hair before securing the cap once more. And another minute to press back the smile still twisting the corners of his mouth.

"I am clearly Marshal Bluff's top investigator," he muttered, shaking his head as he made his way around the corner. Dean would never let him live this one down if he told him what had happened, and the story was too ridiculous not to share.

Instead of saving their office from an attack by a disgruntled criminal or cheater looking for retribution, he'd scared some poor, obviously rattled woman half to death, and nearly gotten a face full of pepper spray for his trouble.

With a little luck, she wouldn't panic and send that photo to the local police station. For starters, that would be terrible for business. And on a personal note, his younger brother, and Marshal's Bluff detective, Finn would surely print and hang the image on every telephone pole between Main Street and the coast.

He'd been certain the vehicle was paying special interest to the office as it passed. But maybe the driver really was lost, and he was losing his touch. He normally sensed trouble from a mile away, sometimes before the person who'd eventually cause the issue even knew that was the path they were on.

He shook out his hands, which had balled uncharacteristically into fists, curled by the tension and distaste of such a total error. He wouldn't blame her if she did call the police. A stranger had approached her in traffic. A guttural sound rumbled low in his chest as Beaumont Investigations came into view. Time to pull it together and focus on the full day he had ahead of him. Vandalism investigations. A stolen stallion worth more than his truck. An allegation of hidden funds amidst a divorce dispute. And those were the tip of the iceberg.

Hopefully the call Dean had taken before Austin went outside to confront an unsuspecting woman was information on one of those cases. Anything to set his day back on course.

A gust of coffee-scented air rushed out to greet him as he pulled open the glass office door. His mother's festive leaf wreath swung wildly under the force.

The SUV driver's face flashed into his mind unbidden. She'd been angry and afraid, but beautiful, with the soft green eyes and plush pink lips of an angel. Maybe it was the morning he was having, or the way his instinctual sense of dread refused to let up, but he couldn't help wondering what had upset her. Why had she been circling the block?

Probably a marital squabble, he told himself. Women

who looked like that didn't stay single. Even if she had the personality of a viper. Though he doubted that was true. She'd seemed vulnerable. And unnaturally quick to raise her pepper spray. Everyone else in town greeted neighbors, and strangers, with a smile and a nod.

He rubbed a hand against the back of his neck and gave one last glance through the window before meeting Dean's curious stare.

"Everything okay?"

"Yep." Austin fell onto his desk chair as Dean rose from his.

"Good." He tugged on his brown leather coat and reached for his cell phone and keys. "Finn called. He's got some information on my missing person's case. I'm headed to the police station to check it out."

Austin nodded, attention fixed on his now tepid coffee. "That was Finn on the phone when I left?" He stretched upright again, in need of caffeine and something to busy his hands.

"No, that was a potential new client, which is why it's good there isn't a disgruntled nut casing this place. I have to take off, and you can handle the client. I've already opened a file and logged the basic information. It's in the shared drive. Give it a read before she gets here."

Austin shut his eyes for a long beat to stop them from rolling. This was hardly his first rodeo, yet something about the older brothers in his family made them think the younger brothers always needed help. Guidance. Or pointers. It wasn't personal, but it was habitual, and he made another mental note not to do the same to Finn and Lincoln. Besides, Dean's sage advice to be prepared was Scouts and cowboy 101. Austin had passed those life courses with gold stars years ago.

He forced himself to refocus on the more important information Big Brother failed to provide. "When's this woman getting here?" And did he have time to pour a fresh cup of coffee? "What's her name and problem?"

"Scarlet Wills, twenty-seven, unmarried, lives alone. Thinks she's being followed," Dean said, narrowing his eyes. "Read the file."

Austin frowned and headed for the coffee maker.

His brother moved toward the door.

The bell dinged, and Dean spoke again, but he didn't say goodbye.

"Ms. Wills?"

Great. She was already there. Austin's head fell forward on an exhale, and he straightened with resolve. No hot coffee for him then.

He forced a polite expression and turned back toward his desk as Dean shook the newcomer's hand.

"I'm Dean Beaumont. This is my brother and business partner, Austin Beaumont. He'll be meeting with you today and getting a feel for your situation. He's military trained, the middle-born of five rowdy brothers and an Eagle Scout. Not to mention he makes a mean cup of joe. You've never been in better hands, I assure you."

Dean's smile was warm and charming as he did his best to break the ice and put Ms. Wills at ease before walking out.

But her wide green eyes were already fixed on him in recognition, and Austin blew out a long, defeated breath. Hopefully the gorgeous blonde before him, the one he'd unintentionally startled in her SUV, would give him a chance to explain before making use of that pepper spray, wherever it was now.

He was definitely going to need that coffee.

Chapter Three

Scarlet froze as Dean Beaumont, the man she'd spoken to on the phone, walked away. Leaving her with his brooding brother. Dean had been kind and polite in person, and for a moment, the mounting tension inside her had faded. It probably helped that he was distractingly handsome. Unfortunately, she never went for the happy, congenial sort. One of her many flaws. Just ask her mother.

Not to ruin her perfect record of bad luck with men, she'd managed to threaten the private detective in front of her with pepper spray. The same man whose help she needed to figure out if there really was a stalker to worry about. Worse? Austin Beaumont looked exactly like the kind of guy she'd cheerfully hitch her wagon to, then get burned.

She scanned the room as he assessed her, taking the opportunity to gather her thoughts and resolve. The office was nicely decorated, with bookshelves and framed photos. Two mahogany desks faced the large front window and glass door, each with a leather executive chair behind it and two padded armchairs before it. The air was warm and smelled of delectable cologne and coffee.

"Ms. Wills," he said finally, tossing his black ball cap onto a shelf and running a hand through his shaggy brown hair. The soft locks fell over his forehead as he moved forward with an outstretched arm.

Manners lifted her hand to his before her brain had made the conscious decision to do so. "Please, call me Scarlet."

The air thickened and tingled between them as his calloused palm curled over hers. The heat from his touch sent sparks of attraction up her arms and into her chest.

He was unfairly handsome without his hat to shield his features, but not at all like his brother. Dean had been light and jovial. Austin had an air of danger around him. His dark, hooded gaze should've felt more like a warning than an invitation.

"I should apologize for frightening you earlier," he said.

Not actually apologizing, she noted and released his hand with some mental effort.

"And I should apologize for threatening you."

His lips quirked in amusement, without quite forming a smile. "Can I get you a cup of coffee?"

"Please."

"You can have a seat, if you'd like." He motioned to the desk on her left, then moved into a narrow hallway beyond the outer office where she stood. "I won't be a minute."

Unnerved by a torrent of emotions, from fear and hope to attraction and anxiety, she remained fixed in place. What did she hope would happen today? What would the PI say about her concerns? She certainly didn't want her fears confirmed, but hearing the danger was all in her imagination didn't seem ideal either. What would that mean about the state of her emotional health?

She bypassed the desk and chairs for a look at the bookshelves and photos. Images of the men she'd just met were accompanied by a collection of other friendly faces. A group shot included the PIs and three other men, roughly the same ages, each with a dauntingly attractive face. An older couple shared an embrace in the background. The Beaumont family?

Smaller frames featured individuals that looked nothing alike. All ages, with a variety of hair and eye colors and skin in every tone from ivory to ebony.

The top shelf held a shadow box with a Purple Heart medal and a dozen images of men in military uniforms or fatigues. A younger version of Austin leaned against a tank. Sweat had applied the cotton of his plain white T-shirt to every perfect muscle and plane of his chest like a sticker. Tan and brown camouflage-patterned pants and black boots completed the ensemble. A sheen of sweat was visible on his brow.

"Cream or sugar?" a low male voice asked, snapping Scarlet back to the moment.

She spun to find Austin barely three feet away, steam rising from the mug in each hand.

"No. Thank you."

He set the drinks on the desk and took a seat. "See anything interesting?"

"Just looking at all these faces," she said, demanding her traitorous gaze not return to the lucky white T-shirt. "You're from a military family?"

"I am."

"Is the Purple Heart yours?" Her voice cracked unexpectedly, and she cleared her throat. Something about the idea of Austin being wounded pressed the air from her lungs.

"No. That belongs to my youngest brother. He had it rough for a while and wasn't interested in keeping the medal around."

"But you were?"

Austin's brows lifted by a fraction, probably making a

note of her nosiness. "I think that medal is a symbol of his survival. Not everyone who earns one lives to see it. I plan to honor and protect it until he's ready to take it back."

She wet her lips and swallowed. This man had heart. If the photos weren't enough to make things crystal clear, his speech had driven the message home. Austin Beaumont had served his country, and he clearly loved his family. Her crush on him was inevitable now. "And all these framed photos of children…" She looked at the images again. All so vastly different. Missing persons he and his brother helped locate? "Kids you helped bring home?"

"I'm afraid that credit goes to my folks," he said. "Those are my brothers and sisters."

Her smile sprouted. "Really? All of them?"

Austin rose and joined her at the bookshelves. "My parents run a ranch where they help troubled young people. They also foster and adopt. Most of these are grown now." He tipped his head toward the photos. "Some were adopted by other families, others aged out of the system, but for at least a little while they were raised by my folks. That makes them siblings for the long haul in my book."

A new warmth spread through her chest, and she turned to him. "Family dinners must be interesting."

"You have no idea."

She didn't, but she would love to. "There are five boys in your immediate family. How many were adopted?"

"Two," he said, stretching a hand in the direction of his desk. "We should get started."

"Oh." She'd nearly forgotten why she was there. "Right."

He hadn't clarified which of his brothers had been adopted, or if he was one of them, but it was clear that didn't matter.

Her heart gave another thud of appreciation.

She returned to the gray armchair in front of his desk. She'd always dreamed of having siblings, but it must've been hard to watch them come and go.

Austin sipped his coffee then moved the wireless mouse in a quick circle, waking up the computer. A moment later, he typed something with the keyboard. "Dean opened a file for you. I'm going to add additional information as we talk."

"Okay." Scarlet rested her hands in her lap, kneading her fingers to stall her nerves. "I'm hoping I'll laugh about this later," she said, planting both feet against the floor. She cursed the unforgiving pencil skirt she'd chosen for the day, unable to cross her legs and bounce her knee as she wanted. The material was too snug and short to make the move smoothly, and a second-rate flashing would be nearly as humiliating as having threatened the man with her pepper spray.

His trained gaze slid over her features and hair, along the length of her neck and torso to her hands. Probably sensing her thoughts and tension. "There's no need to be nervous. You're the one with the weapon."

A soft, unexpected snort of laughter broke on her lips, and her cheeks heated. "I guess you really can read my mind."

"Is that what you think?"

"Don't you know?"

The skin at the corners of his eyes crinkled with mischief, and his lips formed a lazy half smile.

She pushed the moment of lightness aside and hoped her imagined stalker wasn't any more real than mind reading. "I should probably start from the beginning."

She told the story as well as possible with the intensity of Austin's gaze on her, starting with an explanation of the company's website upgrade and her many calls to tech support, because attempting to navigate the system's changes was a low point in her recent career. She moved on to describe the three requests for home showings that had resulted in no-shows and carefully outlined the similarities. She included the homes' locations and absent owners. For her grand finale, she told him about the texts.

"May I see the messages?" he asked.

Scarlet unearthed the phone from her structured leather handbag and unlocked it with her fingerprint before accessing the texts. "The number doesn't match the one given on the contact form from last night. I checked as soon as the shock passed. It also doesn't match the number used for either of the other appointments when no one showed. Which is why I hope I'm overthinking all this."

"Burner phones are cheap and widely available." Austin took the device. His expression hardened as he read the messages but cleared before he raised his eyes to hers once more. "I'd like to take screenshots as evidence."

"Of course." Scarlet nodded woodenly and cringed inwardly at his word choice. Evidence made it sound as if he believed there was enough reason to open a case. As if she was already in the midst of a criminal investigation. "Do you really think someone would go to all that trouble to upset me? Using multiple numbers and sending me on three goose chases just to watch me roam around empty homes?"

Austin caught her in his dark gaze once more, jaw set and expression firm. "What do your instincts say?"

She blew out a slow sigh, deflating against the chair's backrest. She wouldn't be in his office if she could've found a way to let the suspicions go on her own.

"Instincts are rarely wrong," he said, apparently reading the answer in her body language. "People ignore their guts too often, especially women who tend to be more concerned about manners than men. Statistically you're more likely to be in danger of attack or abduction than I am and less likely to be able to fight off your attacker. That alone is reason not to take chances." He tapped the screen a few times then set her phone on his desk between them. "I would encourage you to walk away from anyone and any situation that makes you feel uncomfortable, even if you aren't sure why. Just turn around and leave. As far as these contact forms go, I'd tell your company it's an unsafe practice and you aren't showing homes to anyone else you don't meet in advance, at least by phone. Whatever you need to feel safe."

Scarlet considered his words and her situation for a moment, a new concern itching in her mind. "The contact form has only been in effect for five weeks. If someone is doing this, could they have been one of the first buyers I met through the site, then used the same method to make additional appointments?"

Austin leaned forward on his desk, appearing to weigh his response before giving it. "It's possible someone was watching you before the website changed, and once they realized the new contact form gave them direct access to you, they began to take advantage. He might even see these appointments as dates. Or think you're buying a house together."

Her stomach plummeted and the downy hairs on her arms and neck rose to attention. "You think someone could've been following me, watching me, for more than five weeks?"

"I think anything is possible," he said. "And if last night was the first time he's contacted you afterward, I think he's escalating."

Her mouth opened, and she snapped it shut. Escalating. There was another word she didn't like. A word that made her blood run cold.

"Is there anything else?" he asked. "Even if it's small, it

could matter. Even things from before the website gained a request form? Things you dismissed at the time that might look more pointed now."

She shook her head, prepared to insist nothing else had happened, outside the texts and no-shows. Then something flashed back to mind. "Someone followed me last night when I left the home on Wentworth." She told the story slowly and in detail, watching Austin carefully for a reaction.

His jaw clenched and released several times before he spoke. "Can you describe the car?"

"Not really. It was dark, and I was shaken. I'm sure it was a car though, not a truck or SUV. Black or another dark color, I think. With those bluish headlights."

"That's good," he said, voice soothing and certain. "All those details will help if we come to need them."

Her tension eased by a fragment. She wasn't a confirmed victim yet, but if her fears did come true, she wanted to be useful.

"I'd like to look into this further," he said. "I have some things to tie up and off-load this morning, but I want to get started as soon as possible."

"Tomorrow?" she asked, both thankful and concerned by his decision to take her case.

"I was thinking I could meet you at your office after work today. Maybe interview your coworkers. Meanwhile, I'll check out the company website and do a little reconnaissance at the homes where you felt watched. Can you text me those addresses?" He pulled a sleek black business card from a holder on his desk and slid it in her direction.

She struggled to regain her breath as the reality of things attempted to flatten her to the chair. "You want to meet my coworkers?" She plucked the card from the desk and accepted her cell phone when he passed that to her as well.

"I do, but we can play that however works best for you. Tomorrow, I'd like to begin shadowing you for a day or two. I'll stay in the background. You won't even notice I'm there once we start."

Scarlet highly doubted that. In fact, now that they'd met, she was sure she'd notice him in a stadium full of people. And wasn't one person following her enough? "What do I tell people? My clients?"

He smiled warmly, the picture of calm.

She on the other hand was sure he could hear her erratic heartbeat across the space between them.

"You could tell clients I'm a trainee, if that helps. I'll even wear a suit."

Her mind went fuzzy at the thought of him in dress clothes, the crisp white sleeves of his shirt rolled up to his elbows. "And my coworkers?" she croaked, throat suddenly parched. "I don't want them to know what I'm worried about until I'm sure there's reason for concern."

"Long-lost cousin," he suggested. "New boyfriend? Just let me know what feels right to you."

She swallowed audibly and wished for a bottle of iced water instead of cooling coffee. She took an eager sip anyway. "And your rate?"

"No charge until I know there's a case. We can talk more about it in a day or two."

Scarlet rose and slid her purse strap over one shoulder. "I guess I'll see you tonight. Six o'clock at the Coulter Realty office?"

"I'll be there." Austin walked her to the door and held it open as she passed.

When she buckled into her SUV across the street, he

was still watching, and she tried not to stare. His tan, taut body leaned against the exterior wall. Autumn wind ruffled his hair.

Scarlet released a shaky breath and eased away from the curb, feeling the weight of his gaze on her as she passed.

If suspicions of a stalker weren't her complete undoing, the red-hot attraction she'd felt for Austin Beaumont would be.

Chapter Four

Scarlet drove to work feeling significantly lighter than she had when she'd left home, but also a little flushed. Austin Beaumont had put her mind at ease on the potential stalker situation and given her something altogether different to think about until she saw him again. He'd been a consummate professional in his speech and interactions, but something in his eyes had felt downright inviting. An unspoken dare or challenge.

Or maybe she was projecting.

Regardless, it'd been a long time since she'd experienced a physical reaction while speaking to a man. Yet, as she sat in that PI office, her heart had raced and her thighs had clenched. Her mind had even begun to wonder if he was as capable in private matters as he seemed to be in professional ones. More, what would his lips feel like on hers? What did he taste like? And was he open to entertaining her curiosity?

All thoughts she never had. Clearly the recent paranoia was affecting her mind.

She kept an eye on her rearview mirror as she made her way along familiar downtown streets toward the Coulter Realty offices. No one appeared to be following her, but she still breathed easier when she pulled into the lot behind a coworker. Now she wouldn't have to cross the lot alone.

Lydia Stevens, a newer and younger agent who'd grown up in Marshal's Bluff, climbed out with a grin. A collection of bags hung from her fingertips. Her brown hair was curled into thick beachy waves and hanging loose over her shoulders. The fitted red dress she wore emphasized her runner's figure, and an oversize cream-colored cardigan hung off her narrow frame. She hiked a black laptop bag and a designer purse onto one shoulder then slid a canvas tote and thermal lunch bag into her opposite hand.

Considering the tennis shoes on her feet, Scarlet guessed the canvas tote held Lydia's high heels for appointments. From experience she knew the lunch bag contained a reusable water bottle, a lidded bowl of sliced veggies and a ready-made smoothie or protein shake.

Scarlet admired the ambition, but she stuck with sensible two-inch pumps she could wear comfortably all day. And she ordered lunch on the go, when she had time to eat at all.

Lydia waved as she waited for Scarlet to park and join her. "Hey, you! How was the showing last night? Did you make another sale?"

"No. It was another no-show. My third in five weeks." She considered telling Lydia more about her suspicions and her visit with the local PI, but decided to wait until she knew more. Thinking she had a stalker if she didn't would just make her sound loopy. And telling someone else about her fears would make it all feel more real. Scarlet didn't want either of those things to happen, so she refreshed her smile and locked the car behind her.

Lydia pushed out her bottom lip. "Bummer. So you're still having trouble with the requests from the contact form?"

"Apparently. Have you had any issues?"

"No." Lydia followed her to the office door. "But I don't get a lot of requests that way yet. I'm still too new. I think the system checks senior agents' calendars first. So I only get the lead if everyone else is busy."

Scarlet paused to open and hold the door for her colleague to pass. "Do you ever get appointments through the website?"

"Only a few. Which is why I'm upping my social media game. I'm going to target potential clients by connecting with first-time home buyers, young couples and single career folk."

"Sounds like a plan," Scarlet said, making her way to her desk. She had to get something similar in motion to sell the Perez house before Mr. Perez pulled it from her listings.

A framed photo of Scarlet and her mother greeted her as usual, pulling a more authentic smile across her lips. In the image, the Wills women stood arm in arm beside a SOLD sign and in front of a big white farmhouse. Scarlet had just gotten her real estate license and, under her mom's guidance and tutelage, sold her first property at above the asking price. It was a moment worthy of its ornate silver frame.

She briefly considered calling her mom to tell her about the strange situation she might be in, but Scarlet also hated to upset her without reason. Having a mom for a best friend was wonderful but complicated. She wanted to share everything with her, but occasionally the stories needed editing. And others just weren't Mom appropriate. She couldn't even properly gush about the handsome man she'd met today because of his ties to the potential stalker.

Austin's lean, lithe body flashed back into mind, his dark eyes on her, a wicked half grin on his lips. It was enough to make her want to clutch her pearls, if only she'd been wearing them.

"I bet he has killer abs," she whispered to herself, setting up her laptop for the day.

"Who?" Lydia appeared with her breakfast protein shake, brows arched high.

Scarlet's face heated.

"Oh. You're turning red." Lydia pulled up a chair and sat, crossing her legs and leaning forward. "This is going to be good. Please dish. I love abs."

Scarlet laughed. "I didn't mean to say that out loud."

"But you did. So, let's discuss."

"I met a guy this morning," she admitted reluctantly. "He was...really nice."

Actually, she realized, *this is the perfect setup to our cover story.*

Lydia took a long swig from her shaker and waited for more.

"His name is Austin Beaumont, and he might stop by the office later. If you're here I'll introduce you."

Lydia's jaw nearly unhinged. "No. Way."

Scarlet wrinkled her nose at the strange look of shock on the other woman's face. "You don't want to meet him?"

"Scarlet," she said flatly. "You enormous out-of-towner." The younger agent spun in a dramatic circle on her chair.

"You know I've been here for four years—"

"He's a Beaumont. Of course I want to meet him. The Beaumont brothers are a main component in every Marshal's Bluff woman under fifty's secret fantasy life. And if they're being honest, probably plenty of the men too. The brothers are all older than me, but I've grown up hearing all about them. They're practically legendary. My grandmama says their dad and his brothers were the same way. The one called Dean got engaged last summer and broke a bunch of hearts."

Seeing one of the PIs taken off the market certainly would

be heartbreaking, but not the brother Lydia had mentioned. "I met Dean today too."

Lydia threw up her hands. "Absolutely unfair. You know, that family did a calendar once to raise money for a local farmer who was losing his land. The photographer volunteered her services, and they sold enough calendars to save the farm and hire a crew for harvest."

Also not surprising. But a real missed opportunity. Scarlet would've cheerfully bought three copies of that calendar. One for her office, another for home and one for her mama, who was over fifty, but no one with any amount of good sense would ever mention it.

"How exactly did you meet them before work?" Lydia pressed.

A very good question. Scarlet considered her words. "Austin approached me on the street downtown."

Lydia's eyes bulged. "He just walked right up to you?"

"Yeah." She cringed, recalling him approaching her SUV in traffic. "He startled me, so I threatened to pepper spray him and call the police."

Lydia roared with laughter.

"After we got that misunderstanding sorted, he asked to see me again."

"Wow. Some people have all the luck," Lydia said.

True, though Scarlet had never thought of herself as that person.

Her laptop finished booting up, and she navigated to her email. The number of messages in her inbox knocked her back to reality. "I guess I'd better get busy."

Lydia rose and returned her chair to the empty desk beside her. "Fine, but I'm jealous. Of the guy and the inbox. One day my email will be full," she said, striding to her work space. "Until then, it's time for me to launch the social media campaign of my life."

Scarlet opened the newest email from Mr. Perez, following up on their chat by phone the previous night. He wanted a detailed plan for reaching more potential buyers with information on his property, and something in writing about selling the listing, at his price, in the next two weeks.

She chose to be thankful this was an email and not another phone call.

From there, the correspondences got easier. Past clients planning another move. Referral clients looking for advice. A few showing requests from families and couples she was already working with to find their new home. And three newly accepted offers, which meant a string of phone calls to banks and title agencies after lunch.

By three o'clock, her inbox was looking manageable, and her stomach was filling with butterflies. Just a few more hours before Austin showed up at her office.

An incoming message drew her thoughts back to work. Another showing request sent through the website's online contact form. She opened the email with trepidation and breathed easier to see a woman's name instead of a man's. Better still, the prospective client wanted to see the Perez home. The day just kept getting better.

"Lydia?" Scarlet said, checking the time and responding quickly to the request. "I've got a showing at the Perez home in forty-five minutes. I'm going to head out there now so I can set up before the potential buyer arrives. I want to grab some cookies from the bakery and fresh flowers from the florist. I should be back by six, but if Austin beats me here, will you let him know I won't be long?"

Her coworker smiled. "I will gladly regale him with my many wondrous stories of working with Scarlet Wills."

"I think offering him a bottle of water and a seat will be enough," she said, moving a little more quickly. "But since you said that, I'll definitely be back by six."

Lydia laughed as Scarlet made her exit.

The lines at the florist and bakery were short, and the drive to the Perez home was rural, so she easily avoided traffic.

The home was situated on multiple acres and set back from the road by about two hundred feet. A curving black ribbon of asphalt wound through a lush green lawn and past numerous mature oaks to a turnaround driveway outside the large two-story estate. The annual lawn and landscaping maintenance budget alone was more than Scarlet would make on the sale, and her cut of the asking price was more than some folks made in a year. Motivation to sell was high for more reasons than the owner's persistence.

She climbed out of the car, her purse on one shoulder, cell phone, car keys and a bag with cookies in one hand. A bouquet of fresh-cut flowers rested in the crook of the opposite arm. She closed the door with a flick of one hip and took a moment to admire the estate.

It was nearing five o'clock, making this the perfect time for a showing. There was still enough daylight for a potential buyer to appreciate the exterior beauty on their way inside, and by the time they headed home, an array of auto-timed landscaping lights would illuminate the home and driveway, showcasing the equally brilliant curb appeal by night.

She took two steps before something in the air seemed to change. The soft crack and grind of pebbles underfoot was her only indication she wasn't alone before an arm snaked around her middle and a gloved hand covered her mouth.

Scarlet's scream was squelched by the band of leather crushing her lips against her teeth. Air rushed from her lungs, pressed out by an unyielding grip across her center. The bag of cookies and fresh bouquet crashed to the ground at her feet. She jerked and kicked, fighting uselessly against an unseen attacker.

Hot, sticky breath blew across her temple and cheek. The scratch of his unshaven face scraped against her ear. "Stop fighting, Scarlet," he warned in a low, gravelly whisper. "I'm here to let you know I saw what you did this morning, and I won't tolerate you seeing him again." The rage behind the whisper stilled her limbs. "We can't be happy together if you won't be faithful. Understand?"

She nodded quickly, adapting as he changed the scenario. She'd expected to be dragged off somewhere and killed. Maybe there was hope after all. A warning meant a second chance. Didn't it?

That was all she needed.

"Good," he said, loosening his grip slightly. "Now, I'm sorry to do this, but you have to be punished. Otherwise you might forget we had this little talk or think you can try me again. You can't."

"No. No, no, no, no," she murmured against the glove. "I'm sorry. I'm sorry."

"Shh. This is going to hurt me more than it hurts you."

Scarlet's limbs tightened, and she braced for what would come next.

His hand left her mouth, and for one beat of her heart, she was free.

Then ten long angry fingers curved around her throat and squeezed.

Chapter Five

Austin wiped the back of one hand across his brow and adjusted the brim on his baseball cap to better block the sun. He'd scrambled to off-load as much of his work as possible over the past few hours, clearing his schedule to better focus on Scarlet's case. He now owed multiple favors to Dean, and had a mere hour from meeting with his gorgeous new client again, he was baling hay at the family ranch and hoping his other brother Lincoln would agree to one little thing. "So, you'll handle it?"

Lincoln made a noncommittal sound.

Austin stifled the urge to toss the next bale at his brother.

There wouldn't be time to go home and shower thanks to this delay. He'd have to show up at the Coulter Realty office looking and smelling like someone who'd just filled the bed of a pickup truck with hay. Twice. He was on a real roll with bad impressions today.

"Lincoln," Austin pressed. "Just tell me you'll do it, so I can meet with the new client."

His brother sighed. "You're calling this a reconnaissance to make it sound more appealing, but I'll actually be sitting in my truck alone all night staring at a dark house and trying to stay awake. I can't even drink coffee to pass the time, because then I'd need a restroom, and I can't leave."

"But it's easy money," Austin said. "And it pays in cash."

"I don't need cash."

Austin tugged the work gloves from his hands and frowned. He always forgot that about his brother. Being an officer in the military for several years, most of which he'd spent deployed, had paid him well. And without actual expenses, the money had piled up. Then, he'd come home to reinvent himself as a hermit, working full-time for the ranch. Considering his earn-to-spend ratio and general lifestyle choices, Lincoln wasn't money motivated.

He eyeballed his brother—tan and fit, bearded face and overgrown hair. The picture of a guy with nowhere to be and zero cares to give. Very few things interested him. One was solitude and the other was a blonde. "No one said you had to go alone. Take a friend."

Lincoln's jaw set, and his gaze swept over the stables, likely thinking of the young manager, Josie.

"And if you do this," Austin added, sweetening the pot before he said no. "I won't ask you for another favor for a month."

That raised one of Lincoln's eyebrows and snapped his attention back to Austin. "Six months."

"Two."

"Four."

Austin offered a bland expression. "I can say four, but we both know I'd be lying."

Lincoln rubbed a hand over the back of his neck. "Yeah, all right."

It wasn't abundantly clear if that was an acceptance of the offer or the fact that Austin would definitely need another favor in the next two months, not four, but he took it. "Thank you." Then he checked his watch again. "I might even have time to shower if I do it here instead of running home. And if I borrow some of your clothes."

Lincoln closed the tailgate and leaned against the old farm truck. "What's mine is yours, I guess." He scanned Austin, looking more interested than he had so far. "Do you think there's a real threat for this lady? Or do you just like her?"

"Both," he admitted. "She's beautiful. Successful. Smart. I looked her up online after she left the office. Based on her social media profiles, she doesn't seem to do a lot outside of work. Her personal posts are limited. The accounts for business are another story. I'm guessing that's how she attracted whoever's following her. I'd like to think she's being overly cautious, but if she's concerned enough to meet with a private investigator, there's almost always a problem."

"And you like her."

Austin looked over his shoulder toward their parents' home on instinct. "So far there's nothing not to like. Don't bring it up to Mama. I just met this woman. She's going to be a client. Not an addition to the family."

Lincoln grinned. "That's not what Mama would say."

The sound of tires on gravel pulled their attention to an approaching truck. Their youngest brother, Finn, waved an arm through the open window.

Austin moved in the truck's direction, a sensation of unease rolling down his spine. "Were you expecting him?"

"Yeah." Lincoln kept pace at his side. "One of the new boarders was involved in some petty crimes. The ranch took responsibility for her until the trial. Finn's been around every day or so to check in."

Finn parked beside Austin, then met his brothers halfway across the lawn. "Didn't expect to see you here." He adjusted the dark sunglasses over his eyes. The shiny detective badge on his belt announced his authority, even if he looked far too young for the role.

"I was just here asking for favors," Austin said.

Lincoln grunted. "He pawned his current work onto me so he can meet with some cute new client."

Finn turned widened eyes on Austin. "How'd you manage that?"

"I'm not allowed to ask him for anything else for a month."

"Two," Lincoln corrected.

Finn laughed. "Solitude beats cash, huh?"

"Solitude is priceless."

"Tell me about the cute new client," Finn said, still grinning.

Austin rolled his eyes and explained the situation with Scarlet Wills, then tipped his head toward the house. "I'm going to hit the shower here and try not to be too late reaching her office."

Finn looked up from his phone. He'd started scrolling the minute Austin had given Scarlet's name. "She's got a big web presence. Thousands of followers. If she's picked up a stalker, you're going to have your work cut out for you. She probably talks to a hundred people every week. Buyers, sellers, security companies, maintenance companies, landscapers, home stagers… Could be anyone."

"I'm aware." He'd already made lists to address categorically at their meeting tonight. "This is not my first rodeo," Austin reminded him.

Finn flipped up his palms in innocence. "You're right. You've got this. But let me know if you need an assist."

Austin took a few backward steps in the direction of the farmhouse. "Sounds good. I've got to get moving. I'm officially late."

"You're always late," his brothers called behind him.

They weren't wrong, but it was something he was working on.

Twenty minutes later, he'd showered and dressed in a new T-shirt and jeans from Lincoln's closet. Nice ones that Dean had purchased at Christmas, and Lincoln had promptly stashed in his closet without even removing the tags. Dean liked nice stuff. Lincoln found that entertaining.

Austin was glad for both truths, because now he didn't have to dress in Lincoln's worn-out and holey favorites. He ran a hand through wet hair as he made his way onto the porch.

Finn nearly knocked him down on the steps, more focused on his phone than where he was going.

"Whoa!" Austin sidestepped, barely avoiding the collision. "Where's the fire?"

His brother's brows were gathered low when he lifted his gaze. "The Realtor you're meeting with—Scarlet Wills—"

The chill he'd felt earlier returned to Austin's skin. "Yeah?"

"She's at the ER. Come on. I'll drive."

Tension coiled through Austin's limbs, and he shot a hand out to catch his brother's elbow. "What happened?"

"Someone attacked her this afternoon. Stole her phone, purse and car keys. She managed to get into her car and start it before the key fob was out of range. She locked the doors and used her onboard system to call for help. She was unconscious when they arrived. She had your card in her hand."

Austin was in motion, truck keys in hand. "I'll follow you. Use your lights."

Finn kept pace, making a run for his truck.

Scarlet had been hurt while Austin had bantered with his

brothers. And her attacker had taken everything he needed to find or reach her anywhere she went. Which meant Austin had severely dropped the ball.

That wouldn't happen again.

Chapter Six

Scarlet woke with the sunrise the next morning. She'd been admitted at the hospital for observation after being rescued, treated for her injuries and given a battery of tests. Her head, neck and shoulders screamed with each small movement, but she was glad for the daylight creeping across her windowsill. It'd been a long night of interruptions and drug-hazed nightmares.

Thankfully, aside from being unprecedentedly sore and permanently traumatized, she was more or less fine.

She blinked against the reaching shafts of amber and apricot light and turned to stare into the even brighter hallway. A groan escaped her lips and the sound elicited fresh pain from her tender throat. Memories of the attacker's hands around her neck came rushing back, along with the pungent scent of leather. The once-pleasant smell would forever haunt her now. Just one more way the jerk would continue to ruin things for her, even after she'd physically healed.

Other details about the previous night were fuzzy. She'd spent the wee hours waffling between attempts to fill in the blank spots and not wanting to remember at all. She'd been strangled. That part was crystal clear, and the rest didn't matter.

She hadn't seen the person who did it. Couldn't identify

him by face or voice. Hadn't even gotten a look at what he drove when he made his escape.

There had been pain and fear. Struggle. Then blackness.

She'd climbed into her car and locked the doors, then pushed the starter button, not realizing her keys were no longer in her hand or pocket. The next thing she knew, she'd been on a gurney headed into the hospital. A padded collar around her neck. Straps holding her torso to a backboard. Blinding light everywhere.

Kind of like now.

Except everything smelled of bleach and...flowers?

She squinted at a pair of bouquets beside a pitcher of water and small plastic cup on her nightstand.

"I'm headed that way now," a female voice said.

Scarlet spotted a redheaded nurse moving toward her open door with a wide smile.

Several other women in matching scrubs were gathered outside her room, clutching clipboards and smiling goofily at something unseen.

The redhead stepped inside. "Oh, and it looks like she's awake. Good morning, Scarlet. How are you feeling?"

Scarlet's throat was tight and raw, so she did her best to look pleasant instead of speaking.

"Pardon me, ladies," a familiar tenor declared, seconds before Austin Beaumont strode into the room behind the nurse.

Scarlet's heart rate rose, and her muscles tightened. A million insecurities raced through her addled head. This wasn't the way she wanted to look when he saw her again. Or when anyone who didn't work as medical staff saw her at all. She was hurting and battered, sleep deprived and wearing a hospital gown.

She wanted to order him out. Or at least brush her hair, but her eyes chose to fill with tears of defeat instead.

Austin's right hand curled around a disposable cup. His opposite hand plunged deep into his pocket. The congenial expression he'd worn a moment prior vanished.

"Good morning," the nurse said, turning on a light over the machines and checking the monitors before facing Scarlet. "Your pulse is elevated. How's your pain?"

Scarlet cleared her throat, wincing immediately at the dull throb in her temple.

"Take these," the nurse said, passing her a pair of white pills. "We'll send a prescription home with you." She poured water from the pitcher into the plastic cup and waited while Scarlet took the pills.

"All right. Everything else here looks good. I'll catch the doctor and find out where your discharge stands."

Scarlet watched the nurse leave then slowly turned her eyes to Austin, wishing she was at least wearing her own pajamas, and that she'd been wrong about someone following her.

"I'm sorry," he said, taking a cautious step in her direction. "Scarlet. I'm so very sorry."

Her bottom lip trembled as his compassion pushed her toward the edge. "I didn't want to be right," she croaked. "Celebrities and social media stars get stalkers. Not small-town real estate agents. I just can't—" Her throat ached and words failed her, so she pleaded with her eyes. "I shouldn't have gone to that appointment alone."

"This is not your fault." He set his coffee on the stand beside her bed and gripped the metal rail near her arm. "You did everything right. You sensed something was wrong, and you sought help. I started building your case file and off-loading my work as soon as you left my office so I could concentrate on this. You had no reason to anticipate an attack."

Scarlet bit her lip, knowing that was true. She'd never in her wildest dreams thought she'd be brutally attacked like this. Followed again, maybe, but she'd asked for help with that. "What are you doing here so early? The sun's still rising. How'd you even hear about what happened?"

"My brother Finn is the detective on the case. He filled me in on as much as he can."

She worked the words over in her mind. "I hope he didn't wake you. There isn't much you can do here."

He shrugged. "It seemed smart to come as soon as I could. I feel better knowing you have someone keeping watch."

Scarlet's mouth went dry, and she sipped from her cup again. Did he believe her attacker was still watching? That he'd come to the hospital for her? The thought coiled her gut. "I know it's important to make a statement as soon as possible, before I forget the details, but it's all just—" she moved her hands in circles around her head "—scrambled. Or missing."

"Don't worry about that right now. Finn will check in when he can. Rest. Heal."

A soft rap against the door frame made her jump. Apparently she was more on edge than she'd realized.

The doctor who'd cared for her upon arrival gave a slight nod. His white lab coat had a photo ID clipped to the pocket. The words *Dr. Lanke* were embroidered on the opposite side. "You're up early," he said, moseying forward with a warm, parental smile.

Austin offered the older man his hand. "Austin Beaumont."

"Dr. Lanke." He looked curiously at the PI then swung

his attention to Scarlet. "Would you like your friend to step outside while we go over your details?"

Scarlet glanced at Austin. She wasn't sure which details the doctor planned to share, but she also wasn't in a hurry to be without him. "It's okay. He can stay."

Dr. Lanke explained the results of some tests they'd been waiting on and recapped things she already knew. "Nothing broken or fractured. No signs of a concussion. Bruising and swelling around the throat will reduce on their own. Rest and hydrate. Take the pills for pain as prescribed so your body can relax and heal steadily without becoming over-wrought. Follow up with a counselor within a few weeks, even if you think you don't need further help. Sometimes these things sneak up on us when we're sure we've gotten past them, and something like this should be talked about."

She nodded. "And my missing memories? When will they return?"

He took a breath, releasing it slowly and donning the fatherly smile once more. "The memories will likely return in time. It's not uncommon for patients who've been through trauma like this to suppress the specifics. The mind is a complicated thing, and it will go to great lengths to protect itself."

She slouched, defeated and deflated. It was bad enough that this had happened, but she'd reasoned that everything had a silver lining, or at least a purpose. For example, if she could remember the attacker's face, his car or some other detail that would lead the police to his arrest, then maybe it was worth the trauma, because this would finally be over. But she couldn't remember.

"I'll get the discharge paperwork together, and one of the nurses will bring it around shortly. Alternate ice for swelling and heat for comfort on your sore muscles. Be kind and patient with yourself. Change the bandage on your shoulder daily. I'll send a tube of cream for the stitches."

"Stitches?" she asked, taking a mental inventory. Her shoulder was sore, but so was the rest of her.

"You fell," Austin said, before the doctor could clarify. "Police found blood on a landscaping stone near the driveway's edge. The impact was enough to split the skin."

Dr. Lanke frowned but nodded. "We cleaned the wound and secured it with a couple of stitches to reduce scarring. Nothing serious, but it will be tender as it heals."

"Thank you," she whispered. The words left her lips absently while her mind struggled to imagine the scenario Austin described.

"Pretty flowers," Dr. Lanke said, tucking his clipboard beneath one bent arm. "From you?" His eyes flickered to Austin.

"Yes, sir," Austin said. "My partner and I. The others are from her coworkers."

Scarlet's heart thudded, and her stomach dropped. Did everyone in her immediate world know what had happened? The possibility nauseated her. She wished no one knew, but keeping a secret like this for long in a town as small as Marshal's Bluff would be impossible. Her attack had probably made front-page news.

She rubbed her palms against her arms, trying to scrub away the sensation of her attacker's hands on her skin.

"You're lucky to have such a dedicated fan," the doctor said. "Most boyfriends don't stay all night like this. Not that any of the nurses minded having him around." He chuckled and winked then headed for her door. "I'll get that discharge paperwork moving. You'll be free to go later this morning."

Scarlet's attention snapped to Austin and her lips parted. "You've been here all night?"

Austin looked sheepish. "I couldn't leave you again. I stayed in the waiting room so you could rest. I can't stop thinking this wouldn't have happened if I'd started shadowing you sooner, instead of putting it off until the end of the day. It's possible this happened because you came to see me. If my presence in your life escalated your stalker, then I wasn't there to protect you—" He shook his head, expression darkening.

She let his words roll around in her head, unable to properly focus on or dissect them. Something else was already pressing to the front of her addled mind. "You told the staff you're my new boyfriend?"

"They assumed," he said. "I didn't correct them. I know we hadn't decided on our cover story yet, but I needed a good reason to hang around. Couldn't let them think I might be a stalker." He frowned. "That was very unfortunate and poorly timed wording. Sorry."

Scarlet's lips curled into a small, unexpected smile. She was certain the nurses she'd seen earlier would let Austin do just about anything he wanted without question, but she kept that to herself.

"If I've overstepped, I'm happy to set the record straight with the staff."

"No." She shook her head. "It's okay. I implied as much to my coworker, so—"

"So," he echoed, lips twisting. "I guess it's official."

Her toes curled beneath the scratchy bleach-white blankets. It was definitely official. She was into her new protector in ways that would surely get her hurt in the aftermath. "Yep."

SOMETHING IN SCARLET'S eyes told Austin she liked the sound of them as a couple as much as he did. The fact that she could manage a blush after all she'd been through gave him hope for her full recovery as well. Physical and emotional.

He'd met his share of people who'd experienced terrible things. They all healed at their own pace. Some never spoke of their trauma again. Others addressed their pasts only as necessary. He suspected Scarlet was the type to form an awareness group, hold rallies and raze offenders like hers to the ground. He liked that about her. More than he should.

"I had a second reason for letting the staff believe we're dating," he admitted in the interest of full disclosure. "I can't be sure if your attacker saw you at my office, if he saw us talking on the street or sidewalk, or none of the above. But I don't want him to know you hired a PI. That knowledge could cause him to look more closely at the trail he's leaving while he follows you. We want to keep his focus on you, so Dean, Finn and the local police have the best chance of identifying and locating him quickly."

Scarlet swallowed audibly, and the pulse point in her neck beat faster. She sipped from her little cup again.

"I didn't say that to frighten you. I'm only being forthright." Austin leaned closer, expression firm. "I won't let him get near you again. You can believe that. He can't get past me, and he sure as hell can't go through me."

Her lips parted and her eyes widened as she watched and listened, hopefully realizing every word was true. Austin was more than capable of bringing down any enemy, and she could bank on that.

Satisfied, he nodded and straightened.

"But you can't stay with me forever," she said. "What happens when you're gone?"

It was a solid concern, but clearly she didn't know him. "I won't leave until this guy's caught or you order me away.

Even then, I'll probably still be outside in my truck." He did his best to refresh his smile and lighten the mood. But he'd meant those words too. Whoever had hurt Scarlet was going to pay for it, preferably by way of extensive jail time.

She cringed.

Maybe telling a woman, who was being actively stalked, that he too planned to follow and watch her indefinitely wasn't the encouragement he'd intended. "That sounded less creepy in my head."

Scarlet gave a small laugh, and her eyes fell shut. She opened them a moment later. "Well, the pain pills are kicking in." She raised a hand to her temple, then frowned as her fingers traced the goose egg at the side of her head.

He'd seen worse lumps on himself and all his brothers at one time or another, but it was different seeing the knot on her. The pain of her wounds seemed to form an anvil in his chest.

She lowered her hand to her lap and looked through the open doorway. "What happens after I'm discharged?"

He considered his words before speaking this time, knowing whatever he said would be a shock on some level and wanting to ease that stress if he could. "I'll take you home, if you're comfortable with that. You shouldn't be driving or alone for a while. If you'd prefer someone else, I can call them for you. Or you can borrow my phone."

Her brows furrowed as she looked around the room. "I dropped my phone."

"We believe your attacker took it with him when he left."

She sank back against her pillows. "And my keys. I was in my car, but I remember being surprised when it started. I couldn't drive anyway. My vision was blurry. I was going to pass out."

He nodded, widening his stance for stability. The pain

in her eyes might've knocked him back a step otherwise. "Paramedics broke your window when they arrived. You were unconscious. The police towed your vehicle, which is being treated as a crime scene now. Finn will have the window replaced when they finish. He'll let us know when it's ready, but that might be a few days."

"So I don't have a phone or car?"

"Not at the moment, but I can get you a phone," Austin said. He and Dean kept several at the office for situations like these. He might even have one in his go bag. "And I can be your chauffeur, assuming you don't mind riding in my truck. It's about ten years older than your SUV with none of the added comforts."

She wrapped her arms around her middle. "My purse had my driver's license in it. He's got my home address. And a key to my house."

Austin dipped his chin in acknowledgment. "You won't be alone there, and I'm going to change your locks as soon as we arrive."

"Delivery," a perky female voice called from the doorway.

He turned as a young woman stepped into the room carrying a tall glass vase and two dozen long-stemmed red roses. Austin frowned. "That's quite a bouquet."

"Isn't it?" the woman said, making room for the huge arrangement beside the other, more appropriate-sized ones. "Someone must really love you."

Scarlet's gaze jumped to Austin as the woman took her leave.

"May I?" he asked, already reaching for the card.

"Yes."

He plucked the small white rectangle from a thin plastic stake hidden among the baby's breath and greenery.

Two hastily scrawled words sent fire through his core.

I'm sorry.

Chapter Seven

Austin's focus jerked to Scarlet.

"They're from him, aren't they?" she asked, face pale and expression grim.

"I think so. I'm going to catch the woman who delivered these and find out. I won't be long."

She nodded, and he dove through the door.

"Excuse me," he called, too loud for hospital etiquette. A dozen nearby faces turned in his direction. "Wait," he instructed the woman who'd made the delivery.

Then he turned to the nearest nurse. "I need someone to guard Scarlet Wills's room until I get back. Don't let anyone in or out who isn't already assigned to her care."

The nurse nodded, eyes wide, then dashed toward Scarlet's room. Another nurse followed on her heels.

Austin jogged to the delivery woman's side, noticing the name Marie on her badge for the first time. He passed her the little card. "Did you take the order for these flowers?"

She stared in surprise and nodded. "Yes."

"Can you describe the man who wrote this?"

"I wrote that," she said. "I was in a hurry to complete the order and make my rounds." She motioned to a small rolling cart with an array of flowers, teddy bears and helium balloons. "I like to fill and deliver all the orders that came in after hours as soon as I get in each morning. He ordered the roses before I'd finished loading the cart."

Austin stilled. Marie had written the card. "Was the order placed online? Or did he come into the gift shop? Can you describe him?"

She shook her head. "He called."

"I need you to show me the receipt. Did he pay cash? Does the shop have caller ID?"

The woman looked skeptical, possibly borderline frightened.

"Please," he added, before she could make an excuse or do anything else that would cost him precious time. "I believe the person who sent those roses is the same person who attacked the woman in that room last night. I'm a private investigator, and I'm trying to find him." He pulled his credentials from his wallet as proof and waited while she looked at them. "Help me," he pleaded.

Marie grabbed her cart. "Okay. Let's go."

They hurried to the first-floor gift shop, where she passed her cart and delivery duties to a clerk behind the counter. She took the other woman's position and waved Austin to join her.

"Here." Marie pointed to the phone beside the register.

Blessedly, the device had caller ID.

Next she pulled the receipt tape from the register and matched the time of purchase to the time of the call. Another stroke of luck, likely thanks to the early hour. The phone only stored ten numbers, and his was still in the system.

Austin snapped a photo of the phone number before it was replaced by additional incoming calls. "I assume he paid by credit card. Do you remember the name on the card?"

She pressed her lips together. "It was a prepaid card."

Of course it was. Austin had to give the criminal credit. He was a planner and a thinker.

"May I have the number of the card?" he asked.

The woman frowned. "I think that's crossing some kind of line. I don't want to get fired."

"Can I ask your manager?"

"She comes in this afternoon."

Austin fought the urge to argue. Marie had her protocols too, and she'd already shown him more than she had to. "My brother is the detective on this case. I'll reach out to him. Maybe he can contact your manager."

She nodded. "Thank you. I'm sure that will work."

"Can you help me with one more thing?" he asked, pointing to the handset on the desk. "I'd like to call the suspect. He's more likely to answer if I use the gift shop's phone."

She glanced nervously around. "Okay."

Austin accessed the speaker function and dialed. He pressed one palm against the counter as he listened to the tinny rings.

"Hello?" a low and cautious male voice answered.

Marie's eyes bulged.

Austin motioned for her to talk then scratched a note on a flyer.

"Hi," she said, eyes scanning the paper. "This is Marie from the Marshal's Bluff Memorial Hospital Gift Shop. You placed an order for roses this morning, and I forgot to ask your name."

Austin nodded at her.

She'd done well.

The man's breathing became audible, and a rumbling laugh broke through the line. "Someone told you to call me. Didn't they?"

"No. I was just taking the flowers up and—"

"Don't lie!" he screamed.

Marie jumped back from the receiver, one hand pressed to her chest.

Austin set a palm on her shoulder. "Who is this?" he asked, raising the phone to his ear. "Tell me now, and I'll go easy on you. Make me work for it, and I'll be forced to remind you later that you blew this opportunity."

"Stay away from her," the voice warned. "Stay away. Or you'll regret it."

"I'm definitely not doing that," Austin answered, contrasting the other man's seething tone with a jovial one. "But I am coming for you." He smiled as he spoke, and Marie shot him a curious look.

Scarlet's stalker began to growl. The sound climbed into a wild scream. "She's mine! She's! Mine!"

A round of earsplitting cracks and booms made Austin cringe. It sounded as if the man was beating his phone against something hard, possibly until it burst into pieces, because the line went dead.

"Oh, dear," Marie whispered, moving her trembling hand from her chest to her lips.

Austin dragged a nearby stool from its position in front of the register to within Marie's reach, and she sat. "Do you need me to call someone so you can take a minute to gather yourself?"

She shook her head.

He wasn't sure she was all right, so he kept an eye on her while he dialed Finn and delivered the rundown, then sent the photo of the number on the memory display.

"You should've let me make that call," Finn said. "We could've traced it from the precinct."

"He wouldn't have answered a call from the police station," Austin said. "I called from the gift shop so he'd think there was a question about his order."

"This is the number?" he asked. "In the photo?"

"Yeah." Though Austin was certain that particular phone had been destroyed. "You'll have to come down here and talk with the shop's manager to get the credit card number, but they have it."

"I'm already on my way," Finn said. "If I'm lucky, he paid for the prepaid card with something linked to his name, but I'm rarely lucky. Still, I'll be able to track the card to the store where it was purchased. The store should have a time-stamped receipt. Then I can check the security camera feed from that time to see who bought it."

"He might've bought the card online."

"Don't say stuff like that," Finn said. "You're going to jinx me."

"Okay, Detective." Austin rolled his eyes and waved goodbye to Marie, who was still shell-shocked behind the counter. "Thank you."

She nodded, eyes wide and skin pale.

He should probably send her flowers later for her help. Then again, the stalker might've ruined flowers for her. "I'm going back to Scarlet's room," he said, both to Marie and to Finn. "She's being released this morning, and I want to be there when she gets her instructions."

"Stay with her," Finn said. "I hate everything you've told me about this guy. I don't want you to leave her side again."

"Believe me," Austin said, breaking into a run for the nearest bank of elevators. "I'm not planning on it."

Chapter Eight

It was afternoon before Scarlet was finally discharged. She left in her dirty skirt, socks and underthings, plus a logoed T-shirt from the gift shop. Her top had bloodstains, and she couldn't bring herself to put it on.

The sun was high in the sky when a young man in scrubs wheeled her into the pickup area outside the hospital's sliding glass doors.

"Ready?" Austin asked, opening the passenger door of his truck and offering her his hand.

She didn't answer. She wasn't sure. Much as she wanted to leave the hospital, leaving made her feel vulnerable. She hadn't been hurt at the hospital. She'd been mended there. And going home with Austin meant a whole other set of problems. For starters, he was a perfect stranger, and while she didn't have any reasons not to trust him, she'd been through an ordeal. No one and nothing felt quite as safe as it had before.

In other, more mundane concerns, she didn't have the capacity to be a hostess, and she wasn't in the habit of having company. Her home was her private domain. She met with friends at restaurants or visited their place. Now, she was on the spot to hold herself together and be congenial when all she wanted to do was cry or scream or pack up and move to Timbuktu.

And she still needed to call her mother. She quickly pushed that thought aside.

"Scarlet?"

Her name on his tongue pulled her back to the moment.

Austin stood before her, hand outstretched. The hospital staffer who'd been pushing her wheelchair waited for her to get up so he could move on with his day.

"Sorry." She gingerly set her hand in Austin's and ignored the instant buzz of chemistry as he pulled her onto her feet with ease.

He held the door while she climbed into the truck's cab, then shut it when she was inside.

The interior smelled of earth and hay, warmth and sunshine. The soothing scent of his cologne seemed to underscore everything else.

She winced as she fastened her safety belt; every muscle in her neck, shoulders, back and torso felt tender, overstretched and bruised.

Austin climbed behind the wheel, donned a pair of dark sunglasses and shifted into Drive.

She studied the space around her. He hadn't been kidding about the age of his truck. It was old, a model she remembered from high school, but well maintained. A pair of handcuffs hung from his rearview mirror, and she became suddenly thankful he couldn't read her mind.

"Do you prefer a certain radio station or type of music?" he asked, punching buttons as they turned away from the parking lot.

"I usually listen to audiobooks."

He pointed vents in her direction and turned on the cool air. "What kind of books?"

Heat rushed over her cheeks, and for the smallest moment, she considered dodging the question. Or lying. "Romance," she said finally, uninterested in bending truths. Even less interested in explaining her preferences. "I like books about families and happy endings." She turned her chin away and braced for the joke.

There was always a joke.

"Who are your favorite authors?"

She looked at him. "You know the names of romance authors?"

He shrugged. "A few. Mama is a huge fan. I try to keep up when she tells me about whatever she's reading. I know it's important to her, even if it's not my cup of tea."

"What's your cup of tea?" she asked, more curious about him than his mother's favorite authors.

He glanced at her, then away. "I read a little bit of everything."

"Such as?"

"Mostly nonfiction." He flexed his fingers on the steering wheel. Was he nervous to have the spotlight? "I like information. I don't even care what kind. Everything's fascinating if you give it a chance."

Scarlet waited, curiosity growing. "What have you read about most recently?"

"Cooking, gardening, fishing, aviation, unsolved crimes."

Scarlet smiled. The idea that Austin spent his free time reading was incredibly attractive. The fact that he read indiscriminately about everything from cooking to crime was even better. She wondered how many people knew that about him. And she liked the fact that she did.

"What?" he asked, noticing her stare.

"You're a nerd," she said. "You look like that, and you've still got a big inquisitive brain. I like it."

"You like how I look, or my big, beautiful brain?"

She laughed. Her throat ached in protest, but she couldn't squelch the smile. "I didn't call it beautiful."

"You called it big."

Another laugh broke free, and she grimaced at the pain.

She turned her eyes to the view outside her window, allowing herself a moment to recover while admiring the landscape. Slowly, the scenery morphed from busy downtown streets to quaint little neighborhoods, then to the sprawling countryside.

Within minutes, rolling hills of green grass stretched to the horizon, topped by a cloudless blue sky. Punctuated occasionally with a farmhouse, cattle or a big red barn. The sun was high and hot as it beat against the glass, combating the truck's comfortable AC.

It wasn't until Austin made the turn onto her road that she realized what was happening.

"How did you know where I live?" She hadn't thought to give him her address, and her driver's license was with the stalker.

"Dean put it in the new client file," he said. "But I could've found you without it."

She swung her gaze to him, befuddled and having completely forgotten about the details his brother had asked for when she'd made the appointment. Those moments and that phone call felt like memories from years ago instead of yesterday morning. Even more worrisome was what Austin had meant by the second statement. "How?"

"For starters, you bought your house." He raised his brows and his gaze flicked to hers. "Anyone can visit the county auditor's website and enter your last name in a property search. If they don't know how to do that, they can look at your social media."

"My accounts are all set to private."

"Not your business account." He looked her way once more. "You post daily about available homes, your life as a Realtor, and advice for buyers and sellers. You take pictures of your home and lawn, advising sellers to do this or that to spruce up their properties before listing them on the market."

That was true, but she was careful. "I never give my address or photograph the home directly."

"No, but you showcase landscaping features and additions recommended for curb appeal. Your house number is visible on the mailbox in more than one photo. It's small, but people can use their cell phones to enlarge the image. And anyone familiar with the area knows there are only so many sparsely populated streets with inlet views."

Scarlet rocked slightly as he turned onto her driveway. "You can see the inlet in photos of my patio?"

"Yes." Austin cut the engine and climbed down.

She flipped mentally through an array of her most recent posts, realizing how much she'd unintentionally given away. Sometimes she even took photos of a book on her legs while she sat in the sun. Did her stalker imagine those images were meant for him?

The passenger door opened, and she started.

Austin reached for her hand and helped her onto her feet at his side.

The air between them was charged, and if she hadn't looked like someone recently attacked, wearing yesterday's clothes, she might've thought the tightening of his jaw was a sign of attraction.

She turned to face the house. "Shall we?"

He pulled a large black bag from behind her seat then shut the door and followed her. "After you."

A warm heady breeze wafted through her freshly mulched flower beds, overflowing with native blooms. She inhaled and released several slow breaths, working her pulse back to a more normal range.

"You have a beautiful home," he said. His voice traveled to her ears from a few steps behind her. Appreciation colored the tone.

"Thank you. I got lucky on this one. I helped an older couple find a condo near their grown children, and they offered me first dibs. I bought it before it ever went on the market." And since they'd purchased the place for a tenth of its current value, they were happy with the fair market price she could afford. "I think they liked knowing I planned to preserve it." Anyone else would likely have demolished the little home and built something infinitely grander in its place.

Scarlet loved it just as it was.

She climbed the porch steps and leaned against the doorjamb. "I don't have any keys."

Austin set his bag down and removed a credit card from his wallet. He slid the card into the crack between the door and wall then gave it a shimmy. A moment later, the knob turned, and he opened her door. "Like I said, I'm changing the locks."

Scarlet blinked. Her stomach pitched. "The knobs are original," she said on autopilot. Nearly everything was original. She'd made sure of it, because that had been important until yesterday.

He squinted down at her, big hands on trim hips. "I can drill a hole in the door and add a dead bolt, so we can keep the knobs. Or I can replace the knobs with something more modern and secure. This," he said, tipping his head toward the open door, "doesn't cut it anymore."

"I can order new knobs online," she said. "They'll preserve the aesthetic while offering better security, but delivery will take a few days."

He seemed to consider her words. "Let's place that order tonight."

She nodded then led him inside, flipping on light switches as she moved, hoping her attacker wasn't hiding somewhere in the shadows. Austin closed and locked the door behind them as her limbs began to tremble.

Austin's hand brushed her back. "I'm right here," he said. "You're safe."

Her knees locked, and she looked at her home through new eyes. "What if he's here?"

Austin guided her to the sofa in her living space. "I'll be right back. If you see or hear anything that makes you uncomfortable, just holler, and I'll be back in seconds."

She kneaded her hands as he moved out of sight, listening as his footsteps softened in her adjoining kitchen then went silent in her dining room. She imagined him moving in and out of her two first-floor bedrooms and along the hallway in between. The bathroom and sunroom doors creaked open and closed on the far side of her home.

The steps groaned as he climbed to the second floor.

A few moments later, he reappeared and took the seat at her side. "It's just us. Can I get you anything? Tea? Water?"

She shook her head. "It's my house. I should—"

"You should rest," he said, interrupting. "That's the doctor's orders. Meanwhile, I need to secure your windows and find another way to reinforce your doors until the new knobs arrive."

"It's petty, I know."

"It's not," he said. "This is your home. You've worked hard to make it exactly the way you want it, and this guy doesn't get to change anything more about your life than absolutely necessary for your safety. I can stay here until the new knobs and locks are installed. Longer if he isn't arrested before then. As long as that's okay with you."

Scarlet wiped a renegade tear as it swiveled over her cheek. "Thank you. I'm grateful for your help. I just wish I could do something to contribute. He was close enough to me to do all this—" she motioned to her neck and torso "—and I can't even give the police a description. It's infuriating."

"You've been through a lot. Your memories will likely return. Give it time. I'm sure something will trigger them. Until then, focus on healing." He pushed onto his feet. "Are you hungry? I can make or order something."

"You're supposed to be my guest."

He wrinkled his nose. "I kind of invited myself, and you were just released from the hospital. I'm basically your caretaker," he said. "And if I don't feed you, someone is sure to revoke my privileges."

She kicked off her shoes and stood. "Well, we can't have that." She swallowed a wave of emotion, ready to escape to her room for a proper breakdown.

Of course Austin noticed. "Do you want to talk about it?"

"No. I'm going to take a shower and change into something comfortable and clean." She planned to burn the skirt, socks and underthings in the firepit out back or stuff them into the garbage can at her next opportunity. Anything and everything that could remind her of her attack needed to go. She might even trade in her SUV when it was finished being a crime scene.

"I can make some tea and sandwiches when you're ready," he said. "Or soup if that will be easier for your throat."

Scarlet shook her head. "I think I'll start with a large

glass of red wine and go from there." She didn't wait for his response. She couldn't. Instead, she turned on her heels and marched into her bathroom, where the shower would cover the sounds of her cries.

Chapter Nine

Austin gave himself a second tour of Scarlet's home while she showered. On this round, he took his time to thoroughly inspect every nook and cranny. Not just the places an intruder could hide, but anywhere someone could gain access to the house or install an unnoticed camera.

It'd been too easy to break in, and that fact had stuck with Austin. No one was hiding inside, but that didn't mean someone hadn't let themselves in, done something nefarious then left without a trace. The possibility Scarlet's stalker could've established a way to watch her from inside her home made his skin crawl.

Thankfully, he found no signs of intrusion or surveillance.

He did, however, see an intense attention to detail on Scarlet's part. Visible in the design of each room and the maintenance of the original floors, baseboards and crown molding. It was as if someone had refinished every inch of wood, tile and marble in the place. No wonder she'd cared about the front doorknob. Her home was a personalized work of art.

The decor choices were more feminine than anyplace he'd ever lived, including the ranch, but he didn't object to any of it. It was like walking through a magazine spread. From the floral accents, to the soft color palette, the abundance of pillows, cozy throw blankets and art. It was a different side of Scarlet than he'd seen so far. The serious businesswoman he'd met at his office had shown no indication that she might also wallpaper a half bathroom in butterflies or sleep beneath a wildflower-print duvet. He added these things to the fact that she loved to read and preferred romance books, specifically ones with happy families.

Her small mudroom overlooked the rear patio and the inlet. A washer, dryer and shelf for folding stood before the window. A drying rack with a rainbow of lacy underthings hurried him along before his mind had time to formulate too many ideas.

He was there to protect her, not to want her. Not like that. Yet in two days' time, his ability to maintain professionalism was already being challenged, internally anyway. And that was before he'd essentially moved in with her.

He tried to imagine for the dozenth time how she'd managed to drag herself into her SUV and lock the doors before passing out. Or how she'd had the presence of mind to use her onboard system to call for help. She'd just been attacked. Strangled. Most people panicked in situations far less dire, but she'd maintained a level head and her quick responses might've saved her life.

Satisfied the home's windows and doors were secure, he went to make coffee and pour her wine.

She'd been gone awhile, but he imagined she needed extra time to process what had happened, to appreciate being home and to get through her usual shower routine when she was still so bruised and sore. She likely also needed a minute to adjust to the fact that there was a practical stranger in her kitchen making coffee.

Her bedroom door opened, and she emerged a few short minutes later.

Austin carried a glass of merlot in her direction, meeting her in the small hallway.

Her blond hair was darker, still damp from the shower. She'd piled it on her head and pinned it there. She smelled of shampoo and lotion, a delectable blend of uniquely Scarlet scents. Her cream-colored top clung to her athletic form. A pair of loose pink pajama pants covered her legs. "You remembered," she said, accepting the glass and taking a sip. "Thank you."

He smiled, enjoying the blush that spread across her cheeks and hating the angry red welts, now fully exposed, on her neck. "How are you feeling?"

"Better. It's good to be home with my things, in my space."

"And an uninvited houseguest?" he asked.

She offered a small, sad smile. "As long as he brings me wine, I won't complain much." She glanced down the hall toward her mudroom. "I'm going to sit on the deck. Do you want to join me?"

"I'll meet you there." He turned back to the kitchen for a few things, including a fresh cup of coffee, then headed outside.

Scarlet's bras and panties were off the rack when he passed through the mudroom this time, tossed into a nearby basket instead.

He gave silent thanks for that mercy.

She looked up as he exited her home, wrapped in a soft-looking blanket. "I saved you a seat." She motioned to the white Adirondack chair beside hers; both faced the water.

"Thanks." He lowered onto the wooden seat and stretched his legs out before him. "I have something for you too."

"Oh?"

He lifted his cell phone into view. "I thought you might want to call someone. I still need to set up a phone for you, but you're welcome to use mine now. I'm sure there are plenty of people worried about you."

Scarlet stared at the device. "I think I'll wait. I'm not ready to talk about it."

"They're going to read about it in the paper."

She took another sip of wine. "I only care about my mother, and she doesn't live in Marshal's Bluff. I'll call her as soon as I can manage without crying."

Austin looked at her more carefully, noticing the puffiness around her eyes and slight redness of her nose. She'd been crying in the shower while he'd prowled her home. He should've—the thought stalled in his mind.

What could he have done? It was invasive enough that he'd come to her home and planned to stay. It wasn't as if he could've knocked on her door and offered her a hug.

"How's the wine?" he asked, pushing all thoughts of touching her from his mind.

"Exactly what I needed, though I probably shouldn't mix it with my pain pills."

He shrugged. The doctor had prescribed higher doses of the stuff readily available over the counter, nothing like a narcotic. "I'm sure a glass won't hurt."

"I doubt I'll even finish it," she said. "But a glass of wine on the deck has become symbolic to me. It's part of my routine, especially when I've had a hard day. It's peaceful out here. I swear some nights I can hear my tension rolling away in waves."

"The view is certainly beautiful." He looked away before she caught him watching her, fixing his eyes on the water instead.

"I don't always bring wine. Sometimes I have a cup of tea or a tall glass of ice water. It depends on the kind of day I've had. But the routine is tried and true."

Austin absorbed the autumn sun and salty breeze for several long moments, before moving on to his next gift. "I have something else for you."

She rolled her head against the backrest of her chair, an expression of relaxation on her features. "What?"

He shifted to pull the little weapon from his pocket and held it in the air between them.

She frowned. "What is it?"

"A compact stun gun. I thought you could practice using it a few times until you're comfortable, then keep it with you wherever you go. Especially until this is over."

"I have pepper spray and an air horn. And before you ask how well those worked for me yesterday, I want to point out that I wasn't able to get to them, and I wouldn't have been able to reach this thing either."

He bristled at her words, unhappy with whichever person in her life had made her think that would be anyone's response. "I wasn't going to say that."

She pursed her lips, eyes gliding cautiously over the device in his hand. "I'd probably just wind up shocking myself."

He also despised whoever had given her the idea there was anything she couldn't do right or well. "I'm sure that's not true."

She frowned, clearly unconvinced. "Can I think about it?"

"Absolutely. But just for fun, let me show you how simple it is." He hated pushing, especially now, when she'd finally found a moment of peace, but this seemed important enough to make an exception.

He held the small black cylindrical object on his palm. "It looks like a flashlight."

"It does," he agreed. "And it even has a light, if you need it." He turned the device over until she could see one blunt end. "This little switch powers it on." He demonstrated. "This—" he pointed to a slider, flush with the side "—sets it to charge. And this—" he rested his thumb on a small red button "—stuns."

The device gave a menacing crackle, and Scarlet frowned.

"I have to be close enough to touch that little thing to the person's skin?" she asked.

He gave the device another look. He'd seen its small size as convenient. Looking through her eyes, it was easy to understand the problem. "I hope you'll never again be within arm's distance of someone who wants to cause you harm, but if that day comes, this will send them back a few steps and stop them long enough for you to get away."

He set the device on the small table at his side and turned his eyes to the inlet.

His peace was slowly slipping. He didn't like the thought she'd be alone if he wasn't there. She should be surrounded by friends and family while she pulled through this. If anyone in his family had been hospitalized, the waiting room would've been filled to capacity with folks hoping to wish them well. And a mile-long train of aunties bringing food would've wrapped the blocks outside their home. While her coworkers had sent flowers, the only person Scarlet had spoken of so far was her mama, and she hadn't even called her. "Are you and your mama close?"

She turned bright eyes to his. "Sure. She's my only real family and a great friend."

"And she doesn't live in town?"

Scarlet shook her head. "No. She lives in Holbrook. That's

in the next county. Close enough to arrive quickly in an emergency, but far enough away to keep us from being competitors in the market."

He couldn't help wondering which part of the current situation she thought wasn't an emergency. "Have you considered visiting her for a few days while the police search for your stalker?"

"I have," she said. "I just haven't worked up the nerve to call and break her heart with this news."

Austin raised his coffee and returned his attention to the beautiful afternoon.

Wind rustled through her trees, jostling leaves in every shade from amber to crimson, and knocking a few handfuls loose. They fell like confetti against a backdrop of green grass and brilliant blue water. The view was enough to make him feel as if he was inside a painting. No wonder this was where she came to unwind.

"Do you think the police will find him?" she asked.

He didn't need to ask who she'd meant. And he was sure of his answer. "I do."

"And you'll stay with me until then?"

His heart softened with her wobbling words. He couldn't explain it logically, but he knew he'd stay with her as long as she needed. "I will."

"What if it takes a year? Or ten? You can't just give up your life and all your other clients. What will I do then?"

"Let me worry about my life and my clients. You have enough to think about. Besides, it won't take a year to find him."

Scarlet turned, fixing him with the full intensity of her ethereal green eyes. "How can you be sure?"

Austin leaned in her direction, matching the weight

of her stare. "Because whoever hurt you doesn't stand a chance against my family."

SCARLET WOKE THE next morning at nine. She hadn't slept past six in years, and it felt incredible, until she moved. Her aching body protested as she angled upward in bed.

A glass of water and a note sat on her nightstand, along with the painkillers the doctor had prescribed. The note had simple instructions a la *Through the Looking Glass*. "Eat me. Drink me," she read, smiling at the reminder that Austin Beaumont was running loose in her home.

She took the pills and headed to her bathroom to prepare for her day.

Memories of the previous night flashed in her mind as she combed her hair and brushed her teeth. Sitting with Austin on her deck until the sun had set. Watching movies with him in her living room while sharing snacks on the couch and talking about anything and everything to pass the time. She'd gotten to know him better in a few hours than she knew some of the folks who'd been in her life for years. And she hadn't learned anything she didn't approve of or admire.

He loved his family, all ten million of them. He was also smart, funny and kind. She'd felt safe in his care before, but now, she was looking forward to more nights like the last one.

She swiped her favorite tinted gloss across her lips and gave her lashes two coats of mascara before spending an extra few minutes on her hair. Soft jeans with frayed edges, fuzzy socks and a T-shirt from her office softball league completed the casual look. With any luck, he wouldn't realize how much she hoped he thought she was pretty.

Outside her bedroom, the house was quiet, save for movement in the kitchen.

"Good morning," she called, inching slowly in that direction. Hoping it was Austin and not her attacker shuffling around. "Hello?" she projected her voice as she drew nearer.

The scrape of a chair over tiles met her ears a moment before Austin said, "I have to call you back."

She exhaled in relief and pasted on a smile.

"Hey," Austin said, removing earbuds and rising from her table, where a laptop sat beside a pad of paper and a pen. The enticing scents of coffee and cologne filled the little room. "I hope you don't mind. I helped myself to the shower and your kitchen." He motioned to the pot of fresh brew on her counter. "Can I get you a cup?"

"Please."

"Cream or sugar?"

"Both."

He smiled. His outfit was similar to her own—faded jeans and a T-shirt with his PI company's name on the front. "This was all I had in my go bag," he said, following her gaze to his ensemble. "I borrowed something from my brother yesterday, which left this for today. We should probably visit my place soon for a few staples."

"Sounds good," she said, enthralled by the idea of seeing Austin's home. What did it look like? What secrets would it reveal? The thrill of curiosity thinned when she realized he might live like a frat kid, eating out of pizza boxes and sleeping on sheets he hadn't laundered since moving in.

He passed her a steaming mug.

"Thanks." She inhaled the delectable aroma and exhaled a pound of distress. "I can make breakfast since you made the coffee. As soon as I get to the bottom of this cup and am officially awake."

Austin's gaze flickered to the clock on the wall then back to her. "I hoped to tell you sooner, but I've got breakfast covered."

"What do you mean?" She scanned the kitchen for an indication he'd prepared something already.

The doorbell rang.

"That's for me," he said, tipping his head to indicate she should follow. "Us, actually."

"You ordered breakfast?" She hurried along behind, shamelessly enjoying his use of the word *us*.

"Not exactly."

He opened the door and stepped back so she could move into the space at his side.

A middle-aged woman with a wide smile and milkmaid braids stood on the porch, a casserole in her hands and an insulated bag hooked over her wrist. "Good morning!" she said, big brown eyes swinging from Scarlet to Austin. "Hello, sweet baby boy."

Chapter Ten

"Morning, Mama." Austin stepped forward to kiss his mother's cheek before making room for her to come inside. "Scarlet just woke, and I haven't had time to warn her about your arrival."

She pinched his cheek. "Warn her? I'm here to help. Now, where's the kitchen?"

Scarlet blinked as the woman moved past, following her son to the stove.

"Scarlet," he said with an apologetic grin. "That's my mama. Mary Beaumont."

They followed on the older woman's heels. "Mama, this is Scarlet Wills."

"It's lovely to meet you," she said, setting the temperature on Scarlet's oven. "This just needs to be warmed a little. I hurried to get here so you wouldn't have to wait long."

"Thank you," Scarlet said, half amused, half in shock.

Austin's mom made casseroles and dropped what she was doing to race them to his clients? Scarlet's mom never cooked, barely ate and only rushed to get to business appointments.

"I made your favorite," Mary said, speaking to her son. "Fajita breakfast casserole. I brought all the fixings and some things for lunch and dinner. Snacks too. But y'all can come to the ranch for dinner if you'd like. It must be dull staying here around the clock. It might be good to get out."

"Said the spider to the fly," Austin muttered, causing his mama's smile to widen.

Scarlet watched them, mesmerized at the ease of their interactions and the way they moved in practically choreographed steps around the room. Putting things into her refrigerator, sliding the dish into the oven, setting the table for three. Clearly Austin had familiarized himself with her small kitchen while she'd slept.

Mrs. Beaumont made small talk as they worked, complimenting Scarlet's home and asking how she felt. She asked about her mother too and if Austin was being a good houseguest.

The initial shock of her presence was gone in minutes, and Scarlet was unprecedentedly at ease with another stranger. Like with Austin, Scarlet suddenly felt as if she'd known the older woman forever. And she laughed when Mrs. Beaumont told stories about life on the ranch raising five boys.

"And that's how this one got a scar above his eye," she said, poking Austin on the forehead. "He likes to say he fell from a bull, but that wasn't the story I heard."

Austin leaned away with a grin. "Dean said a blanket would work like a parachute if I jumped off the barn. He was fifteen, and I was ten. I thought he knew everything."

"Brothers," she said, pride evident in her eyes. "Do you have any siblings, Scarlet?"

"No, ma'am."

Mary reached across the small table and covered Scarlet's hand with hers. She searched her face a moment then said, "I know things probably seem pretty scary right now, but I promise you, my boys are working hard to change that, and they never fail."

She grinned, thinking of Austin's comment on her deck last night. "So I've heard."

"It's true," Mary said. "They're all very good at what they do, and they always get their man. Or woman." She winked.

"Mama," Austin warned. "Don't."

"What?" she asked, raising her shoulders to her ears. "I'm just offering her a little comfort. My boys never get involved unless they know it's worth the trouble, and they give 110 percent when it is."

Scarlet couldn't help wondering if Mary was still talking about finding a stalker, or if she'd moved on to something else.

"Did Austin tell you Dean just got engaged?" she asked. "I can't wait for the wedding. And the grandbabies. Do you want children, Scarlet?"

Scarlet's gaze jumped to Austin, who dropped his forehead into one waiting palm. "Yes?"

"Excellent," Mary said. "I know it's every couple's choice, but I like to imagine the ranch filled with children one day when my husband and I are too old to keep all the teenagers. Then it will just be us, our children and our grandbabies."

Austin straightened with a laugh. "Mama would like to see my brothers and I populate a small town."

Mary beamed. "There's nothing wrong with wanting a big family."

"I always wanted five children," Scarlet said, unsure why the secret, silly fantasy slipped out.

"Really?" Austin and his mom asked in unison.

"Yeah." Scarlet laughed. "I don't know why five, exactly. Maybe it was a result of being a lonely only child, but I decided a long time ago five was the perfect number. Unfortunately, at twenty-seven and single, five is probably not in the cards these days."

"Well," Mary said. "You never know, do you? Twins are a possibility. So is adoption and being pregnant a lot." She laughed.

Austin looked horrified. "Mama."

"We're just having a little girl talk," she said. "I suppose you'd prefer to talk shop."

He looked as if he'd prefer to talk about anything else, and Scarlet regretted her candor. It wasn't as if she'd included him in her fictional family of seven. Still, he looked paler than she'd ever seen him, and it felt like she was the cause.

"Have you given her a Taser?" Mary asked.

"I tried," he said. "I offered a stun gun, but she wouldn't take it."

Her thin brows furrowed. "How about a pistol?"

Scarlet laughed. "No, thank you. I think I'd sooner carry the Taser."

Mary smiled. "Then it's settled."

The apple really didn't fall far.

The oven dinged, and Mary popped to her feet. "Time to eat."

"She loves us with food," Austin said.

"I'd never say no to that." Scarlet smiled. She'd only known Mary Beaumont a few minutes, but it was evident she loved her family in every possible way.

Scents of roasted red peppers, eggs, onions and cheese floated through the room, and her stomach groaned in anticipation.

"Eat up," Mary said, setting the casserole on the table between them. "Because I think the next thing we should talk about is how soon you can relocate."

"We're going to my place later," Austin said. "I need to

pick up some things if I'm going to stay here, but you can always see what you think while we're there." He looked to Scarlet, avoiding his mama's knowing eyes. "It might be the better choice."

AUSTIN KNEW THE moment he suggested his place as a possible location for Scarlet's respite, his mama would latch onto it. But the words had practically leaped from his mouth the moment she'd mentioned relocation, which was an idea he wouldn't argue with. And he couldn't backpedal now.

His mama hitched a brow.

Everyone who knew the Beaumont family assumed it was their father, a former police chief, who inspired the boys to get involved in law enforcement or investigation. But anyone who'd spent any amount of time at the ranch knew Mama as the best detective among them. She saw, heard and sensed everything. The only time he or his brothers got away with something as kids and teens was when she'd decided to ignore it. Even then, she let them know she hadn't missed their transgression. Usually by doubling their chores for a week or two without comment.

Scarlet raised her mug, looking pleasantly calm on the outside, but her hand trembled as the drink reached her lips.

He didn't want to take her away from her home, and he'd been thinking of how to avoid it, but his mama was right. Scarlet's place wasn't the safest option. Changing the locks would help, but it would be days before the new ones arrived. Until then, the problem was sleep, or the lack of it. He couldn't remain perpetually awake and on the move for days, making his rounds from the front to back door all through the nights.

"Has Austin told you about our ranch?" Mama asked. "It's beautiful. Peaceful. There's always plenty of good food and even better people. There are animals too. A stable with horses if you like to ride. And you'd be safe. If you'd prefer someplace like that."

Scarlet returned her cup to the saucer with a soft clatter. "I'd like to stay here, if that's possible."

Mama tipped her head. "Anything's possible, but is it safe?" She looked to Austin. "How long before the door locks are changed?"

"By the end of the week," Scarlet answered. "I placed the order last night."

"And who will keep watch at your front and back doors until then?"

Austin fought a smile. He and his brothers had a running theory she was a mind reader. Times like these seemed to support that.

Scarlet's eyes darted to him. "How did you watch both doors?"

"I was on the move most of the night."

"You didn't sleep," she said flatly, and he could practically see the reality of the situation sinking in. The set of her mouth turned grim. "I slept better than I have in a long while."

Silence stretched around them.

Scarlet sat taller and turned to his mama. "I wouldn't want to risk bringing my danger to your ranch and the folks you're helping there. I hear you do wonderful things for young people with troubles of their own. I don't want to see this spread to anyone else."

His mama's gaze roamed Scarlet's features, and Austin wondered if she saw the things he did. Scarlet was brave and selfless. She'd been through hell, but still worried more about potentially exposing strangers to her attacker than about the added protection the ranch could offer her. "That's why you don't want to stay with your mama."

"Yes, ma'am."

"Hotels aren't ideal," Mama said, dusting her lips with a napkin. "They can be hard to guard properly if they're breached. But if you can check in unnoticed, under a false name, you might not be found. If you decide not to stay with Austin. There will be an added expense of course. And he'd still need to be there. At least with adjoining rooms."

Scarlet nodded, accepting his mama's input, which had obviously been worded to sway her against the notion.

Austin rested his clasped hands on the table, drawing both sets of eyes. "I can talk to my brothers about setting up shifts to keep watch here for a few days. Staying won't be a problem if that's what you want to do."

Scarlet frowned. "I hate to put out anyone else. You're all doing so much already. And if they're here all night, they'll be exhausted all day. That will only diminish their ability to search for whoever did this to me." She sighed. "That's counterproductive."

He dipped his chin once in agreement. "My place is still an option. It's not listed on the auditor's website as owned by me. Very few people know where I live. Dean and I went to great lengths to hide our addresses when we opened the PI business. I keep a top-notch security system, and I'm an excellent shot."

He bit the insides of his cheeks, regretting the comment about shooting trespassers, even if he had been joking. A little.

Scarlet snorted a small laugh, and his mother's smile widened at the poorly timed words.

"Well." Mama stood. "I should be getting back to help your father. Let me know what you decide and if there's anything you need. I've put a cowboy casserole in the freezer for dinner. Just take it out while the oven preheats, then pop it in for about half an hour, and it'll be ready to eat."

"Thank you," Scarlet said, rising to walk her to the door. "For everything. It was really nice to meet you, and your offer for me to stay at the ranch was very generous. I can see where Austin gets his kindness."

Mama's eyes flashed with pride, and she fixed him with a look over Scarlet's shoulder that could only be interpreted as immense approval.

He was sure to hear about it later.

Chapter Eleven

Austin and Scarlet waved from the porch as Mama drove away, and the moment felt so oddly natural, he wondered if his lack of sleep had pushed him toward delirium.

Scarlet turned on her toes, teeth pressed into her bottom lip and looking strangely excited. "I have an idea."

He frowned. "About?"

She shifted, averting her gaze before seeming to steel her resolve. "There's something I think we should do. You gave me the idea last night when you were encouraging me to relax and not worry."

His lips parted and all sensible thoughts left his brain. "What did I say?"

"That something would eventually trigger my memories, and they'd come back."

He fought a smile. He hadn't been sure what he'd unintentionally motivated her to do when this conversation started, but recovering her memories wasn't even on his radar. "What's your idea?"

"I want to go back to the place where I was attacked. Maybe being there will jar something loose." She pretended to knock on her forehead. "What do you think?"

Austin grimaced, uncomfortable for all new reasons. "Are you sure about that? It hasn't even been forty-eight hours.

There's no need to rush. I think your memories will return on their own, if you're patient. Your doctor told you to rest."

"Maybe I don't want to rest." She crossed her arms and squared her shoulders. "It's not as if I'm asking to run a marathon." She winced. "That sounded angry, but it wasn't directed at you. I'm mad because I can't remember anything about this guy. Meanwhile, he's out there running free, doing whatever he wants, when he wants, and my life is a wreck. I'm hurt. I've got a live-in bodyguard. I might have to leave my home. I can't go to work. And I hate that I can't be more helpful to you and your brothers when everyone else is doing so much for me."

Austin stepped closer, leaving only a foot of space between them, unsure if she needed a hug, or if he did. He'd already assured her, multiple times, that she didn't owe anyone anything for their help. "Returning to the scene of your attack will likely be traumatic. Your mind hid what it did to protect you, and going back might feel a lot like unloading a dump truck of stress onto your brain."

"Or it might not."

Austin crossed his arms, matching her stance. He wouldn't willingly cause her distress. But he wasn't sure he could deny her either.

"You said you were here to help." Her expression softened and so did her voice. "I think this will help."

Austin sighed. She was right. Her happiness outweighed his concerns, and he was in way over his head.

An hour later, Scarlet was finally moving toward the front door.

She'd dragged her feet a bit while getting ready to leave. Mostly second-guessing herself, battling nerves and putting off the trip she'd suggested.

She stuffed her feet into brown suede booties and pulled her wool peacoat from the hook near her door. "Ready?"

"Yep."

She spun in the direction of his voice, hating the joy and comfort it brought when they'd only known one another a short time.

He stopped before her, having added a leather jacket and baseball cap to his ensemble. "I forgot to give this to you earlier," he said, reaching into his pocket. "You'd only been awake a short time before Mama arrived. By the time she left, you wanted to head out. Time got away from me." He passed her a cell phone.

She accepted the device, searching his eyes for more information.

"It's a new disposable," he said. "I had one in my bag like I thought. I opened it last night and set it up. I added myself, Dean, Finn and Mama to your contacts. Now you can call your mom when you're ready. Or a friend. Whoever you want."

A knot of unexpected emotion clogged her throat. It'd been her experience that most people said lots of things they didn't mean. But every time Austin made a promise, he followed through as if it was the most normal behavior in the world. He probably had no idea how much little things like reliability and truth meant to someone who'd been played, scammed and generally run around by men since the moment she'd started dating. "Thank you."

She gave herself an internal kick for her constantly increasing interest in him. He was here because she'd hired him. Not because he wanted to spend the rest of his life in her arms, watching sunsets from the deck, raising children who'd never doubt how much they were loved.

The sound of keys pulled her out of the fantasy, and she followed Austin across the porch toward the driveway.

They were on the road, closing the distance between her home and the scene of her attack, in minutes.

She stared at the phone in her hands, trying not to think too hard about their destination. It had been her idea after all, and it was far too late to chicken out now.

"Thinking of calling your mama?" Austin asked.

"Yes, but I might call the office first. Lydia sent flowers to the hospital, and I never thanked her." She dialed without letting herself overthink the decision. Whether she wanted to talk about what had happened or not, Lydia deserved to know she was safe and healing.

"Coulter Realty," Lydia answered on the first ring.

"Hey." Scarlet's throat tightened, and she had to clear it before going on. "It's me."

"Scarlet!" Lydia gasped. "Oh, thank goodness! I've been worried sick. I almost drove to your house this morning when I didn't hear from you. I stopped at the hospital after work, and they said you'd already been discharged."

"I'm home and doing well," she said. "The flowers were pretty and very appreciated. I'm sorry I didn't call you sooner."

"The morning paper said you were robbed. How are you doing? Do you need anything?"

Scarlet cringed, having forgotten to worry about what the paper said, and hating that Lydia's voice was laced with pity. "I'm fine. I didn't see the paper."

Austin glanced her way.

"The article was awful," Lydia said. "I cried reading it. I can't believe something like that could happen here, and to someone like you."

Scarlet wasn't sure what her friend had meant by the last

part, but her eyes misted with unshed tears anyway. "I'm okay," she croaked. "Or I will be. I'm with Austin, and he's taking good care of me."

Lydia made a wild sound in the back of her throat then squealed. "Oh, now I am definitely coming to visit you."

Scarlet slid her eyes in Austin's direction. The slight upturn of his lips suggested he'd heard the squeal, if not Lydia's very loud words. "Don't do that just yet," she said. "We might stay at his place for a few days. The person who attacked me has my purse, so we know he has my address."

Lydia gasped again.

Had she always been so dramatic, or had Scarlet been emotionally numbed by recent events?

"Which reminds me," Scarlet added, pressing on. "I sent an email to the home office last night letting human resources know I wouldn't be in for the rest of the week. I can't exactly sell houses looking like I do." The knot at the side of her head seemed to throb on cue, and her fingers trailed up to touch the bruising around her neck. "I've reached out to all my appointments and asked if they'd like to reschedule. I've given your email to everyone who wasn't interested in waiting. I thought that was best. You can do the showings. Make the sales. Build your client list. And I won't look like a flake for canceling last minute. I hope that's okay."

"Are you sure?" Lydia asked.

"Absolutely. You're a fantastic agent, and I know they'll be in good hands. Call me back at this number if you need anything."

"Thank you."

Scarlet smiled. "Don't mention it."

She disconnected the call and refocused on the view outside. Her stomach tightened as Austin turned off the main road and onto Mr. Perez's driveway.

It was time to find her memories.

Chapter Twelve

Scarlet dropped the phone into the truck's cup holder, a rush of foreboding crashing over her as she stared through the windshield.

Austin cut the engine but didn't make a move to get out. Probably waiting for her to decide if she was sure she wanted to do this.

The Perez home was beautiful as always, a handsome estate on a gorgeous plot of land.

She was safe. She wasn't alone, and what had happened once at this location wouldn't happen again.

She repeated the ideas silently until they felt more like truth, then she reached for her door handle. "Okay. I'm ready."

"I brought the stun gun," Austin said. "In case you want to carry it for peace of mind or try powering it up while we're here."

She shook her head, releasing a slow breath. "One thing at a time."

Austin followed her lead when she opened her door and climbed out. Then he hung back while she moved to the driver's side.

Sunlight glinted off pebbles of broken glass on the driveway.

"They had to break your window to get to you," Austin said.

She nodded, feeling his eyes on her as she walked along his truck, pretending it was her SUV. Her limbs began to tremble and her breaths quickened, but her mind went numb.

She scanned everything in sight, willing the blank spots in her memory to be revived.

"You doing okay?" Austin asked.

Scarlet clenched her teeth. "Everything looks different," she said, trying out reasons her stubborn brain refused to cooperate. "It's earlier in the day. My SUV isn't here. I know this is where it happened, but nothing feels the same."

"That's good," Austin said, stepping nearer and setting a gentle palm on her arm.

Scarlet turned to glare. "How can you say that? This place was supposed to give me answers."

"It's good because you're not losing your mind right now. Some people can't ever return to the places where things like this happened to them. Even seeing similar scenes in a movie can be enough to trigger their fear and panic. I'm saying I'm glad you're doing okay right now."

She considered his words, and the soft pressure of his palm against the fabric of her coat. "Yeah, well, I'm on a mission, and I'd hoped this would be easier."

He pulled his hand away and wiped it across his mouth, possibly fighting a grin. "All right. What's next?"

She wet her lips, making the procedure up as she went along. If being there wasn't enough, maybe the gruesome details would help. "Tell me what the police said," she suggested. "Maybe that will get the mental imagery going."

Austin looked skyward a moment, as if gathering his thoughts. "Finn said he spent about an hour out here walking the space, then circling the area in his car. There wasn't a lot to go on. He found some tire tracks in the grass along the road's edge, tucked behind that cluster of trees."

She followed his gaze and pointed finger to a dense cluster of pines. "I didn't come from that direction. I wouldn't have seen beyond the trees."

Austin nodded. "Your stalker probably knew that."

"He's smart," she said, wishing it wasn't true. "Like a conniving little fox."

"Pretty much. All the more reason to carry a stun gun."

She rolled her eyes. "You're persistent."

"I am," he said, releasing the mischievous grin she loved. The one sure to do her in if the unnamed stalker didn't.

Then another idea came to mind.

"I don't like that look," he said.

"What look?"

He stepped back. "The last time you made that face, you asked me to bring you here, and you wouldn't take no for an answer."

"Sometimes I can be persistent too," she said. "Especially when I'm right about something, which is most of the time. Like now." She twisted at her waist, scanning the area. "You won't like it, but I want you to humor me."

The apprehension on his face was nearly comical. As if she'd asked him to kindly remove his fingers. "Can you be more specific?"

"I want you to grab me from behind."

His eyes widened and his brows rose. "What?"

"Like an attacker," she clarified. "I think that could help."

"That is definitely not a good idea," he said. "For a whole host of reasons, I'm going to decline."

"You can't."

"I can." He took another step back. "I won't pretend to

attack you. I don't want to upset you or put that terrible idea in your head, even if you think you want it. You don't."

"I decide what I want," she said. "Now, stop backing up. That's where I was standing when it happened."

Austin's gaze fell to the broken glass at his feet.

"I'd just gotten out of my SUV. I'd barely taken two steps before his hands were on me. He dragged me back to where I'd started. I thought he was going to take me to a secondary location and murder me."

Austin paled as she marched forward then turned in front of him, putting her back to his chest.

"Scarlet," he warned.

She shivered at the sound of her name on his lips and the feel of his breath against her hair. "Hush, please." She reached back and caught his wrists then pulled them forward. "One arm came around me here." She curved his arm around her rib cage. "The other covered my mouth." She guided his fingers to her lips, but he tensed, refusing to actually touch her. "Put your face against mine. On the right."

Two long beats passed before he did as she'd asked. His skin was warm and smooth as it brushed against hers, and her heart rate quickened.

"I don't like this," he complained.

"Shh." She closed her eyes and imagined the scene, allowing the fear to build inside her. "I think he had a beard or hadn't shaved." Her breaths grew shallow as she chased the memories. "I felt stubble on my cheek."

"Good," he said, attempting to lower his arms. "That's something."

"Wait!" She caught his wrists and jerked them back into place, momentarily crashing one arm against her tender torso and the fingers of his other hand against her mouth.

Austin cussed and sprang back.

Scarlet's eyes flashed open, catching his reflection in the truck's side-view mirror. But it wasn't Austin she saw there.

He looked horrified when she spun to face him, hot tears on her wind-chilled cheeks.

"I saw him in the SUV's mirror. He was tall, but shorter than you, and he had a beard," she said, the words pouring out faster than she could sort them. "He wore a dark gray hoodie. The hood was up, pulled over his hair. I don't know what color it was, and his eyes were cut off in the image."

Joy and adrenaline flooded her system, and she bumped the toes of her boots against his. "His shoulders were narrower than yours. His arms were thinner. I didn't know him. Or he didn't seem familiar."

Austin's hands rose to grip her elbows as a tremor rocked through her. "Breathe, Scarlet. This is all good, but you have to breathe. Do you want to sit?"

She shook her head, tears coming heavily as relief mixed with residual terror. "I did it."

"Yeah, you did." Austin pulled her against him, engulfing her in his embrace and resting his cheek against the top of her head. "You were fearless. And you're safe now. Okay?"

She nodded, tears soaking the thin cotton of his shirt. Her arms wrapped around him, beneath the unzipped bomber jacket. And another memory returned. "I think he wore leather gloves." A small, unexpected sob broke on her lips.

"It's okay," he whispered. "Just breathe."

AUSTIN CURVED HIS body around hers, holding her close and feeling his protective instincts surge. She'd been through so much, and she'd willfully returned to this place, hoping to make a difference, even knowing the experience could break her. That was a whole other level of bravery. And he admired her for it. He'd seen soldiers behave similarly during his time in the military, and the mental connection was jarring. Scarlet was a civilian, but she was fighting her own war, where the enemy was violent and invisible. And she was alone in her experience, but still, she persisted.

He stepped back, dropping his arms to his sides, stunned by the turn his thoughts continued to take. He was too taken by her, and he didn't like the way it left him unsettled.

"Sorry," she said, looking embarrassed. "I didn't mean to—" She motioned between them.

"No. You're fine. I just—"

They stared at one another, tension twisting in the air.

"What would you like to do now?" he asked, hoping to appear more calm and centered than he felt. "We can swing by my place to get some things, or your office if you have anything you need to do."

"Can we go to the police station?" she asked. "Maybe I can tell Detective Beaumont what I remembered."

"Finn," Austin said, raking a hand through his hair. "Yeah. That sounds good. I'll call and let him know we're on the way."

They climbed back into his truck, and the air seemed thicker as he reversed down the driveway. He hadn't intended to hold her. Hadn't expected her to hug him. But she had, and he did, and now he knew what her heart felt like beating against his.

And he had no idea what to do with that information, but it was all he could think about.

She looked at him as he pulled onto the road and pointed them toward town.

He dialed his brother.

"Detective Beaumont," Finn said, voice rising from the truck's speakers.

"It's me," Austin said. "You're on speaker, and I'm with

Scarlet Wills. She's remembered a few details about her assailant and would like to meet with you if you've got some time."

"Nice," Finn said. "Did she remember what he looks like?"

"Kind of," Scarlet said, answering for herself. "I don't think it'd be worth meeting with a sketch artist, but I might be able to pick him out in a lineup."

"Can y'all meet me at the station in about twenty minutes?" Finn asked. "I'm headed that way now."

"Not a problem," Austin said.

"Good. Once we have some suspects, we'll call you in for that. How do you feel about taking a look in the mug shot database?"

A bright smile split her pretty face. "I can do that."

"Finn," Austin said. "Any news on the phone number used to order those flowers yesterday?"

"Unfortunately," he said, "it was a disposable unit like we suspected. Unregistered. I'm still working to track down the prepaid credit card's origin. So we could still get lucky on that."

Austin doubted it. This criminal was proving to be a real planner.

Chapter Thirteen

Scarlet trembled as she crossed the parking lot to the Marshal's Bluff police station. Her body couldn't seem to understand the reason for her recent jolt of adrenaline, and her fight-or-flight response was going haywire.

She took a calming breath with every step and hoped the rush would soon pass. She wanted to thank the detective on her case for all the effort he was making to protect her, and she hoped the news about her attacker's description would help speed up his capture.

She was also eager to talk to another member of Austin's family. Mostly because she was an only child, and siblings had always interested her. Nothing more.

Austin held the door to the lobby for her to pass, then greeted a uniformed officer behind a sliding glass window by name.

The men exchanged a few words while Scarlet took in her surroundings. The space was pleasant, if she didn't get caught up in the fact that everything heavier than a magazine was bolted to the floor.

A nearby buzz set them in motion once more. Austin steered her through another door, one hand on her back.

They passed several offices in a narrow corridor before a

ridiculously attractive man in a gray dress shirt, black slacks and a blue tie leaned into the hall ahead of them.

"Hey." His gaze moved from Austin to Scarlet, and recognition hit. This was Detective Beaumont.

Lydia was right. These men came from an unfair gene pool.

"Hey," Austin echoed. "Finn, you remember Scarlet Wills. Scarlet, you've met my little brother Finn."

Finn offered her his hand and she shook it. "I remember. You're looking well. It's nice to see you under better circumstances."

"Thanks," she said, following him into an office. He'd visited her on the night of her attack, but she'd been too out of sorts to hold much of a conversation.

Austin closed the door behind them then motioned for her to take a seat in one of the two chairs in front of his brother's desk.

Finn returned to the rolling chair on the other side.

She hadn't noticed before, but the resemblance between brothers was profound. Brown hair and eyes. Straight noses and teeth. Broad shoulders and square jaws.

Finn swiveled an open laptop to face her. "This is our mug shot database. It's fairly easy to navigate. You input the things you know here." He pointed to a set of drop-down lists on the left side bar. "Then click search."

Like online shopping, she thought. Except instead of sorting by price or pattern, she'd set the physical characteristics she wanted to see.

"It helps to sort by known offenses," he said. "Since we don't know if this guy has a criminal record, we'll have to work with what we've got. In the event he's never been arrested, this exercise will be futile, but at least it's somewhere to start."

Scarlet made a few selections and clicked search.

Finn slid a pad of paper and pen across the desk to her. "It might also be helpful to list all the men you see regularly or would recognize if you saw them on the street. Specifically those who live in town or nearby."

She straightened. "Like coworkers and clients? Or the barista at Java Jim's and the clerk at the grocery?"

"All of the above," Finn said. "Dry cleaner, mailman, guys from your gym. Anyone you've interacted with in the time since this began, or just before you started feeling watched. Even a simple exchange, a polite word or smile can be misconstrued as interest to these types of perpetrators."

She pursed her lips, hating that idea. She spoke to dozens of people every day. "Okay."

She switched gears, pulling the paper closer and starting a list while faces appeared in her mind like popcorn. She began with real estate agents and clients, then moved on to groundskeepers, bank representatives and title clerks, the man who cleaned the office, and a handful of workers at businesses she frequented. "You won't tell all these people I named them as potential criminals, will you?"

Finn chuckled. "No. And feel free to flag the ones you're sure don't fit the physical description. I'll still want to talk to them in case we're looking for someone peripherally connected."

She wrote until her hand cramped and she'd exhausted the list inside her brain. Then she returned the paper to Finn and her attention to the database search results.

"This is good," he said. "Thank you."

"Mom stopped by," Austin said.

Finn snorted a small laugh. "I had no doubt she would."

"She brought food."

"Uh-huh."

The brothers dove headlong into a discussion on their allegedly meddling mother, whom Scarlet thought was lovely. So she quickly tuned them out.

Her attacker's shadowed face, the hoodie and beard played on a loop in her mind. Little flashes. Tiny pieces of a larger picture. And something more. There was something about his mouth. She tried to hold on to the image for inspection. His lips hadn't been snarled or curled in anger as he'd choked her. The expression was flat, resigned. As if his strangling Scarlet was merely necessary. Something he simply had to do so he could go home and get on with his night.

She shivered, wondering what he was doing now. Was he afraid he'd soon be caught? Or did he like the chase? *Maybe*, she thought, *he's eating a hamburger with friends at the sports bar down the street.* Completely unaffected by what he'd done.

She forced her attention back to the screen where she'd been mindlessly scrolling. How many photos had she missed?

None of the faces before her now seemed right, and the more she scrolled, the more uncertain she became. Maybe she wouldn't recognize him after all.

A ringing phone broke her concentration once more.

The Beaumonts stilled as well, but no one made a move to answer the call.

A long moment seemed to pass before she realized the ringing phone belonged to her.

"Oh!" She pulled the device from her jacket pocket, having completely forgotten she'd tucked it in there when she left Austin's truck.

Her heart sank as she looked to the screen.

"Who is it?" Austin asked, swiveling on his seat with interest.

A reasonable question, considering she'd only had the phone for an hour or so, and she didn't even know its number. She did, however, recognize the digits onscreen.

"It's my mother."

AUSTIN WATCHED AS Scarlet's expression moved from confusion to astonishment, then resignation as she answered the call. She scanned Finn's small office, likely seeking but not finding anyplace for privacy.

Finn raised his brows, noticing Austin's interest.

He shrugged.

"Hello, Mom," Scarlet said, turning slightly away. "I'm fine. How did you get this number?" A soft groan left her lips. "Lydia."

Finn knocked gently on the desk, returning Austin's attention to him once more. "Is she close to her mama?"

He nodded. "I think it's the reason she's been putting this off. She called her office earlier. Lydia must've passed the number along."

Finn cringed. "Can you imagine if that was our mama?"

Austin matched his expression. "No."

"I'm serious," Scarlet said. "I'm barely injured. I was only kept for observations. A bump on the head and some bruising." She rubbed a hand over her eyes. "I asked them if they wanted to reschedule, and Lydia's handling the ones who don't."

Austin frowned. Had her mama moved on to shoptalk in the span of a couple sentences?

"Mom," Scarlet said, voice firming on the single syllable. "I'm at the police station right now, and I need to go so I can concentrate. We're trying to identify the man who did this." She glanced at the Beaumonts.

Austin and Finn looked at one another, both caught silent and staring.

"No, I don't need you to come to Marshal's Bluff. I'm staying with a friend for a few days... Because I didn't want to bother you."

Finn tented his brows. "Who's the friend?"

"Me." Austin slid his gaze away. "We might stay at my place until I can get her locks changed."

"We?"

"Yes," Austin said under his breath, returning his attention to his brother. "Obviously."

"When did y'all become a we?" Finn whispered back.

Austin scowled. "What?"

Finn raised his palms and leaned farther in his brother's direction. "You could've said you invited her to your place, or that she agreed to stay with you for now. You didn't have to use the word *we*. But you did."

"That's ridiculous." Austin mouthed the words.

"Sorry," Scarlet said, sliding the phone into her coat pocket. "That was my mom."

Finn dragged his gaze away from Austin and worked up a polite smile. "I hope she wasn't too worried."

"She took it better than expected," Scarlet said. "Of course, I didn't give her a lot of details, and apparently she hasn't looked online. Lydia said the morning paper covered things pretty well."

"It did indeed," Finn said. "Normally I would've played this close to the vest, but in your case I felt it was best to make an offensive move over a defensive one. By announcing this man's out there strangling women, folks will be cautious and vigilant. Hopefully people will be talking about him everywhere he goes and the spotlight will put a dent in his confidence."

She blinked. "You're trying to rattle him?"

"I want to make him think twice before acting out again. I need time to review all the materials related to this case, and considering how involved you are in the community, there are a lot of interviews to conduct." He lifted his notepad and turned it in her direction. "You have interactions with so many people on a regular basis that you broke them into categories. And each of these names is more than a potential suspect, it's a link." He looked at the paper then back to Scarlet. "You order coffee from Dustin a few days a week at Java Jim's, but when I talk to him, I might learn there's a cook in back on the days you normally visit, and a pastry delivery is also made around that time. Then I need to talk to the cook and pastry guy too."

She slumped in her chair. "So my list of fifty names could lead you to speak with a hundred people."

"Yep, and I can't have your attacker lashing out while I'm still doing the preliminary data collection."

"What if he gets a thrill from everyone talking about him?" she asked. "Like those bombers and pyromaniacs who stand around the crime scene, enjoying the trouble they caused."

"Right now, I'm willing to let his ego inflate a little, especially if that means he's not out there looking for you."

Austin rested a palm against the side of her chair, wishing he could squeeze her hand instead. "You okay? We can always come back later if you're getting tired or sore. Finn's got a nice long list of people to talk to now. He can use that to get started."

She looked to the screen then back. "Give me a few more minutes?"

"Sure."

He watched as she pushed herself to refocus. Then he dropped his hands into his lap and faced his brother. "Anything I can do to help you? I'll be at my place for a few days laying low, but I can research."

Finn worked his jaw, eyes seeking and hands clasped on the desk. "I'll let you know. Maybe I'll send you a copy of this list." He tapped the notepad. "Right now, you've got a witness to protect."

"Thank you," Scarlet said, still scrolling through mug shots. "For calling me a witness. Not a victim."

Finn opened his mouth then closed it and grunted.

Austin grinned. Scarlet Wills was a lot of things, but she wasn't a victim.

Eventually, her recent injuries got the best of her and she began to squirm, tipping her head side to side, stretching her neck and kneading her shoulders.

Austin nudged her with an elbow. "Let's go. You've done enough today, and we can always come back."

She sighed and slumped against the chair. "Yeah, okay."

Finn walked them down the hall and bid his farewell, leaving Austin to escort her back to his truck.

"You did a good job today," he said. "Did I tell you?"

She smiled. "I think I might've heard that."

"What do you think about getting that glass of wine and watching the sunset from my deck tonight?"

Her eyes lit. "You have a deck?"

"I do."

"And wine?" she asked.

He beeped his truck doors unlocked. "I've got hard cider. It's fruity, so that's a little like wine. Right?"

"Wine adjacent," she said. "I accept."

"Then let's call it a day. We can spend the rest of the afternoon relaxing in a pair of rockers like retirees."

A sharp whistle turned Austin toward the police department before she could respond.

Finn jogged in their direction as Austin opened the passenger door for Scarlet. "Wait. I just got a call from Dispatch. A fire was reported at 1611 Inlet Way. The fire department is already en route."

Austin's eyes snapped to Scarlet.

She gasped. "That's my place!"

Chapter Fourteen

Scarlet sat numbly in the passenger side of Austin's truck as they raced through town, hot on Finn's tail. The detective's lights and sirens parted traffic for him, and Austin glided his truck through in the wake, like the second line to the world's worst parade.

Austin used voice commands to call Dean and a few others, attempting to get information about how bad the situation was, but everyone was still en route as they were.

Scarlet kneaded her hands, certain some part of her would die if her home was unsalvageable. She'd put her heart and soul into the restoration of the property, not to mention most of her money. Those walls were her safe haven. No amount of insurance money could rebuild it. The structure was historic. And some modern throwback or replica would never be the same.

Worrying about installing the wrong doorknobs seemed incredibly trivial when the place was on fire.

"We're arriving now," an unfamiliar male voice explained through the truck speakers. The sound of waning sirens faded in the background. "No visible flames," he said. "What's your ETA?"

"Three minutes," Austin reported. "See you soon."

The call disconnected, and Scarlet stared at his face.

"Who was that?" she asked. "What did he mean? No visible flames. There's no fire?"

"Mark's a volunteer EMT. We'll know what he meant soon."

She swallowed a lump of fear rising in her throat and fixed her gaze outside the windshield.

The fire trucks were first to come into view. One had parked in her driveway. Another along the roadside. A police cruiser and an ambulance were angled into the space between the trucks.

"Someone called 911," Austin said. "I'm guessing it was the same person who set the fire, wanting to make sure you got the call while you were out and had to hurry back and find all this madness."

All Scarlet cared about in the moment was that Austin's friend had been right. There weren't any flames visible from the road. She placed a hand over her heart and sent up prayers of gratitude.

Austin parked behind the first responders. "Let's see what these guys know."

She hopped out and met him at the front bumper then hurried in the direction of her home.

Finn had jammed his vehicle into her driveway behind the first fire truck, two of his wheels on her lawn. He spoke to a passing fireman on his way to meet Austin and Scarlet. "We're going to get an update and report in a minute. Whatever happened in there, it looks like he's escalating again. I'm glad you made plans to stay elsewhere for a while."

Austin curved his fingers around hers, offering a small squeeze. "Do we have any idea how bad it looks inside?"

Scarlet's mind reeled. Fire could've ruined, charred or weakened the internal structure. There could be irrevocable smoke damage. Or chemical and water damage caused by whatever was done to stop the flames and smoke from spreading.

"Escalating," she said, repeating Finn's word. Her voice sounded foreign to her ears.

The word rolled in her mind, circling and itching.

"Yeah," Finn said. "And this is exactly the kind of lashing out I'd hoped to avoid."

Austin tugged her hand gently. "Are you okay? Scarlet?"

The Beaumonts' words sounded as if they were underwater. Flashes of her attacker holding her in place whipped in and out of her mind. *He is escalating.*

"I think he spoke to me," she said.

"Who?" Finn asked.

She shook her head, unwilling to be sidetracked as she clung to the sensation of her attacker's hands on her mouth and middle. "He whispered something into my ear when he pressed his cheek to mine." She closed her eyes, imagining the scratch of his whiskers, and her lids flew open. "He said he wanted us to be together." She looked from Finn to Austin, heart racing and stomach souring. "Something like that. There's more, but I can't—"

The brothers exchanged a look.

Scarlet's fuzzy thoughts suddenly cleared. Wasn't escalation supposed to move more slowly? "When I came to you, I thought I was being followed," she told Austin. "You said it was possible that had been going on for weeks. Then out of nowhere, he attacked me. Now two days later he lit my home on fire. It feels more like he's unraveling."

Austin rubbed his forehead then the back of his neck. "I think he saw you with me and became territorial. The attack might've been the warning you mentioned. Maybe that's why he let you live."

Her mouth twisted in disgust. "Then he tried to apologize by sending flowers."

"But I was there, and I called him."

Finn hooked his hands on his hips. "I'm guessing by all this." He motioned to the abundance of emergency vehicles surrounding her property. "He knows Austin spent the night here last night."

Nausea twisted in Scarlet's core. What if the person who'd set a fire in her home while she was away had acted last night instead? When she was sleeping and Austin was circling her home, trying to watch both doors by himself.

She stepped away from Austin and wrapped one arm around her middle, covering her mouth with the other hand.

A fireman strode in their direction, and Finn stepped forward with an outstretched hand. "How does it look in there?"

Their small circle turned expectantly.

The fireman made eye contact with her, then Austin, nodding to each, before returning his attention to the detective. "Small fire. No damage."

"I don't understand," she said. How could there be a fire without damage?

The fireman glanced over his shoulder at her house. "It appears as if a contained fire was intentionally started in the master bedroom. Nothing else seems amiss. It's safe to go inside and take a look when you're ready."

Finn tipped his head. "After you."

Austin turned to Scarlet, but her feet felt like lead.

He slid his hand in hers once more and gave that familiar, gentle squeeze. "Scarlet." He dipped his head closer. "I've got you."

Then they were in motion.

First responders milled around, chatting and watching as

Scarlet and Austin passed. This small, contained fire was sure to be tomorrow's front-page news. It probably wouldn't take long for the dark cloud to settle over her name as a Realtor. The lady with a stalker. A bad luck human to be avoided. Then where would she be?

She'd have to start over. Again.

A million unkind words flooded into her mind. Nasty comments from her mother's many companions, snide words from Scarlet's former boyfriends. Unkind teachers who'd assumed she was the problem when her dyslexia made it harder for her to learn new material, before she'd gotten the help she'd needed. Anyone and everyone in her past who'd seemed to believe all their problems started and ended with her.

She'd overcome a lot of those burdens with regular trips to the therapist and remediation training for her dyslexia, but she was sixteen and miserable again as she marched into her home. Even with Austin at her side.

"No signs of forced entry," an officer stated to Finn as he reached the porch. The man in uniform nodded to her as she passed.

"He has my keys," Scarlet said, mostly to herself. There wasn't any reason to break in now. And if the criminal lost her keys, he could always use a credit card to gain access.

She followed the parade of men into her bedroom where another person in uniform took photos of the metal bucket, normally used to collect ashes from the living room fireplace. Now seated on her bed. Black soot marks marred the beautiful eyelet cover.

"Books were used to kindle the fire," the fireman said, pointing to the bucket. "A liquid accelerant enhanced the flames. Smoke detectors were going off when we arrived."

Finn made a path from one side of her bed to the other. "Who called this in?"

The fireman shrugged.

Scarlet supposed Finn already knew that answer, and the number was likely tied to another untraceable, disposable phone. "He wanted me to know he was angry," she said, feeling as if she was finally catching up, but very late to the game. "Another warning. Not a punishment."

The final word stuck in her head and itched in her throat. Another memory hovered just out of reach. Another awful thought pushed the curiosity aside.

The man who'd nearly killed her had been in her home while she was away. He'd been in her bedroom. Invaded her space, used her keys as if he belonged there. And for those reasons, this threat felt inexplicably more personal than the physical attack. If nothing more had gone wrong, she might've been able to convince herself she'd been in the wrong place at the wrong time when she was strangled. But there wasn't any way to deny this threat was intended for one person. This was absolutely about her.

Finn and the firemen left her room.

She turned to watch them go, having missed whatever they'd said.

Austin stepped closer. He released her hand in favor of sliding his palms along her forearms. "How are you doing?"

She exhaled a thin breath. "Not good."

He pulled her against him for a quick hug. "They have one more thing to show us, then you can gather your things and we'll get out of here."

Scarlet straightened and followed him through her open bedroom door.

Finn and the fireman stood before a small built-in desk in her parlor. Floor-to-ceiling bookshelves stood on either side. Several tomes were missing. Likely the ones used to start the fire.

A photo of Scarlet in a long white beaded gown centered her small desk. Her image beamed back at them. The gown had been spectacular, rented from one of those big LA shops and returned when the event had ended. The plunging neckline and slit up one side had made her feel confident and sexy.

The party had been amazing, attended by top real estate agents, bank execs and related industry stars. All to see her and a handful of others receive awards for excellence.

"When was this taken?" Finn asked.

"Last summer," she said, then thought better of it. "Not a few months ago," she clarified. "The year before. Maybe fifteen months back. It was a banquet thrown by Coulter Realty executives."

Finn stretched blue gloves over his hands and lifted the photo. "Fifteen months, huh?"

A slip of paper scooted across the desk in the picture's absence, revealed and set free by Finn's action.

The air thickened, and Scarlet's chest grew tight as she stared at the message and read the tidy script.

You betrayed me.

Chapter Fifteen

Austin spent the next half hour with his fists clenched and jaw set, taking in every comment and detail traded between Finn and the other officials. Hoping to hear some magic words that would give the stalker's identity away.

Scarlet had excused herself to collect her things and probably do some internal screaming.

The simmering rage was real and very thinly veiled, for him at least.

He'd promised to be her eyes and ears, so she wouldn't miss anything while she packed.

Eventually, the fire trucks and ambulance took their leave, carrying the first responders with them. Finn and his team stayed a bit longer, attempting to pull fingerprints from the doorjambs and knobs, as well as the desk, bookshelves and the fireplace bucket.

Austin hoped they'd find something but suspected they wouldn't. Whoever they were dealing with was meticulous. Worse, Scarlet said he'd worn leather gloves to attack her. He'd likely worn them for this as well.

Finn leaned against the archway between Scarlet's living room and kitchen. "I'm going back to the station," he said. "I need food and a little time to make sense of the information we have. Hopefully I can get it to lead somewhere."

"Good luck," Austin said, meaning it to his core.

"Thanks. I'm just glad he continues to leave clues." Finn sighed and tented his brows. "It's obvious I don't have to say this, but I will anyway."

Austin frowned.

"Keep her close." Finn flicked his gaze over Austin's shoulder, presumably toward the room where Scarlet was packing. "I know you like to get involved and take action. We all do, but this time your energies will be best used to entertain her. Distract her. Keep her away from town."

Finn was right. That didn't need saying.

Austin bit his tongue and nodded.

Finn released a small puff of air and rolled his shoulders. "I know you know what you're doing, but it's also my job to say the words. Speaking as your brother now," he said, voice lowering drastically. "She's hurting, scared and hunted. This situation could become an issue."

Austin crossed his arms and straightened. "You don't think I can protect her?" Was he kidding?

"That's not what I'm concerned about."

Austin narrowed his eyes, and the brothers exchanged a long silent look.

He imagined Finn was attempting to telepathically point out that Scarlet was vulnerable and Austin wasn't the sort to get serious about a woman, yet he'd been seen holding her hand by half the emergency responders in town. And that could be confusing for many people.

Knowing he'd probably think the same things in Finn's shoes, he settled for a curt dip of his chin.

Finn relaxed, glanced around the home then headed for the door. "Call if you need anything."

"Back at you," Austin said, following. "Keep us in the

loop if something new comes up. Even a small thing. We want to know."

Finn stopped on the porch to puff out his cheeks. "We." He shook his head then jogged to his truck and climbed inside.

Austin stared after him. He had started thinking of himself and Scarlet as a we. He didn't want to think about why. It wouldn't end well. His relationships never did. Other than his mama, all the women he knew took issue with his job. It kept him out too late, gone too long and unable to discuss what he'd been up to most of the time. Since he couldn't imagine doing anything else for a living, he'd stopped trying to find a significant other.

A small crash in the next room set Austin in motion, heading toward the source of the sound.

Scarlet stood before her dresser, picking up a collection of books she'd apparently dropped while packing.

He crouched to help, but his heart stopped at the sight of her.

Tears tracked over her cheeks. Her eyes were glossy, her face pink.

They stood at the same time, and she wiped her face. "Sorry. I'm a little shaky, and I thought I had them stacked better."

He stepped forward without thinking and pulled her into his arms. A bad habit he couldn't seem to break. "You don't have to apologize. Let me help you."

"No. I've got it." She edged away, face cleared of emotion. "I'm ready." She tucked the books into a bag on her bed then lifted the handle of a large suitcase. "This looks like a lot, but it's not all clothing. I'm bringing some of the smaller things I wouldn't want destroyed in a fire if he comes back."

Austin pressed his lips together, feeling irrationally rejected by the way she'd pulled away. He'd crossed a line by hugging her, and he needed to be more professional. "It's no problem. Bring as much as you want."

He made a mental note to keep a more polite distance moving forward. He wouldn't allow her to be hurt again on his watch. Not by the criminal currently tormenting her. And certainly not by himself.

SCARLET BOUNCED ALONG in Austin's truck, moving away from town and the sea. It was strange to her, not to live near the water. But he'd grown up on a ranch, so maybe it wasn't as important to him as it was to her. Still, she'd be even more of a mess than she was if not for her deck and the inlet views to calm her.

The reaching limbs of ancient trees stretched over them, crowding the sky into little more than a pale blue ribbon above. The narrow gravel road ahead was spattered with autumn leaves in every color and utterly devoid of other vehicles.

He glanced at her as the truck waddled along, more and more slowly as the path they traveled grew infinitely less accommodating of their apparent trespass. "Are you worried yet?"

She dared a look in his direction, then returned her eyes to the road, if that's what she was supposed to call it. "Have I wondered if I accidentally let a serial killer drive me into the mountains to escape a stalker? Nope. That's never crossed my mind."

Austin chuckled, and the road began to smooth. Fresh chunks of gray gravel led to a short, covered bridge, then bent around another corner in the distance. Every board of the bridge appeared new.

"Wow." She leaned forward, admiring the structure.

"There aren't many covered bridges left in North Carolina. What on earth is one doing here?"

"My brothers and I put it here," he said. "With a little help from our dad. It took us more than a decade."

She turned to gape at him.

He rolled onto the bridge's center and shifted into park. "Do you want to get out and look?"

"Absolutely." She climbed down and ran her hands over the treated wood, taking in the obvious craftsmanship. "You really built this?"

His smile was proud as he approached. "We started when I was a kid. My grandma owned the land, and she liked covered bridges. She had a lot of memories of the one in the town where she grew up. Grandpa proposed there. So, when she was getting older, Dad made her foreman on this project, and he enlisted my brothers and I for free labor. We took turns leaving for the military and college, but eventually we got the job done."

"And your grandma?"

He shook his head. "She was around for most of it, but she was too ill to see it finished. We promised to bring her here on the next nice day, but she passed during the winter. I guess it wasn't meant to be."

Scarlet moved to his side and folded her hands in front of her, determined not to touch him like she wanted. All the touching only made things more confusing. "I'm sorry you lost your grandma. She must've felt so loved, seeing you do this for her." Scarlet couldn't imagine. The possibility love like that existed, even between a grandparent and their grandchildren, tightened her lungs and filled her heart with hope.

"I like to think so," he said. "She was very special to us all."

Scarlet moved to the bridge's edge, drawn by the sounds

of running water. "I can't believe your dad knew how to do this. And that he was able to teach children."

"Grandpa was a carpenter. Dad learned a lot growing up with him, and we learned a lot working with Dad. Our family didn't always have tangibles to pass down, like family jewels or antique whatnots. But our parents and grandparents did what they could to give us their morals, values and skills."

She rested her hands on the wide railing and peered through a cutout in the bridge's side. Initials had been carved into the wood. D.B., F.B., A.B., L.B., J.B. She traced the set in the center. "Is J.B. your dad?"

"My oldest brother, Jake."

She wondered which face was Jake's in the family photo at Austin's office, but the image had already faded in her mind.

Below them, water burbled over rocks and around fallen trees, cutting an arched path through the hillsides. A hundred yards ahead, on the freshly graveled road, stood an old mill, its waterwheel motionless in the creek.

Austin leaned a hip against the railing. "These aren't quite inlet views, but they make me happy when I've had a tough day."

She turned to squint at him. "You live nearby?"

He hitched his chin toward the mill. "Grandma left the property to me. My brothers got other things. They wouldn't have wanted this, and I wouldn't have wanted anything else."

"And you live here now?" she asked, attempting to make sense of it.

He nodded. "I'm restoring the place a little at a time. I'll have the rest of the road repaired and covered with gravel in the spring. Living back here is the main reason I keep my old truck. I've never gone anywhere it couldn't take me."

Scarlet smiled, fitting another piece of the Austin Beaumont puzzle into place. She already knew he loved his family, history and the outdoors. Now she knew he was good with his hands.

He smiled, and her face heated. "Are you cold?" he asked, likely mistaking the color in her cheeks.

She shrugged, unwilling to lie and not trusting her mouth while her brain felt a little on the fritz.

"Let's go inside." He opened her door and waited while she climbed in. Then he drove the rest of the way to his home.

The former mill was a two-story rectangle with a triangular roof, like the ones children draw on paper. Weathered old boards ran lengthwise like a log cabin, making up the body of the structure. Red metal panels replaced the original roof. Thick beds of black mulch and a row of brightly colored mums lined the brick walkway. A grapevine wreath with a burlap bow hung on the painted black door.

"Pretty," she said, climbing steps cut from stone as old as time.

"Mama decorates everything," he said, unlocking and opening the door. "She says pretty things put folks at ease."

"She's not wrong," Scarlet said, following him inside.

Battered hardwood floors spread out before them to an exposed brick wall. A small table sat against the stone with a framed sketch of the mill hanging above and an empty vase. A set of steps anchored the wall to her left. A pass-through arch in the bricks drew her forward.

The space beyond was wholly unfinished, covered in dust and fallen plaster from a crumbling ceiling. A row of tall, skinny windows lined the far wall and overlooked the waterwheel.

"This will eventually be my office," Austin said, motioning to a set of sawhorses topped with a sheet of wood and a stack of files. A ladder-back chair stood behind it. "Come on. Let's get you settled upstairs."

He led her up the sturdy, visibly reinforced staircase, past strips of insulation rolled between two-by-fours. Clearly a work in progress with much more to be done.

She began to worry about what she'd find on the second floor.

Those fears subsided as she rounded the bend in the stairs.

A spacious, open floor plan rolled out before her. On this level, the exposed bricks from below became a fireplace dividing the studio. A small island stood before multiple sets of French doors overlooking a rear deck. Stainless steel appliances and painted cabinets hugged the corner, careful not to interrupt the view. Living room furniture had been arranged on an earthen-colored rug before the fireplace, and a large bed with scrolled iron head and footboards anchored the wall opposite the creek views.

"There's only one bedroom and bathroom," he said. "I can set up a cot in my office or sleep on the couch if you're okay with me being up here. You're welcome to the bed, and the bath is around the corner there." He pointed.

She stared, trying to reconcile what lay before her with the exterior views and the barely passable road.

He frowned. "You don't like it."

"No. I love it. It's like living in a tree house." A really modern, very cool tree house. She moved to the bank of glass doors, mouth hanging unashamedly agape. "How do you ever make yourself leave?"

"I'm money motivated. I like to eat and keep the lights on. Plus, there's a lot still to be done here, and that all takes cash."

"Have you applied for historical property grants?"

He smiled. "I have. I might be able to get some help with restoration of the wheel and road, but not the mill. I've altered too many things, and the updates have negated eligibility."

She gazed at the granite countertop and Edison lights over the island. She supposed he had changed a lot, but the structure was still original. Wasn't it? Not the roof. Her mind whirled with new purpose. Maybe when her stalker was jailed, she could help Austin look for available funds.

Assuming he wanted to remain friends.

Austin's stomach growled, and she grinned.

"I don't suppose you get pizza delivery here?"

"No." He moved toward the fridge and opened the doors. "But I've got a grill and some free time. How do you feel about burgers?"

"I feel very good about burgers," she assured him.

And Austin went to work.

Chapter Sixteen

They sat on Austin's deck long after the meal was finished and the sun dipped low in the sky. Scarlet actively reminded herself that the last few days, and the current moment, were real. She wasn't dreaming and wouldn't wake up to her formerly predictable and satisfying life. That era was over. It wasn't safe to go home.

Austin excused himself and returned with two brown bottles. "As promised, my special wine."

She smiled as he approached with the hard cider. "Those look perfect for fall."

He twisted the cap from one bottle and passed it her way. "What?"

"What?" she repeated, accepting the offer.

"You made a face when I took off the cap. I'm sure you could've done it yourself. I was just being—"

"Kind," she said. "I know. I'm starting to pick up on the pattern."

He returned to the rocking chair at her side. "I've noticed some of your routines too."

"Like?"

"You frown a lot when anyone does anything for you. The simplest things. Like when Finn held the door. Or Mama brought breakfast. When I breathe."

She smiled and took a sip of her cider. "Habit. I'm not used to the help, I guess. I've been on my own a long time, and I don't have siblings or close friends. So I just do everything myself."

He looked offended.

She bristled. "There's nothing wrong with being self-sufficient. Don't look like I just told you I hate your truck."

He kicked back in the chair, swigging from his bottle before speaking. "What about your mama? You must've been her top priority, since it was just the two of you."

Scarlet debated her response. She hated talking about herself, and especially about her life before moving to Marshal's Bluff. But she also longed for someone in her life she could be real with. *And if Austin has a problem with my truth, he doesn't have to stick around when this is over*, she reasoned.

She watched the water flowing through the creek below, letting it soothe her nerves and urge her on. Maybe it was time to be transparent for a change. Time to stop putting on a show. Everything else was changing. Why not this too? Besides, she was almost certain Austin wouldn't hold her past or secrets against her. If not because he was genuinely honorable, then because she'd soon be out of his life if that was what he wanted.

He waited patiently while she chose her words.

"My mom started selling homes when I was in elementary school. I don't remember much about my dad, but after he moved out, she told me he only came back to ask her for money, and we didn't have any. He'd threaten to take me with him sometimes, and Mom would empty her tiny bank account for him. She said whatever amount she had was always enough to make him go away, but never enough for a lawyer."

Austin's jaw flexed. Unhappy or uncomfortable. She couldn't be sure which, but he'd asked, so she was answering.

"When Mom heard how much money she could earn selling houses, she made it her mission to be the very best agent she could. We drove all day once, visiting every thrift store in three counties looking for suits and costume jewelry on the cheap. Then she studied every night after her shifts at the diner and got her real estate license. She was my age then, beautiful, witty, motivated. She did well and made a shrewd businesswoman. I never doubted I'd follow in her footsteps."

"Why do I sense a but?" he asked. "I know you sell real estate."

Scarlet inhaled deeply and released it slowly. "She was busy making a living and thriving on the attention that comes with mastering something, and I was home alone more often than not. I was rarely her priority, but I couldn't complain without feeling guilty because I knew I was the reason she worked so much. She was making ends meet for me. But she was never very...maternal. She did the best she could, and I doubt she has any idea she could've done better."

"You raised yourself and ended up caring for her too," he guessed.

"I did what I could, which wasn't much while I was small, but I got older and I learned. She hired a lawyer to protect me from my dad in the times he was out of jail and on the take." Scarlet forced herself to meet Austin's eyes, waiting for the judgment that came when anyone found out one of her parents had been in jail.

He nodded in understanding, processing without judgment. So, she carried on.

"I was in high school when I discovered I had dyslexia.

Until a kind and attentive young teacher caught it, everyone else just thought I wasn't very smart, or that the girl with the uninvolved mom didn't try. By that time, I'd already decided who I was, and I wasn't proud of her. And Mom's continued absence seemed to say I wasn't worth the time. Having dyslexia made it all worse, because once I'd been diagnosed, I couldn't just pretend my grades were low because I was too cool to care. Everyone knew my grades were low because something was wrong with me. I didn't want a label, and I hated being pulled out of class for extra help. I tried to quit school my junior year. Mom wasn't having that, so I rebelled however I could and our relationship suffered for a while."

"Rebelled?" he asked.

"Endlessly." She smiled a little at the lengths she'd gone to push back at a life she thought had pushed her too far. "I got a fake ID, then a tattoo and piercings. I dyed my hair jet-black then cut it off. I skipped classes, and some nights I didn't come home. And I always dated the wrong kinds of men."

Austin rocked in his chair, head turned to face her, the picture of ease. "I'm not going to pretend to know what it's like to be you, then or now. But I will say I grew up on a ranch for troubled youths, and what you've described is practically troubled teen 101. Kids try to regain control however they can. My brothers and I all did similar things too."

She frowned. "Sure."

"We did," he assured her. "We didn't even have it rough in life. We just hated rules and authority. And living on a ranch for struggling kids put a spotlight on us. There was pressure to be some kind of models for appropriate teen behavior. None of us were good with spotlights."

She tried to imagine the pressure he described and wondered if it wasn't easier for her in the house alone. No one caring if she slipped up. She probably would've failed her teen years either way. "I think I dated bad boys to goad my mom. It never worked, and I wound up wanting them to care about me, but they didn't."

"You were young, angry and trusted the wrong people," he said. "Then those people perpetuated your low self-image."

She looked away, hating the truth. "I created my own misery."

"You were a kid, and you were hurting," he corrected. "You turned out pretty great, so it might be worth forgiving yourself."

She opened her mouth to say she already had. Of course she had. She was twenty-seven years old. But she couldn't say the words. Because maybe they weren't true.

"Is it why you listen to so many audiobooks?" he asked. "Because of the dyslexia?"

"I can read as well as anyone now," she said. "I like audiobooks because I spend a lot of time in my car, driving from showing to showing. The books help pass my time. And I listen at an advanced speed, which means I read more books a year than I could otherwise."

Austin took a deep pull from his cider, tipping his head back as he drank.

Her eyes dropped to the long, tan column of his throat. Then, a little lower, to the bit of exposed collarbone, where his shirt was tugged down at the side. "I started over when I moved here," she said. "I put the past behind me, and I began a new story."

"I get that," he said, setting the bottle aside. "You faced some demons in your teen years and you conquered them in your twenties. Sounds like victory to me."

"I have a tattoo of a broken heart on my hip." She bit her lip hard, unsure why she'd told him, but needing him to understand her past wasn't behind her—it was etched into her heart and inked on her skin.

"As far as any men who broke your heart," he said, shifting forward on his seat and glaring at her. "They didn't deserve you and probably didn't deserve the company or attention of anyone, especially a woman. They probably also had their own emotional issues and mistreating you made them feel a little bigger. Either way, you weren't the cause of their behavior. That was all on them."

Her eyes stung, and she blinked back the tears. "It's very nice of you to say." No one else ever had.

"It's very true of me to say."

"Why aren't you dating anyone?" she asked, unable to quench her curiosity, and hoping he'd be as candid with her as she had been with him.

Maybe he'd say he hated marriage, believed in open relationships or didn't want kids. Maybe then she could get her head on straight where he was concerned.

He rolled his eyes, looking unprecedentedly self-deprecating. "I live in a small town with three eligible brothers relatively my age. The dating pool got incredibly small, really fast. Aside from that, women don't seem interested in a partner who works long hours, stays out late, often overnight, and can't talk about who he's with or what he's doing."

"So you aren't opposed to dating?"

"No." A small smile played on his lips. "Why? Are you asking?"

She laughed. "It's just good to know there's at least one nice guy out there, willing to treat a partner right."

Austin made a disgruntled sound. "There are lots and lots of men like that. You found the bad ones because you were in a bad place. Those guys were the exceptions, not the rule. I promise you. Now you've got me rethinking my life's mission."

She gave a startled laugh. "You have a life's mission?"

"Don't you?"

She rocked and smiled. "I guess I try to do the best job I can every day at whatever comes my way."

"See?" he said. "And I help and protect anyone I can, however I can. I'm adding you to this list. I will convince you good men exist and there's one out there for you, if you want him."

She wet her lips, hoping that man was him, and not caring that it was silly to want him. Even if they were from two very different upbringings. "You've got lofty goals, Beaumont."

His lips twitched. "More than you know."

Chapter Seventeen

Austin woke groggy and restless the next morning. He hadn't slept well following a long night of research on the potential stalkers in Scarlet's life. And countless replays of his conversation with her before she'd gone to bed.

They'd talked about deep and real things on his deck, things he didn't generally discuss. Not with his friends. Not with his brothers. Absolutely not with someone he'd only known for a few days. Yet, there he was. Scarlet made it so easy to open up, and he could see some of her shared stories had cost her as well. The worst things she'd confided were about her father and the boyfriends of her youth. Too many men had treated her poorly, and those experiences had evidently chipped away at her self-worth. Though no one would know it by talking to her more casually. She hid the dark and bruised parts well. And he wanted more than anything to spend as long as it took to help her heal every past scratch and scrape, because those injuries had nothing to do with her and everything to do with unworthy men.

She'd been especially understanding when he'd shared his reluctance to settle down over the years. He'd been in love once, but she'd had no patience for his work and no trust when he was away. The relationship had gone from the best days of his life to the worst in less than a year. And evoking the fool-me-once motto, he hadn't planned to waste his time, or offer his heart for another punching, ever again.

Scarlet had just nodded and said the whole experience must've been hard.

He'd spent a long while wondering if he was an unintentional hypocrite. He'd insisted Scarlet be open to the possibilities that her bad experiences were exceptions to the rule. Yet he hadn't been willing to take the same chance himself. At least, not before meeting her.

Worse, what if she held him to his challenge? Was he actually supposed to introduce her to someone else so they could fall in love?

His fingers flexed and curled, tempted to knock the hypothetical other guy's lights out.

Living with Scarlet Wills was going to be the death of him.

He sighed in relief when the shower in the next room finally silenced. Knowing she'd been naked and wet on the other side of the wall had conjured a thousand unbidden ideas. The concentration it'd taken to push the thoughts from his mind was exhausting, and he blamed his lack of sleep.

He poured a glass of iced water from his pitcher in the refrigerator and started a fresh pot of coffee. Finn and Dean were on their way over, and they'd likely be exhausted. They too had been working on Scarlet's case long into the night. In fact, everyone he knew with the ability to look for this criminal was on the job and taking it seriously. Austin had never been so thankful for his network of lawmen and related professionals.

The coffee finished brewing several minutes later, and Scarlet still hadn't made an appearance. Something about her prolonged absence struck him as odd.

Maybe he was just looking for a reason to see her sooner, but he went to check on her anyway.

He crossed the floor to his bedroom then rounded the corner to a closed bathroom door.

A low curse and sharp yip sounded inside.

Austin's heart thundered, but he knocked casually. "Everything okay?"

"No!" Scarlet snapped. "It's this ridiculous cut on my shoulder. Of all my injuries, this is the one I hate most."

His muscles tensed. He hated every bump and bruise on her body, but he'd admittedly forgotten about that one. "Are you in pain?" he asked. "Is it bleeding? Should I call your doctor?"

The lock clicked, and the bathroom door crept open. "No. It's healing fine, I think. I just can't reach it to use the cream," she said, shame thick in her voice. "I've only been replacing the bandage for the last couple of days, but it's itchy now, and I have to deal with it. Except I can't."

He looked at the door, now cracked open by an inch, and he imagined her bare shoulder. The long line of her neck, the gentle sway of her hips. The supple fullness of her breasts. He swallowed a groan. The universe was testing him. "Can I help?"

"I feel like a completely helpless human, which I hate," she said. "But yes. Will you please?"

His hand was already on the knob. "Of course."

Scarlet stood inside, looking sheepish and frustrated in a pair of navy blue leggings and a plaid flannel shirt. The buttons at the top were unfastened. She gripped the material at her breastbone, allowing the shirt to drape loosely over her shoulder and down her back. "I can get the bandage on if I prepare it first, then kind of slap it in the right direction, but I can't see what I'm doing to get the cream on. I don't think I could reach it properly, even if I could see."

He stepped inside and closed the door, hoping that would make her feel less exposed. "Just tell me what to do."

She turned her back to him, loosening her grip on the shirt. Their gazes met in the reflection of his bathroom mirror.

An inch or two of slightly puckered skin was visible on one shoulder blade, striped with three small stitches. "It's healing," he said. "That's why it's beginning to itch."

"That's good news, I guess." She sighed, apparently still coming down from her frustration. "I'm supposed to put this cream on the stitches then replace the bandage." She slid a tube of prescription medicine around her middle to him. "The new bandage is set up on the counter, but I can't get this part accomplished."

Austin checked the cluster of materials near his sink. As promised, one square gauze pad was outlined with medical tape and waiting, sticky side up, on the counter. Her shoulder was smeared with the cream nowhere near the wound. "I've got this," he said, smiling at her reflection. "Someone's always injured on the ranch. I've had my fair share of first-aid experience."

"I haven't," she said. "I've never broken a bone, needed my tonsils out or been admitted to a hospital before the other night. I never even needed braces."

He guffawed at her reflection. "Brag a little, why don't you?"

She laughed.

"Hold still." He lifted the tube and squeezed a dollop of cream onto her little wound, thankful the injury wasn't any worse and that the doctor had chosen stitches. Austin had suffered much worse without stitches, but those wounds had left scars. He hated the thought of her being scarred for life by this creep. The emotional and mental aftermath alone would be bad enough. Scarlet didn't need physical reminders too.

Her body swayed closer, leaning back as he gently dabbed at her shoulder, then smoothed the bandage on. He took his time wiping the extra, accidental spots of cream she'd applied before he came to help, and shamelessly savored the feel of her soft, supple skin.

"I'm happy to make this my daily job, if it reduces your stress," he suggested, lingering where he shouldn't.

"I accept," she whispered, relaxing fully against his chest, eviscerating the space between them from hips to shoulders. Her head lolled to one side, and their gazes met in his mirror once more.

Tension ratcheted in him as he watched for signs of uncertainty in her eyes. When he found only curiosity and interest, he stroked his fingers over the curve of her shoulder, tracing her honey-scented skin to the crook of her neck. "Is this okay?"

"Yes." She sighed softly, and his body stiffened.

Austin's heart rate doubled as he thought of a dozen other ways he wanted to touch her and elicit those little sounds. But he was supposed to be her protector. She was hurt, scared and vulnerable. The things he wanted weren't right. At least not right now.

She turned to face him, and his hands fell to his sides. Her chin lifted, and she fixed him with those beautiful moss green eyes. The longing and trust he saw there twisted and tightened his core.

His hands rose again, cupping her hips. He warned himself not to cross a line.

Not to take her mouth with his. Not to toss her unbuttoned shirt and everything else she wore onto the floor so he could worship her. He definitely shouldn't lift her onto the countertop and lose himself inside her.

Scarlet's hands glided over his chest and shoulders, fingertips tangling in his unshorn hair. Her pink lips parted and she rose onto her toes. The slide of her body and warm press of her breasts against him tightened his grip on her hips.

The heat in her gaze set a fire in him, and he felt a fissure form in his already too thin resolve.

"Austin," she whispered, her breath dancing on his lips, inviting them closer.

The sound of his doorbell pushed a curse through his gritted teeth. He forced his hands away from her with the final frayed tether of his self-control. "My brothers are here," he said, voice too deep and gravelly. "Excuse me."

He turned on his toes and headed for the door, forcing his mind and body back into submission with each measured step. And knowing his brothers would still see right through him.

SCARLET STUMBLED BACK, gripping the countertop and wondering what had happened. She'd imagined Austin's mouth on her a thousand times, and she'd practically thrown herself at him in the hopes of experiencing the real thing. But he'd walked away.

Hot, delicious tension seemed to coil around them anytime they were near, and she'd been sure he'd felt it too. She'd spent a long, restless night wondering if the mutual attraction had been only in her mind, but his assistance this morning had been electrified. He'd touched and held her as if he wanted her too.

Hadn't he?

He'd practically run away when the doorbell rang. Actually, he'd cussed first, then run. Had he been upset about the interruption or about what they'd almost done?

The latter seemed silly since he'd offered to find a good man for her, so she'd see they still existed. When he'd said it, she'd hoped he meant himself. Maybe she'd misread everything. Maybe her confused, overwrought emotions had made her brain unreliable.

She shook the circling thought away and buttoned her shirt. She left the bathroom with her shoulders square and expression flat.

Male voices rose up the staircase as she moved through the bedroom. "What do you look so guilty about?" someone asked.

She thought the voice might belong to Dean, but she hadn't spoken to him since their initial meeting and phone call.

"I don't know what you're talking about," Austin said.

Was Dean right? Did Austin feeling guilty?

Why?

Maybe she'd completely misread it all.

"I've been waiting for you guys," Austin said. "I'm just impatient."

"That doesn't explain the look on your face," Dean pressed. "What happened?"

"What happened to you?" Austin asked. "I don't live that far out of town."

"No, but it's not as if it's easy to get here," Finn answered as a herd of footfalls arrived on the second floor. "Where's Scarlet?"

She waved. "Here."

The brothers stopped in a cluster at the top of the stairs. And they all looked a little guilty in her opinion.

Chapter Eighteen

Dean was first to speak, seeming to break the spell around them. "Hello." He stepped toward her, hand outstretched. "We met at the office. Dean Beaumont."

"I remember," she said, accepting the shake and fighting the urge to more fully cover herself despite the yoga pants and long-sleeved top. She felt exposed, as if all three brothers could see far more than she wanted them to see.

Finn simply raised a hand then slid his eyes at Austin before heading into the kitchen and helping himself to a mug of coffee. Dean followed.

Austin seemed frozen for a long beat.

Scarlet's heart squeezed when their eyes met. Humiliation and confusion heated her cheeks. She'd come on to Austin, and he'd made a polite, but speedy, escape.

Would he ask her to leave now? Maybe send her to his family's farm?

Did his brothers know?

"Looks like you're healing up nicely," Dean said, kindly breaking the silence once more. "How do you feel?"

Scarlet jerked her attention away from Austin and forced a polite smile for the slightly taller, older Beaumont brother. "Thank you." She hadn't noticed how bright his blue eyes were before. After looking into Austin's deep brown gaze for so long, the contrast was slightly jarring. "I'm feeling better. It's been good to get out of town, I think."

Finn unpacked a bag she hadn't noticed him carrying and set up a laptop on the table. "I thought you might want to give the mug shot database another try while I'm here."

She moved in his direction, eager to be useful and glad to have a purpose. The strange energy moving between brothers put her a little on edge. "Sure," she said. "I'd love to."

Finn ran his fingers over the keyboard briefly, then looked at her once more. "All set." He pulled out a chair at the table and motioned for her to sit. "Can I get you some coffee?"

"That sounds nice. Thank you."

The oven dinged, and Dean grabbed potholders from a drawer. "Tell me this is Mama's ham and cheese quiche."

"It is," Austin said, striding stoically into the kitchen to help.

A few minutes later, the four-seat table was covered in plates, mugs and food. And three-quarters of it was surrounded by Beaumonts.

The conversation flowed between small talk and shoptalk seamlessly, each brother easily keeping up as the direction ebbed and flowed, moving in a half dozen directions.

She tried to concentrate on the mug shot database and her coffee. She'd made short work of her breakfast, including two servings of chopped fruit from a bowl.

"I'm hung up on the photo of you in white," Dean said, catching her eye over the laptop's screen. "You looked like a bride."

"Afraid not," she said, glancing up at him. "It was a company event."

Finn shifted. "I've contacted Coulter Realty's home office and asked for a guest list from that night. Can you identify everyone visible in the photo with you? Including folks in the background? It might help us focus our search."

Her knee began to bob beneath the table, unsettled by the implication. "You think it could be someone from my company?"

"Or someone peripherally related, yes."

She wasn't sure why that information made her situation feel worse, but it did.

"Do you commonly use the same service people when you're preparing homes for sale?" Finn asked.

"Frequently." Scarlet took a big drink from her coffee. "We have preferred companies for lawn maintenance, home inspections, stagers, bankers and title companies to name a few. Representatives from all of those companies were at the party, plus Realtors and their guests, event staff and valets."

Dean wiped his mouth with a napkin. "Sounds like a lot of interviews to arrange."

"Will you discount the people from my daily life now?" she asked. "From the list I gave you before the fire?"

"Not completely," Finn said. "I'm just shifting my focus a bit. That photo is significant to your attacker. I want to know why and how he came to have a copy."

"Have you checked online?" she asked. "The company website sometimes uses shots from special events to build the Coulter Realty brand."

"I have, and I didn't see it. I'd like to start contacting the people you remember seeing at the party."

Scarlet nodded, hating that everyone she knew professionally would receive a call from a detective regarding her attack. She returned her focus to the database and soon re-filled her coffee.

Dean was the first to leave after breakfast. He offered fist bumps and warm smiles when he headed out. The love and respect between brothers were something she admired. If she'd had siblings, she would've wanted to be their friend too.

Even if her interest in Austin was one-sided, she'd always remember that he showed her what a family could be. And that families like those she read about in books really existed. Because if this existed for the Beaumonts, it could exist for her too one day. That kind of hope was priceless.

Scarlet rubbed her eyes a long while later, tired and stinging from screen fatigue. The mug shots were endless, but she'd begun to wonder if her attacker had ever been arrested. Maybe he was too young. Or too careful. Maybe his stalking tendencies were new, or maybe he'd been content to just watch until now. There were too many unknowns. Too little she could control and too few assurances.

Austin's phone buzzed on the table and Finn's phone rang. Austin frowned. "Well, that's not good."

"Dean?" Finn asked, phone already at his ear.

Scarlet tensed, hoping nothing bad had happened to their kind, congenial, blue-eyed brother.

Austin stared at his phone then at Finn.

Finn tapped the phone's screen and lowered the device onto the table, speaker function engaged. "Say that again."

"Y'all better come down to our office," Dean said. "I just got here, and there's been trouble."

AUSTIN WAS GETTING tired of following Finn through town from crime scene to crime scene. He hated that all these awful events led back to Scarlet's attacker, and that his office was now involved in something sure to make the paper. Whatever they were driving into this time was a double whammy. Scarlet would be unfairly rattled. And his business would receive bad press.

No one wanted to hire a private investigator everyone was talking about. The most important thing a PI could do was be discreet. But that was out the window now.

He parked his truck along the curb near his office, behind a police cruiser and Dean's truck. A small crowd lined the sidewalk. Several onlookers snapped pictures.

"Take a look at the people," he told Scarlet. She'd barely said ten words to him since asking for help with her bandage this morning, and he needed to apologize, but now wasn't the time. "Let me know if you recognize anyone in the crowd."

"Okay."

"We might want to adjust our plan moving forward," he said, drawing her eyes to his.

"What do you mean?"

"We think this guy was following you for weeks, but he attacked after you met with me. I think he saw us together, either at my office or outside it. Then, he apologized by sending flowers to the hospital, but I called him back and he lost it. I stayed at your house overnight and he lashed out again the next day when we left. He said you betrayed him. There's a pattern forming, and it's not a good one. I think he imagines himself in love with you and doesn't like you spending so much time with me."

"Are you sending me to the farm?" she asked. The words came quick and flat, as if she'd been expecting the possibility to arise.

"No." He frowned. "I won't suggest that again. You want to stay with me, and I want you with me. Now we're making the detail decisions together."

She unbuckled her seat belt and turned on the seat to face him. "Okay. So, what are you suggesting?"

"Maybe we should go out in public as a united front. It

might be a good idea to make it clear that I'm not going away soon."

Scarlet chewed her bottom lip. "How?"

"I'd like to stay a little closer to you, if you'd be comfortable with that. Hold your hand, keep you near. Disrupt the misconstrued fantasy that you're his somehow. Make it clear he cannot lay claim to you."

She blinked and scowled. "Like when I tell a guy I'm not interested, but they won't leave me alone until I lie and say I have a boyfriend? Because they have more respect for a fictional boyfriend they've never met than me, the woman they're trying to hit on?"

Austin rubbed a hand against his cheek. "Seriously. We've got to introduce you to nicer people."

The anger bled from her face, replaced by something that looked a lot like hope. "Like you and your brothers?"

"Not my brothers."

Her lips quirked, and the teasing little motion was nearly enough to make him lean in and kiss her.

"About earlier," he said instead. "I'm sorry. I shouldn't have run away."

"I wish you wouldn't have," she whispered.

The urge to kiss her hit again.

Someone rapped on his window, and he turned slowly to see who'd ruined his very pleasant moment.

Dean grinned and waved through the glass. "Are y'all getting out, or did you just come to be near the action?"

Beside him, Scarlet's door opened. She cast a knowing look in his direction as she rounded the hood toward him and his brother.

Austin climbed out as well.

"Ready," she said upon arrival. Then she offered Austin her hand.

He folded his fingers with hers and drew her closer.

"Mama's going to hear about that," Dean muttered, leading the way through the crowd. "Half the people out here know her in one way or another. And everyone knows how she is."

Scarlet stopped short a few paces later, and he did as well.

Big red letters had been spray-painted across the office windows, spelling three familiar words.

SHE IS MINE

Dean stuffed his hands into his pockets. "Our security camera was down, so we don't have any footage of who did this."

Austin struggled to maintain his calm. "What do you mean our cameras were down? That's a top-notch system." He'd made sure of it, chosen every component with exacting care.

"I don't know." Dean frowned, eyes trailing over the red-lettered threat. "It doesn't make any sense. Everything was working fine, then it just...wasn't. At least the glass wasn't broken. The office wasn't breached."

He didn't care about the windows. Those could be replaced. But he loathed the fact that some unhinged, dangerous individual was out there, watching and believing that Scarlet was his. That he had some twisted claim to her. As if she was property instead of a person. And that she was his.

Finn cut through the crowd in their direction, scratching his head. "One of the officers on my team found a few neighbors near Scarlet's place and the Perez home who are willing to share video footage from their doorbell cameras around the times of those crimes. We'll talk to business owners on this block too. If we're lucky, we might catch the same vehicle near more than one crime scene at the times of the crimes."

Scarlet stared at the big red letters. "This feels less significant than his earlier attacks. Doesn't it? Spray paint instead of fire or destruction."

"Only at first glance," Finn said. "Yes, the person who vandalized the windows could've easily chosen to destroy the office or smash the windows instead, but that destruction would've been open to interpretation. He wanted to leave an exacting message. And it's for Austin this time, not you."

Austin clenched and flexed his jaw. "This is what he said when I called him from the hospital gift shop."

Scarlet squeezed his hand, a small, silent, secret gesture. And he felt a bit of the tension ease.

"If he's moved on from heartbreak over his imagined loss to rage at Austin for his interference, this could get much worse before it gets any better," Finn said.

Dean snorted a small laugh as his keen gaze drifted over the onlookers. "Keep coming at us, guy. You're only creating more chances to be found."

Austin nodded. He didn't like the idea of a criminal's rage pointed anywhere near Scarlet, but it would certainly help Finn and his team if the stalker continued to lash out. Everything this guy did provided another clue. Another sliver of his identity. And soon the pieces would come together enough to see the big picture.

"Finn?" Scarlet asked.

All eyes in their little circle turned to her. "I thought I was followed away from a home showing the night before I decided to meet with a private investigator. I don't know if it was or wasn't the stalker, but it was a car, not a truck or SUV. I don't know if that will help your team as you review the video footage, but I wanted to say it."

Finn's gaze slid from Scarlet's face to their joined hands. "I'll let the team know." He raised his eyes to Austin and shook his head. "And I can almost guarantee you about five people on this sidewalk have already let Mama know about that."

Dean covered his mouth, failing to hide a wide, toothy smile.

"I've been warned," Austin said.

Scarlet wiggled her fingers, but Austin cupped his free hand over their joined ones and leveled her with a no-nonsense grin. "I'm not worried about Mama, and you don't need to be either."

His brothers broke into laughter and walked away.

Chapter Nineteen

Scarlet rolled her tender shoulders and rubbed the bunching muscles along the back of her neck. Sitting inside the Beaumonts' PI office had red flags of panic flying high in her head, and tension building steadily in her muscles. The last time she'd been here, sitting at this desk, a brutal attack followed, and the trauma from that night sizzled inside her. She might've been followed long before meeting Austin, but it felt as if this was where her nightmare had begun.

Austin placed a bottle of water on the desk before her. "Did you bring your pain pills?"

"Yes." She dug into the small purse she'd brought from home, large enough to carry everything she needed, which was only a phone and pills these days. "Thanks. I almost forgot they existed."

He took a seat on the edge of his desk and watched as she took the medication. "Are you hurting? We can take off anytime if you want to get out of here and lay down. You're supposed to be resting, but I feel as if we're constantly on the move. That must be taking a toll."

"No. I'm okay," she said. "I'd rather be here than somewhere else waiting to know what happened. I can work with facts. The waiting and wondering are worse."

Dean clicked the mouse at his desk, reviewing the feed

from their security camera before it went offline. Finn hovered at his side.

Scarlet's phone rang as she tucked the pill bottle back into her purse, and she glanced at the screen. "It's my mom."

Austin nodded and moved to join his brother, giving her space to talk.

"Hey," she answered, forcing enthusiasm she didn't feel into her voice. "How's it going?"

"That's what I called to ask you," her mom said. "I've been thinking of you, and I wondered if you want to come and visit. I can't get out of town because I have a showing first thing tomorrow, but I'm home for the rest of the day, and you said you were taking a little time off, so why don't we meet somewhere for dinner?"

"I'm not sure that's a great idea," she said, gaze flickering to the window washers attempting to scrub the most recent threat off the glass. "The police haven't been able to identify the man who attacked me, and he's making it clear he'll try again."

Her mom was silent.

Finn looked her way, an expression of apology on his handsome face.

She made a mental note to remember she had an audience.

Austin returned to her and waited for acknowledgment.

"Hold on a second," she told her mom, lowering the phone from her ear.

"It might be a good idea to get out of town for the evening," he said. "If your mom wouldn't mind an extra guest, we can head that way now. Spend a few hours. If you want."

She squinted, unsure if seeing her mom was what she needed right now.

Austin bent forward at the waist. "I would love to meet

your mama," he said, voice low. "Besides, I already showed you mine. You've got to show me yours."

One of his brothers snorted, and she smiled.

"I suppose fair's fair." She delivered the news to her mom, with one caveat. "Mom? Sounds like I can come, but I'm bringing a friend, and I'd be more comfortable if we had dinner at home, considering the circumstance."

"That's fine," her mom answered. "I'll get my carryout menus together and see what's for dinner."

Scarlet said her goodbyes and disconnected, then she stood.

"Looks like we're taking off," Austin announced.

"Yeah, yeah," Dean said, motioning him away with a teasing smile. "You take the pretty woman to dinner, and we'll stay here working."

Finn shook his head in feigned remorse.

Austin held her hand as they walked to his truck and opened her door. "Don't be afraid to let me know when you're ready to leave your mom's place. Even if we've barely arrived. Or if you need to lay down while we're there. I can entertain myself and your mother if necessary."

"You will definitely entertain my mother," she said dryly. She only hoped her mother wouldn't make an obvious show of her delight when she saw him. Handsome men were on the top of Trina's favorite things list. Having their undivided attention was another.

He smiled. "I'm just saying that I'm here to help, and you're not a bother. Sometimes I get the feeling you could use the reminder."

Scarlet nodded as she climbed inside and buckled up, deeply grateful fate had brought her to this man, and equally sad for the day they'd say goodbye.

AUSTIN PARKED OUTSIDE a grand two-story estate in the historic district of Trina Wills's town. He whistled appreciatively.

"Yeah," Scarlet agreed, looking up at the large Tudor-style home through the windshield. "I spent my teen years here. Mom got a good deal and worked hard to restore it."

"Just like you," he said.

"I picked up a thing or two from the project that made the work at my house a lot easier." She reached for the door handle and paused, as if steadying herself. "I've learned everything I know from her. The good and the bad."

Austin wanted to respond but didn't know how, so he climbed out and walked with her to the door. Scarlet rang the bell.

It only took a few moments for the large wooden barrier to swing open. An older version of Scarlet appeared before them with a smile. She wore dress pants and heels with a crimson blouse. Her fair hair was blown out and teased like a pageant woman, and her makeup was fully done.

"Baby," the older woman said, pulling her daughter into a hug. "I'm so glad you came. It's been too long. Come in. Come in." She motioned them into the two-story foyer. "Let me take your coats."

They removed their coats, and Mrs. Wills examined Scarlet. "Are you wearing pajamas?"

"No, Mom," she said. "This is Austin Beaumont, my—"

He stepped forward, offering his most respectable smile. "Nice to meet you, Mrs. Wills. I've heard so many nice things."

"Me too," she said. Her gaze traveled the length of him, appraising. She placed a stiff hand beside her mouth, as if to hide her next words. "You're right. He is handsome."

Scarlet's lids drifted momentarily shut. She reopened them with a resigned expression. "Dinner smells delicious."

Her mom cast another look in Austin's direction. "Call me Trina." Then she turned to lead them to a dining room table large enough for twelve. "I ordered Italian. Hope you like it."

Trina sat at the head of the long table, pushing salad around a plate while Austin and Scarlet each took a chair on either side of her and enjoyed two helpings of stuffed shells.

"How's Lydia doing with your clients while you're out?" Trina asked.

Scarlet paused, a forkful of pasta halfway to her mouth, and tension zinged in the air. "I haven't heard from her today."

Trina blinked. "You didn't call her? Have you at least checked in with the clients to see if they're happy with her level of service?"

"No." She returned her fork to the plate. "It's been a busy day."

"Every day is a busy one," her mom said. "Either that, or you aren't making the most of it. Am I right, Austin?"

He narrowed his eyes, certain he'd been snared in some sort of trap. "I'm not sure that's always the case," he said, unwilling to support her, but trying hard not to flat-out disagree. "Scarlet's right about our day. We've been on the move since breakfast. The only call she made time for was yours."

Trina stopped pretending to eat her salad and rested her hands on her middle. "My. I'd better stop before I need stretchy pants too."

Scarlet rolled her eyes, and Austin stifled a laugh. She changed the subject to her mom's workday, and things got lighter.

Trina obviously loved talking about herself, her sales and the new clients she'd be working with soon. She also mentioned a new boyfriend who thought she could stand to lose a couple of pounds and who was currently between jobs.

Scarlet's expression implied this was all par for the course with Trina.

Austin made a mental note to hug his mama a little tighter the next time he saw her. And to thank her for all the fussing she did to make his life nicer just because she could.

Despite the strange dynamic between mother and daughter, they seemed to enjoy their time together, more or less. And Trina boxed up the leftover food for them to take home.

She asked very little about what Scarlet was going through, and while he didn't understand that either, he was glad not to rehash it all. Scarlet seemed like she needed the break.

He drove home in the dark, Scarlet dozing beside him, and he couldn't help wondering what it would be like to have meals with Trina more often. And to see his family include Scarlet as well.

He was thankful for the peek inside her life, and he felt as if he understood her a little better now. Scarlet was the focused and giving one in their mother-daughter relationship, while Trina was the workaholic, driven by attention and supported at home by her child.

Regardless of their differences, it was clear they loved one another.

In hindsight, it made sense Trina hadn't asked more about the hell Scarlet was going through. The conversation would've steered too far away from her as the topic. And Scarlet had a lifetime of doing what she could to keep the spotlight on her mother.

A long practiced dance.

All the more reason Austin would work to make Scarlet the center of her world and his.

And he planned to tell her as much in the morning.

Chapter Twenty

Austin finished his third cup of coffee on the deck after breakfast. Scarlet sat beside him, still in her pajamas and bundled in the woven throw from the back of his couch. It was an image he wanted to see for years to come. And he'd promised himself he'd say so today. Which was the reason he planned to pour a fourth cup of coffee. He'd been up all night trying to decide how to broach the subject.

I know your life is in constant danger right now, emotions are high, you probably feel overwhelmed and confused about many things and my timing is terrible, but I'm falling in love with you. Let's discuss.

"You okay?" she asked, peering over her steamy mug. "You look stressed. Not that we don't have enough reasons for that. I've just never seen you actually look rattled until now. And we're here. Doing this." She extended an arm toward the mountains around them, the rocking chairs, the blue sky and the picturesque view of the creek rushing beneath. "So, what's up?"

He thought of a few reasonable ways to say he'd developed an attachment to her and didn't want to see it end, but none of them seemed right or worthy.

He'd become far more than attached.

"Lost in thought, I guess," he said, forcing a smile. "You?"

"A little," she said. "I've never thanked you for all this. For taking my case. For believing me when I came to you that day, when I wasn't even sure I believed myself. Then showing up and staying the course when everything went promptly to hell. You've catered and comforted. Now you're hosting me. It's a lot, and I was up half the night thinking I'm kind of awful for not saying this sooner."

The idea they'd both been awake last night but not together made him sad. He liked being with her and talking to her. They could've been happy instead of restless.

"Are you usually this involved in your cases?"

He frowned. She couldn't mean what he thought she meant. Could she? "No. Not like this."

He'd never once been attracted to a client. Never wanted to get to know them personally or have them in his life. He'd always done his best to help, nothing more.

There had just been something about Scarlet from the start. And the more he'd gotten to know her, the more he wanted to know. The more he wanted her to stay when this was over. Which was what he should be saying to her right now.

But the risk could outweigh the potential gain.

If Scarlet didn't feel the same way, there was a chance she wouldn't be comfortable staying with him. He'd regret her absence in his home, but more importantly, he'd worry about her safety anywhere else. After what had happened at his office yesterday, he wasn't convinced the culprit wouldn't go to his family's farm for her. And the farm was the only other place he'd consider safe enough for anyone under constant threat of attack.

All reasons to wait until the criminal was captured and the danger gone before making an already complicated situation worse.

"So, your past girlfriends didn't get upset about your job because you'd started living with other women?"

He barked an unexpected laugh. "No. It's the time involved. Unless I'm on a stakeout, I always come home. Alone. But it's still a lot of long hours. Even after I get here, I work online, create files, paperwork, process contracts. I don't have a lot of time to go places. To date. I work, make time for my family and this place, then scrape together a little sliver of downtime when I can."

She set her coffee on the table at her side and turned to him, expression caught somewhere between contemplative and resolved. "I need to ask you something important, and I need you to answer me directly. Will you do that?"

He shifted, matching her position in the chair beside his. "If that's what you want." He swallowed and braced himself for what came next.

Her green eyes flickered away then back. "Yesterday, in the bathroom," she began. A blush spread across her face, pinking her cheeks, and her gaze dropped to his lips for one quick beat. "I thought you might've wanted to kiss me. I've spent the time since then wondering if I read everything wrong, or if something changed your mind. I stepped up and put my arms around your neck because I wanted you to kiss me, but if I misread you, I think I should apologize and let you know it won't happen again." She wrinkled her nose. "You've been so kind, and if I crossed a line or made you uncomfortable, I'm sorry."

His mouth opened to speak and his mind raced. He hadn't been able to make himself broach the subject, and she'd simply put it out there. No wonder he was falling for her. Scarlet was fearless. Unlike him, apparently. "I definitely wanted to kiss you in the bathroom yesterday."

Her eyes widened and her lips twitched. "Well, then I'm not sorry."

He smiled. "If I'm being fully honest, I've been thinking of kissing you a lot more often than I should."

She blushed, and his gaze dropped to her full pink lips.

He could practically taste them, almost feel them pressed to his. When his gaze returned to hers, she was watching him.

And like magnets, they both began to lean closer.

She laughed and pulled away when the distance between rocking chairs proved too much.

He stretched to his feet as Scarlet fell back into her chair, shaking her head at the temporary defeat. He offered his hand and pulled her up beside him, then wound an arm around her back. "We can't give up that easily."

"Agreed," she said. "We should try that again." The delight in her eyes thrilled him, and her contagious smile parted his lips as well.

Austin cradled her jaw in his palm, memorizing the lines of her face and absorbing this moment.

She closed her eyes and tipped her chin, then rose onto her toes.

The simple, openhearted gesture cracked something loose inside him, and he knew there wasn't any going back from there. He could only hope she'd feel the same when all was said and done.

And his phone rang.

Scarlet stepped away, brows raised. "Whoever's calling you right now is the absolute worst."

He laughed, dipping forward quickly and pressing a kiss against her temple before pulling the phone off the table at his side. "It's Finn."

She sighed, sobering a bit. "It's back to reality then."

He puzzled briefly at her meaning as he answered. "Hey, what's up?" Did she know being with her was the only reality he wanted?

Probably not because he'd yet to say so.

"I'm at the Coulter Realty office in town," Finn said. "Is Scarlet right there, or do you need to get her?"

"She's here."

Scarlet's brow furrowed.

"Hold on." Austin tapped his screen and lowered the phone between them. "All right. You're on speaker," he told his brother.

"Morning, Scarlet," Finn said, his voice oddly flat. "I'm at your office."

"More window paint?" she asked.

"No," Finn said. "A woman was attacked here this morning, and there's a threat at your desk. You two should probably get down here."

Fear flashed in Scarlet's eyes, and Austin's heart ached for her.

The stalker had crossed another line, bypassing destruction of property and trespassing. He'd attacked again, and this time it was someone Scarlet knew and likely cared for.

"What woman?" she asked, voice quaking.

"Lydia Stevens."

SCARLET BOUNCED DOWN the gravel lane on the seat in Austin's old truck then flew with him over paved country roads into town. Her heart raced and stomach lurched with flashbacks of her attack and fear for Lydia. Would she be hospitalized too? Would she be okay?

Did Lydia know Scarlet was the reason for her attack?

She was sure Austin would tell her this wasn't her fault, but he couldn't deny the truth. Scarlet's stalker wouldn't have been at the Coulter Realty office if not for Scarlet. He wouldn't have been so upset if she wasn't hiding out with Austin. And even if Scarlet wasn't sure what she could've done differently, Lydia's suffering was still directly linked to her. Scarlet should've predicted this somehow and protected her.

Austin covered her hand with his on the seat between them, gently stroking his thumb over her clenched fist.

"Did he say how badly she's hurt?" Scarlet asked. She'd barely heard anything Finn had said after Lydia's name.

"No. The paramedics were still working on her when he called."

Scarlet closed her eyes and sent up endless prayers for Lydia's well-being. For her stalker's capture and for no one else to be hurt this way.

The crowd outside her office was thick and deep, significantly larger than the group that had gathered outside the PI office the day before. The full gamut of emergency responders were there as well. An ambulance, a fire truck and three police cruisers crowded into the employee parking lot. Red and white lights flashed against the surrounding buildings on repeat, reflecting off the glass of nearby windows.

She and Austin jumped down from the truck and met at the hood, catching one another's hand then jogging the rest of the way to the building.

Uniformed officers had formed a barricade on the sidewalk. Thankfully, they recognized Austin and let them pass without question.

A moment later, he held the door so she could enter the office.

The space was full of people in uniforms. Cameras flashed and low voices murmured.

Time slipped beneath her, and the world seemed to tilt.

Lydia was laid out on a stretcher, eyes closed and a padded collar around her neck. Dark bruises and fresh cuts peppered her jaw, forehead, eyes and nose.

Scarlet pressed her lips together, willing herself not to be sick on the office floor. And she hurried to the gurney's side. "Is she going to be okay?" she asked, clutching Lydia's hand.

Her friend's fingers didn't curl or grip back in response.

And Scarlet's tears began to fall.

The gurney inched forward as an EMT dislodged its brake. "I'm sorry," the man said, looking as if he meant it. "We'll do everything we can, but we have to go."

Scarlet pulled her hand away, and the paramedics guided an unconscious Lydia through the door.

Austin's arms curled around her, and she turned to bury her face against his chest. "We'll go to the hospital when we finish here, and I'll see if I can learn more."

"Thank you."

He stroked her hair, and she fought the urge to break down.

A sharp whistle cut through the air, and Scarlet forced herself upright, shoulders square and chin high.

Finn waved a hand overhead.

Austin pulled her against his side. "Time to see what he found."

The sea of uniformed personnel parted as they made their way down the aisle toward Scarlet's desk.

Finn stepped back, making room for her and Austin to take a look.

Her chair had been overturned and everything had been scribbled on. Her files, papers, the monitor. Even the fabric of her rolling chair and the desk itself. Two haunting words repeated again and again.

She's mine. She's mine. She's mine.

Chapter Twenty-One

Austin swore under his breath as Scarlet fell against his chest, breath rushing from her body. Even while doing all he could to protect her physically, the stalker was still getting in his jabs. Taking mental and emotional hits wherever he could.

"I can't believe this is happening," she whispered.

Austin wound his arms around her, gritting his teeth and pulling her in tight.

A storm of fury and heartbreak thundered inside him. Whoever was responsible for these attacks had clearly snapped. And wherever he was, he was a danger. The expressions on the medics' faces had made it clear that Lydia wasn't as lucky as Scarlet had been. Her injuries were more severe and would take far longer to heal. Though, she too would carry a lifetime of trauma from this man's hands.

The mere idea that Scarlet, who'd been strangled and left unconscious, was lucky compared to anyone was another sign of just how bad things had gotten.

Her fingers curled against his back as she clung to him. Her ragged breaths vibrated his chest and pierced his heart. Whatever thread of connection he'd imagined between them before had fast become a heavy rope. One he was sure could tow freight trains without a single tear.

"I've got you," he whispered, lowering his mouth to her ear. "Finn and the others are going to find the man who did this."

A camera flash straightened his spine. Behind her, a member of the crime scene unit documented evidence of the struggle.

Finn's and Dean's eyes were on Austin. They gave nods of understanding and acceptance before turning away. They saw what he'd yet to verbalize.

He was in love with Scarlet Wills.

"Come on," Austin said, sliding his hands onto her biceps. "Let's go to the hospital and see what we can find out."

Finn took a step in their direction as they broke their embrace. "I'll be there as soon as I can. We'll touch base then if you're still around."

Scarlet curled her arms around her middle, eyes haunted. "I want to stay at the hospital until I can see her," she said. "Her siblings are out of state now. I think I should wait with her mom until the rest of the family arrives. She shouldn't be alone."

Austin checked his watch. If they hurried, they'd arrive before his favorite volunteer headed home. "We'd better get moving." He guided Scarlet back to his truck and helped her inside. "You're very kind to think of Lydia's mother," he said. "She and Lydia will appreciate that."

"It seems like the least I can do." Scarlet's eyes were woeful as he closed the door.

He rounded the cab to the driver's side and climbed behind the wheel. "There's only one person to blame for any of this," he said softly. "And that person isn't you."

The drive to the hospital was silent, save for the sounds of Scarlet's unsteady breaths and tires on warped brick roads.

He parked beneath the nearest streetlight just outside the visitors' lot and held her hand as they hurried inside.

Curious eyes turned briefly in their direction then away, not finding whoever or whatever they'd been seeking.

"What now?" Scarlet asked. "We're not family, so the staff won't talk to us. Do we wait for Finn to arrive?"

"We can, but it's a small town," he said, steering her toward a pair of chairs near the interior doors. "We won't have to wait long for information."

She offered a quizzical look, but sat.

"Do you know Mrs. Thatcher?" he asked.

"No. Does she work here?"

"She's a volunteer who makes those little knitted hats for newborns and fills in just about anywhere she can."

One of the paramedics from the real estate office moved into view before Scarlet could ask more questions.

Austin stood and offered his hand. "Were you able to get her stabilized?"

The other man nodded, expression grim. "She's undergoing tests, then they'll admit her for monitoring. She's stable, and that's something."

Scarlet rose. "Is she awake?"

"No, ma'am. Not yet." He opened his mouth to say something more, but his partner appeared behind him moving double time.

"We've got another call," she said. "One of the Briar kids fell from his horse."

The man gave a quick goodbye nod and hustled away.

Scarlet sighed. "Maybe I can steal a lab coat from the back of a chair and sneak around until I find her. It always works in sitcoms."

Austin fought a smile. "No need," he said, gaze locking on the woman he'd hoped to catch. "Here comes Mrs. Thatcher."

The older woman carried a large, quilted bag in one hand with an array of yarn strands hanging over the edge. Her white hair formed a crown on her head, and her milky blue eyes twinkled at the sight of him.

"Mrs. Thatcher," he said, lifting a wide smile. "How are you?"

She kissed his cheek and beamed. "Very well. Thank you. How's your mother?"

"Missing you," he said. "When will you get out to the ranch for lunch again?"

"Oh." She shrugged. "It's hard to say. I spend all my time knitting lately. This town has become a baby factory. There were four new little ones born since I arrived this morning." Her gaze slid to Scarlet. "All girls."

Scarlet offered a small smile.

"You remember Scarlet Wills," Austin prompted. "You were here when I got here on the evening she was attacked. You knew where I could find her."

The woman's eyes widened, and her gaze moved to Scarlet's throat. "I remember. Why are you back? Are you unwell?"

"I'm worried about my friend," Scarlet said. "The man who did this to me attacked another woman today. She was brought here a few minutes ago, and we're waiting to see her, if someone will allow it."

Mrs. Thatcher released a puff of air. "Oh, dear. You should sit."

Scarlet and Austin returned to their seats, and Mrs. Thatcher sat beside Scarlet. She took her hand and offered a cautious look in Austin's direction.

"Did you see her come through?" he asked.

"I might've," she said. "Would she have arrived in the last fifteen minutes?"

Austin nodded. "She was with the paramedics who left as you arrived just now."

Mrs. Thatcher's expression fell. "Then I know the one you mean. I thought she'd been in a car accident."

Austin shook his head.

The older woman turned her eyes to Scarlet, who was listening silently. "I'm so sorry."

"Mrs. Thatcher is the eyes and ears of this hospital," he said. Even better, she was a shameless gossip, and a little flattery usually loosened her lips.

"My husband was the chief of surgery," she said proudly. "Rest his soul. He practically lived here, and so did I until our children were born, then again after they'd grown. I know everything about this old girl." She glanced around the room. "Always changing. Full of life and tragedy."

"And the woman?" Austin asked. "Any chance you know where we can find her?"

"I don't want her to be alone," Scarlet interjected. "And I'd like to be with her mom when she arrives."

"They took her straight to the CT room for a scan," Mrs. Thatcher said. "The paramedics told the doctors she'd had severe head trauma, was unconscious, and they were concerned."

"How'd the scan look?" Scarlet asked.

"I don't know about that, but she's in the ICU now for observation. You should go up to the third floor waiting room. They keep fresh coffee and hot water for tea. I'll bring something sweet when I come around tomorrow."

"Thank you, Mrs. Thatcher," Austin said.

"Anytime, dear." She rose, and Austin did as well. "Now,

I'd better go see how the ladies at intake are doing. Tell your mother I'll call soon."

"I will." He reached for Scarlet and pulled her up with him. "This way."

HOURS SLOGGED BY in the little waiting room outside the ICU. There wasn't anything to do and no real reason to stay, but Scarlet insisted, so Austin did his best to accommodate.

He requested a pillow and blanket from a volunteer to help Scarlet sleep more comfortably, and he'd even begun to refill the waiting room coffee when it ran low or got cold.

Finn had come and gone with minimal news to share. Lydia's head scans had been clear, but she'd had significant neck trauma and was sedated to help with the pain. Her mother, who was local, had been visiting Lydia's brother in Texas. The family was flying in as soon as they could.

Yet another reason Scarlet wouldn't leave. She couldn't bear the thought of Lydia not having anyone waiting for her when she woke.

A guard had been positioned outside Lydia's room for due diligence. Just in case the attacker returned to silence her, if she'd seen his face.

The whole set of events had pushed Austin to his limits, and he'd spent a long while reviewing the evidence available while Scarlet slept. He'd seen his share of awful things, but he'd never seen them keep coming like this, and not at someone he loved.

He pulled the compact stun gun from his pocket and slid it into her jacket. She didn't want it, and he hoped she'd never have reason to use it, but knowing it was within her reach, even while she was safe beside him, offered a world of comfort. Only then, as the sunlight of a new day began to climb the windowsills, did Austin finally fall asleep.

SCARLET WOKE WITH a stiff back and aching neck. Her head pounded and her throat was dry. Austin was asleep in the chair beside her, long legs stretched out before him, while she and her pillow had leaned against his side.

A travel pack of pain pills sat on the table before them with a bottle of water.

She rubbed her eyes and rolled her shoulders, working out the kinks in her tender muscles, then opened the pain pills and water to take the medication.

The hospital bustled around her, and she was thankful for every hushed voice and hurried footfall. The halls had become eerie in the night, too quiet and still. Occasionally punctuated by a tragedy, racing crash team or other emergencies that left Scarlet on edge. Fearing Lydia had taken a turn for the worse and knowing no one would tell her if she had.

A trio of swiftly moving men appeared in the hallway, visible through the wall of waiting room windows. Her heart raced at the sight of a familiar face.

"Finn!" She clutched Austin's hand to wake him then creaked to her feet, wincing at the discomfort.

Austin stood instantly. "What happened? Are you okay?"

"Finn's here," she said, tracking the detective with her gaze. "And he's not alone. That means something, right?"

She moved into the hall as Finn and the officers approached.

"You're still here?" Finn asked, brows furrowed. He motioned the officers to continue on.

"I couldn't leave," Scarlet said. "Lydia's family isn't here yet." She glanced at the empty waiting room to be sure that was still true, and they hadn't arrived during the night.

His gaze shifted to his brother. "I'm on my way to see her now. Why don't y'all come back with me? It might soothe her to have a friend present when we talk. Officer Pratt is here to relieve Officer Grant of his shift, and Officer Meade will speak with the nurses."

Scarlet's heart swelled with hope. "Speak with her?"

"Yes. Lydia's awake."

Scarlet stifled the urge to hug him. She settled for following him into Lydia's room with Austin at her side.

Her friend's eyes opened and shut several times before opening to stay. "Scarlet?"

"Yes." Tears burst into existence as Scarlet hurried to Lydia's side. She clutched her right hand, avoiding the one with an IV, and did her best to remain calm and composed. "I'm here."

Lydia made a weak attempt to hold on to Scarlet's hand. "He came for me," she whispered, voice rough and raw.

"I know. I'm so sorry."

"Lydia?" Finn said. "I'm Detective Beaumont. I was assigned to Scarlet's case and I'll be working on yours as well. I promise I'm going to do everything in my power to apprehend the man who did this as soon as possible."

Lydia turned to watch and listen as he spoke. The wide red marks on her face from the day before were now swollen and black. A deep cut on her lip had been patched with a stitch, and there was blood on the white of one eye. A thick padded collar still circled her neck.

She released Scarlet's hand, brows furrowed and gaze distant, as if the reality of things was just filtering in. She lifted her fingers to the injuries on her face, and her expression crumbled.

"It's going to be okay," Scarlet said, voice quaking. "I'm here now and you're safe. No one will hurt you again. I promise. And I won't leave unless someone makes me. Even then I won't be far." She glanced to Austin, who'd made a similar promise to her once.

Finn pulled a little notepad from his pocket. "Were you able to get a look at the man who did this?"

She nodded then searched the ceiling with her eyes. "I think he was—" Her gaze snapped back to Scarlet. "He was looking for you. I said you weren't at work, and he said he knew that. He wanted to know where you were, but I didn't know. I said maybe at home."

"Can you describe him?" Finn asked again, rewording the question and working to regain her attention. "I know this is hard."

A sob broke on Lydia's lips and tears began to roll.

Her monitors beeped and a nurse came to check the situation. "Lydia? Morning, hon. Can you breathe for me? Nice and slow?" She frowned at Finn, then Austin, and slid her eyes over Scarlet. "This is an ICU. She's permitted to have one guest at a time, and all guests should be family. You know that, Detective."

"Her family is en route," he said. "Scarlet went through something similar this week, and we hoped her presence would put Lydia at ease."

"How's that working?" she asked, gaze hard. "Wrap it up."

Austin raised his palms in innocence. "I'll step outside." He moved into the hall just beyond the door, outside Lydia's sight, but within Scarlet's view.

Lydia's lips quivered and her face contorted, fighting the tears. "He was tall with a beard. Not old. Not a kid either. I don't know. He wanted Scarlet. It was all he would say. Over and over. Where was she? Who was she with? Why was I lying?"

She sobbed.

Scarlet passed her a tissue. "I'm so sorry." The words

were small and pathetic, but they were all she had to offer. The horror of the moment was too heavy to bear.

Lydia wiped her eyes, sucking in shallow, shuddered breaths.

Finn cast a cautious look at the nurse before trying again. He worked his jaw. "Was he familiar to you?"

"No." She shook her head and cringed, presumably at the pain. Her gaze flipped back to Scarlet. "But he knew me. He said my name."

"That's good information," Scarlet said, hoping to look calm and reassuring, while inside she cracked apart. "Detective Beaumont can use all of this to build a profile. To try to find him."

"Can you think of anything else?" Finn asked. "Even something small. A limp or lisp. A logo on his hoodie? A scar or tattoo?"

Lydia's eyes shifted, possibly sorting her thoughts or searching her memories. Her monitors beeped more frequently.

The nurse's expression tightened. "Remember to breathe, sweetie. Last warning, Detective."

"He went to your desk," Lydia said. Her hand latched onto Scarlet's with unexpected fervor. "He left me on the floor and I watched—I watched him—"

"I saw," Scarlet said, covering her squeezing hand. "It's okay. We were at the office yesterday. Everything's been photographed."

"Photograph," Lydia repeated, gaze distant, as if recalling the moment.

"That's right. It's all being processed."

"No." A tear slid over her cheek. "He took your photograph."

"When?" Finn asked, voice harder than it had been since

entering the room. "At the office party? Could he have been the photographer?"

Lydia shook her head again, skin paling and a sheen of sweat breaking across her brow.

"All right. That's enough." The nurse stretched her arms wide, as if to herd and push them from Lydia's room.

"No!" Lydia shoved onto her elbows. "He took the photograph from your desk."

The words hit Scarlet like an anvil as images from the day before returned. Everything had been covered in ink. Scribbled with that horrid message. *She's mine. She's mine.* Her desk had been overturned. Her papers scattered.

Austin stepped back inside, eyes darting from Scarlet to his brother. "Did you find a framed picture with her things?"

"No," Finn said, turning to Scarlet. "Why? What was in the photo?"

Her world came crashing down with the answer. "Me and my mother."

Chapter Twenty-Two

Scarlet dialed her mother for the thirtieth time as she and Austin raced along the highway between Marshal's Bluff and Holbrook. "Voice mail," she reported. "She's not answering her landline or cell phone. And no one at her office has seen her yet today."

"Hang in there," he said. "Finn's been in touch with her local police department, and they're looking for her too. All we can do is get there and help. Meanwhile, we have to keep trying."

"What if we don't find her?"

"We will," he said, reaching across the seat to grip her clasped hands, which were kneaded into a ball on her lap. "Can you think of anyone else she might've spoken with recently?"

Scarlet shook her head. Her mother didn't have friends. She had coworkers and clients, plus the occasional boyfriend. "I knew some of her coworkers before I moved, but there's a lot of turnover in this business. I don't know how many still work with her."

"If you know how to reach them, give it a try. Meanwhile, we'll stop at her home, then move to her office," he said. "We'll talk to neighbors and anyone else who might've seen her coming or going at either location. And we'll visit the local police department to introduce ourselves. Whoever is on this case will want to talk to you too."

Scarlet closed her eyes, combatting a swell of nausea and fatigue. Each time she was sure things couldn't get worse, they did. And this was far more horrible than anything she'd imagined.

This guy had her mother.

"He attacked Lydia yesterday," she said. "He's had enough time to drag my mom into another state and do anything he wants to her."

Austin gave her fingers a squeeze, and she braced for more words of false comfort that didn't come. "I know."

And those words were even worse.

Her mom's historic Tudor home appeared a while later, tucked neatly behind its brick fence. The limbs of mature trees swayed on the lawn, losing hordes of multicolored leaves with each bluster of the late fall wind.

Scarlet made a run for the front door. She rang the bell and knocked then peered through the windows, praying for signs of life inside. Hoping her mom would trundle into the foyer with a new man on her arm and a mimosa in one hand, having turned off her phone's ringer to embrace ir-responsibility and new love.

"Car's gone," Austin said, hands cupped near his eyes as he peeked through the narrow garage windows.

"That's good," she said. "Right? I don't see any signs of a struggle inside the home, so maybe she's just…out."

She wrapped icy arms around her middle, recognizing her words as a lie. The unseasonably cold day burrowed ice into her veins. Her mother wasn't out shopping or meeting someone for an early dinner. She wasn't with a new boy-friend. She was gone. Taken against her will.

"Do you have a key?" Austin asked. "We should check inside if we can."

Scarlet shook her head and glanced toward the home. "No." She hadn't had a key to her mom's place since the day she'd moved out and Trina had asked for it back. Scarlet tried the doorknob just in case. "Locked."

"All right." Austin moved toward the waiting truck. "We'll check her office next."

The drive into town was short. A cruiser sat in the parking lot when they arrived.

"Why do you think the cops are here?" Scarlet asked, climbing down from the truck and hoping she didn't already know. Her teeth began to chatter as her exhausted body flooded with adrenaline she had no way to process.

The last time they'd arrived at an office like this with a police presence, they'd found Lydia beaten and unconscious.

"This is routine," Austin said, matching his stride to hers across the parking lot. "No flashers. No other first responders. My best guess is that these officers are just following up like Finn requested."

She exhaled, shaking her hands out hard at the wrists. "Okay. That makes sense."

"I always make sense," Austin said, drawing her eyes to his.

A small smile tugged her lips.

"I've got you," he told her, swinging open the glass office door and waiting for her to pass. "Whatever comes, we'll face it together."

Her heart swelled, and her lips quivered. "Thank you."

Unlike the more modern satellite location in Marshal's Bluff, her mom's office was set in a historic brick building with a row of curtained windows and tidy flower beds along a stone walkway.

The homey theme carried through to the interior. Each agent had a large wooden desk on a colorful rug with two armchairs positioned before it and a matching chair on wheels behind it. A refreshments area with coffee, tea and a minifridge for bottled water and juices anchored a wall near the restrooms. Vases with fall-colored blooms sat on side tables with framed photos of top-selling agents and printed lists of company attributes.

"This is cozy," Austin said, pausing in the entryway to look around.

"Each office is designed to be most attractive to the clientele in that area," Scarlet said. "It's all about the outdoor views in our town. People move there to enjoy the seaside."

The Marshal's Bluff office was utilitarian, mostly glass and metal, meant for brief visits on a client's way back outside. The interior was pale blue and the art featured boats, gulls and images of the sea. No one wanted to be indoors in Marshal's Bluff. Whereas Holbrook was all about history and hospitality.

A uniformed officer spoke to a woman at a desk near the back. "And this is her calendar?" he asked.

"Yes. We keep our own schedules. Trina's is always full. We don't see a lot of her, unless it's a paperwork day and she's here playing catch-up." The woman's gaze jumped to Scarlet and Austin as they stepped forward. She gasped. "Oh, my stars, I thought you were her."

The stern-faced officer looked their way. His pale blue eyes were creased at the corners and tight with concern. He was older than Scarlet, probably older than her mother, but fit with an air of authority that gave Scarlet hope. "I'm afraid this isn't a good time," he said. "Can Ms. Reese take your name and number and give you a call in a bit?"

"No." Scarlet moved in their direction. "I'm Scarlet Wills. This is Austin Beaumont. My mother's Trina Wills."

The man's expression morphed from politely patient to apologetic. "I'm sorry. Come on in. I'm Officer Barrow and this is Cindy Reese, a coworker of your mother's."

"Please sit," Cindy said, pointing to a seat at the desk beside hers. Her white sweater set and long, shapeless blue skirt reminded Scarlet of her elementary school librarian. Her gray bun and pencil tucked through the knot finished the look perfectly. "That's your mama's desk," Cindy said. "You look just like her. Anyone ever told you?"

Scarlet tried to smile. "It's been a while, but I used to hear it all the time." She lowered herself into the seat and covered her mouth at the sight of her mother's things. All neat as a pin. All untouched, waiting for her return. And the same framed photo that Scarlet kept on her desk stood beside her mother's monitor as well. "Austin," she whispered. "Look."

He placed his hands on her shoulders, and she did her best to soak up his strength.

Scarlet ran a fingertip over the glass, tracing her mother's cheek.

The large paper calendar beneath her opposite hand was lined in client names, addresses and times. The color-coded system had been in use for her mother long before the realty company they worked for had a website and apps to organize an agent's schedule.

"It looks as if your mother had an appointment on the books for first thing this morning," the officer said, drawing Scarlet's eyes to the paper calendar. "I'm guessing she went straight to the home on Elm after leaving her place. We've tried the number for the client, but no one answered." He pointed to the digits written with the name and address where her mother planned to meet a client at 9:00 a.m.

Austin set his hands on his hips. "He's been using disposable phones for related crimes in Marshal's Bluff."

Officer Barrow grunted, clearly unimpressed but unsurprised. "Detective Beaumont gave me a pretty solid rundown," he told Austin before returning his gaze to Scarlet. "I'm very sorry for what you're going through. My team and I are working in tandem with the Marshal's Bluff police force, and we'll do everything we can to locate your mother and make sure she's safe."

"Thank you," Austin said.

Scarlet nodded, throat tight.

The desk phone rang, and the room stilled. Air thickened around her shoulders as she stared at the screen.

"That's the number I called earlier," Officer Barrow said. "From the morning appointment. Let's see if your mother arrived as planned." He leaned forward, arm outstretched, as if intending to answer the call.

Scarlet lifted a hand to block him. Her gaze swept the caller ID screen then the paper calendar under her hand. And a sense of foreboding curled around her spine. She pressed the speaker button on the phone. "Coulter Realty," she said warily. "Scarlet speaking."

"Hello, darling," a low voice seethed. "I knew you'd answer my call."

Austin was at her side in the next moment, his cell phone poised before the speaker, a recording app already in use.

Scarlet gripped his arm then pushed on. "You did?"

"I know everything about you. And I see you right now," he said. "Still with that man. Still unwilling to listen."

"Is my mom with you?" Scarlet asked, ignoring his menace. "Can I talk to her?"

"Not while you're keeping him around."

"What if I ask him to go outside?" she asked, cringing slightly at the thought.

"Tell him you're mine!" he roared, voice vibrating the little speaker and sending Scarlet's hammering heart into her throat.

She reeled back, feeling as if she'd been slapped and remembering women got hurt when he got angry. "I'm sorry," she said, rising to lean over the phone and beg. "I'm so sorry. Please don't be mad at my mom. I didn't mean to upset you. It's not her fault. I'll do better."

"You will," he said, voice lower and assured. "Because infidelity has a price."

The line went silent, and Scarlet's world collapsed around her.

Chapter Twenty-Three

Austin sent the audio recording to Finn, then he turned his focus to Scarlet, who looked as if she was in shock.

Officer Barrow had cracked immediately into action, voice rumbling through the quiet office as he recounted the details to Finn and his team. The front door quickly opened and closed as he moved outside.

Cindy Reese stared after him. "Where's he going?"

"Looking for the caller, I imagine," Austin said. "Are you okay?"

She nodded woodenly then cast her attention to Scarlet, staring and motionless, before heading to the refreshments table. "I'll find something for her to drink. I think she's in shock. Heaven knows I can't blame her."

"Thank you."

"I'm not in shock," Scarlet whispered, still staring blankly ahead.

Austin crouched at her side. "Are you sure?"

Her chest rose and fell in steady breaths. The hairs on her arms stood at attention, bolstered by a cascade of goose bumps.

"Scarlet?"

Cindy returned with a steaming mug and a half-sized

bottle of water. "I wasn't sure you liked tea, so I brought water too," she said, setting both on the desk.

Scarlet didn't move or respond.

"Is she okay?" Cindy whispered. "Should she see a doctor?"

"I'm thinking," Scarlet said.

"Oh." Cindy set a packet of crackers beside the water and backed up. "That's good. I'll leave you to it."

Austin raised his palm in thanks as the older woman turned away.

"Do you think he's still out there?" Scarlet asked. "Parked across the street or lurking on the corner?"

"I'm sure he's already moved on," Austin said. Leaving them to chase their tails as usual.

"He knew I was here. Sitting at her desk. Knew I'd answer the phone. How?"

Austin looked at the windows, each with a slatted wooden miniblind and sheer curtains parted at the center. "I don't know. He likely guessed."

"After following us here," she said. "Knowing I'd look for my mother."

"That, or he saw my truck in the lot. From there he could've assumed you were at her desk. Just because he said he saw you, doesn't mean he did. And there's a chance he was speaking figuratively when he said he saw you. As if he knows you, not that you were literally in view." Though even Austin had trouble believing that theory. Whoever this guy was, he'd been clinging to Scarlet like a second skin from day one. And he'd yet to figure out how he was doing it.

And now he had her mother.

The door opened again, and Officer Barrow strode back inside, cell phone no longer at his ear. "There weren't any signs of the caller on the street, but he could've easily walked or driven away. A team's been dispatched to review local security footage in search of a car matching the description provided by Detective Beaumont. For now, it's probably best that Ms. Wills find someplace safe to stay out of sight."

Austin nodded, his mind already working through their prospects. His place was the safest, but it was back in Marshal's Bluff, and he knew better than to ask Scarlet to leave this town, where her mother had gone missing. She'd want to stay close to the places and things in her mother's world. There were a handful of inns on the way into town, but those wouldn't be any easier to guard than any other house, which only left hotels. Something outside Holbrook, but not as far as home, would be best. Some place within a ten-to fifteen-minute drive, in case they were needed in a hurry.

Scarlet tugged on his coat sleeve, gaze still fixed on the paper calendar under hand. "Look."

Officer Barrow moved to his side. "What is it?"

One slender finger touched a set of initials at the top of Trina Wills's schedule for the prior day. TS.

Austin examined the script, then looked to her for explanation. The letters were written near the date without indication of time or purpose. "What does it mean?"

Scarlet turned bewildered green eyes to him. "Tech Services."

His mental wheels spun as the pieces of the puzzle began to fall into place.

Cindy returned, an expectant look on her brow. "Trina has been having issues with her company laptop and accounts. Maybe she scheduled a meeting to sort it out."

Scarlet paled. She'd had her share of similar problems not long ago. "What if the person who left the image of me from the party didn't actually attend the party or take the picture?" she asked. "What if he had access to the photos from that night because he was the one selecting which ones to use?"

Austin recalled the Coulter Realty website, where images from events like the one in question were featured on the About page.

"Tech Services would've been given all the images, so they could upload a few to the site."

Austin's fingers curled. The culprit had been in Scarlet's life all along. Tucked neatly into the background.

"I'll call Detective Beaumont," Officer Barrow announced.

Scarlet moved her cell phone onto the desk and navigated to Coulter Realty's corporate page, then to the staff directory.

"Smart," Austin said, crouching for a clearer view over her shoulder.

"Tech Services," she said, zooming in on a candid shot of the men and women who made up the department. "I talked to someone from TS almost every day during the transition to the new website. Something was always going wrong or haywire with my new email or the password. I must've had it reset a half dozen times. Then I needed help with the contact form when I began to receive showing requests. They were assigned to me, but I didn't always get a notification in time to make the appointments. It was a long process filled with hiccups. But what if they weren't all hiccups?"

"Who did you talk to?" he asked. "You said you spoke to someone every day. Was it always the same person?"

"Yes," she said, the word barely a whisper. "Him."

Her hand trembled violently as she passed the phone to Austin, nearly dropping it in the process. She'd zoomed in on one man in a group of smiling, carefree faces around a table. Sandy hair. Dark eyes. A narrow face and build. "Greg. I've never met him in person or seen him before now." An ugly sound ripped from her core. "That's the man who attacked me."

Austin returned the image to normal size, temper raging silently beneath his surface. The man who'd attacked two women, threatened, stalked and now abducted someone looked just like everyone else in the photo. A perfect wolf in sheep's clothing.

He wrapped Scarlet in a hug.

"Tech Services," Officer Barrow said, back on his cell phone nearby. "I need the contact information on a man called Greg."

A tremor spread through Scarlet as they listened to the seasoned officer command someone at Coulter's corporate location.

"That's the one." His gaze flickered to Scarlet then Austin. "Greg Marten."

Austin held his eye contact, jaw locked, and a silent understanding passed between them. Greg Marten's reign of terror was ending now.

"I need Marten's contact information and everything you know about him. I'd also like to speak with the other members of his department... He's a person of interest in several ongoing investigations with both the Holbrook and Marshal's Bluff police..." Barrow rubbed his forehead, apparently unhappy with the response he received. "Then I'll be there with a warrant inside the hour." He disconnected the call and made another while heading for the door. "Get her somewhere safe while I run this guy down," he told Austin, before pulling his attention back to the phone. "This is Barrow. I need to speak to someone in Judge Touran's office." He raised a hand in goodbye and strode back into the day.

Scarlet stood, gripping Austin's elbow for balance. "Greg tampered with my account and had access to my schedule. That's why he always knew where I would be. He could've even watched me through my laptop camera. It was company-issued after all. So was my phone. And I'll bet he's the reason your security cameras weren't working when your office windows were vandalized."

"We've got his name now. Finn will know everything else about him soon. Let's go somewhere and lay low."

"I don't want to leave town until my mom is found."

"I know," he said. "I have an idea."

SCARLET FOLLOWED AUSTIN into the lobby of an upscale boutique hotel on the edge of town. The building was grand, with a crimson awning, doorman and the year 1912 carved into a stone beside double-glass doors.

The parking lot had been relatively full considering it wasn't tourist season, and they didn't seem to be near anything of significant importance. But she supposed staying here was a treat any time of year.

The arching foyer was inlaid with golden accents and a mural of the sky. Crimson carpet ran underfoot, outlined in large marble squares. An ornate round table centered the space, topped with a massive floral arrangement that had probably required two people to carry it.

A man in a suit stood ready at the desk beyond. "Welcome to The Carolina Grand. How can I help you?"

"Hello," Austin said. "We'd like a room."

"You're in luck," he said, without referencing the computer screen at his side. "We have one left."

Men and women crisscrossed the space around them in bunches, all clearly delighted. Their voices and laughter echoed off the high ceiling, walls and floor.

Austin frowned at the busyness. "Is there something going on?" he asked. "A convention?"

"A weekend wedding," the man said. "If you're looking for peace and quiet, it might not be the right place for you. But, if you're fans of music, there'll be a live quartet at meal times in the house restaurant and a local band in the bar, which could make for fun evenings."

Austin grinded his teeth in consideration, keen eyes scanning the exits and doorways. "Where is the available room located? Which floor?"

"First."

His frown deepened, and he glanced at Scarlet.

The man behind the counter furrowed his brow. "Is that all right?"

"Maybe," Austin said. "Does your restaurant have a private entrance?"

"No. All guests use the main doors. Why?"

"What about the bar and kitchen?" Austin asked. "How many entrances are on this floor?"

The other man reared back his head and looked to Scarlet. This time, a bit concerned.

"I'm okay," she said, offering a small smile. "He's just incredibly diligent."

The man's attempt to match her smile failed.

"How many entrances in total?" Austin repeated.

"Four. One on each face of the building. North. South. East. West." He moved his hand from wall to wall, as if the exits were visible from where they stood.

"And on which side is the room located?"

He pointed again. "The Thurston Suite is east facing and well equipped. Anything you don't find there can be delivered to you from our pantry or closet, and our concierge is full-service. Anything you need, he can acquire."

"I doubt that," Austin muttered.

The man leaned forward, looking pointedly near their feet. "Do you have any luggage?"

"No."

Scarlet sighed at the ridiculousness of the conversation, and how utterly bizarre they must look and sound to this man. Eager to take the last available room, but worried about the building's entry points, and all the while without a single duffel bag or suitcase between them.

"We didn't expect to stay in town when we arrived," she said. "But circumstances have changed."

"And you want the room?"

"Yes," Austin answered. "And I'll need to speak to your manager."

The desk clerk took his time checking them in, probably wishing he'd told them the hotel was full. Then, Austin spoke briefly with the shift manager, delivering the details of their situation. He promised to pass the information on to the hotel manager when her shift began.

The walk to their room was long and slightly convoluted in the historic building. They turned left twice before finding the hallway with the last available suite. They were each given a key card to access the door, though she had no intention of going anywhere without Austin. And he let them inside with a swipe.

The space was small, as promised—a large four-post bed at the center took the lion's share of space. An armchair in the corner shared a stand with the bed. A table with two chairs stood before a window at the far wall, and a restroom was just inside the door from the hallway. Plush blue carpet covered the floor, and large oil portraits in gilded frames adorned the walls. A minifridge and small television were the only signs of the millennium.

In another life, in a room like this with a man like Austin Beaumont, she'd never have time to turn the television on. But in that life, her mother wouldn't be in the violent hands of a deluded, dangerous man.

Chapter Twenty-Four

Scarlet showered and slipped into a T-shirt and underthings they'd ordered after settling in.

Austin had arranged for anything not provided in the room, like clothing, to be picked up from a local store by the hotel concierge, who really did handle everything. He'd also ordered a tray of soups and breads from the restaurant for their dinner, and he hadn't forgotten her glass of red wine.

He'd met her every need without being asked, and though Scarlet's world was crumbling, she felt utterly cared for. A new sensation she never wanted to let go of. In fact, she hoped to do the same for him someday.

Austin rose from his chair at the table when she stepped away from the steamy bathroom in her big T-shirt and fuzzy socks. Damp hair hung loose over her shoulders, and she shivered, suddenly regretting not wrapping herself in the cushy terry cloth robe.

"It's all yours," she said, hoping to look less self-conscious than she felt and moving to one side of the bed to peel back the covers.

A new show had started on the television, which had been playing softly for hours since their arrival. They'd watched a marathon of sitcoms from her childhood while intermittently eating and touching base with Finn for new information. He never had much to offer, but he and Officer Barrow were exhausting even the tiniest leads, which made a terrible situation slightly better.

The last update had come more than two hours before, and all that was left for her to do now was wait. She wasn't sure she'd be able to rest well, but it was late and sleeping was the fastest way to pass the time until he called again.

"Thanks." He gathered his things and headed for the bathroom, which was still seeping steam.

The closet door was ajar in the corner, and a stack of folded blankets sat on the armchair, topped with a pillow. Somehow, the time they'd spent collecting updates on the search for her mother and watching television had distracted her from the implications of sharing a room with one bed. She'd felt comfortable and safe, despite the overarching circumstances, just as she had in the days shared at her home and his.

Now thoughts of their sleeping arrangements were front and center in jarring and slightly thrilling ways. She couldn't ask him to sleep in a chair while she had a queen-size bed to herself. That was just bad manners. And impractical.

She dragged her attention to the bathroom, where a shower had started running, then made up her mind. She put the pillow and blankets away, closed the closet door and slid into bed as planned.

Every splash of water in the next room brought an image with it that she couldn't ignore. Memories of his arms curved gently, protectively around her. His hands on her skin offering comfort. His breath on her lips when they'd nearly kissed.

She squirmed beneath the cool cotton sheets, restless for something she didn't want to name.

When the bathroom door opened again, Austin appeared

in pajama pants and bare feet. His hair was wet and a T-shirt clung to the damp planes of his chest.

Scarlet felt a rush of heat from the crown of her head to her toes.

He stared at the empty chair then turned his eyes to her. "You put the blankets away?"

She nodded and pulled the comforter back. "I think we should share the bed. It doesn't make any sense for you to sit in a chair all night. Given the days we've had lately, we both need some rest, and you won't get it there." She nodded to the place where his blanket stack had been. "We need to be ready for whatever the morning brings."

Austin released a breath. "You're not wrong there." He dropped the pile of clothes he'd worn all day onto the table then climbed into bed beside Scarlet and turned out the light. A moment later, he rolled over and leveled his face with hers.

The soft glow from the television flickered in the darkness.

"On or off?" he asked, raising the remote he'd grabbed from his nightstand.

"Off."

Her eyes adjusted quickly to the darkness, and she smiled at him lying so close to her. "Do you think we'll hear any more from Finn tonight?"

"It's possible," he said.

Finn and his team were working every angle. Interviewing Greg's friends, family and coworkers. Looking for properties he or his family might own that went unused this time of year, like a cabin or lake house. Checking the vehicle databases for anything he could be driving, including boats he could use to hole up on the water. On top of that, Tech

Services had spent the day digging into his work computer, and Marshal's Bluff officers had combed his home.

"It's just a matter of time now," Austin said.

She nodded, liking the way that sounded. "It seems impossible for him to hide."

"I think it is," Austin said confidently. "It would be hard enough for someone in their right mind to stay out of Finn's grasp for long. Add in the fact that Greg's juggling some kind of mental break, and he's got your mom in tow, and I don't think he'll last another twenty-four hours. I suspect they'll close in soon. He'll know he's caught and be forced to leave Trina behind to make a break for it."

Scarlet raised a hand to wipe a renegade tear. "I hope you're right. I hope he won't hurt her before he leaves her." At least no more than he'd likely hurt her already, forcing her into his control.

"Hey." Austin brushed hair away from her face with the backs of his fingers. "You okay?"

"My emotions are everywhere, but I'm fine. It's a lot to think about, and it's been a long week."

"All the more reason to rest." He tucked the lock of hair behind her ear then stroked his palm over her shoulder and down her arm.

Heat from his touch sizzled a path across her skin, and she shivered.

Austin pulled back, but she caught his fingers and rested their joined hands on the blankets between them.

Their eyes locked and breaths mingled in the darkness. Electricity charged the air.

"Are you still thinking about kissing me?" Scarlet asked, releasing his hand. "Because I'm thinking of kissing you." She slid her fingers along the curve of his neck then stroked his jaw with her thumb.

He stilled beneath her touch, and his Adam's apple bobbed. "I am."

"And?" she asked, somehow closer to him than she'd been a moment before.

He crooked one arm beneath the pillow supporting his head and let his free hand trail the curve of her hip. Then he pressed against the small of her back, eviscerating the little space left between them. Austin's lips curved into a small, mischievous grin as he pressed his mouth gently to hers.

Scarlet's body melted against him. She'd never wanted to be kissed by any man so much in her life. And unlike so many people liked to say, the anticipation was not better than the reality. It was as if his mouth was made for hers, and every fiber of her ignited at his touch. The soft moan that escaped her drew a full smile across his lips.

He pulled back and stared, heat and longing in his eyes. His heart hammered beneath her palm on his muscled chest. "I won't ever let anyone hurt you again," he vowed, voice low and thick with truth. "And I don't want to leave you when this man is caught. I'm hoping you'll ask me to stay."

Emotions rose and bloomed in her as she kissed him in response. His perfect words filled her, because she didn't want him to go. She found the hem of his shirt and tugged until he pulled it over his head and tossed it onto the floor. She removed her shirt as well.

Austin cussed at the sight of her bare breasts. He cupped them reverently in his hands as he kissed her once more.

When her head was light and her body boneless, he moved his skilled tongue along the plane between her breasts. She gasped as he stroked and suckled one taut nipple, angling his body more firmly against hers.

Her hands fisted in his outgrown hair and his mouth drifted lower. "Austin."

"Still okay?" he asked, as he continued to explore.

She arched in answer and invitation.

"Yes?" he asked between kisses, working a magic rhythm with his touch.

"Yes."

He dragged his lips up the column of her throat.

The gentle slide of his tongue on her skin sent shock waves of pleasure through her limbs. She rocked her hips with every pulse of his hand. Austin's kisses were devouring and he swallowed her needy moans. She wanted nothing more than to be consumed by every inch of him.

She gripped the waistband of his pajama pants, desperate to feel more of his bare skin on hers.

"Scarlet?" he whispered, as her body tipped toward the brink of unraveling. "Are you sure this is what you want?"

"You are the only thing I want," she said, and his eyes flashed hot with pleasure.

Then he brought her swiftly over the edge.

AUSTIN WOKE THE next morning with Scarlet's hand in his. Her lithe body curled against his side. He stroked the hair from her cheek, pressed a gentle kiss to her forehead and hoped like hell she'd want him today the way she had last night. Because there wasn't anything he wanted more than her, and he didn't see a future where that would change.

He longed to kiss her awake and love her once more, before the busyness of their day began. More than that, he needed to reiterate his feelings and intentions so there'd be no questions or misunderstandings by the light of day. His heart was hers for the taking.

A shrill ring interrupted his thoughts, turning his eyes to the phone on his nightstand.

He grabbed the receiver quickly, silencing the sound, but his shifting body roused Scarlet anyway.

"Who is it?" she asked.

"I don't know." He pulled the phone to his ear. "Hello?"

"Mr. Beaumont?" a strained male voice asked.

"Yes." He slid upright against the headboard, senses on sudden alert. "Who's this?"

"This is the hotel manager," the voice continued. "There's a man in the lobby looking for the woman you arrived with yesterday. He has her photo and is claiming that she's his wife and she's been abducted. He's making quite a scene."

"What does he look like?"

"Sandy hair, brown eyes. He's wearing jeans and a hooded sweatshirt."

Adrenaline surged in Austin's body as he swung out of bed and began to dress on autopilot. "Where is he now?"

"In the lobby. He's arguing with the desk clerk who's refusing to give any information. I sneaked into my office to call you."

"Good work. I'm on my way. Call the local authorities and tell them what you've just told me." Austin returned the receiver to its cradle and swiped his cell phone off the nightstand.

Scarlet sat, clutching blankets to her chest. "What's going on?"

"Greg's in the lobby trying to find out which room we're in. The hotel manager is calling local authorities, and I'm going out there to see if I can get my hands on him before he gets away." Austin tucked a pair of handcuffs into his pocket and grabbed his wallet and key card. "Get dressed and be ready when I come back. Don't answer the door for anyone."

She nodded, already scrambling for the bathroom. "Be careful."

SCARLET WAS IN turbo mode. She dressed in seconds and headed back into the main room, preparing to stuff their things into bags in case they needed to leave in a rush.

The door clicked again, stilling her in her tracks. Austin had barely been gone a minute. What had he forgotten? Or had something big already gone wrong?

She pulled on her coat as she hurried to meet him. "Everything okay?"

A familiar figure moved into view as she rounded the corner.

Greg Marten glared, wild eyed, and raised the gun in his hand.

Chapter Twenty-Five

"This way," Greg said with a flick of his wrist, pointing to the door with his gun.

Scarlet held her ground, mind racing. If he shot her, everyone would hear and she might live. If she went with him, her odds of survival would be infinitely thinner. What she needed to do was stall. Austin would be back soon. "How did you get in here?"

"Key card." He grinned. "They're not hard to copy if you know what you're doing and can get close enough to the one you want. I know what I'm doing, and it's surprising how careless the housekeeping staff is these days."

She struggled to swallow. The harmless guy from Tech Services had somehow become the ultimate modern-day villain. "The manager is on to you," she said. "He called the police. You'd be smarter to run now than to add another crime to your spree." If he valued being clever, maybe he'd take her advice and go.

Greg grimaced and marched forward, extending his gun in her direction until her eyes closed. "I am very smart." A hand clamped over her wrist, and he jerked her hard, nearly knocking her off her feet. "Don't give me any trouble, or I will leave without you, and I'll kill your mother as punishment."

Scarlet's ears rang, and her thoughts clouded. Everything dissipated from her mind except her mother. And she let Greg tow her into the hall.

"No one's coming to save you this time," he said, guiding her along with a stern hand. "A bunch of hotel guests are in the restaurant making a ton of noise, and your PI is chasing his tail in the lobby. I've got you all to myself. Now, out you go." He shoved her through an exit door, into a small lot where a large truck was making a delivery.

She scanned the traffic-packed streets nearby and winced at the sight of the old navy sedan local police had been searching for.

Greg opened the passenger door. "Get in and climb over. You're driving."

"What?"

He pushed her across the armrests and into the driver's seat then planted the keys on her lap. His hand lingered unnecessarily. "Drive. Make a left onto Main Street and hurry, or we'll be too late to save your mother."

Terror seized her lungs as she dug the key from beneath his palm and started the car. She glanced through the window as she shifted into gear, wishing for Austin to burst from the hotel and save her.

"Do you hear any sirens?" Greg asked, turning her attention to his smug face.

She blinked away the tears forming in her eyes. "No."

"That's because I'm the one who called your room, not a manager. I'm the one who drew your PI away. No one called the cops. There's no help on the way. Right now, your friend is standing around wondering what happened. He'll probably demand to speak to the manager who will have no idea what he's talking about. I've outmaneuvered all of them. Now you and I can start the life we're meant to have."

Austin raced down the hallway, past a housekeeping cart. The staffer's lanyard hung from one side. He considered stopping for a fleeting moment, to tell her not to disturb his room, not to frighten Scarlet who was already terrified and alone, but he couldn't spare the time. Not if Greg Marten was in the lobby and local police were on their way. This was Austin's time to take down their enemy and see that he was cuffed and charged.

The hotel restaurant was packed as he jogged over the crimson carpet to the desk. Guests spilled from the open French doors, bringing a cacophony of voices, laughter and music along with them. Greg could blend easily into the rambunctious morning crowd and vanish through a side door if Austin didn't hurry.

"Where did he go?" Austin called, erasing the final few yards to the welcome desk.

The young man behind the counter blinked. "Who?"

"The man who was here looking for his wife. Your manager called me. I'm Austin Beaumont." He dug his wallet and PI license from one pocket and flashed it across the counter.

The man frowned. "I don't know anything about that, sir."

"Who was working here a minute ago? I need to talk to them. No." He waved a panicked hand, feeling the world tilt beneath him. "I need to speak to your manager."

"Can I help you?" A regal-looking blonde woman in a black pantsuit and heels strode confidently from a nearby doorway. "I'm the hotel manager, Eva Branson."

Austin stilled then stumbled back, realization gripping his heart and chest like a vise. The hotel manager he'd spoken to only minutes before had been a man. "Call the police," he demanded. "Tell them Austin Beaumont said to get here. Now!"

He tore back through the cavernous lobby, down the hallway and past the housekeeping cart to his room. He pressed the key card to the door and swung it open, his heart and final thread of hope in the balance.

But as expected, the room was empty.

"WHERE IS MY MOTHER?" Scarlet asked, fingers aching from her grip on the wheel, fear stiffening her posture.

The old sedan smelled of motor oil and cigarette smoke. Both scents likely permeated the fabric seats long before Greg made the purchase. A pair of orange tree-shaped air fresheners dangled from the rearview mirror on white springy cords. The back seat was empty, the car otherwise immaculate.

"Turn right," he said, ignoring her question and pointing to the upcoming highway entrance. "Get on the interstate, then stay in the left lane and keep up with traffic until I say otherwise."

She looked at the car beside her, wishing the other driver would make eye contact and see her distress. The young man behind the wheel of the SUV sang along to the radio, oblivious to her terror. She changed lanes, losing hope, and something thumped softly in the trunk.

"Good," Greg said, satisfied she was cooperating.

Her heart sank. Getting on the highway would mean disappearing, maybe permanently. Somewhere Austin and local law enforcement would never find her.

A flash of red and white in her side-view mirror caught her eyes. Austin's old truck appeared, cutting in and out of traffic with ease.

"Use your signal," Greg said. "Make the turn."

She shot him a venomous look and eased her foot off the

gas pedal. Surely he wouldn't kill her while she was driving. "First tell me where my mother is!"

The muted thumping she'd heard earlier grew louder and more fervent. Scarlet jerked her head around to face the back seat, earning her a honk as she swerved.

"Is someone in the trunk?" Scarlet gasped. "Is that my mom?"

Greg pressed the gun's barrel to her ribs. "She's fine. Now pay attention and drive. Getting into a car accident won't be good for her."

Scarlet bit her lip, eyes darting to Austin's truck in her rearview mirror. He was a block away but gaining on them. She slowed, poking along, allowing cars to pass her.

"What are you doing?" Greg demanded. "Drive faster!"

"I'm nervous," she snapped. "I don't like traffic or having guns pointed at me. I think you locked my mom in the trunk. How am I supposed to handle this? Why did you even take her? Do you want me to hate you?"

"I want you to do what I say. She's your motivation," he said. "Mommy stays safe as long as you obey and stop seeing that man. She's in the trunk so you stay calm and don't try anything ridiculous while you're behind the wheel."

Scarlet's mouth opened then shut. She could be angry, and she could be mean. But her mom would be the one he punished, and she couldn't allow that.

"Get on the highway."

She checked the rearview again. Austin had moved ahead by another car length, but the traffic light was yellow. He wouldn't make it through the intersection with her.

Greg pointed the gun into the back seat then cocked it. "Run the light or a bullet goes into the trunk."

Scarlet released a defeated sob as she jammed the gas, launching them onto the highway.

AUSTIN POUNDED HIS hand against the horn as the sedan carrying Scarlet and her abductor made the turn onto the highway.

The phone rang as he angled out of line and onto the berm, tossing dirt and gravel into the air behind him.

"Beaumont," he answered, skirting around waiting traffic.

"This is Officer Barrow," a familiar voice announced. "What's going on? One minute Dispatch has me en route to The Carolina Grand, and the next minute, I'm told you're in vehicular pursuit of Greg Marten."

"I made both calls to Dispatch," Austin said. "He tricked me, came right into the hotel and took her. They're headed southwest on Highway 17." His truck hit the on-ramp with a growl and shot him up to speed. "They're in his Toyota with a two-or three-minute head start I plan to eliminate."

"We've got his vehicle registration. I'll put a notice out on the car and access cameras along 17 to scan for his license plate."

Austin pushed his truck's engine to its limits, determined not to let Scarlet and her abductor get away.

Soon, a car resembling Greg's appeared.

"I think I see it," he said, nudging the gas pedal lower. "They're passing the Camden exit, heading toward Elizabeth City."

"Copy that."

A caravan of semitrucks appeared on the horizon, stretching down the center lane. He'd barely considered the possibility of the trucks becoming a barrier and obstacle when the sedan began to change lanes, cutting in front of the convoy as Austin drew alongside the second truck from the rear.

When he reached the front of the line, the sedan was gone.

A FORK APPEARED on the highway, dividing one interstate into two. "Where are we going?" Scarlet asked. "What do I do at the fork?"

She needed information, and she needed a plan.

"Stay right. We'll get off at the next opportunity."

Scarlet used her signal and began sliding across four lanes in a mess of traffic, barely avoiding a caravan of 18-wheelers. "But where are we going?"

"I don't know."

"What do you mean you don't know?" She pursed her lips, reeling in her temper. "You said we're going to start a life together. Where are we doing that? You have to talk to me."

"How can I trust you?" he snapped. His formerly placid expression suddenly filled with rage. "After you spent the night with that man? How can I ever trust you?"

She winced, hoping he hadn't somehow seen what they'd done. Like he seemed to see everything else she did.

"I warned you and warned you," he said. "I told you to knock it off or you'd be punished. And it's as if you don't even care!" he screamed. "What is wrong with you?"

Scarlet focused on the road, muscles tight.

Spittle flew from his mouth with each lament, and he pounded his fists against the dashboard.

"I'm sorry," she said, voice wobbling and tears threatening. "Please don't be angry."

"I thought we had a connection," Greg complained. "You called me for help with the system, with your email, with passwords, and I helped you. I thought we bonded. We got to know one another. You even helped me pick out our house."

"You bought a house?"

His glare burned the skin of her cheek. "I bought the one

you told me was perfect for a new family. One that could grow with me."

Her stomach dropped, and the severity of her situation grew infinitely clearer. She remembered the conversation about the house. She'd encouraged him to buy the bigger home, because he had his eye on someone special and hoped to settle down. Maybe start a family.

Greg's expression became affronted, and his mouth set into a grimace. "I can't believe you don't remember."

"I do," she croaked. Suddenly, she saw all those innocent chats with a stranger at the corporate help desk in a drastically different light. And she couldn't help wondering if all her computer issues had really been a result of the new system, or if they'd happened at his hand and by his design, so she'd have to keep calling.

"You said I was your hero," he whispered. "And I believed you."

Heat climbed Scarlet's neck, and nausea rolled in the pit of her stomach. She struggled to breathe, certain she'd be sick or black out and kill them all in traffic. She'd been so thankful for Greg's help every time. She might've even been flirty. And he was right, after a particularly frustrating issue with her email password, she'd called him her hero.

Had that been his tipping point?

"I saved you before, and I'm saving you now," he said, voice lighter. "You see the kinds of choices you make on your own. How easily someone can get to you. Harm you." He lifted the gun from his lap, as if she could've forgotten it was there. "I'm going to keep you safe. You just have to stop fighting me. I can make you happy."

She made eye contact with another driver as she reached the far right lane. The other driver pulled swiftly ahead. A hundred witnesses and no one saw anything, when it felt as if the entire car should be flashing with her distress. Why couldn't others see the dark cloud preparing to consume her?

Greg's hand landed on her thigh again, and her stomach pitched. "Take this exit."

Rolling fields of grass spread into the distance. A forest rose on the right.

Her foot eased off the pedal a bit, not ready to leave the safety of a hundred moving cars.

He pointed his gun into the back seat again, and she took the exit to nowhere.

They rolled along the curving county route with no homes or businesses in sight, and infinite reasons not to go any farther.

Left without options, she burst into a dramatic round of tears. She was out of time for making a good plan, so she'd have to improvise and settle for making any plan and hoping it worked.

Since he seemed hung up on being her hero, tears felt like a good start.

She breathed harder and faster, making each puff audible, and shuddered. Then she pulled onto the side of the road with a series of desperate sobs.

There weren't any cameras to find them here. No passing vehicles to notice they'd stopped. Just them and a whole lot of nature. So she'd focus on getting him out of the car. Then she could drive away with her mom in the trunk and not stop until she found a police station.

"What are you doing?" he demanded. "Drive!"

"I can't," she cried. "I can't. I can't." The tears ran freely now, her true emotions mixing with the show. "Help me. Please!"

Greg swiveled on his seat, looking through the rear window then back to her. "What's wrong? What do you want me to do?"

"You have to drive. I'm shaking. I'll crash if I keep going. I'm—" she considered her believable options "—I think I'm having a panic attack." She shifted into Park and pressed her palms against her face, hoping to make her skin redder, eyes puffier and her overall look more unwell.

"What do you need?" he asked. "A paper bag? Water?"

"Just drive," she said. "I can't do it."

A long beat of silence passed before he spoke again, distrust evident in his voice. "I know what you're doing."

Scarlet steeled her resolve, unfastened her safety belt and reached for him across the armrest.

It was possible he'd take a shot at the car after he climbed out and she drove away. Possible a bullet would hit the trunk. But at least if that happened, she'd already be in motion, able to find a hospital for her mother. She had to take the risk, because staying with him was a death sentence.

"You're still my hero," she whispered, swallowing bile that rose with the words. "Help me. Please."

Slowly, his tense muscles relaxed beneath her hands, and he pressed his gun-free palm against her back. "Shh," he cooed. "Breathe."

The shudders of repulsion that followed seemed to convince him she truly wasn't in any shape to drive.

"Okay," he said. "But no one's getting out of the car to make this switch. We'll have to slide across the seat to trade places." He pushed the armrests up, creating a flat bench between them, and patted the space.

Scarlet released him, heart thundering, mind racing. She couldn't actually let him drive. He'd have all the control.

Greg scooted into the center of the seat and swung one foot into the well beside hers. "Come on."

She turned and rose, attempting to awkwardly climb over him, but he caught her hips and drew her onto his lap in a straddle. Gooseflesh crawled over her arms like a thousand baby spiders and another hard round of shivers racked her form. She dropped her hands to her sides.

"Hey," he said softly, peering into her eyes. "I've got you." The handle of his gun pressed against her left thigh.

Something heavy registered inside her jacket pocket on the right. An impossible thought rose in her mind, a tiny sliver of hope.

She maintained eye contact with Greg as she felt the cylindrical shape with her fingertips, then slid her hand into the pocket.

Austin had given her the Taser.

Chapter Twenty-Six

Scarlet wet her lips in concentration as she located the narrow switch at the bottom of the stun gun and slid it into the on position as Austin had shown her. Then she pushed the slider along the device's side to arm it. Now she'd have to choose her moment and be quick.

Greg's gaze moved to her mouth, and his hand skimmed her ribs, apparently misinterpreting her still exterior as submission. He leaned in for a kiss, and she let her head fall to the side, allowing him to access her neck instead.

Ignoring the nauseating feel of his lips on her skin, she gripped the compact stun gun and rested her thumb on the button. When Greg finally sought her mouth, eyelids at half-mast and an eager expression on his face, she thrust forward, connecting her forehead with his. The teeth-rattling collision drew a shout from her captor. His hands flew to his forehead.

The gun's barrel angled toward the roof.

Scarlet squinted against the pain and grabbed his raised wrist, holding the handgun in place while she pressed the stun gun to his neck.

A sickening crackle carved the air, and Greg's gun went off in a burst. The bullet ripped a hole through the roof before his hand opened and the weapon toppled into the back seat.

Scarlet grabbed the keys and threw herself toward the passenger door.

He sputtered and roared, fingers clutching at her shirt as she scrambled away.

She pressed the trunk release button on the key fob, and the lid swung open.

The car rocked as Greg raged, pounding a hand against something inside.

Her mother's curled form came into view as Scarlet reached the trunk.

Trina blinked against the sun. Her usually perfect hair and makeup were in unprecedented ruin. Her skin was pale, and a large bruise marred her cheek. "Scarlet!"

"We've got to go," she said, reaching for her mom.

The driver's door opened, and Greg bumbled into the grass, still spewing horrific strings of swears and clutching a palm to his neck.

"Stay back," Scarlet warned, releasing her mother in favor of resetting her stun gun. "Stay away from us."

Trina wobbled at her side, shaken but alive, then clutched her daughter's arm for balance.

Their assailant glared as he yanked open the door to the back seat. "Oh, I'm going to stay far away from you now. I'm done trying to set you straight. So it's time to end this instead." He stretched inside, and Scarlet spun away, pulling her mother with her.

"Run!" she cried, and the women headed for the trees.

Trina struggled to keep up with Scarlet, despite the fact that she was in far better shape.

Scarlet added that to her ever-growing list of concerns.

"Come on, Mom," she panted. "Just a little farther." They

had to make it into the trees before Greg. "We need to find somewhere to hide."

Soon, shade poured over them, and a small measure of relief set in. The forest stretched in three directions, providing plenty of options for cover.

"Here," Trina rasped, pulling her daughter sideways. She ducked behind the broad trunk of a moss-drenched oak then doubled over to vomit on the forest floor.

"Oh, my goodness." Scarlet crouched at her side. "Are you okay?"

"I think I have a concussion," she said, sliding down to sit in the leaves and dirt. "I can't keep running. My head is pounding and spinning. It might explode, if I don't straight-up collapse."

Scarlet pressed a gentle palm to her mother's sweaty face. They couldn't stay there long. They'd be sitting ducks if they didn't keep moving. "How long were you in the trunk?"

"I don't know. Hours maybe," she said. "I was attacked outside my morning showing. I don't even know if that was today. I woke up in a trunk."

Scarlet smoothed her mom's hair away from her eyes. "That was yesterday."

"Scar-let!" Greg's voice echoed through the trees. He broke her name into syllables and sang them like a nursery rhyme. "You can't hide from me, Scarlet," he taunted. "Don't you know that by now?"

She pressed a finger to her lips, and the women became still as statues.

Leaves crunched and twigs snapped in the distance.

Scarlet held her breath as she peeked around the ancient tree.

Greg was visible through a dense thicket of brush and

patch of evergreens. He scanned the forest in the opposite direction.

Her mother tugged her arm then pointed away. A massive boulder stood near the tree line. "Do you still have the car keys?"

She nodded. If they could get to the boulder, they could take another break for Trina's sake then make a run for the car.

She locked eyes with her mother, and Trina stood on trembling legs. Scarlet used her fingers to count to three.

They burst into crouched runs, darting toward the massive stone.

Maniacal laughter erupted behind them. "There you are!" Greg jeered. "No need to bother running now. I've found you, and it's time for your punishment."

The earsplitting crack of a gunshot sent birds into flight from the treetops.

And her mother fell to the ground.

AUSTIN EXITED THE HIGHWAY, certain the sedan must've done the same. He'd only lost sight of it for a few seconds, and it had to have gone somewhere. He slowed to consider his options, which were few. He could return to the highway, but if they were there, his detour would've afforded them a more than generous lead, one he'd likely never make up. Or he could continue on the winding country road, hoping to catch them, assuming they had gotten off the interstate.

Another set of questions crowded into mind before he could sort the last. If Scarlet and Greg had taken the rural exit as suspected, where were they now? And where were they going? According to the big green signs at the bottom of the ramp, the nearest town was twelve miles away. The nearest town with a population over a thousand was nearly fifty miles farther.

A gunshot broke the silence, and Austin went on alert. His truck rocketed forward as he listened carefully for another round of gunfire to break the silence. And he prayed he wouldn't discover a fatality along the roadside. He redialed Officer Barrow.

"What do you know, Beaumont?" the cop asked, answering on the first ring.

"I'm heading east on a county route off exit 113. There's been a shot fired."

"Any sign of the cause?" Barrow asked.

"Not yet," Austin said, floating around the next curve.

Greg's sedan appeared as the road straightened. Trunk lid up. Three doors open.

"I've got eyes on the sedan. Two miles east of the exit. I'm approaching now."

Austin skidded to a stop behind the sedan, and he leaped from the truck's cab, cell phone in one hand, sidearm in the other. "No signs of the passengers."

He turned in a small circle, scanning the scene in all directions. Wondering what to make of the abandoned car. Hoping things weren't as bad as they appeared. "I think she got away somehow and made a run for the trees." That was where he'd go if he needed cover and time to make a plan.

"Copy that," Barrow said. "Help's on the way."

Austin pocketed the cell phone and jogged across the field toward the tree line, phone tucked into his back pocket, sidearm in hand.

SCARLET'S EARS RANG, and the breath left her body. She fell to the earth beside her mother, scooping her into shaky arms. "Mom!"

Trina's eyes opened, then shut.

Scarlet scanned her body for a bullet wound, then frantically searched the forest for signs of her shooter. Trina wasn't bleeding, but she also wasn't responding.

Scarlet's world tilted, and tears fell from her eyes as she imagined all the scenarios where they didn't make it out alive. And all the things she wished she'd told her mother long ago. "I'm so sorry," she whispered.

A gut-wrenching wail rose through the forest.

Scarlet froze, unsure what to make of the sound.

Then someone called her name.

She lifted her head, straining to see without being seen. A familiar silhouette came into view. "Austin?"

"Scarlet!"

She stretched onto her feet and ran to meet him, careful to watch for signs of the shooter.

Austin caught her in his embrace and cupped her face in his hands. "You're okay," he said, stroking her head and holding her tight. "I thought I'd lost you. I don't ever want to lose you."

Emotion clogged her throat and fresh tears stung her eyes. "Mom's hurt, and Greg's got a gun. We have to get her out of here."

Austin shook his head. "I shot Greg and took his weapon. He'll live, but he won't go far. I aimed for his knee."

Scarlet fell against him in relief as sirens wound to life in the distance.

"Let's get your mama," Austin said, and he followed her back to Trina's side.

Chapter Twenty-Seven

Three months later

Scarlet jammed the sale sign into her front yard with equal feelings of relief and remorse. Greg Marten had been charged with multiple counts of assault, attempted murder, abduction, stalking and a bevy of lesser crimes. He'd been convicted of them all. And though she knew, logically, that he'd be behind bars for many years to come, she still felt his eyes on her some days. Especially in places she knew he'd been. Like her beloved waterfront home.

"You okay?" Austin asked, rubbing her shoulders and gazing at the historic cottage he'd tried to help her redeem.

Weekly counseling sessions for her trauma and a thorough cleansing of every room on the property had made a dent in her unease. But she knew now that nothing would fully erase the unsettling sensations she felt there. Not even the brand-new locks and dead bolts had brought her peace.

She raised one gloved hand to cover his. "It's bittersweet," she said, her breath rising on the frigid air in little white clouds. "I love this place, but I can't stay."

"Well," Austin said, moving to stand before her. "How about we go home and get warm? I have a surprise there for you."

"I love everything about those suggestions," she said, curling into his embrace.

He pressed cool lips to her forehead. "Let's go."

The sun was setting as they climbed back into his truck and cranked the heat and defroster. She'd moved the bulk of her regular-use items to Austin's house weeks before, and the Beaumonts had helped her transport the last of her other things into storage last weekend. Now all that was left to do was sell her home.

She peeled off her gloves and held her icy hands in front of the hot air vent. "I hope your surprise involves a fire, a glass of wine and lots of naked cuddling with my favorite human."

"Please let that be me," he said breathlessly.

Scarlet laughed and leaned closer, planting a kiss on his handsome face. "Take me home, Mr. Beaumont."

The drive to Austin's place was borderline perilous in the winter. An exceptionally cold snap had created ice in the ruts and grooves before the covered bridge. Driveway repair would be top priority come spring, or she'd be stuck there permanently.

"What on earth?" she asked, tipping forward as an abundance of twinkle lights became visible on the bridge and in a number of surrounding trees.

Someone had also lined the road with candles burning inside canning jars.

"Do you like it?" he asked.

"I love it! Can we get out? Is this the surprise?"

Austin chuckled and rolled on.

Scarlet twisted on her seat, seeking the beautiful lights and making plans to take photographs from his deck when they got home.

A collection of 4x4s had gathered in the parking space outside the mill.

"Is this a party?" she asked, recognizing a few of the vehicles as belonging to his family. "Or just dinner?" She could never be sure with his family. There were just so many of them, and they gathered for any reason.

Austin parked then turned to grin at her in the darkness. "I'm hoping it's a celebration."

She narrowed suspicious eyes on him. "What are we celebrating?"

"Us." Austin leaned in her direction and kissed her absolutely senseless.

The porch lights flashed on, and Scarlet took a moment to regain her composure.

Hopefully partygoers weren't planning to stay long. She had plans for snuggling that couldn't be ignored.

Mrs. Beaumont waved one arm overhead on Austin's front step. A wool cape clasped around her shoulders. "Come in!" she called, her words muffled through the glass. "It's cold! What are you doing?"

Austin ran the pad of one thumb across his bottom lip, returning her gaze to what she was missing. "Ready?"

Oh, she was ready. Not necessarily for a party, but she would like to see the Beaumonts. Austin's family had embraced her as one of their own, and she loved every encounter. She especially looked forward to his mother's hugs and his brothers' banter. And she deeply appreciated her new sort-of sister too, Dean's fiancée, Nicole.

Scarlet opened her truck door and slid into the cold. Austin met her with a kiss on her nose.

"Finally," his mama said, greeting them with hugs before ushering them inside.

The air smelled of cinnamon and vanilla. Merry chatter rattled down from the second floor.

"Hurry up," Mrs. Beaumont pushed, nudging them toward the stairs. "Everyone's waiting."

Austin took Scarlet's hand and escorted her to the party.

A round of cheers erupted as they reached the little crowd. At least two dozen people raised their glasses. Dean and Nicole, Mr. Beaumont and Finn. Lincoln and Josie, the stable manager at the family ranch. Plus a fully recovered Lydia and Scarlet's mother, to name a few.

"Mom?" She moved in Trina's direction and pulled her into an embrace. The time they'd spent in the forest together had sparked a sort of healing between them that had been long overdue. "What are you doing here?" she asked, grateful and downright shocked to see her outside Holbrook on a work night. Then she remembered the treacherous road. "How did you manage it?"

"Wisely," Trina said, answering the latter question first. "I left my car at the Coulter office in town, and I rode here with Lydia and Finn."

Lydia beamed at Trina's side. The pair had formed a bond in the days since their ugly run-ins with Greg Marten. "Hi, Scarlet. Austin."

Austin shook the ladies' hands.

"Thank you for being here," Scarlet said. "I had no idea we were having a party, or I would've invited you myself." She turned to pin Austin with a playful look of reproach and found him pulling a small velvet box from his pocket.

"It's happening!" Mrs. Beaumont yelled.

Austin laughed, and a hush rolled over their guests. "Scarlet," he said, voice warm and thick with his sexy southern drawl.

"What are you doing?" she whispered, staring at the box and certain she must be wrong.

"I love you," he said. "I was lost for you the moment you walked into my office, and I just keep falling a little further every day you're around. You are strong and smart. Steadfast and sexy."

The crowd chuckled, and Mrs. Beaumont covered her mouth with obvious delight.

"I can't imagine my life without you in it," he said. "And I don't want to. I hope you feel the same way."

"I do." She nodded, head and heart so light she could blow away.

His eyes misted with emotion as he opened the little box and lowered to one knee. "Marry me," he pleaded.

Hot tears swiveled over Scarlet's cheeks as she pulled him up to kiss her.

Then she said yes.

* * * * *

HOTSHOT HERO FOR
THE HOLIDAYS

LISA CHILDS

For my hero for the holidays and every day,
Andrew Ahearne. Love you so much!

Chapter One

The big box in the corner of the firehouse was filling up, wrapped and unwrapped toys overflowing from it, and the box was nearly as tall as Trent Miles's six-foot-four-inch height and twice as wide around as he was. Trent tossed a toy fire truck onto the top of the pile and grinned. Black Friday wasn't even over yet, and they'd already filled one box. They would definitely beat the local police precinct in their usual competition to see who could collect more for Toys for Tots. Not that it was all about the competition.

Just mostly.

"You're back," the captain said as he stepped out of his office off the main area of the firehouse.

Trent nodded.

"Hell of a thing to have to fight a wildfire over Thanksgiving," the captain remarked. "Sure you're not ready to give up being a hotshot?" Captain Rodriguez was in charge of this firehouse here in Detroit; Trent's US Forest Service hotshot team was comprised of firefighters from all over and operated out of a small town in northern Michigan with a superintendent in charge.

Trent chuckled, as the captain probably expected, and shook his head. But the truth was that he didn't love being a hotshot firefighter as much as he once had. He still loved flying off to wherever he was needed to fight wildfires, but he hated what had been happening with his team over the past year. He hated how his team wasn't the team he'd known and loved like family.

He'd always thought he was so close to those guys, closer than even with his crew here at the firehouse in Detroit where he worked full-time. The hotshot gig, with the US Forest Service Department, was on an as-needed basis. But with the number of wildfires over the past five years that Trent had been a member, he'd worked with the Huron Hotshots almost as much as he had out of his local firehouse in Detroit.

"But do you have the fan club in Northern Lakes that you have here?" the captain asked, his dark eyes sparkling with amusement. Manny Rodriguez had served in the US Marine Corps with Trent's dad, who had died during a deployment when Trent was young. Manny had known Trent his whole life and would have taken him in after his mom died, too, if someone else hadn't stepped up. Someone who hadn't had to welcome a traumatized, almost-teenage boy into their home but had chosen to anyway.

"What fan club?" Trent asked, wondering what the joke was. Manny didn't usually tease him like Trent's fellow hotshots did.

The captain opened his office door and stepped back inside for a moment. When he came out, he had a small stack of envelopes in his hand. "Christmas cards from your fan club."

"Christmas cards?"

Manny shrugged. "Guess my wife isn't the only one who still sends them out in November."

"I thought she was the only one who still sends them out at all." Trent counted out five of them, not quite enough for the fan club his boss claimed he had.

"Open them up," Manny said. "Maybe they're all from my wife."

Trent chuckled. "Maybe so…" He held up one of the envelopes. "'To the hot firefighter'? How do you know this is for me?"

"This motley crew isn't your hotshot team," Manny said. "Nobody's knocking on our doors to put out a calendar." He patted his belly that protruded over his belt.

Because of how dangerous fighting wildfires was, hotshots were required to be in peak physical condition. Their lives literally depended on it. But Trent respected every fire he fought. He knew all too well how an innocuous one in an abandoned warehouse could suddenly consume a city block and claim multiple lives. Or how what looked to be a rundown, empty apartment building could still have residents. He knew that too damn well. And because of the nightmares he had over it, he would never forget.

"My hotshot team has never done a calendar," Trent said. He'd just recently found out that they'd been asked, but other hotshots had pressured the superintendent to turn down the offer. Now he knew why. One of his team members wasn't really who he'd claimed he was for the past five years.

And that was just one of the secrets that had recently been revealed. That was why his hotshot team didn't feel like the family he'd once thought they were—because of all the damn secrets and lies. Hell, even his *family* didn't feel like his family anymore, not after his sister put his team at risk just to further her own damn career.

"You okay?" Manny asked.

Trent nodded. "Yeah, just tired."

"You've been out West for two weeks. You don't need to be here after just getting back," Manny said. "Forget about the cards for now. Go home. Get some sleep. You know things will also be getting crazy around here given the time of year. Holidays mean home fires."

Trent groaned. More candles burning, dried-out Christmas trees and hot lights, if they were still using the old, non-LED ones, never made a good combination. But he didn't want to go home either. Knowing how much he was gone during the wildfire season, he'd opened his place up to other people living with him. Or just using it while he was gone.

He doubted he would go home to the empty house he wanted it to be right now so he could actually unwind. "No, I'm still pretty keyed up," Trent said. More at the people who'd used him and kept secrets from him than from the wildfire. "I better open up these cards and make sure they're not really for you, Manny." Only a couple had "to the hot firefighter" on them; the rest were addressed directly to Trent Miles, care of the firehouse.

Manny chuckled. "I can only hope this old man would get fan mail like you do."

The two cards to the hot fireman contained flattering and flirty personal messages with cell numbers scribbled under the names of the senders. A couple of other cards expressed gratitude for him saving them in the past. That was why he did what he did. For the people he could save.

If only he could save them all…

But he couldn't. Despite his best efforts, they lost people in fires. They weren't able to get them out in time. Weren't able to save them.

The last card he opened was also addressed to him by name. But it wasn't thanking him. Not at all. Dread twisted his stomach when he read the message written inside. Maybe it was from a family member of someone who hadn't survived.

Or maybe it was about that other thing, the thing he'd just

learned was going on with his hotshot crew. The sabotage. The attempts on their lives and the notes his boss and some of his teammates had been receiving. The threats.

This note, scrawled inside a card with a gold Christmas tree on the outside, was definitely as threatening as some of those had been. *You're going to find out what it feels like to lose someone close to you. Soon.*

"What the hell…" he muttered, the dread in his gut growing even heavier.

"What is it?" Manny asked with concern.

Trent shook his head. "Nothing." He didn't want to worry his boss. Not like Trent had been worrying even before receiving this card. He had already lost more than one *someone* close to him. A few of them before he had even become a firefighter. And more recently, he'd lost a hotshot buddy, and a few other teammates, really close ones, had nearly died as well. He didn't want anyone else getting hurt or worse, and especially not because of him.

"Trent, I know you've had a lot going on with the Huron Hotshots," Manny said. "But I hope you know that I'm always here for you."

Trent bear-hugged his boss and chuckled. "I swear, none of these cards are from your wife."

Manny laughed and slapped his back. "I don't know if that is a relief or a disappointment. I might like a break from her nagging. Speaking of which, I better get home before another call—"

An alarm pealed, echoing off the concrete and metal of the firehouse walls and floor.

Manny cursed.

"You can leave, man. I'm sure the crew's got this," Trent assured the captain.

The firehouse erupted with movement: firefighters

coming down from the floor above while others rushed in through the open doors, getting their gear, starting the engines.

"What's the address?" Manny asked the lieutenant in charge of the crew. "What kind of fire?"

"Sounds like arson. Fire started after a report of shots fired at the same address," Lieutenant Ken Stokes replied.

Manny gripped Ken's broad shoulder and advised him, "Be careful. Make sure police have secured the scene and that there is no active shooter before you guys get anywhere close to it."

"Where is it?" Trent asked since Ken hadn't answered that part of the boss's question yet.

Ken glanced down at his tablet that held the information from Dispatch and read off the street number and name.

Panic gripped Trent, pressing so hard on his lungs that he had to cough to clear his throat. "I'm going with you," he told the lieutenant.

"What? Why?" Manny asked. "You just got back from a hotshot run."

"That's my address," Trent replied.

The lieutenant sucked in a breath. "There's already a possible fatality, Trent."

Just moments ago, Trent had read that ominous note that warned he would find out how it felt to lose someone close to him. Soon. Had that warning already come to pass? Had he just lost someone close to him?

Who?

SHOTS FIRED. SOMETHING had definitely happened here tonight before the fire. But would Detective Heather Bolton be able to figure it out?

She leaned against the side of her vehicle, studying the

scene playing out across the street in the faint glow of the streetlamps. The firefighters rushed around the house, spraying water onto the flames. If the fire hadn't already destroyed whatever evidence might have been left at the scene, the water was probably washing away anything that might have survived the fire.

The victim hadn't. The body had come out first. In a body bag. But the smoke or the flames hadn't killed the victim. The bullet hole in her skull had. The coroner had confirmed that before even loading the body into his van and driving away.

Heather could leave now, too. She'd already talked to the neighbor who'd called 9-1-1 about the gunshots she'd heard. The woman hadn't seen anything; she'd only heard the shots. And while she'd called the police, she'd been too afraid to look out the window.

"People are always coming and going at that house," she'd told Heather in a conspiratorial whisper. "I heard the owner is or was a member of a gang."

Heather had widened her eyes with surprise over that speculation. The burning house in question was located in an upper-middle-class neighborhood. But she knew from her year and a half working with the vice unit that drugs could be dealt and manufactured anywhere and a lot of the time gangs were involved.

That was why Heather had decided to stick around; to wait for the owner to show up. The owner wasn't the person who had left zipped inside that body bag in the coroner's van. As well as determining cause of death at the scene, the coroner had also been able to determine sex. Female. Heather had already accessed the property records and had found out that the name of the owner was Trent Miles.

The name had a ring of familiarity to Heather. Either

she'd heard it before or their paths had previously crossed. Had she investigated him? No charges or convictions had come up in the quick criminal check she'd done on him.

Not even prior arrests or warrants. So if he was a gang member, he hadn't gotten caught doing anything criminal. Yet.

But Heather was working toward the highest case clearance rate in the department right now. She was so close that she could taste the victory. So close that Detective Bob Bernard could probably just about taste the crow he was going to have to eat over his remarks about girl detectives not earning their jobs. He claimed that females were only promoted to detective so that the police department could avoid getting sued for sex discrimination.

Heather couldn't wait to tell the misogynistic jerk to suck it when she surpassed his record. She needed to close this case and at least one more before Christmas in order to secure bragging rights before the office holiday party. Because who knew—maybe Bob was actually working on improving his own closing rate. Though she doubted it.

She also doubted that this fire was an accident; it had obviously been set in order to destroy evidence of the murder. The flames were out now. Only smoke rose from the blackened structure. She crossed the street and stepped closer to the crime scene tape that she'd given to the uniformed officers to cordon off the area.

One of the firefighters stood just inside that tape, staring very intently at the damaged house. His square jaw was clenched so tightly that a muscle twitched in his lean cheek.

"Did all of the firefighters make it out?" she asked with concern.

She wasn't a fan of firefighters, not after having dated a couple of them back when she'd been a uniformed officer. Most of them were like Bob Bernard, chauvinists who didn't respect women and just wanted to brag about the dangers of their careers. How they were such he-men for fighting fires. While she didn't want to date any of them again, she didn't deny that their jobs were dangerous. She also appreciated what they did and didn't want any of them to get hurt doing it.

"All of the crew made it out," the man confirmed, and he turned back to tip up his hat and stare at her.

His face was streaked with soot; he'd definitely been in the fire. The dirt on his face made his eyes glow even more; they were an eerie light brown, topaz, like the eyes of the cat that had shown up at her house a year ago.

"Are you a reporter?" he asked.

She reached for the badge that dangled from the chain she wore around her neck; one of the links of the chain snagged the red scarf partially tucked inside her long puffer coat. Winter had come early to Michigan this year; even now snowflakes drifted down around them. "I'm a detective with Detroit PD. Detective Bolton," she said. "This is my case."

"Do you know what happened?" he asked. "There was a report of shots being fired and the first fire crew on the scene said that a body was found inside. Was it identified yet?"

She narrowed her eyes and studied his face. He was damn good-looking. And curious, so curious that he stayed with her instead of helping his crew with the hoses and equipment. No. He was more than curious. His eyes glistened a bit, and she didn't think it was from the smoke because his big, broad body was nearly shaking. "What's your interest in my case?" she asked.

"This is my house," the firefighter replied, and his voice cracked. "I need to know who was inside."

"So do I," she said. "You must know who would have been here, who was living with you or visiting you."

He shook his head. "I've been out of town for two weeks. I just got back to Michigan earlier today."

"Who can confirm that for you?" she asked.

"My hotshot crew. My superintendent is in Northern Lakes. My captain, at the firehouse here, can confirm it, too. Manny Rodriguez," he replied, and he glanced around as if looking for the man.

So Trent Miles was a hotshot.

She nearly groaned. He wasn't just a firefighter. He was an elite firefighter. And probably an even bigger daredevil than those couple of jerks she'd gone out with.

"How long ago did you get back to Michigan?" she asked.

"Just a few hours."

"A few hours is a long time," she pointed out. Especially when the 9-1-1 call had come in just a little over an hour ago. "And you didn't come by your own house? Not even to drop off your bags?"

He shook his head. "My one bag is still in my truck at the firehouse."

"Where have you been since you got back?" she asked.

He shrugged. "I stopped at the outlet mall on my drive down from Northern Lakes and did some shopping and got something to eat. Gassed up my truck, too."

"Got any receipts to back that up?" she asked.

"I—I don't know," he said. "Are you saying I need an alibi?"

She shrugged now. "It's your house."

"But I don't even know who was here, who was in the fire," he said, staring as intently at her as he'd been staring at the house. His strange eyes were hard with indignation and frustration. "Why won't you tell me who was inside?"

"The body hasn't been identified yet," she said.

"The coroner had already taken it away when I got here. So let me see it," he said, his deep voice gruff with emotion or maybe the smoke he'd inhaled in the fire.

When had he inhaled it? When he'd been fighting the fire just now? Or when he'd set the fire?

"I need to know who it is that..." His throat moved as if he was struggling to swallow. Then he finished, "...that I lost..."

Heather had a pretty good bullshit meter. She could usually tell when someone was lying or trying to manipulate her. That was why she went on a lot of first dates but very few second dates. While low-key and trying to maintain control, Trent Miles seemed genuinely upset. He attempted to control his emotions instead of what Heather considered putting on a performance. She never trusted the people who were overly dramatic when the cameras were rolling and then showed no emotion when nobody was watching.

A couple of news crews had arrived at the scene and were setting up behind the police barricade. But instead of turning toward the cameras, Trent Miles turned away and ducked his head down inside the raised collar of his coat as if he didn't want to be caught on film.

He could have another reason for that, though. He didn't want there to be evidence of him at the scene. But if that was the case, he would have walked away from her instead of asking her questions, instead of asking about the body.

Unless he was lying about who he really was. Or maybe he just wasn't taking her seriously, like so many other people failed to do. With her long blond hair pulled back in a ponytail and minimal makeup, she looked younger than her thirty years, which often had people underestimating her. Like Bob Bernard.

The old man was going to realize soon how wrong he was when she closed this case. But to close it, she needed to find out who the victim was, just as Trent Miles claimed he needed to know. "You really have no idea who was staying in your house?" she asked skeptically. "What? Do you Airbnb it?"

He shook his head. "No. I just… A lot of people know the code to the digital locks and may have shared it with other people."

She swallowed a groan of frustration. That was going to make it a lot harder to identify the body and the killer. Unless…the killer was standing right in front of her.

"Your neighbor said something about people coming and going all the time…" she said, watching his face carefully as she trailed off, giving him the chance to add more.

"Did they see who was here tonight?" he asked, and again that intensity was back on his face, that fear, as the muscle twitched along his square jaw again. "I need to know!"

He wasn't the only one.

She nodded. "Okay. Let's take a trip to the coroner's office. See what we can find out. My car's just over here." She gestured to the other side of the street where her unmarked cruiser was parked in front of the house of the neighbor who'd reported hearing the shots. She waited, expecting an argument. A stall. Something.

"Let me tell my crew," he said. And he headed toward one of the fire engines.

A few of the guys hugged him. And an older man, who was in a DFD uniform but not his gear, handed Trent something and then glanced in her direction. Envelopes. Trent Miles wrapped his gloved hand around them like he was holding a snake. Just what the hell had the older guy given him?

Trent shoved the envelopes into one of the deep pockets of his coat and headed back toward her. He had to duck low and hold up the crime scene tape to maneuver underneath it and join her in the street.

"Over here! Over here!" a male reporter shouted. "We have questions for you about the fire!"

Trent turned away again and focused on her. "Let's go."

"You don't want to talk to the reporters?" she asked.

He shook his head. "Not that one," he murmured.

"Why not?" she asked. "Bad blood between you?"

He shook his head again. "I don't know him."

"Over here! Over here!" another reporter yelled out. "Detective!"

Either that reporter or one of the crew must have noticed the badge dangling around her neck. Heather ignored the media and clicked the fob for her vehicle.

"You don't want to talk to them either," Trent observed as he walked beside her as they crossed the street. With his long legs, he probably had to slow his stride to match hers.

"Nope. I don't want to talk to any reporters." She didn't have enough information yet. About the fire, the victim or the possible suspect.

Trent stopped on the passenger's side of the unmarked vehicle. "Want me to ride in the back?"

Her questioning him about his alibi had probably clued him in to the fact that he was a suspect. But just a suspect...

"You can ride in the front." She doubted he would try anything. And if he did, she was armed.

He opened the front passenger door while she went around to the driver's side. When they'd both closed their doors and she started the ignition, she asked, "Have you ever ridden in the back of a police car?"

He released a ragged-sounding sigh and nodded. "I have…a long time ago…"

Heather was intrigued, more than she should be about the man when she had a murder to solve. But in order to find out who the killer was, she first had to find out who the victim was.

Or had she already met the killer? And was he sitting right next to her?

Chapter Two

Trent was surprised the detective hadn't had him ride in the back behind the shield that would have protected her if he tried anything while she was driving. She clearly suspected he knew more than he was telling her about whoever had died in the fire at his home.

He wished like hell that he did. But the calls he'd made on the way to the fire, to his sister's cell, had gone unanswered. And Brittney hadn't shown up at the scene like he'd expected she would, if she could. And if she couldn't...

Tears stung his eyes, and they weren't from the smoke. He blinked and glanced across the console at the detective. She had just one gloved hand wrapped around the steering wheel as she drove away from the scene of his burned home. Her other hand was close to her side. Or maybe her weapon?

She really did have suspicions about him. He probably hadn't helped his case when he'd admitted to having ridden in the back of a police car before. He was kind of surprised she hadn't frisked him before letting him get into the front with her.

"So what was the reason you were picked up in the past?" she asked.

"Traffic accident," he replied.

She glanced across at him. "You were at fault?"

He shook his head. "I wasn't the driver. My mom was. She didn't make it. The police officer drove me to social services."

She sucked in a breath. "I'm sorry. How old were you?"

"Twelve."

"Why didn't they have your dad come pick you up?"

"He was already dead," Trent said. "Died the year before during a deployment with his Marine unit."

She glanced at him again, sympathy in her green eyes. A deep, vibrant green. "Tough childhood you've had, Mr. Miles."

"Trent."

"Trent," she said. "Is that when you got into a gang?"

He snorted derisively. "Why do people assume a young half Black man growing up in Detroit must have been a gang member at some point?"

"I wasn't the one who made the assumption," she said. "Your neighbor, the one who called in about the gunshots, told me that."

"Then she probably told you my name, and you checked my record. I don't have one."

"Just because you never got convicted doesn't mean you never did anything illegal."

"Doesn't mean that I did." He couldn't deny that he'd done some stupid things in his life, though. And getting into this car with Detective Bolton was probably another one. Even though he had nothing to hide, he would have been smarter to talk to her with a lawyer present. Just like Moe had taught him growing up because of all those times the police had picked him up for something he hadn't done. Thank God Moe was a lawyer, or his record probably wouldn't be as clean as it was. She would lecture the hell out of him over talking to Detective Bolton without her present, but he couldn't call her until he knew whose body that was.

Who had been shot in his house? He didn't want to devastate her until he knew for sure that it was Brittney. It couldn't be Brittney.

"What else did my neighbor tell you?" he asked. "Did she say who she saw going in there tonight?" People tended to recognize his sister, especially after the big story she'd done at the expense of his hotshot team.

"She just heard the shots. She didn't see anything tonight," the detective replied. "But she said that a lot of people come and go at your place."

He snorted again. "So what? You think I'm dealing drugs out of my home?"

"I think someone got shot in the head and killed in your house before it was set on fire in order to destroy evidence, and I'd like to find out who that was and why they were killed," she replied.

Feeling like she'd just punched him in the gut, he lost his breath for a second and had to gulp in another before speaking. "I want to find that out, too. Since you know the person was shot in the head, you must know more about whoever it was. What else did the coroner tell you?"

She peered straight ahead as if focused on the road. But this late at night, there wasn't much traffic, despite it being Black Friday. Maybe all the shoppers were back home, exhausted from getting up so early and standing in lines for deals. They were probably eating Thanksgiving leftovers while sacked out on their sofas.

His sofa was gone. Most of his house, too. What else had he lost? And more importantly, who else? He'd already lost too damn many people, and his pulse quickened with the fear that someone else he cared about might have died. Brittney?

He had to know.

"Detective Bolton," he prodded her, his heart beating heavy with dread. He could tell that she knew more than she'd revealed.

"The body is female," she said.

Panic pressed on his chest so heavily that he jerked open his jacket, trying to breathe. But he couldn't draw in any air as that pressure intensified, squeezing his chest. His heart...

She pulled over to the curb and parked. "Are you okay? You know who it is? Your wife?"

He shook his head. "Not married..." was all he could rasp out.

"Girlfriend?"

He shook his head again. "No..."

"You obviously have some idea," she said. "Who are you afraid that it is?"

He pressed his hand harder against his aching chest. "My sister..."

"She lives with you?"

"Sometimes," he said. "She knows the key code and lets herself in and out when she needs a place to stay in the city." Otherwise, she lived in the suburbs with her mom, Moe, and her stepdad. Moe had been his dad's second wife, after Trent's mom, but due to his frequent deployments, their marriage hadn't lasted either.

"Have you tried calling her?"

"Yes," he said, choking out the word through the lump of fear in his throat.

"And she hasn't answered?"

He shook his head.

"When did you talk to her last?" she asked.

"Uh…it's been a while," he admitted, that pressure even heavier on his heart now.

"You didn't have time to talk to her when you were gone with your hotshot team?" she asked.

He swallowed the emotion rushing up on him. "No. And I didn't talk to her for a couple weeks before I left with my team."

"Was she staying with you then?" the detective asked, her brow furrowing beneath her wispy blond bangs.

He shrugged. "I don't know if she was here. I was mostly staying at the firehouse. I've been avoiding her," he admitted. But maybe not well enough that whoever had sent that card didn't think it would hurt him to lose her. That wasn't why he'd been avoiding her, though. He'd had no idea someone had it out for him.

"Sibling squabble?" she asked. "I can relate. I have sisters, too. We fight over the stupidest things."

"It wasn't like that," he said. "It wasn't over something stupid." Not when it had nearly cost Ethan his life.

"Then what was it like? Just how pissed off are you at your sister, Trent?"

He groaned. "God, you are determined to think I'm the one who shot that person…" It couldn't be Brittney. It just couldn't be. He would never forgive himself for not forgiving her or at least speaking to her again. Guilt and regret rushed up to choke him, but he cleared his throat and finished, "…and set fire to my own house."

"Well, doesn't sound like *you* actually spend a lot of time there," she remarked dryly. "So whoever was in there shooting probably wasn't after you. Is there a reason someone would be after your sister?"

He shuddered with the heaviness of the sigh he expelled. "A lot of reasons. She's a reporter. Brittney Townsend."

"Townsend? Is she married?"

"No," he said. "She's my half sister." He hated saying that, though. She was wholly his sister in his heart even when he was pissed at her. She had to be okay. But why hadn't she called him back? He'd left her voice mails. He reached into his pocket for his cell and pulled out the envelopes with it. The screen was black; it had died on him. He couldn't remember when he'd charged it last.

"So different dads?" the detective asked.

He glanced at her with irritation, wondering if she was making assumptions about him again. "Same dad. She took her stepfather's last name. She was so little when our dad died that she didn't remember him."

"Brittney Townsend," the detective repeated, and her eyes widened with recognition. "She's that reporter. Used to do fluff pieces but has stepped it up lately."

At his expense and the expense of his hotshot team.

The detective's eyes narrowed again and she nodded. "Oh, now I know why you haven't been talking to her. She blew up the lives of your hotshot team."

And his best friend had nearly been blown up because of that, because Brittney had exposed his true identity and his whereabouts to a man who wanted him dead.

"I'm pissed at my sister, but I would never hurt her." He was in pain just worrying that something might have happened to her. If she was truly gone...

HE DEFINITELY WASN'T ACTING. The pain on Trent Miles's handsome face was real, so real that Heather felt a twinge of it striking her heart. Which was weird.

She'd never experienced anything like that. In fact, her two sisters often accused Heather of having no empathy. What they probably meant was sympathy, because she refused to give them any when they complained about their lazy husbands and their screaming, spoiled kids. They'd married the immature idiots whose moms had waited on them hand and foot growing up, and they'd somehow expected them to not expect their wives to continue to coddle them?

She sighed and focused again on the man in her passenger seat. While she struggled to hang on to any suspicion about his guilt, she still suspected he knew more than he had admitted to her. He was holding something back.

She glanced at those envelopes on his lap, lying beneath his cell. His finger was pressed against the power button, but the screen remained black.

"Your phone dead?" she asked. She flipped open the console and pulled out a cord. "Here's a charger. I think we have the same cell." Probably the model that the city ordered for all their employees. She plugged the end into that charging portal on the console and held the other end out over his lap, her hand coming dangerously close to his thighs that were so muscular they strained even the thick material of his uniform pants.

The man was built like a...hotshot firefighter, like the ones from every calendar she'd ever seen. The ones her sisters had bought for her when she'd dated the couple of firemen.

Neither of her dates had looked like those calendar pages, though. Not like Trent Miles did.

His fingers brushed hers as he took the end of the cord from her. And she experienced a curious little jolt, like she was getting charged. He plugged in his phone, but the screen stayed black.

"How long was it dead?" she asked.

"I called Brittney on the way to the fire," he said. "She

didn't pick up, so I left her a message, and I sent a…" His voice trailed off, gruff with emotion. With fear for his sister.

She could empathize with that. Even as crazy as her sisters drove her, she loved them and wouldn't want anything to happen to them. Ever.

"She might have been busy when you called, and then when she tried to call you back, your phone was already dead," she pointed out.

He released a shaky breath and nodded. "Yeah, yeah, that could be why."

She reached across the console again and squeezed his arm. Through the heavy material of his firefighter jacket and her gloves, she shouldn't have felt another jolt, but she did. *What the hell…*

He jumped, too, and grabbed his vibrating phone.

The cell.

That was it; she'd felt the vibration. But still, it was good that they were parked or she might have jerked the wheel when she'd jumped.

His breath shuddered out in a ragged sigh. "It's a text from her."

Heather read it off the screen. "'So you're talking to me again?'" The time the text had come through was also on the screen. "She sent that after the report of gunshots being fired at this address and also after the body had been removed from the house."

Relief surged through her. She wasn't sure why; it wasn't as if she knew Brittney Townsend. She'd only watched a few of her reports over the years because Heather didn't really care where the hot spots in town were and what the upcoming fashion trends were going to be. But she cared about people, more than she would ever admit to her sisters. Even more than she cared about her case clearance rate.

"You can call her back," Heather told him. "She might know whose body was found in your house."

He nodded, but he didn't make any move to return his sister's text or calls. There were missed calls from her, too. "I don't know if I should."

"Just don't reveal anything specific about the investigation," she said. After what his sister had done to his hotshot team, he probably didn't trust her, and neither should Heather.

"It's not that..." He pulled the envelopes out from under his cell and flipped through them.

She smiled as she noticed some addressed "to the hot firefighter." But a few had his name on them. He handed one of those across the console to her. "What is this?" she asked.

"A Christmas card."

"A Christmas card?" A body had been found in his house and he was showing her his holiday mail?

But the tension was still in his body even after finding out his sister was not the person who'd been killed in his house. Maybe he had some idea, despite denying it, who that person was.

She pulled the card out of the envelope and stared down at the gold Christmas tree on the red background. "Pretty..." she murmured. Then she flipped it open. On one side the printed message from the card company told him to enjoy the holiday season with those he loved. On the other...

"'You're going to find out how it feels to lose someone close to you. Soon,'" she read aloud. Then she turned back toward him. "When did you get this?"

"It came to the firehouse here in Detroit while I was out West with my hotshot team. I don't know when it arrived."

She focused on the envelope. The postmark was smudged. "I can't read that...the date or the place from where it had been mailed." It was already pretty light and then must have gotten damp and the ink bled into the paper. "And of course they didn't include a return address."

"It was mailed, though? Not dropped off?" He flipped through the other envelopes on his lap. "These were dropped off."

She reached across and took those envelopes from his hand to look through them herself. Once again, despite the thickness of her gloves, her fingertips tingled from touching him. *Must be a lot of static electricity in the car.*

"It probably would have been kind of hard to mail out something addressed 'to the hot firefighter,'" she said, amusement tugging her lips into a smile. "But if they'd had the address for the firehouse…" They'd probably wanted to see him, though, which was why they'd personally dropped off the cards.

She didn't blame his fans for being fans. Trent Miles was one of the best-looking guys she'd ever seen in person and not on a movie screen. Hell, he was probably even better looking than those Hollywood superstars because he wasn't wearing makeup, just that fine sheen of soot from the fire.

She pulled her gaze from him to focus on the smeared postmark. "I'll see if the techs can figure out where it was mailed from," she said. She had a favorite in the unit who managed to pull off magic for her all the time.

"Have them check if it was mailed from Northern Lakes," he suggested.

"Northern Lakes? Where that Canterbury heir was found hiding out while letting everyone believe that he was dead for the past five years?" She knew, though, that had been his sister's big break, the scoop that had taken her off the restaurant and fashion beat.

"*Ethan* was actually hiding out in a national forest,"

Trent said, "but he is part of my hotshot team and one of my best friends."

"That's why you don't want to talk to your sister. Because she let the world know he faked his death and was living under an assumed identity?"

"There's more to the story than that. He didn't fake anything. He was in a plane crash five years ago. He just…" Trent sighed. "The details don't matter now. That is why I haven't been talking to her. When she exposed Ethan's secret, she put his life in danger. Now I'm worried that, if I start talking to her again, I'll put her life in danger. That message in the card is threatening to take away someone close to me, and Brittney is the closest family member I have."

"Oh…" Heather murmured over the clarification. He wasn't hanging on to his righteous anger with his sister, like she probably would have; he was trying to protect her. "That makes sense." And was probably safer for Heather, too, so she didn't have to worry about the reporter revealing too much about the case before she'd had the chance to really start her investigation. "Do you think that whoever died in that fire might have been mistaken for her?"

He shrugged. "I don't know."

"You really have no idea who else it could have been?"

He shook his head. "No. I'm just relieved it's not my sister. But I hope that someone else didn't die because of me."

"We don't know anything for sure yet," she reminded him and herself. She didn't really know that he'd had nothing to do with those gunshots and that fire. She had to verify his alibi first. Had to make sure that he wasn't a suspect.

But…

Wouldn't it be easier for her if he was? If he was, she could close this case quicker and move on to the next. If he had no alibi, then he had the most means and opportunity to have committed this murder.

She glanced down at that strange Christmas card someone had mailed him. It made more sense that whoever had sent this threat was behind the murder. They'd thought the person in his house was the "someone close to him" they'd wanted him to feel the pain over losing.

But he had no idea whose body that even was.

Heather had some idea, not about the identity of the dead victim, but about how to flush out the person who'd sent that card. It was a dangerous plan, though.

Probably the most dangerous for her.

TRENT MILES HAD to suffer. Really suffer.

He had to be forced to feel the pain that his actions—no, his inactions—had caused others. From the image playing across the television screen in the dark room, it was hard to see if Miles was suffering or feeling anything at all. As the reporters called out to him from the scene of the fire, he ducked his face into his coat, hiding it from the cameras like he'd been hiding these past two weeks.

The reporters didn't know who Miles was, but the person watching the television knew. Then Miles maneuvered around the crime scene tape and joined someone else in the street. The watcher sat forward, leaning close to the television.

Was it…?

The detective. Bolton with her blond hair and her pretty face and her bitchy ways.

She deserved to suffer, too.

Chapter Three

The body was burned beyond recognition. But even if it hadn't been, if *she* hadn't been, Trent doubted he would have recognized the victim. And she was a victim. The hole in her head proved that she'd been dead even before the fire. This had been no accident. Someone had wanted her dead.

But why? Was it about him or was there some other reason someone had wanted this woman dead?

Even if he hadn't talked to Brittney, he would have known it wasn't her. His sister was taller than this woman. Hank was also taller than the body. Henrietta "Hank" Rowlins and Michaela were the female members of the hotshot team, and they were like family to him, too. Fortunately, they were both in Northern Lakes or maybe just north of it in the little town of St. Paul, where they worked out of a small firehouse.

"You really have no idea who she is?" the detective asked.

He glanced up to find her staring at him as intently as he'd been staring at the body. He shook his head.

"No girlfriend? No female friend that might have been crashing at your place?"

"I already told you no. The only female I know who would have been in my house is Brittney." And that pressure in his chest eased again knowing she was alive. This wasn't her lying on the cold metal table in the morgue.

"She's wearing a wedding band," the detective said, pointing to one of the victim's hands where a ring was fused in with the charred flesh.

He'd seen bodies before, victims of fires, but knowing this person had been in his home and might have died because of him made it even more horrifying and sickening. And he felt some of the pain that note had promised he'd feel, but he didn't know this person. Or…

"What is it?" Detective Bolton asked. "Did you think of someone?"

"The body is so badly damaged." Maybe he'd been wrong to dismiss everyone he knew. "Moe, but I don't think it would be her…" There was a reason, but at the moment, exhausted and emotional, he struggled to remember why it couldn't be her.

"Who's Moe?" the detective asked.

"Brittney's mom." He'd been worried about having to call her about Brittney. But could she have come by his house? She had the key code.

"What's her full name?"

"It's Maureen Townsend." Relief rushed over him as he remembered why it couldn't be her lying in front of him, burned beyond recognition. "No. No. She's gone. She always goes away over Thanksgiving. She and her husband take a cruise over this week because the courts are shut down."

"She's a lawyer?"

"Used to be," he said. "She's a judge now."

"Of course. Judge Townsend. Impressive family. A lot to live up to."

Maybe that was why Brittney was so ambitious. She was trying to live up to her mother's success. Despite the realization, Trent couldn't cut his sister any slack. Not right now. Not without the risk of putting her in danger like she'd put Ethan.

And him. Trent had nearly died in one of those attempts on Ethan's life. He would rather be at risk himself, though, than put his younger sister in danger.

"If your sister is the only person you can think who might have been staying at your place—"

"She's not the only one," he said. "Coworkers crash at my place a lot because it's close to the firehouse. Brittney is just the only female."

She narrowed her startling deep green eyes and stared at him with obvious skepticism. "Really? You never date? Never have anyone who might have been waiting at your house to greet you when you returned from that wildfire?"

Heat crawled into his face, despite the cool temperature in the morgue. He usually dated. A lot. And women had tried to surprise him at his place. "That's happened in the past," he admitted. "But I've been taking a break from dating."

He'd recently lost a fellow hotshot because his cheating wife had murdered him, brutally, gruesomely, and another hotshot had been stalked and nearly killed by some woman who had been obsessed with him for years. After that tragedy and near-tragedy, Trent had decided it was smarter, with so much going on right now with his professional life, to forego a personal one and focus instead on being safe rather than having sex.

Maybe going without for a while explained why he was so damn aware of the detective. Every time she'd touched him, while they'd been parked at the curb in her car, tension had gripped him, tightening his muscles. At first he'd thought it was just because she clearly suspected him of murder and he was feeling fear.

He'd been concerned that he'd broken Moe's rule, the advice she'd given him in his youth to never speak to police without legal representation. But he had nothing to hide, then or now, except this attraction for the detective.

Even in the weird fluorescent glow of the morgue lights, she was beautiful. Her eyes were so heavily lashed and vibrant, skin so silky-looking and features so delicate. And when she'd unzipped that puffy jacket, she'd revealed two things: the holster holding her weapon and a curvy, athletic body that had brought all that tension back.

"You might be taking a break, but maybe somebody isn't happy about that," she said.

He flinched. There had been a few snippy texts. A few voice mails from disgruntled female friends with benefits, but that had been months ago. "It doesn't matter. I changed my locks to digital ones, and I only gave the code out to my coworkers, my sister and Moe, but I have no idea who they might have shared it with," he said. He stared down at the body again, that horror gripping him. "This isn't anybody that I personally know."

Or so he hoped.

"I'm going to need a list of everybody who has that code," she said. "And I'm going to need to speak to them and find out who else they might have shared the code with. Maybe this is a spouse or girlfriend of one of them. Maybe this has nothing to do with you."

"I want to believe that," he said. But that card, and all the sabotage and other things that had happened in Northern Lakes, made him think otherwise.

"But you don't," she said.

"Do you?"

"I'm not going to make any assumptions until I've done more investigating."

The coroner had left them alone in the morgue. Maybe

that was why, despite the chill, the detective had unzipped her jacket. Not because she was warm but to show Trent her gun, to warn him that she was armed.

And dangerous?

The way she affected him, this weird attraction despite the circumstances, made her very dangerous to Trent. But he couldn't stop himself from moving a little closer to her, from staring at her with some of that heat starting to burn inside him, starting to dispel the cold. "So you haven't made a decision about me yet?" he asked. "About my guilt or innocence?"

She shook her head, and that blond ponytail bobbed around her shoulders. "No."

"What will it take to prove to you that I could never hurt anyone?"

She snorted. "Everyone is capable of hurting someone else. Maybe not purposely but…it happens. We hurt people without trying. That note in the card makes it sound like you hurt someone."

He tensed as he realized now what the note meant. "You think someone blames me for losing someone they loved?"

She glanced at the body on the table. "Like a husband who lost a wife…"

"Even when I was dating, I never dated a married woman," he said. "I would never mess with someone else's marriage." That was how his hotshot friend had died, because someone had messed with his, and Dirk Brown had suffered a horrible fate because of it. Fortunately, the lover was in jail now as an accomplice. And the wife who'd killed him…

She was dead.

Trent glanced at the table. This person had suffered a horrible fate, too. Why? Because of him?

"We need to figure out who this is," he said.

"The coroner is going to see what DNA he can get from the remains, and he's also going to check dental records, but it'll be easier for him if he can have something to compare that DNA and dental records to, if we can come up with some possible identities of the victim."

He nodded. "Right. I'll get you the names of everyone who had the code."

"I'll have to talk to your sister, too," she said, as if warning him.

Ever since his phone had charged, it had been vibrating with more incoming texts and voice mails from Brittney. "I'm pretty sure she knows my house burned down. She's going to want to interview you about it."

"You're the one she wants to talk to now," the detective said. Obviously she hadn't missed what had been going on with his phone.

He shook his head. "I can't. I can't risk whoever sent that damn card realizing just how close she is to me." Or how much he would miss her if he lost her, despite the way she infuriated him.

"There is nobody else that close to you?" she asked with skepticism.

"My mom and dad are both gone," he said. "Brittney is it for my blood relatives, but then there's my hotshot family." And they were family, but since the sabotage had started on their equipment and there had been real attempts on their lives and losses, everything had been different. Tense. Distrustful. But maybe that was like real family, too.

"Seems like a lot is going on with them, according to that report your sister ran," the detective remarked. "I should talk to them, also."

He sighed. "They're all over the place now since we just

got back from that wildfire." But he knew when they would all be together.

She seemed to know it, because she arched a dark blond brow over one of those vibrant green eyes. "But they will be getting together again sometime?"

He sighed again. "For the hotshot holiday party," he admitted. "But that's over a week away."

"If I don't talk to them sooner, we'll make it a date," she said.

"You're going to go with me to my Christmas party?"

"If I haven't closed the case by then, I will," she replied matter-of-factly. "I have a plan to flush out whoever sent you that card and determine if they're the one who killed the person found in your house."

"They must be," he said. "I have no idea why else anyone would have been shot and killed in my home."

She shrugged. "Who knows? It might have nothing to do with you."

"I hope that's true. But I think we both doubt that."

"The card, the murder, the fire..." She shook her head. "I don't believe in that many coincidences."

"So what's your plan to find out the truth?" he asked, and all that tension returned to his body.

"You're going to have to start dating again."

"You read that card. You know that'll put that person in danger," he said.

She smiled. "That's what I'm counting on, to flush out whoever sent that card when they make an attempt on the life of your date."

He narrowed his eyes as suspicion gripped him. "Who is my date going to be?"

"Me."

"You want me to start dating you?" he asked, and despite the coldness of the morgue, heat surged through him again. For her, he would be tempted to think about having a personal life again. If it wouldn't put her life in danger…

TRENT MILES PROBABLY thought she was as sex-crazed as those fans who'd addressed their Christmas cards "to the hot firefighter." They'd also written notes inside, but they had offered to get close to him. *Very close.* Not threaten to take away someone close to him.

The coroner returned before she'd had the chance to explain what she had really meant. And she hadn't wanted to lay out her plan in front of someone else in case it was as impulsive and reckless as she suspected. So they'd left the morgue to head over to the police department. She had Trent sitting in an empty interrogation room to make the list of people with the key code for his digital locks while she checked out his alibi.

With his permission, she accessed the GPS on his truck, which proved he hadn't been anywhere near his house since returning from Northern Lakes. He couldn't have fired the shot that killed the woman or set the fire to cover up the murder. His stops at the outlet mall and burger place checked out, too, and quite easily. People tended to remember someone who looked like Trent Miles. They also had security footage they emailed to back up his alibi.

He'd had nothing to do with the murder. But did he really have no idea who the victim was? He'd changed the locks on his house for a reason; there must have been someone he'd wanted to keep out.

An obsessed former girlfriend?

Heather jumped up from her desk in the detective bullpen of cubicles and headed down the hall to the interview room. This close to midnight there weren't many people in this area. Most of them were down on the lower floors. The holding cells, the front desk. This floor was quiet, so Trent had probably heard her coming, her boots pounding on the worn linoleum floor. But he didn't look up when she opened the door to the interrogation room. He was focused instead on the pad of paper she'd given him, staring down at his writing on the top sheet as he clutched the pen in his hand.

"Is that your confession?" she asked but was only teasing. She had proof now of his innocence, which made her strangely happy. Strange because it would have been easier for her to close the case if he'd been guilty. She wouldn't have had to look for other suspects.

He looked up then, but he didn't seem surprised to see her standing in the doorway. He must have been aware that she'd opened the door. "I confess that I have no idea who could have been in my house tonight. I keep looking over these names that I wrote down for you, and Brittney was the only one who could have…" His gruff voice trailed off and his throat moved as if he was struggling to swallow.

No matter how betrayed and used he felt from his sister exposing his friend, he obviously still loved her. Somebody else might have betrayed him, too, and given out that key code to someone Trent wouldn't have wanted to have it.

She stepped inside the room and let the door close behind her. "We'll figure it out," she vowed.

"Yes, you have a plan." He leaned back in his chair and stared at her with those intriguing topaz-colored eyes. He'd taken off his jacket; it hung over the back of the chair. His shirt was thin enough that it molded to the sculpted muscles of his chest. It wasn't just his face that was good-looking. "You're going to date me."

Her pulse quickened until she reminded herself about the

cover. "To flush out whoever wants to hurt someone close to you," she said. "That's the only reason why."

"That puts you in danger," he said. "You might get hurt, and maybe it won't be by whoever's after me."

"So who do you think is going to hurt me, then?" she asked.

He arched a dark brow. "Your husband? Your lover?"

She snorted. "If I had either of those, they would probably hurt you instead."

"Someone could still hurt you." The tension was back in his handsome face, making him clench his jaw so tightly that muscle twitched again.

"Who?" she asked. "The killer or you? Don't worry. I can take care of myself. I have a gun and a hard heart. I won't forget that we're just faking and fall for you."

His mouth curved into a slight grin. "What if I forget and fall for you?"

She laughed at the thought. "Yeah, I doubt that you're looking for a relationship any more than I am. Or you wouldn't have changed your locks. Any particular reason why you did that? Any former girlfriend so obsessed that she would have let herself in like that woman probably did tonight?" Unless someone had lured her there, someone who had his key code, which would have been someone he considered a friend. Or a relative, like his sister and stepmom.

She definitely needed to speak to his sister.

His face flushed a little. "There were a couple of women I was seeing who wanted more serious relationships than I wanted," he admitted.

She nodded in appreciation of his honesty. "Write down their names, too."

"But they don't have the key code," he said. "And I think one of them even got married..." His eyes widened with surprise as he probably realized what Heather had already been considering, that the dead woman could be someone he had been involved with before her marriage.

"Married," she said, "like the woman found in your burned house."

He shook his head. "No, she wouldn't have been there. She moved on. She got marri—"

"How do you know that?" she asked. "Was she communicating with you even after she got involved with someone else?"

His face flushed slightly beneath the soot, and he rubbed his hand along his jaw. "Uh…"

"Maybe she thought you would pull a Dustin Hoffman in *The Graduate* and barge in to stop her wedding, and when you didn't…"

"She what?" Trent asked. "She showed up at my place? She didn't have the key code."

"And she didn't know any of your coworkers? Anyone that might give it to her?"

He sighed. "Maybe she could have gotten it from someone who had it."

She stepped closer to the table and grabbed the pad. There were a lot of names on it. A lot of people she would have to call. But first she would call the married woman to find out if she was alive or if hers was the body found in the fire. "This might not be what you think. Maybe she got the code, got in your house, started the fire and then shot herself. The fire might not have had a chance to get going for the smoke or flames to show when your neighbor called 9-1-1 about the shots she heard. That was why she didn't mention the fire during her call to Dispatch."

"You think what happened could have been a suicide?" he asked, clearly horrified. "But that card…"

"Maybe she was the one who sent it. She figured she was closer to you than you did."

He didn't reach for the pad. Instead, he pulled out his phone and scrolled through his contacts. "Her number is in here, but I still don't get it. We didn't even go out that long."

"*You* weren't that close to her," she said. "But she obviously felt more than you did." If that was the effect Trent Miles had on women, maybe Heather should have concerns about going undercover as his girlfriend. But she might not have to; if her suicide theory was right, she could close this case tonight.

She pulled out her cell and dialed the number he showed on his screen for Caitlin. It rang a few times. But it was late. Maybe her phone was off. Or maybe, because the woman didn't recognize the number, she was just going to let it go to voice mail.

"Hello?" The woman's voice, husky with sleep, emanated from the speaker of Heather's cell.

"Caitlin?"

"Yes. Who is this?"

"Detective Bolton with Detroit PD," she replied.

The woman gasped. "Oh, my God. What's happened? Has someone been in an accident?"

"Probably no one you know," Heather said. "But your name did come up in the course of an investigation into a fire at Trent Miles's house."

"Oh, my God!" she exclaimed again, her voice cracking with sobs. "Is Trent okay?"

A male voice grumbled in the background of the call. Heather couldn't make out his words, but he sounded irritated. Maybe his irritation was over the late-night call or maybe over the subject of the call. He obviously wasn't as concerned about Caitlin's ex-boyfriend as she was.

"Trent is fine," Heather assured her. Actually, he was *damn* fine. She wasn't going to have to stretch her acting abilities to pretend to be his girlfriend.

The woman released a shaky sigh. "That's good. I— Is there anything I can do?"

"No. You answered the question I had just by answering the phone," Heather assured her.

"I don't understand."

"Thank you," she said and disconnected the call.

Trent released a shaky sigh of his own. "That's good. It wasn't her." His cell vibrated, and the same number Heather had just dialed showed up on his screen. He ignored the call.

"You really aren't much of a phone talker, huh?" she asked. "You don't take many of your calls."

"You know why," he said. "I don't want to put anyone in danger. That's the reason I'm not sure your plan is a good idea."

"I told you. I can take care of myself. I have a lot of training and a gun."

His lips curved into that slight grin again. "And a hard heart," he added.

She smiled. "Very hard," she assured him with pride. "I've never even been close to falling in love, let alone getting obsessed with anyone." That was mostly because she'd dated idiots, though, and hadn't wanted to wind up as unhappy as her older sisters. "I'm not going to get hurt."

"Then maybe I should be worried about me."

"Remember, I'm armed," she said. "I can protect you."

"But who's going to protect me from you, Detective?" he asked with a slight, sexy grin.

She could keep him safe, and she wasn't worried about him falling for her. Nobody else had yet. Probably because she was too independent and focused on her job to give anyone the time or attention necessary to sustain a relationship. But despite her gun, and her resolve to never get involved, she was a little worried about herself.

Because he was so damn good-looking.

BRITTNEY WAS FRUSTRATED. One, because her brother would not return her calls and texts. And two, because she was trapped at the station, editing some fluff piece that she'd shot a while ago.

They'd promised her that she would cover more important stories after she'd gotten such a scoop. But then they'd changed their minds, using the holidays as an excuse and that people needed feel-good stories right now.

Brittney didn't feel good. She felt sick over upsetting Trent, sick that he wasn't even talking to her. And sick that something had happened to him, because she'd heard about the fire.

What the hell was going on?

Chapter Four

Trent hadn't been entirely joking when he'd said he was worried about himself. He had no home. No possessions but for the duffel bag of clothes in his truck at the firehouse, and they needed to be washed. But that was the least of his concerns because the house and possessions were just things. He was worried about people, about feeling the pain of loss like the Christmas card note threatened. He didn't want to lose anyone, especially not Detective Bolton, which was strange since he'd just met her.

And under the worst of circumstances. Somebody had been murdered in his home. Who?

He glanced across the console at the detective. He didn't want her to wind up like that woman had: dead. Sure, she had a gun and training and could take care of herself. But if she got hurt because of him...

"You didn't need to do this," he said.

"Do what?" she asked.

"Drive me back to my truck." It was already after midnight.

"I couldn't let you walk."

"I could have taken an Uber or a cab or called a friend," he said. She wasn't a friend. He wasn't even sure that she still didn't consider him a suspect. Maybe that was why she'd proposed the plan of pretending to be his girlfriend, so she could get close enough to him to get evidence against him.

"You weren't going to call a friend. You don't want anyone that you consider a friend near you right now."

"No, I don't," he agreed. "So I would have called a cab."

"The least I can do is give you a ride back to your vehicle," she said. "You're a victim, Trent."

He cringed at the word and shook his head. "No. That woman lying in the morgue is the victim."

"You lost your house, and you've been threatened," she said. "That makes you a victim, too."

He groaned. "I hate that word. But I guess I should be happy you're calling me that instead of a suspect. Or do you still have your doubts about me?"

She shook her head, and that long ponytail bobbed around her shoulders. "Not anymore. Your alibi checked out."

He expelled a ragged sigh. "Good."

"Did you have doubts?"

"Not me. I know I'm innocent."

"Somebody doesn't think so," she replied. "Or why else would they want you to know what it feels like to lose someone close to you, unless they held you responsible for them losing someone close to them?"

He sucked in a breath, pain jabbing him. "I have never purposely hurt anyone."

"But inadvertently…?"

He shrugged. "I don't know. But I must have or why would someone have sent that card?" Why had someone been killed in his house?

She sighed. "We'll figure it out. We need to find out who that woman was."

"I gave you that list."

However, she hadn't called anyone but Caitlin. Instead, she'd offered to drive him back to his vehicle. Actually, she hadn't offered; she'd insisted. She probably hadn't wanted to make those calls in front of him or leave him too long in the interrogation room after clearing him as a suspect. He'd almost rather have stayed there than return to the firehouse.

He didn't want the pity of his crew. Didn't want them offering him sympathy over a house or over that body found inside when he didn't even know who she was and what she'd been doing there. She was the one who deserved all the sympathy.

"Who's going to be around the firehouse when we get there?" she asked.

He glanced at the clock on the dash of the unmarked vehicle. They'd been at the morgue and the police station for a couple of hours. "The guys who were on call and responded to the fire at my house are probably gone now, unless there was another fire. And the night crew is probably asleep, unless there was another fire."

"So you're telling me if I want to find any of them at your station, I better hope there was another fire after yours?" she asked.

Tension gripped him at the thought. "I hope there wasn't another one."

"Because you missed it?" she asked.

"Because I don't want anyone else getting hurt."

She braked at a traffic light and glanced over at him. "You're not like the firefighters I've met in the past," she said. "They were adrenaline junkies who couldn't wait for the next fire. Maybe just because it gave them the chance to talk about that fire, how dangerous it was, how close they came to dying in it."

"Sounds like the firefighters you met were idiots," he said.

"You haven't worked with any like that?" she asked with another pointed glance. Then she focused on the road, driving through the green light.

They were nearly at his firehouse, where probably a few of the guys were up talking about the fire, about the body they'd found. There were some who thrived on the adrenaline of the job. He sighed.

She chuckled. "Thought so."

"But most of us do this job because we want to help people," he insisted. That was the motive for every single member of his hotshot team, except maybe one. The one who was sabotaging the equipment, getting people hurt.

Was a member of the team really responsible for those accidents? For the faulty equipment? The superintendent of the team, Braden Zimmer, had received an ominous note of his own a while back claiming that one of them wasn't who he thought he was.

Braden had assumed the person was referring either to the arsonist who'd terrorized Northern Lakes several months ago or to whoever had been sabotaging the equipment. The arsonist hadn't been a member of the team, so the note must have been referring to the saboteur.

Or Ethan Sommerly. He wasn't who everyone had thought he was, as Trent's own sister had revealed. His cell vibrated again, probably with another text from Brittney. He'd have to talk to her eventually, but he hoped he could put it off until Detective Bolton figured out who had sent him that card, who wanted him to suffer. He was already suffering at the thought that someone might have died because of him.

What had he done or failed to do that made this person want revenge on him? His head throbbed, and he raised one of his hands to rub his temples.

"That's why I'm driving you back here," the detective remarked. "You're clearly exhausted."

She didn't even know the half of it, of everything that had been going on with his hotshot team. And he needed to tell her just in case that murder and that fire had something to do with all that.

With the saboteur...

TRENT HAD FALLEN strangely silent on the last few miles to the firehouse, as if he dreaded going back there. Or maybe he dreaded her being there with him, interrogating his co-workers. Heather had no choice. She had to do her job. She had to find out the identity of the woman who'd died in his house, as well as the person responsible for her death.

Or maybe he was just, as she'd mentioned moments ago, exhausted. He'd just recently returned from a wildfire out West and then had helped out fighting the fire at his own house. Despite their efforts, the house was probably another casualty, like the woman found inside it.

Where was he going to stay? She knew he wouldn't put one of his friends and certainly not his sister in danger and stay with them. What about the firehouse?

Or a hotel?

Would he be safe at either of those places?

But this person, the one who'd written that ominous note, didn't sound as if he or she wanted Trent dead. They just wanted him to suffer.

For what?

"You really have no idea who would have sent you that note?" she asked as she turned onto the street where his firehouse was located. All the buildings around it were dark but for security lighting. It was late. That was why she hadn't made any more calls tonight. Chances were the family of that woman would report her missing if they hadn't already. She'd asked Dispatch to contact her immediately if anyone called about a missing woman.

Unfortunately, Heather knew where the woman was: the morgue. DNA or dental records would be necessary to determine her identity. Even family members wouldn't recognize her in that condition, and Heather wouldn't want to put them through that.

But she'd put Trent Miles through it. A twinge of guilt struck her, and she grimaced. She'd still considered him a suspect at the time, so she'd wanted to shake him. And she had, but not into a confession. He hadn't done anything wrong, at least not that she knew about. But he'd curiously remained silent in response to her question.

"Did you think of someone?" she asked. Or maybe of something he'd done to someone?

Maybe he wasn't as perfect as he looked.

But then who could be?

She certainly wasn't. She was probably handling this whole case incorrectly, and not just because she wanted to close it so quickly, but because of him.

He was distracting. Unsettling. So unsettling and distracting that she drove past the firehouse. But a parking lot, with an assortment of trucks in it, was on the other side. She slowed and steered into the lot and breathed a soft sigh of relief that he probably hadn't noticed how he got to her.

She found an open parking space near the street. "Looks like a lot of people are still here," she remarked.

Trent didn't look around the lot but looked at her with his

brow furrowed slightly and an intensity in his light brown eyes. But still he remained silent.

"What is it?" she asked. "Who did you think of?"

He shook his head. "It's not… I don't have a name. I don't have any idea…"

"Then what is it?" she asked. Because he was holding something back, something weighing on him that he hadn't shared with her, that he almost seemed to want to share. "What's wrong?"

He released a shaky sigh. "When we go in there, what are we going to say to the crew? What's your *plan* for this?"

A smile twitched her lips. "Ah, you're worried about my plan to play your girlfriend."

"Yes. I'm worried you're going to get hurt."

"I told you not to worry about me. I thought you were worried now about yourself, about you getting hurt," she said, reminding him of what he'd said back in the interrogation room. "I figured then that you were referring to your life or your heart, but you must have really been talking about your image. Don't I measure up to your dating standards?"

He was probably only attracted to women who made an effort with their appearance, who wore makeup and curled or flat-ironed their hair into submission. Heather just dragged hers back into a hair tie and swiped a little mascara onto her lashes if she remembered. And she certainly didn't dress to attract male attention, usually the opposite. On duty and off, she wore black pants, a sweater and long coat in the winter. And in the summer, black pants and a tank top with an oversize blouse, so she could hide her holster.

He laughed. "Fishing for compliments, Detective? You've got to know you're gorgeous."

Her pulse sped up so much it seemed to skip a beat.

His tone was too matter-of-fact for him to be just trying to charm her. Or maybe he was that good of a charmer, and if he was, she might have to work a little harder to protect her heart than she'd thought.

"You're already the best boyfriend I've had in a while," she said with a smile.

"But I don't even know your first name," he said. "So I'm not sure any of my coworkers are really going to buy this relationship, especially when they all know I haven't been dating for a while. And a detective? Are you sure we should tell them what you do?"

She wasn't charmed anymore. She glared at him. "What's wrong with *me* being a detective?" Too many men had a problem with her career. The ones she'd dated and the ones she worked with; even her dad thought it was too dangerous for her, that she should have a nice safe career or be a stay-at-home mom like her older sisters and her own mother had been. While her mom had been happy with that choice, Heather would be even more miserable than her older sisters were.

He held up his hands as if she was pointing a gun at him and looked about to shoot. "Nothing's wrong with detectives. But you know there's always been a rivalry between the fire department and the police department."

She shrugged. "So? I've dated firemen before, and they obviously dated me."

He sucked in a breath as if she had shot him. "You have?" Then he nodded. "Guess that explains why you think we're all daredevils who want fires to happen just so we can brag about them. You dated the wrong firemen."

She nodded now. "You'll get no argument from me on that. But even though I dated duds, I know of a lot of relationships between cops and firefighters, as well as between cops and paramedics and cops and nurses—"

"Okay, okay," he said. "You don't have to convince me."

Heat rushed to her face. Had she sounded like she was begging him to date her? "This is just for pretend, you know," she reminded him. "Just a ruse to flush out whoever the hell is out to hurt someone close to you."

"I know," he said. "But if we don't want everyone else to know that this is just a pretend relationship, I really think I should know your first name. Calling you Detective Bolton in front of my friends isn't going to fool them into thinking we're really romantically involved."

A smile twitched up her lips again. "Maybe that's my kink," she said. "I prefer you call me Detective, and if you don't, I use my handcuffs and my nightstick on you."

He closed his eyes and groaned. "You have a wicked sense of humor, Detective."

"Who says I'm kidding?" she asked, but she was only joking.

"I think you're wrong about nobody falling for you. I think plenty of men have."

"I was just messing with you. I'm not really kinky," she admitted.

"You're funny, and that's even sexier than kinky." He opened his eyes, which were suddenly dark, the pupils dilated.

Was he actually attracted to her? Or was he just getting into the role she'd talked him into playing? Her boyfriend. She nearly snorted at the possibility of that ever becoming a reality. A guy like him, this good-looking, was probably used to women throwing themselves at him and lavishing him with time and attention.

Heather was too busy to dote on anyone, which reminded

her that she should be busy trying to clear this case. Trying to find out who that poor woman was.

"We better go inside," she said. "Find out if anyone knows who might have been in your house tonight."

He nodded. "Okay, so you're just going to ask…"

"What are you nervous about?"

"How do I act like we're a couple?" he asked. "I've never gone undercover before."

Maybe not this way, but Trent Miles had definitely spent some time under the covers playing the part of boyfriend. Since he'd admitted that he hadn't had any lasting relationships, maybe all he'd ever done was play.

She smiled and assured him, "I think you'll be just fine. And my name is Heather."

"Heather…" he repeated in that deep, sexy voice.

And she had to resist the urge to shiver as her skin tingled a bit, like he'd touched her, when all he'd done was say her name. She would have to keep reminding herself that this was just a ploy, a way to find out who a victim was and how she'd become one, and to close a case. She couldn't get distracted again. Next time she might miss more than a firehouse.

She drew in a breath and reached for the door handle. "Okay, when we get inside, you need to let me know which of your coworkers are on that list you gave me of who had the key code to your place."

"So we're just going to be straight that you're investigating, even though we're involved? Wouldn't that be a conflict of interest?" he asked.

Damn him and his logic.

"It would be if we were really dating," she agreed. "But since we're only pretending, it's fine for me to investigate.

Do you think any of your coworkers are really going to be concerned about police protocol anyway?"

He shrugged. "I don't know. If you're right, and one of them might be involved in what happened at my house, that person could be very concerned."

"Agreed," she said. "That's the reason for the pretend relationship. And we can just say we've been keeping it quiet because of our careers, being so busy, you being gone so much, we didn't know if it would last, yada yada…"

He chuckled. "So my real reasons for not having a relationship."

"Mine, too," she said. "And then we say that, now with this happening at your house and the fire, we need to continue to keep it quiet at least for my job. We bring them in on the secret with us and hope that inspires them to share some secrets of their own."

"I'm not sure that'll work," he said.

She sighed. "It might not. But if the person who sent you the card is behind what happened at your house, then they'll want to try to take me out if we can convince them we're together."

"That's what worries me," he said and then uttered a sigh of his own. A heavy one that sounded resigned; by now he had to know he wasn't going to win this argument with her.

"Okay," she said. "Go time." She opened the door and stepped out into the parking lot. The temperature had dropped, the cold in such sharp contrast to the heat they'd generated in the car that she sucked in a breath and a few of the snowflakes that drifted down.

"Okay?" Trent asked as he came around the vehicle to join her on the driver's side.

She nodded. "Just colder than I thought."

"'Tis the season," he said but shivered a little as well.

"The entrance I have the key to is over here." He moved his hand to her back, planting it just above the curve of her hips as he turned her toward the building.

Heat streaked through Heather, chasing away the chill. As they walked across the parking lot, an engine started and revved. Then lights flashed on high beams, bright and blinding as the vehicle turned toward them.

Heather squinted against the light, trying to see the driver as she unzipped and reached inside her coat for her weapon.

Tires squealed and the engine roared as the vehicle bore down on them. And they stood, frozen, in that bright light.

WERE THE FIREFIGHTER and the detective dead? A glance in the rearview mirror as the driver sped away confirmed they were lying on the pavement. It had all happened so fast. The driver wasn't even sure if they'd struck them. The vehicle was so big and had been moving so fast. And their bodies were lying there, unmoving. Had they just jumped out of the way? Or had the vehicle struck them but the driver was so high on adrenaline they hadn't noticed?

Hopefully they were dead.

Both of them. So Trent Miles hadn't just lost someone close to him. He'd lost his own life as well.

Chapter Five

Had the vehicle struck her? Trent wasn't even sure if it had struck him. Everything had happened so fast. One second they were standing in the bright beams of those headlights and the next they were somersaulting through the air, trying to leap out of the way of the bumper of the speeding vehicle.

He'd struck the pavement so hard it had knocked the breath from his lungs. She'd grunted then, too, but now she was frighteningly quiet as she lay beside him on the pavement in the shadow of the firehouse. He couldn't see her face, couldn't see if she was conscious or even hear if she was breathing.

"Detect—Heather," he said, his voice gruff with the fear he hadn't had time to feel when that vehicle had tried to run them down. Tried…?

Maybe it had succeeded. While it hadn't hit him, maybe it had struck the detective.

"Heather!" he called louder, his heart pounding fast and furiously.

Still lying on her back, she turned only her head toward him, and her eyes gleamed in the shadows. "Are you okay?" she asked.

His heart skipped a beat now that her first concern was for him. But she was an officer of the law and had vowed to serve and protect. So this was just her professional reaction, not a personal one. He nodded. "Yeah, I'm fine. What about you?"

She rolled to her side and pushed herself up from the pavement. A grimace gripped her beautiful face for a moment before she sighed and nodded. "Yeah, I'm fine. I didn't get hit. Just hit the ground hard."

Trent shoved himself up and to his feet, ignoring the slight shakiness of his legs. He had bumps and bruises, too; he could feel the ache in his muscles already. And he grimaced, too.

"Are you sure?" she asked. "Nothing broken? Do we need to call an ambulance or make a trip to the ER?"

He shook his head. "I'm fine. Are you sure you are? You said you hit the ground hard, and I know I did."

She took a few steps and nodded. "Yeah. Nothing broken on me."

"That was too damn close!" Hopefully it had just been an accident, someone who hadn't seen them starting across the parking lot.

"It was perfect!" she exclaimed, excitement quivering in her voice. "The plan is already working!"

Metal creaked as the back door of the firehouse opened.

Heather reached for her weapon, but Trent caught her arm as he turned toward one of his bosses.

"What the hell happened?" the lieutenant asked. "Did that vehicle just run you down? Are you two all right?"

"Yes, we're fine," Trent said.

"Did you get a good look at it?" Heather asked. "Do you know who was driving it?"

The man stared at her for a moment. "I don't know who you are."

"Detective Bolton," Trent said. "And, Heather, this is

Lieutenant Ken Stokes. He was in charge of the crew that responded to the fire at my house."

The lieutenant extended his hand to her. "I'm not sure I'll be able to help you. Our fire investigator is who you'll want to coordinate your investigation with…"

"I will follow up with him, too," Heather said. "This is a possible murder investigation."

Trent almost hoped the woman had killed herself in the scenario Heather had suggested in the morgue. Then he wouldn't have to worry about anyone else getting hurt. But still a life had been lost, a life that wouldn't have been lost if not for him. A pang of guilt struck him, and he grimaced again.

"Are you really okay?" the lieutenant asked.

Trent nodded.

"You must have seen something, to come out here like you did," Heather prodded the man.

"Oh, yeah, I was on the second floor, in the kitchen." He gestured toward a window that overlooked the parking lot. "I heard the revving engine and squeal of tires, but all I saw was the roof of the vehicle. I couldn't see what it even was or who was driving it."

"What color was it?" Heather asked. "Was it long, like an SUV, or shorter like a truck?"

The man shrugged and shook his head. "I don't know. It all happened so fast. Didn't you two see what it was? Who it was?"

Heather cursed. "No. The lights blinded me." She glanced at Trent, as if asking him.

And he shook his head. "Just the lights. That's all I saw." Then he focused on the lieutenant again. "What are you doing here still?"

"I stuck around, figuring you'd need to come back for

your truck. And that you'd probably wind up staying here since your house is uninhabitable now."

"He's going to stay with me," Heather said. "We just came by to pick up his truck."

The lieutenant's brow furrowed as he stared at them with confusion. "I thought you were just investigating…"

"My interest in the fire at Trent's is personal as well as professional," Heather said. "But that's not something a lot of people need to know."

But it was too late for that. The door behind the lieutenant had remained open, and a few of the crew slipped out from behind it. From the looks of shock and speculation on their faces, it was clear they'd heard what she'd said.

While Trent's stomach muscles tightened with apprehension, she smiled slightly. This was all part of her plan. To do what? Find out the identity of the woman in his house? Find who'd sent Trent that card? Or to get herself killed?

He shuddered over how close they'd just come to that happening. But except for that initial silence from her, when the wind had probably been knocked out of her like from him, she was unfazed. He couldn't say the same. Even after everything that had happened recently with the hotshots, he wasn't used to this, wasn't used to being the target of someone's rage and violence.

He didn't like it. Not one bit. Especially if whoever was after him was someone close to him. Someone he worked with.

Heather stepped closer to him, and he didn't know if it was part of the act until she nudged her elbow into his ribs. And he remembered what she'd wanted him to do. So he introduced her to the guys.

"You met my lieutenant. These guys are Gordy Stutz,

Harold Wyzocky and Tom Johnson. You all stranded here since my place burned down?"

Gordy, an older guy with thinning hair, shook his head. "Your beds are more comfortable than the bunks, but I've been staying here during my shifts. It's been quieter at the firehouse than your place the past couple of weeks."

"What's been going on while I was out of town?" Trent asked.

Tom, a young Black man, snorted. "Ask Barry. He's been the one using it the most since your sister hasn't been around." The guy grinned. "Speaking of your sister..."

Trent glared at the younger man. "My sister's off-limits." He'd had to tell his crew that a few times. Unlike his hotshot team, who hadn't known about his relationship to Brittney Townsend until a week or so after she'd shown up in Northern Lakes, the local crew had always known about their relationship. She tended to drop by the firehouse a lot, much to Tom's delight.

She hadn't been doing that lately, though, not since her betrayal and his refusal to talk to her. If she had been the one found in his house...

He swallowed down the guilt threatening to gag him. He couldn't make up with her now, especially not after what had just happened. Heather had nearly been run down just for walking next to him.

"Where is Barry?" Heather asked the question.

The guys glanced around the lot. "He was here a little while ago. He must have just left."

Heather glanced up at Trent, and he read the question in her eyes. Could it have been Barry who'd tried to run them down? He shook his head.

"Where's he going?" she asked. "Since Trent's house burned down? Why wouldn't he stay here?"

"His shift was over," Tom replied. "He was going home to his place in the burbs and his wife and kids." He grimaced as if the thought of a family disgusted him.

"Were his wife and kids staying at my place, too?" he asked Gordy. "Is that why it was too loud?"

Gordy smirked, then glanced at Heather and shook his head. "I don't know what was going on."

Trent didn't have to be a trained investigator to realize Gordy was lying. They must have heard the part about her being a detective, and it was clear they weren't going to reveal any more information.

Heather was determined, though. "You all had the key code to Trent's place," she said. "You know that a body was found inside. Do you have any idea who she was?"

Tom's mouth dropped open, and his eyes went wide. "She? Was it your sis—"

Trent shook his head. "No. Brittney is fine." From the number of texts and voice mails she'd left for him, she was probably frustrated as hell that he wasn't talking to her. But that was for the best right now, or hers might have been that body found inside his place.

"That's why we need to know if any of you gave the code out to anyone else," Heather said. "We need to know if you have any idea who that might have been."

"You're not able to identify her with DNA or dental records?" the lieutenant asked.

"We need some DNA or dental records to use for comparison, so we can determine a match," Heather explained.

"I really don't know," Harold said with a glance at the others, as if he suspected one of them might.

But they crossed their arms and shook their heads. And Trent knew that none of them was going to talk, at least not to the detective. Remembering they had another role to play, Trent slid his arm around her.

She tensed at his touch. Maybe she'd forgotten their game. Then she slid her arm around him and smiled up at him.

His body tensed also, muscles tightening as desire gripped him. Or maybe it was just the adrenaline from their near miss moments ago. "Hon, my truck is over here," he said. "I'll grab it and follow you back to your place." Because he had absolutely no idea where she lived. He wasn't even sure he was really going to follow her. He just wanted to get the hell out of that parking lot where they could have died. He wanted to get away from the crew that he couldn't trust.

"The captain told me to tell you to take as long as you need off," Lieutenant Stokes told him.

"Of course he did," Gordy murmured with a trace of the resentment Trent had detected in him before.

Some of the crew at this firehouse thought he got special treatment because the captain had been friends with his dad, because the two men had served together. And because Trent had been a Marine as well. Maybe they weren't wrong. Manny had never made him choose between Trent's full-time position at the local firehouse and his gig as a hotshot. Other team members hadn't been as fortunate with the flexibility as Trent had.

But none of them had lost their house to a fire and maybe someone they knew along with it, or at least someone who'd been killed because of being in their house. Someone else could have just been killed as well. He tightened his arm around Heather for a moment before releasing her. Even though he walked toward his truck and she toward her vehicle, he wasn't sure he should really follow her home or just keep driving. It would probably be best for her. And maybe for him as well…if he kept going, getting as far as he could away from her.

USUALLY, HEATHER MONITORED her rearview mirror to make sure nobody was following her. With all the cases she'd cleared, and the criminals she'd sent to prison, she'd gotten a few warnings like Trent had. But hers didn't come in Christmas cards, and the postmarks were easy enough to read because they generally came from prison. So she didn't worry much about a vengeful criminal following her home, but she was cautious.

Now she kept glancing into her rearview mirror to make sure she was being followed, that Trent was sticking with the plan. It was working. After nearly getting hit in the parking lot, he must have realized that.

Too bad they hadn't gotten a good look at the vehicle that had nearly run them down, and would have had they not leaped out of the way. Tomorrow she would pull all the security footage in the area, but for tonight…

She wanted to get Trent back to her place. He had to be exhausted. Physically and probably emotionally as well. He'd been so worried that the body found in his house was his sister's. Despite being angry with her, he obviously still loved Brittney Townsend very much, so much that he wanted her to stay away from him.

He didn't love Heather. Hell, after she'd treated him like a suspect, he probably didn't even like her, but he clearly wanted to keep her safe, too. So she kept watching, making sure that the lights of his truck stayed behind her, that he was following her home. Because she was so focused on him, she would probably miss anyone else who might be following them. Was that vehicle that had nearly run them down behind Trent, following him? Waiting for another opportunity to try to kill them?

Because it wasn't just Heather who'd nearly been struck. Trent could have been hurt as well. Probably was hurt and just too proud to admit it. Was he too proud to stay with her? Or too stubborn?

His lights remained behind her, but there was more than just his back there. Light shone through the cab of his truck, illuminating the dark shadow of his tall body behind the wheel. He was a big man, but he could have been hurt just as badly as she if that vehicle had struck them.

Maybe the killer had decided that, after killing whoever had been in Trent's house, it was time to kill him now. Heather was definitely not the only one in danger. He was, too. And he needed her help and her protection; she wasn't sure if he would actually accept it, though.

If he didn't, the next time he might not be so lucky. Instead of surviving with probably just the same bumps and bruises, he could wind up dead…like the woman in his house.

BRITTNEY GRASPED HER cell phone in one hand as she stepped out of her small SUV. Maybe Trent would call her back or at least text her. But she doubted it.

Was he that mad at her? Or was it this…?

Crime scene tape, cordoning off the area around his house, fluttered in the slight evening breeze. Beyond the tape, faint plumes of smoke rose from the burned-out structure. The acrid odor hung in the air, burning her nose and lungs with each breath she took.

"What the hell…" She rasped the words out of her scratchy throat.

When the call had come into the TV station about a fire,

she'd been trying to edit that damn fluff piece so that when it aired she didn't undo all the strides she'd made to become a serious journalist. She'd wanted to take that call about the fire, especially when she learned there had also been a report of shots fired at the same address, but the producer had assigned it to one of the male reporters like he usually did with anything that might be a crime or at all interesting.

She really needed to find another job, one where they would take her seriously. But right now she needed to find her brother. He'd left her the voice mail and texts after the call had come into the station about the fire, so he had to be okay. He wasn't the body that had been found inside the house.

That person was still unidentified, or so the coroner's office had claimed. Did Trent know who it was? Had he thought it was her? Was that why he'd finally contacted her again after weeks of the silent treatment? Probably. Because he clearly hadn't forgiven her, or he would have returned her calls or texts. Unless he was busy dealing with this, with the fire, with the investigation.

There was a detective on the case already: Heather Bolton. From what Brittney had learned about her from her contacts in the police department, Bolton was a badass with the best case clearance rate in the precinct.

The right person was on the case for Trent as long as he had nothing to do with this. And he couldn't...

Brittney had spent so much of her life idolizing her big brother that she worried she wasn't always objective when it came to him. She'd recently learned how many secrets people were capable of keeping, even from those closest to them.

Trent had certainly been keeping secrets from her about what had been going on with his hotshot team. After that arsonist had been caught all those months ago, Brittney had thought the only danger he faced were the fires he'd fought. But there had been so much more going on, with sabotage, with one hotshot's death, with the attempts on the lives of so many other hotshots.

Was this fire and that body related to his hotshot team and what had been happening in Northern Lakes?

Was Trent the next target of whoever had been targeting his team? She turned her attention to her cell again. Still no response from Trent.

So she called. Predictably it went right to voice mail. Was it just her calls that he wasn't taking, though? Or was he unable to take anyone's calls right now?

She held up her cell and snapped a picture of his smoking house. Then she sent it to him with the caption: What the hell is going on, big brother?

Chapter Six

What the hell was he thinking? Trent had no business following Heather home like some stray dog. She was a detective working a case, not a bodyguard. Not that he needed one. She probably needed one more, if whoever had nearly run them down believed that they were together. That they were close.

But was Trent following her home going to protect her or put her in more danger? He wasn't sure, but he suspected that someone might be following him. The same set of lights had stayed pretty steady behind him. With few other vehicles on the road this late, it was easy to track them. A big vehicle, like the one that had nearly run them down.

He shuddered as he considered how close it had come to striking them. How badly they could have been hurt, or worse, if it had struck them. He eased his foot off the accelerator, leaving more space between his truck and the back of Detective Bolton's unmarked police vehicle. He shouldn't go home with her, shouldn't put her in any more danger than she already was. But...

The vehicle behind him slowed as well, then stopped, and a signal light blinked just before it turned left onto another street. Ahead of him, Heather's right signal light blinked, and she slowed before turning onto a residential street. But she didn't continue driving. She braked just around that turn, as if waiting for him.

He had no doubt she would probably follow him if he drove past. She might even turn on the siren and flash the light all but hidden on the dash of her vehicle. He wasn't going to escape her, but he didn't necessarily want to.

He really didn't have any place else to go but a hotel or motel. And it wasn't as if Heather Bolton couldn't take care of herself and him.

He braked and turned onto the street she had, and her vehicle started forward again. He followed her down a couple of blocks until she turned again, this time into a driveway. She parked outside a closed garage door. The driveway wasn't long enough to accommodate his truck, so he parked at the curb in front of the bungalow that outside lights illuminated. Unlike the bungalows on either side of it that had aluminum siding and dark shutters, this one had been updated with cedar shake siding and some stone.

He'd always wanted to make his place look like this, but with as much as he'd worked, he hadn't had the time. Maybe one of his neighbors had torched the place because it had been the ugliest house on the block with its faded beige aluminum siding and sagging black shutters. Or maybe they'd torched it because they thought he was a drug-dealing gangbanger like the neighbor had led Heather to believe.

She didn't believe that anymore or she wouldn't have invited him to stay with her. Had she invited or ordered him? He didn't know for certain.

A fist tapped the passenger's window, and he jumped, startled. Then her face appeared, her eyes intent as she stared through the glass at him. He pressed the power locks, unlocking the door, and she opened it. "You going to sit out here what's left of the night?"

"I've slept in my truck before," he said.

"What? After your parents died?" she asked.

"No, I wasn't homeless. Brittney's mother and stepfather took me in then," he said. Probably because Brittney had begged them to and they'd refused her nothing. A pang of guilt struck his heart that he kept refusing to even talk to her. Inside his pocket, his cell kept vibrating with texts and reminders that he had unread texts. Probably several of them by now. He didn't want her in the middle of this, though, didn't want her in danger because of him. "But I was twelve then," he reminded her. "I don't need anyone to take me in now."

"I'm not taking you in out of pity or anything else," she said. "This is just a ploy to flush out a killer, and it's working."

"Too well," he said. "Shouldn't I park someplace else in case I was followed?"

"I hope you were followed. That's the whole point of this. They need to see your vehicle here, at my house, to believe that we're together. This is getting personal for me, too, now. I want to catch whoever tried to run us down." Her green eyes glinted with the determination in her voice.

"Do you always get your man, Detective Bolton?"

She snorted. "I don't want a man. It's criminals I want and only to put them behind bars. They are my fires to put out."

He drew in a breath and nodded. "Okay…" For some reason he trusted her, trusted that she would catch whoever was behind that fire and the incident in the firehouse parking lot.

He wasn't sure he should trust himself right now, though. Maybe his instincts were wrong. Obviously, he'd already trusted someone he shouldn't have. A couple of someones, actually. His sister and whoever had burned down his house, which was probably someone who had the key code. Someone with whom he worked.

HEATHER HAD COME up to his truck for two reasons. One, because she wasn't sure he was going to get out of it and come up to the house. The other, so she could check the street, see if any other vehicle besides theirs had turned onto it. She didn't notice any other headlights, but a strange foreboding gripped her. And despite the thickness of her puffy jacket, goose bumps lifted her skin beneath it. Was someone out there, in the shadows, watching them?

Or was her sense of foreboding because of the hotshot firefighter she'd invited into her home? This was the plan, though, she had to remind herself. To fool whoever was after him.

Trent grabbed a duffel bag off the passenger's seat and stepped out of his truck. After clicking the fob to lock it, he came around the box of the truck to where she stood on the sidewalk. "Nice place," he remarked as he stared over her head at the house.

She smiled. "Yes, it has become my dad's retirement project." She chuckled. "Probably a way for him to get some time away from my mother and eat and drink what he wants." She often found an empty can or two of beer in her recycling and greasy wrappers from takeout in her trash.

Trent tensed. "If he comes and goes, is this a good idea for me to stay here?"

"Afraid he might threaten you to make an honest woman out of me?" she asked.

"Afraid he might get hurt, just like I'm afraid that you might, especially after that vehicle nearly ran us down." He shuddered as if cold. And maybe he was since he must have taken off his firefighter jacket in his truck and wore just his shirt and the firefighter pants. But she had a feeling that what chilled him was how close they'd come to getting hurt.

"Don't worry about my dad," she said as she started walking toward the side door of her house. "Mom has him working on some projects at their house, getting it ready for the holidays. He won't be allowed over here until he finishes up there, and knowing how they can never agree, that won't be until after the holidays."

She pulled open the screen door and punched in her key code for the lock on her cedar-stained wood door. "These are easier than handing out keys," she said as the light on the lock blinked green and clicked. "Especially since my dad tends to lose them and my sisters tend to overuse them. That's why I put in separate codes for each person. You didn't do that with yours?"

He shook his head. "No. I just bought the lock that has the one code in it. I travel so much, I didn't want to have to remember more than one. I just wish now that I hadn't let so many people use my place."

"I'll work on that list tomorrow," she said. "It's late now." She pushed open her door and stepped inside the dark house.

Trent hesitated, standing outside under the small gabled roof over the side door. The wind kicked up, swirling snowflakes around the house with a blast of cold air.

She sucked in a breath as the cold swept through the open door and hit her even inside the house. He had to be freezing. "You don't have to be scared," she teased him. "I didn't lure you here to take advantage of you."

Finally he stepped across the threshold, and in the limited space between the stairs leading down to the basement and the ones leading up to the kitchen, he stood close to her. So close that his body brushed against hers, and heat shot through her. "That's too bad…" he murmured as he stared down at her.

Ignoring the heat and the mad pounding of her heart, she laughed. "I shouldn't be surprised that you would play with fire. It's your job, after all."

"That's not playing," he said with a heavy sigh.

This close to him, she could smell the smoke on his clothes, probably in his hair and on his skin. "And neither is this," she reminded him. "We're trying to catch whoever is after you."

"They're after you now, too," he said.

"Yes, the plan is working," she reminded him. And feeling that sudden chill, that sense of being watched, she peered around him through the open door. But even with her yard lights on, she couldn't see anyone. If they were out there, they were standing deep in the shadows. Hiding…

Waiting…

Like that person must have waited for them at the firehouse. They must have assumed Trent would have to return for his truck or to stay in the bunk room since his home was a total loss. That threat in the Christmas card wasn't just against whoever was close to him. It was against Trent, too.

He must have felt the chill, because he pulled the door shut and turned the dead bolt.

She climbed up the couple of steps into the kitchen. But when she reached out to flip on the lights, Trent caught her wrist in his big hand.

"Wait," he whispered, his mouth close to her ear.

She tried not to shiver at the heat of his breath against her skin. "What?" she whispered back.

"There's someone in here…" he whispered. "I hear something…"

She tensed and reached for her weapon. But as she listened, she recognized the stealthy noise. The creeping foot-falls and then the whoosh of air as the cat jumped onto the counter and stared at them with his eyes gleaming in the dark. Eyes nearly the same color as Trent's.

He gasped and stepped around her, as if to protect her. And Heather flipped on the lights then. The cat hissed at the stranger in their home, the black fur rising on his neck and his suddenly arched back. Then he jumped down from the counter and ran off, footfalls louder now than when he'd sneaked out from wherever he'd probably been sleep-ing. "Some watchdog you have there," Trent said with a deep chuckle.

"Oh, Sammy would tear you to pieces if he thought I was in danger," Heather assured him. "You should see what he's done to my reading chair in my bedroom. It must look awful threatening in the middle of the night."

"Are you inviting me into your bedroom?" he asked.

She snorted. "You get the guest room, buddy. This rela-tionship is only pretend. Remember that." That last warn-ing wasn't just for him but for herself as well. "But feel free to raid the fridge."

She pulled open the door of the stainless-steel appliance and glanced inside at the mostly empty shelves and groaned. "But you better like pickles." A jar of baby dills and some bottles of condiments were about all that were inside, as well as a few cans of beer her father must have left behind and her green teas. She couldn't have one of those now or she would be awake all night.

She would probably be awake all night anyway, though. And it wouldn't be just because she had to stay vigilant in case they had been followed back to her place.

"I'm not hungry. I'd just really like to take a shower." He held up his duffel bag. "And use your washer and dryer if you have them. I haven't had a chance to wash my stuff from out West yet."

An acrid smoke smell emanated from that bag just as it did from his hair and the clothes he was wearing. "That must have been some wildfire," she mused. And he'd returned from that to battle a blaze at his own home. "The washer and dryer are downstairs." She pointed back down the steps they'd walked up. "And there's a hall bathroom with a great shower my dad recently remodeled."

"Do you want to use it first?" he asked.

She shook her head. "I have an en suite. Dad took out a tiny third bedroom to make a big primary suite."

"With your reading chair," he said.

"Yes." She wouldn't be reading tonight, though. She would be listening for any sign of an intruder. After pointing out the guest room and bath to him, she headed into her suite. She took a quick shower and then pulled out her laptop and cell to check messages and send messages, following up with the crime scene techs and the fire investigator.

It was late, though, so she didn't expect responses. It was so late that she should get some rest. She'd also requested extra patrols in her area overnight; they would be vigilant and close in case she needed backup. She was a light sleeper and would notice if someone tried to get inside. She was such a light sleeper that the sound of Trent showering kept her awake, imagining how he must look standing under the spray, the water rushing over his muscles and sleek skin. Not only was there the possibility of an intruder coming into her house but also into her mind: Trent.

Heat rushed over her, so hot that beads of sweat formed on her forehead and above her lip and trickled between her breasts. Needing some ice water, she tossed back her covers and headed to the kitchen. Her suite was at the end of the hall, so she had to walk past the bathroom where the water continued to run and steam slipped out from beneath the door. Steam with the scent of soap and man.

She hadn't had the smell of man in her house in a long while. Too long. That probably explained why the thought of him naked had her so hot and bothered. No. The thought of Trent naked would bother her no matter what; the man was gorgeous. But he was also in danger, and now, thanks to her plan, so was she. So she had to stay focused.

Had to stay alert. She opened a cabinet and pulled out a large insulated glass, then pushed it against the automatic ice maker. The machine rumbled, then chucked shards of crushed ice into her glass. Maybe instead of water, she should pour one of her green teas over the ice. That way she would stay awake and aware of every noise.

But this late at night, the caffeine would make her jittery, and she wanted to be alert, not trigger-happy. So she switched the ice maker to water. Once her glass was filled, she turned to head back to her bedroom and nearly collided with a big, bare, muscular chest. So much for being alert.

The noise of the ice maker had drowned out the sounds of his approach. She sucked in a breath that smelled like the steam that had escaped from the bathroom, of soap and man. But this close to him, the scent was even more intense.

Her reaction was, too. Her nipples tightened beneath the thin material of the oversize T-shirt she wore as a nightgown. His gaze, those topaz eyes gleaming in the faint glow of the under-cabinet lighting, dropped to her shirt, and he sucked in a breath.

Heather lowered her gaze, too, following the rippling ridges of abdomen muscles to the towel knotted low around his lean hips. The man was the next level of fitness, like there wasn't an ounce of fat on him. Anywhere.

She only saw those sculpted muscles and some red patches that were maybe bruises from when they'd hit the asphalt in the firehouse parking lot, possibly burns from that wildfire or the fire at his house. "Are you okay?" she asked.

He groaned a little. "Just going down to get my clothes out of the dryer." And to do that he had to pass through the kitchen, past her.

She should have stayed in her room, because seeing him like this, standing so close to him, had her even hotter and more restless than before. Maybe she needed to pour that ice water over her head. "I'll…" Her voice was just a husky rasp. "…get out of your way, then." She moved to step around him, but he was so big and the space in her galley kitchen so narrow that she touched him. Her hip bumped against his thigh, and one of her breasts brushed his muscled arm. She nearly moaned as desire shot from her tightened nipple to her core.

He reached out, clasping her hips in his big hands. "You're not in my way," he said, but his voice was so low, so gruff, and the look on his face, the heat in his eyes…

She had no doubt that he felt this, too. This intense attraction, desire.

Need.

We're just supposed to be playing. Pretending…

This wasn't real. The relationship or the attraction. But it felt more intense than anything Heather had experienced before. Maybe because he was so unreal. So handsome, so fit that he couldn't be human. She reached out with her free hand and touched his chest. His heart leaped beneath her palm, then pounded hard and fast.

He drew in a long, ragged breath, as if bracing himself to step away. But instead of releasing her, he clutched her hips tighter and pulled her just a little closer. "I know this isn't what you intended when you told me to stay here…with you…" He closed his eyes and grimaced, as if struggling.

She was struggling, too, and her usual reaction in tense situations like this was to ease the tension with humor. "How do you know?" she asked. "Maybe this was exactly what I intended." And she slid her palm across his chest.

"You're killing me," he said, his jaw clenched as he opened his eyes and stared so intently at her. "I'm trying to resist temptation right now."

"I'm tempting?"

"You're gorgeous. So damn sexy with your hair down and that shirt…" He groaned and closed his eyes again, definitely trying to shut her out.

If only he could turn her off…

Maybe if she closed her eyes…

If she shut him out…

But she could still see him in her mind, all those sculpted muscles and sleek naked skin. Now she could smell him even more intensely and hear him breathe. She was so aware and so damn attracted to him.

His breaths were coming faster and shallower, but his chest moved beneath her hand as if those breaths were hard to come by. She could also feel the heat of his body, the smoothness of his skin.

She opened her eyes just as his thick lashes fluttered open. And he stared down at her with the same raw desire that coursed through her.

And suddenly it was hard for her to breathe.

To not get caught following, a turn had been taken a while ago. A turn that had let Trent Miles and the female detective slip away. For a moment.

Driving up and down the side streets they might have

taken eventually led to the discovery of the hotshot firefighter's truck parked outside a small house with cedar siding and stone. The detective's unmarked police vehicle was parked in the driveway. Like being unmarked fooled anyone…

Like everybody didn't know what and who she was. And now where she lived for however long she remained living.

She should have already been dead. Her and Trent Miles. They'd avoided getting hurt in the parking lot of the firehouse. But their luck wouldn't last.

And now that they had so easily been found, neither would their lives…

Chapter Seven

Trent awoke slowly…due to a strange niggling sensation that someone was watching him. Staring at him…

Through him…

He hadn't slept alone last night like he'd expected to, like he'd been spending his nights unless he was in the bunk room at one of the firehouses. He opened his eyes and returned the unblinking stare focused on his face. A stare probably eerily similar to his in color.

Small paws kneaded his chest, claws nipping slightly into his skin, as the black cat stood on him. It had been somewhere in the bed all night, sneaking in with him when he'd carried in his armload of laundry.

The alarm on the dryer had sounded at the worst time last night, right when he and Heather had been standing so close in the kitchen. Her hand on his chest, both of his clenching the curves of her hips. And the way she'd been looking at him…

At his lips…

She might have even been rising up on her toes to reach for him, to slide her hands around his head and pull it down for her kiss. Or at least that was what he wanted to think…

That she would have kissed him. Instead, when that dryer signal had sounded, she'd jumped back and sloshed the contents of her glass onto that thin T-shirt she apparently wore as a nightgown. Or to drive him out of his mind.

To him that soft heathered cotton was sexier than silk and lace, especially when the water seeped into the fabric, making it transparent over her ample breasts. Over the nipples he'd already been able to see pressing against the shirt. His body hardened just thinking about last night, about her... about how damn badly he'd wanted her.

But the dryer signal and the ice water had apparently brought her to her senses. She'd let out a long, shaky breath and laughed. "I never knew how good firefighters were at starting fires. Good thing I had this water handy to put it out." Then she'd slipped around him and disappeared down the hall.

He'd wanted to follow her. So damn badly...

But she'd obviously changed her mind about acting on the attraction between them. And he couldn't blame her. His life was a mess right now, and she didn't even know the half of it. He hadn't told her about everything that had been happening with the hotshots. And he hadn't put any of their names on the list he'd given her, even though a few of them did have the key code. With everything they'd been through, he wanted to talk to them before she did.

He could hear her talking now, not the words, just the sound of her voice drifting beneath the closed door of the guest room. The cat heard her, too, because he cocked his head and froze, one claw nipping into Trent's skin again. "Hey," he protested.

The cat leaped off him, hitting the hardwood floor with a noise that was surprisingly loud for his slight weight. Before Sammy could get to the door, it swung open.

"Everything okay in here?" Heather asked. She was dressed in faded jeans and an oversize red sweater, probably oversize to hide her weapon. She hadn't been wearing it last night, though. She hadn't been wearing anything but that thin cotton T-shirt.

Just thinking of how she'd looked in the dim lighting had his body reacting, tension and attraction gripping him. He groaned and shifted beneath the quilt, trying to hide that reaction.

She stepped farther into the room. "Are you okay? Did you get hurt worse than you admitted when we hit the asphalt last night?"

He did have some new aches and bruises to go with some of the ones he'd already had from working that wildfire. "I'll live," he said.

"You might not if whoever was driving that vehicle last night has their way. I don't think that's the last time they're going to try for you."

"It's whoever is close to me that's in danger, not me," Trent said.

"We could have both been killed last night."

He shifted against the bed and flinched, the aches and pains proving how true her words were. Hitting the asphalt wasn't the only reason his body was aching, though. Getting so close to her, wanting her so badly and not even kissing her had him aching, too. With longing.

With desire.

He groaned again.

"Don't worry," she said. "I'll do my best to keep you safe and find out who the hell tried to run us down."

"But how are you going to solve this case if you're baby-sitting me instead?"

"Shh," she said. "Never talk about me babysitting. My sisters will get the idea to try to drop their kids on my doorstep again." She shuddered.

He laughed.

She was so funny and smart and beautiful and sexy. He wasn't sure how he would handle being so close to her and not being able to kiss her, touch her or make love with her.

"I don't have to protect you," she said. "Looks like Sammy stood guard all night in here with you." The cat wound around her legs, purring loudly as if marking her as his and making sure that Trent knew he didn't have a chance of claiming her.

He probably didn't, but for a little while last night she had seemed to want him as badly as he'd wanted her. She was barely even looking at him this morning, though, and certainly not with that look of desire gleaming in her eyes like last night. Maybe he'd just imagined it all. Had he imagined hearing her voice earlier?

"Was someone here or were you on the phone?" he asked.

"Phone," she said. "I was making calls to everyone on that list."

"Who did you talk to?" he asked, uneasily. Hopefully not Brittney, because the more she knew, the more involved she would get, and the more in danger. He didn't want that; he would do anything to protect her, even freeze her out. Last night he had relented and returned her latest text with a text of his own: I'm okay. Back off.

"Not many," she said. "I mostly left messages." Her cell, clutched in her hand, rang now. "Somebody must be calling back…"

Before he could ask her, she ducked out of the guest room, closing the door behind her, as if she didn't want him to hear. These were people he knew, people he'd trusted, but to her, they must be suspects. Could one of them, his friends or co-workers or family, be responsible for that woman's death? For the fire? For the threat against him?

TECHNOLOGY SEEMED TO be conspiring to bring Heather to her senses. Last night, the signal on the dryer had brought her out of that sensual spell she'd been so deeply under that she'd nearly kissed Trent Miles. She was pretty damn sure if she'd given in to that temptation, then she would have given in to all her desires.

So it was good that the dryer signal had startled her into spilling the water on her shirt. The cold had jolted her out of that spell and to her senses. Just as the ringing cell had now. Or she might have given in to the temptation to crawl into bed with Trent like Sammy had.

"Traitor," she hissed at the cat in a soft whisper.

The cat hissed back.

"What?" the voice rumbled out of the cell speaker, bringing Heather's attention back to the caller.

It wasn't one of the firefighters. This call was from a crime scene investigator.

"Did you find anything on the traffic cam footage from near the area where the house burned and the woman died?" she asked.

"There are no cams close enough to that address to confirm that any of the vehicles came off that street," the tech replied.

"Damn…" she murmured. She had some uniforms canvassing the immediate area to request neighbors' home security and doorbell footage. Hopefully something useful would turn up to help identify the woman and her killer or at least who actually used Trent's house, since the other guys last night had denied that they had. Nobody else she'd talked to so far seemed willing to admit they used it, if they'd even talked to her at all. She'd left a message for the elusive Barry Coats, but he had yet to return her call.

Had they just missed him last night at the firehouse? Or

had he just missed them? Why would he have tried to run them down unless he'd had something to hide? Like his guilt...

Just what had he been using Trent's house for that caused his other coworkers to stop using it? She needed more information about the guy.

"Is there anything else you want me to check?" the tech asked.

"Yes," she said. "Traffic cam and security footage near the firehouse on Front Street."

There was another hiss of breath, and she glanced down to see if Sammy had made the sound. But she saw only denim and long, bare feet. Trent had stepped out of the guest room. He'd pulled on a pair of jeans but hadn't done up the top button yet. While he'd pulled on a button-down flannel shirt, he hadn't done up those buttons either, leaving it open over his bare, muscular chest.

Damn him.

She closed her eyes for a moment and drew in a deep breath.

"Detective?" the tech asked. "Any particular time you want me to check the video?"

"Uh..." What time had that vehicle nearly struck them? She'd been so distracted then that she was lucky it hadn't hit them.

"One a.m.," Trent answered for her.

"One a.m.," she repeated. At least he'd been more aware than she'd been. She wasn't sure if he'd shoved her out of the way, or they'd simultaneously jumped out of the way. "A firefighter, Trent Miles, and I were nearly run down in the parking lot," she explained. She should have filed the report last night, after she'd questioned the lieutenant, but she would file it soon.

She needed to get it together or she wasn't going to close any of these cases, and they were starting to pile up. The shooting, the death, the fire and the attempted vehicular manslaughter, or murder, if it had been premeditated.

Had the person been waiting for them, knowing that, with Trent's house burned down, he might return to the firehouse to sleep?

Or had it been a crime of opportunity?

She had no idea, but she had to get her act together and figure things out. Or she wouldn't have just her case clearance rate to worry about but her life as well.

"Detective Bolton?" The tech called her name a little louder, as if he'd called it before and she hadn't heard him.

"Yes, I'm here."

"Are you all right? Was anyone hurt?" he asked with concern.

Craig. That was his name. She knew it because she always asked for him. He was young. Bob Bernard complained about his hiring, saying he couldn't even grow a beard, how could he handle his job?

Bob was such an idiot. But that was fine. Craig was smart and strove to be the best at his job, just like Heather did. She liked him. "I'm fine, Craig. Thanks so much for checking into all of this for me. You're the best."

"Thanks, Detective," he said, his voice full of pride. "I'll let you know what I find for that time frame and location."

"Thank you!" she said and then clicked off her cell.

"Not one of my crew," Trent said.

"No, one of mine," Heather said.

"Sounds like an admirer."

"A really good tech," she said. If anything turned up, Craig would find it. "Not a lot of your crew have accepted my calls and even fewer have called me back."

"They worked late last night," he said in their defense.

She didn't think that was why they hadn't called her back, especially Barry Coats.

"But you talked to or left messages for everyone on that list?" he asked, his long body suddenly tense as if he was uneasy.

Was he worried about her talking to his coworkers or his family?

"I haven't contacted your stepmom and your sister yet," she said, thinking that might be who he was concerned about. "I figured you might want to call them and tell them about the fire before handing the phone to me." She still had to question them. "That way they can hear your voice and know for sure that you're fine."

"I guarantee Brittney already knows about the fire," he said and held up his cell, showing her a dark photo on the screen.

She had to step closer to him, to his bare chest, to try to decipher what the image was. But she forced herself to focus just on the phone, not him. Only streetlamps illuminated the scene in the picture, the crime scene, the tape marking off the area around his still-smoking house. The caption on the photo read: What the hell is going on, big brother?

Heather smiled. "I think I'm going to like your sister."

Trent groaned. "That's what worries me."

She laughed now. "So let's give Brittney a call."

He shook his head. "Not until I've had some coffee and figure out how to talk to her and get her to stay the hell out of it so she doesn't get killed."

As well as the text his sister had sent him, she'd seen the one he'd sent to her. Clearly he didn't think she was going to heed his warning to back off.

"I have every strength of coffee pod in the kitchen, and

the water in the machine is heated up," she said. "Once you have your coffee, we need to contact the rest of the names on your list and maybe follow up with some in-person visits if I don't get calls back from the others I've left messages for, like that firefighter we just missed last night." Or had he just missed them with his vehicle?

"There might not be enough caffeine for me..." Trent murmured, then passed her in the hall to head toward the kitchen. He passed her so closely that his bare chest brushed across the front of her sweater.

And heat shot through her body, making her jump back like she'd been burned. She had probably just had too many cups of coffee since waking up. Hell, she hadn't really woken up because she hadn't really slept at all.

She'd lain in her bed wishing that Trent was in it with her. That was definitely a temptation she had to fight. She'd already crossed so many lines by having him come home with her. She'd done it for his protection, but she couldn't protect him or herself while being so distracted.

She had to stay focused for both their sakes. For both their lives.

"WHERE THE HELL is he?" Brittney asked, frustration gripping her. She'd checked everywhere for Trent last night. At her mom's. At the firehouse. She'd even checked some hotels in the vicinity. The hotels had offered her more information than anyone at the firehouse had last night.

The lieutenant who'd answered the door had been short with her and hadn't let her inside the building. A lot of firefighters didn't like reporters. Her brother included lately.

And now every one of his hotshot team members.

A few of his local crew didn't dislike her, though. In fact, there was one of them who liked her a little too much.

So she waited in the parking lot for him to leave after his night shift ended.

The minute he exited the firehouse, she pushed open the driver's door of her small SUV and stepped out. "Tom!" she called out to him.

A grin crossed his face. He was cute and young and eager to impress her. A little too eager for Brittney. But at the moment, she was counting on that eagerness.

"Hey, beautiful Brittney," he said.

She tried not to grimace at the compliment he'd given her so many times that it irritated instead of charmed her now. *Come up with something a little more original.* And something that wasn't just about her looks. She was sick of being judged for those and deemed capable of handling only the fluff instead of the hard stuff, like the smart, savvy reporter she was.

So smart that she smiled back at Tom. "Hey, handsome," she said.

He chuckled. "What do you want, Brittney?"

"My brother," she replied. "I can't find him anywhere." Her voice cracked a little with the concern gripping her. She was worried. Very worried. And frustrated as hell that he wouldn't return her calls. And his response to her text hadn't reassured her at all. I'm okay. Back off.

"He didn't tell you?" Tom asked.

Which meant he knew where Trent was, so some of that pressure inside Brittney eased. "He's not returning my calls," she admitted. "I know that with the fire and all he must be busy…" She trailed off to see if his crew member would fill in the blanks.

Tom snorted. "I'll say he's been busy. A lot busier than any of us knew."

The comment left Brittney with more questions than answers. Was he talking about the fire? The body found in the house? The shots fired? Or something else? He could have even been talking about her exposé on the hotshot team, but that had really only exposed one member who'd been living his life as a dead man. He'd almost become a dead man because of Brittney's exposé, and her brother could have been killed as well.

Just as he could have been last night if he'd been home when the fire started. Had he been?

She didn't even know, and they'd once been pretty close. So close that she could have been in his house last night. She stayed there a lot when she was working a story in the city and didn't want to drive to her mom's place in the burbs.

Could she be the reason his house had been burned down? That someone else had died? Was she the one someone really wanted to hurt, because of the story she'd done? Guilt gripped her for a moment, and she sucked in a breath.

"You okay?" Tom asked with genuine concern.

She shook her head. "I need to know what the hell is going on." And if it was because of her. She'd had that strange sensation lately of being watched, but maybe that was just because she'd made the national news with her scoop on the Canterbury heir, so she was more recognizable.

Tom stepped closer, his arms open as if he was about to give her a hug. Was it that bad?

Someone had died in Trent's house. Of course it was that bad.

But she held up a hand to ward off the man. "I'm fine," she said. "I'm just worried about my brother."

Tom's face drew into a tight grimace. "Me, too," he admitted, his voice gruff. "He and his girlfriend could have been killed last night."

"Girlfriend?" She hadn't even known that Trent had

started dating again. "And wasn't someone killed in the fire?" A female.

"Not in the fire," Tom said. "Here, last night, in the parking lot. The lieu said he saw from the kitchen window—" he gestured toward the second story "—someone nearly ran them down in the parking lot." He shuddered.

She gasped as a sharp pain jabbed her heart. "Nearly? What happened?"

Tom shrugged. "I didn't see it. But the lieu heard the engine rev and tires squealing. That's why he looked out the window. They got out of the way just in time, and they insisted they were okay."

So the fire hadn't been about Brittney, but she wasn't relieved. She was even more concerned that it was about her brother, and maybe his new girlfriend. While she hadn't met many of his past girlfriends, usually because he didn't date them long, she always knew when he was dating.

She didn't know anything about what had been happening with her brother lately. She knew why: her damn exposé on his best friend and his hotshot team. And what if something happened to him and he never forgave her? What if something already had happened to him and that was why he hadn't returned her calls? Anyone could have sent her that text telling her to back off. Even his killer...

Chapter Eight

"Ready to call her?" Heather asked as she held out his phone to him. That picture Brittney had taken and sent last night stared up at him from the screen. His house, or what was left of it, with plumes of smoke rising from the blackened structure.

The house didn't mean anything to him. He hadn't even spent that much time there. It was the woman who concerned him. Who was she?

He doubted that Brittney would know.

"She'll ask more questions than she'll be able to answer," he warned her. "And are you sure you want her to know about you? About whatever we're claiming we are?"

Her lips curved into a smile. "Can't even say the words? *Boyfriend and girlfriend? In a relationship?*" She grimaced after she said them. "Those words are hard for me to spit out, too."

He found himself smiling but was curious. "Why?" he asked. "Why is it hard for you?"

She wriggled her dark blond brows. "What are we talking about now?"

He chuckled. "I thought you didn't want to play with fire," he reminded her. But the way she looked at him across the table in her breakfast nook had his body hardening again, just as she'd teased.

"I'll leave that to the firefighters," she said.

"Calling Brittney will be playing with fire," he said. "She might do a story, especially if she senses a scandal, like the detective investigating a murder being involved with one of the suspects."

"You're not a suspect. Your alibi checked out, and you're in danger. So you're in police protection."

"I thought Sammy was my bodyguard," he said, his gaze moving to the cat sleeping on the pad on the window seat in the nook.

She glanced over at her cat and smiled at him with affection. "He's exhausted from pulling the overnight shift."

Trent touched the small scratches on his chest. "I think I needed protection from him." He grinned at her. "Too bad you chickened out last night."

Her green eyes widened, and her mouth dropped open with shock. "You think I chickened out? I'm brave," she insisted. "I'm not stupid. And last night…that would have been stupid."

He couldn't argue with her. Really. "Yeah, but it would have been fun."

Instead of agreeing, she narrowed her eyes as if skeptical of his claim.

He arched a brow. "Want me to prove it?"

"Wow…" She shook her head. "You are really trying to stall me talking to your sister."

He sighed and admitted, "I'm trying to stall *me* talking to my sister."

"Are you really just worried about her doing a story on all of this?" she asked. "Or are you still mad at her over that one she did on the Canterbury heir?"

"My best friend," he said.

Heather glanced down at his list. "What name is he going under now? In fact, most of the numbers you gave me have local exchanges, but your hotshot crew wouldn't..." She looked back up at him, her eyes narrowed with suspicion. "You didn't put any of them on your list? None of them have the key code for your place? Not even your *best* friend?"

God, she was smart.

"Nobody's around the Detroit area," he pointed out.

"So? They never visit? You've never given any of them your key code and the offer to stay if they are in the area?" she asked.

He felt like a suspect again.

A CALL COMING in on her cell momentarily suspended Heather's interrogation of Trent. One of his local crew had returned her voice mail.

"I haven't stayed at Trent's for a while," Jerome Whittaker insisted.

Heather wasn't sure if she believed him. "Why not?" she asked.

"What? What do you mean?"

"He gave you the key code, so you've used his place in the past, so why not recently?" she asked. "I looked up your address. You don't live far from the firehouse. Why wouldn't you just stay there?"

"Snoring. I'm a light sleeper, and some of the crew snore."

"So get earplugs or go back to your own house. As I said, you don't live that far—"

"My wife and I were having problems," he confessed. "But we got back on track. I don't need to stay there anymore."

"And you didn't give that key code out to anyone else?" she asked.

"No. Everybody I know already had it."

"Your wife?"

His words sputtered incoherently into the phone until he cleared his voice and asked, "Why would I give it to her?"

"Why wouldn't you? If she had to find you and you were asleep—"

"I— She didn't know I was staying there," he said.

"I need to speak to her," Heather said. She needed to confirm that she wasn't the woman whose body had been found in the fire.

"Uh—I— Why? I just told you she doesn't know that I ever used Trent's place."

Heather glanced across the table at Trent, who was silently studying his coffee mug. Then she focused on his friend again. "Apparently, you don't want her to know. Why not? What exactly did you use his house for?"

"I—I told you," he said. "We were going through a rough patch. But everything's fine now."

Maybe because his wife was dead. Heather's detective mind always went with the worst-case scenario. "I need to talk to her and confirm that she's alive—"

"Alive? What the hell are you talking about?"

"The body found in Trent's house has not been identified. I need to talk to your wife. But I'll do that in person." She disconnected the call as Jerome was sputtering in protest again.

"My turn for the interrogation now?" Trent asked.

"What the hell was your house? A brothel?" she asked.

He shrugged. "I really thought my crew was just using it to crash because Lieutenant Stokes snores really loudly."

"You didn't know some of them might be using it to cheat on their wives?" she asked. She glanced around her house. With all the changes her dad had made, it was so damn cute with its white cabinets, light quartz countertops and sun-drenched breakfast nook. She couldn't imagine letting anyone use it but her dad. And she even sometimes worried about him, but that was just because of his eating junk food and drinking beer.

"No wonder the neighbors thought it was a drug house, what with everyone coming and going like they were," she commented. "And I think there are more people that you haven't even included on this list who were using it, like your hotshot team."

"None of them could have beat me down here after our return to Northern Lakes," he said.

"You stopped at the outlet mall and to eat," she said, reminding him, and herself, of his alibi. "They could have driven straight through."

He sighed, and his broad shoulders drooped slightly. "I'll put them on the list. But can we follow up with everyone else here first?"

She nodded. "I will. I think it's more likely someone local. Like Jerome Whittaker or the Barry dude…"

He clenched his jaw, his expression grim.

It clearly bothered him that his house had been used as it had. That his coworkers might have taken advantage of his kind offer to cheat on their spouses.

"I believe you that you didn't know," she said.

He let out another sigh and the tension eased from his face. "I really didn't. I know relationships are hard for hotshots, with being gone so much, but I didn't realize what was going on with the local crew."

"Could one of your hotshots have been using the place for the same reason?"

He chuckled. "No." But then the amusement left his face and his topaz eyes returned to that grim expression. "But one of them was hurt by infidelity like that. We lost him earlier this year to a horrific *accident*," he said, with his emphasis on *accident* implying it really wasn't.

"I take it that it wasn't actually an accident," she surmised. "I remember your sister's report referring to a string of bad luck or sabotage befalling your hotshot team."

His jaw clenched again.

"That's what you've been reluctant to talk about?" she asked.

"My hotshot team has been through a lot over the past year," he said. "I don't want to put them through anything else, especially if this has nothing to do with them."

She sighed. "I want to clear this case quickly. So I don't want to close any avenue of investigation yet. But I will put off contacting any of them for a bit."

"Until after the Christmas party?" he asked, his eyes looking hopeful. "It's just a week away."

"I hope we close the case before then," she admitted. She wasn't sure how long she could last just pretending to be his girlfriend when she was so damn attracted to him. If she ran into him in the kitchen again in the middle of the night, she wasn't sure she would be able to resist temptation.

Hell, in broad daylight now, her skin tingled with awareness, and her pulse beat faster than normal. Maybe that was from the lack of sleep and all the caffeine she'd drunk that morning.

But…

She suspected it was just him.

She jumped up from the table then to grab another cup, not that she needed it with as jittery as she already was. Trent must have wanted a refill as well, because he got up from the table, too, and joined her in the kitchen. That small galley kitchen with not much space between the fresh white cabinets. It was enough for Heather when she was alone, and she was usually alone.

But not now...

Trent's big body crowded into the space with hers, brushing against her. They were fully dressed now; he'd done up his shirt and the button on his jeans before joining her in the kitchen. But she was still affected by his nearness. So much so that she closed her eyes and imagined how he'd looked last night and this morning, lying in the guest-room bed when she would have preferred that he spent the night in hers.

"Thank you," Trent said, his deep voice low with sincerity.

She opened her eyes and stared up into his handsome, oh-so-serious face. "For what?"

He lifted his hand and gestured around him. "For giving me a place to stay and for protection. But most especially for understanding about my hotshot team and my sister."

She smiled. "I can tell that they mean a lot to you." And she hoped like hell that it hadn't been one of his team in the house. He'd said there were a couple of women on the team, but he'd claimed they were the wrong build to match that body in the morgue.

He wasn't a coroner, though.

And she was probably remiss in not investigating the hotshot angle right now as well as his local crew. She'd focus first on the locals, and if she didn't find the perp, she'd go with him to his hotshot holiday party.

"Thank you," he said again, and he reached out and slid his fingertips along her jawline. "You are very understanding as well as..."

She sucked in a breath as his eyes dilated. "As well as

what?" she asked. He'd complimented her last night, but that had been last night...in the heat of the moment.

After their near-death experience.

This was daylight. And reality. The night before just seemed like a dream now.

"You're understanding as well as smart and beautiful..." As he trailed off, he drew in a shaky breath. Then he released it in a sigh and added, "And so damn sexy..."

In a baggy sweater and old, loose jeans? She'd purposely dressed this morning so that he wouldn't see her physical reaction to him like he had last night in that thin T-shirt.

But while he couldn't see it, she could feel it. The heat spreading through her, the tightening of her nipples, the pull deep inside her. She wanted him so damn badly.

"This is dangerous," she murmured.

"Yes," he agreed, but he stepped a little closer so that his body touched hers.

She could feel his heart beating, as hard and fast as hers. "Stupid even," she said but found herself reaching up, sliding her arms around his neck. She cupped the back of his head and pulled it down toward hers.

"Really stupid," he agreed.

She smiled, but then she brushed her mouth across his. And that fire ignited, not just inside her but between them.

He kissed her back, his mouth moving over hers. His lips were both hard and soft as he parted hers and deepened the kiss. His tongue slid inside her mouth, and she met it with hers.

Like last night, his hands gripped her hips, but instead of just hanging on, like he had last night, he lifted her until her butt settled onto the countertop. He'd probably done it so he didn't have to lean down so far since he was so tall.

She was glad he'd done it, because her legs had been

threatening to fold beneath her as desire overwhelmed her. Shook her. She couldn't remember ever feeling such heat and passion. She nipped his bottom lip lightly with her teeth.

He groaned. Then he nipped her back before sliding his lips across her cheek and down her neck.

Her pulse leaped beneath his mouth. She moaned as the desire intensified, pulling at her core. She wrapped her legs around his hips, dragging him closer. Through his jeans, she could feel the hard ridge of the evidence of his desire for her. She moaned again with the need that gripped her.

"Heather…" he murmured.

Maybe it was a question. Maybe he was asking how far he could go as his hands tugged at the bottom of her sweater. Was he thinking about lifting it?

Her breasts swelled as her heart pounded even harder with anticipation. She wanted his hands on her body.

"Heather." His voice was a rough whisper, and his body had tensed.

Then she heard the noise, too. This time it wasn't Sammy making it. He was still on the window seat in the breakfast nook but awake now. His little furry body as tense as Trent's against hers.

It wasn't footsteps, but a rattling noise as if someone was trying to open the door. Trying to get in…

Her dad had the code; he would have already unlocked it if it was him. No. This was someone else. Someone she'd not given access to her home. Someone she didn't want to have access to her home, like the person who'd set Trent's on fire and had tried to run them down.

What was he going to try now? And would Heather have time to retrieve her weapon from her bedroom before he got inside?

USUALLY AFTER A wildfire assignment, like the one the Huron Hotshot team had just been on, Ethan Sommerly would have returned to his job as a forest ranger and the seclusion of his post in the middle of the Upper Peninsula of Michigan. But since his real identity, as Jonathan Michael Canterbury IV, had been revealed, he knew there was no place he could hide. He didn't care, though. Since the man who'd wanted him dead, his own brother-in-law, was no longer a threat, Ethan didn't want to hide anymore.

And he definitely didn't want to be alone anymore. He reached across the bed then. The sheets were cool; Tammy had gotten up a while ago to open her salon. It was just downstairs. If he listened, he could probably hear the whir of the hair dryers and the faint rumble of voices. He tilted his head, but the rumble he heard was his cell phone vibrating against the tabletop next to the bed.

He groaned and reached for it. When he saw the name Brittney Townsend lighting up the screen, he groaned again. Trent had given her his number a few weeks ago, but he couldn't be mad at his best friend over that. Brittney had witnessed Tammy's abduction and called to inform him. While she'd helped save Tammy's life, she'd also been the one who'd put it in danger when she'd revealed his true identity, so he swiped to ignore her call.

Tammy was safe now. So he had no reason to talk to the reporter anymore, especially when she was probably going to ask him again to do a follow-up interview with her. While he wasn't going to hide anymore, he had no intention of doing any interviews with any reporter, but most especially not her.

Was Trent talking to her yet? He'd been so pissed at her. Maybe that was why she was calling.

He wasn't going to get in the middle of family drama;

he'd already gone through enough of his own. That drama exhausted him even more than fighting the wildfire. Or maybe how he and Tammy had celebrated his return yesterday had exhausted him. How they'd celebrated all night long...

His body hardened just thinking about it, about her. She was so amazing. He was the luckiest man alive that she'd fallen as deeply in love with him as he had with her. He grinned over the irony of that, over the man who'd once thought himself cursed with the Canterbury family's notorious bad luck now relishing his good fortune.

The steps creaked slightly under her weight, and he could hear her voice as she ascended the stairwell from her salon. "He's probably still asleep," she was saying. Was she bringing up someone with her?

Only one set of footsteps was coming down the hall toward her bedroom, though, and it was the distinctive click of Tammy's high heels. But he heard another voice now. "I think he's probably just ignoring my call."

Brittney Townsend was smart. She was also too damn persistent. Of course she had Tammy's cell number; they had become friends when she'd been up here tearing his world apart. But it had come back together now, better than it had ever been before. As Jonathan Michael Canterbury IV and even as Ethan Sommerly.

He wasn't keeping any more secrets from people he cared about, like Brittney's brother and the rest of his team. And he was happy. Begrudgingly, he had to admit he probably owed some of that to Brittney and her damn persistence.

"Thank *you* for taking my call." Brittney's voice wafted out of the speaker of Tammy's cell. She'd stepped just inside the doorway, her phone held out.

Tammy looked like a model with her streaked hair and

stylish clothes, clothes she'd bought from her best friend Courtney Beaumont's new boutique. The black leather skirt and lacy blouse had his body hardening all over again with desire for her.

Then Brittney continued. "I wouldn't have bothered him, but I'm really worried about Trent. His house burned down last night, and a body was found in it—"

"What?" Ethan exclaimed, swinging his legs over the bed as he reached for Tammy's phone. "What the hell happened?"

"I don't really know," Brittney said. "Sometime last night there was first a report of shots fired at Trent's house and then a fire started and—"

"Is he okay? Did he get out?" Ethan asked, his heart pounding hard and fast with fear. How the hell could they do what they did, battle monster wildfires, and lose their own homes to a fire?

But was his home all that Trent had lost?

"You said a body was found inside…" His voice cracked with emotion. Not Trent. He was one of the best damn firefighters Ethan had met since becoming a hotshot. Trent would have gotten out. He'd had to…

"It was a female."

"I didn't think Trent was even dating."

"I didn't think so either," Brittney said. "But one of his local crew told me that after the fire, Trent and his girlfriend nearly got run down in the firehouse parking lot."

Ethan's breath shuddered out with relief. "So he's alive."

But Brittney didn't confirm his statement.

"Isn't he?" he prodded her.

"I haven't talked to him. He left me a voice mail after the fire and sent some texts. I think he wanted to make sure that body wasn't mine."

"Of course he did," Ethan said. "He loves you."

The reporter snorted. "Sure. That's why he's torturing me with no contact."

"Or he knows he's in danger and he's protecting you," Ethan said. Maybe that was why Ethan hadn't heard from him yet either. But why, while they'd been out West, hadn't Trent mentioned he had a girlfriend? What the hell was going on?

A sniffle emanated from Tammy's cell speaker, and Brittney audibly drew in a breath. "Of course. That sounds like my big brother."

And Ethan's best friend. "I haven't heard from him," he told her.

"I thought he would call you for sure, or come up there…"

Ethan sighed. "I haven't even gotten a text from him. I don't know where he is."

"Or who he's dating? Tom, from the local firehouse, thinks Trent is with her, whoever she is."

"I don't know about her either."

"Apparently, you aren't the only one of your hotshot team keeping secrets," Brittney remarked.

Ethan already knew that because he knew who else was keeping a secret, but he suspected Rory VanDam wasn't the only one. Whoever the hell had been sabotaging the equipment was also keeping a secret. Was it one of them? And had that person gone after Trent now?

"Will you let me know if you hear from him?" Brittney asked.

Ethan held his breath for a moment, knowing that he would do whatever Trent asked of him. If Trent didn't want his sister to know that he'd been in contact…

"I'll make sure that he does," Tammy said. "And please let us know if you hear from him first."

"I doubt that will happen," Brittney replied. "I just wish I knew if he was still giving me the silent treatment or if something else happened to him."

Like maybe the person who'd tried twice to kill him had succeeded with another attempt?

Chapter Nine

"Stay here," Heather whispered at Trent.

He wished he could stay exactly where he'd been, pressed up against her warm, curvy body. But she was wriggling down from the countertop; then she slipped past him.

To investigate that noise on her own.

Someone was trying to get into the house. Someone who didn't have her access code. Someone who had no right to be there. And no reason...

But for him.

He'd brought this danger to her home. God, he shouldn't have followed her back here last night. He should have kept driving. Out of Detroit...

But where?

He hadn't wanted to return to Northern Lakes either. His team had already been through enough. They couldn't lose anyone else. And neither could he.

Despite her order for him to stay in the kitchen, he stepped out of the small space between the cabinets and stumbled forward, over the soft body of the cat.

Sammy let out a yowl, hissed and streaked past him, heading toward the basement and what he probably considered safety.

"Some bodyguard you are," Trent murmured, keeping his voice low as he listened.

Floorboards creaked. Had the intruder gotten inside? Trent hadn't heard the squeak of any door hinges. But with everything as new as it was, maybe it hadn't made any sound from that initial rattling at the front door. The noise had come farther away from them than the side door.

Trent walked past the breakfast nook and was just about to duck through the archway into the living room when a hand grabbed his arm.

"I told you to stay put," Heather said, her voice shaking in a furious whisper. "Get down just in case they have a gun."

She had a tall and wide picture window in the living room, so it would have been easy to see if someone was still out front, near that door. Trent couldn't see anything but the top of the neatly trimmed bushes of the landscaping.

Then he couldn't see anything as Heather jerked him to the floor. "Stay down," she said. She was crouching herself as she slunk toward that front door with her gun drawn, the barrel pointing down at the refinished hardwood floor.

Following the line of that barrel, Trent saw what the rattling had been. The little metal mail chute toward the bottom of her arched oak door was stuck open, a bunch of mail jammed into the slot. He chuckled. "Guess we overreacted."

But Heather didn't reholster her weapon while she peered through the front window. She shook her head. "There's someone out there."

Then he felt that creepy sensation that chilled his skin and his blood. Someone was out there, watching them. He tried to get closer, tried to look out, but Heather jerked him down again.

"You're going to get your head shot off," she warned him. "Stay out of sight." She glanced toward that mail slot again, toward the envelopes jammed in it. But there was more than that; there was something inside that bundle of envelopes. A little box.

Was it an explosive device?

Was that what had started the fire at Trent's house? Something with a detonator?

He'd just been sitting around while she'd made all those calls this morning. He should have been making some of his own to the fire department arson investigation unit. He should have found out if they'd determined the cause of that fire and how it had started.

He knew it was arson. He just didn't know if someone had set a match to a trail of gasoline or if something more sophisticated had started it. Like the bomb that had blown up his best friend Ethan's truck and nearly Ethan along with Annie, the Northern Lakes firehouse dog. Annie had saved Ethan's life that day. Trent had to make sure he saved Heather's, especially since he kept putting it in danger.

He tugged on her arm now, pulling back from the front door. "We need to get the hell out of here," he said. "There could be explosives in that box."

With the things people found nowadays on the internet, it didn't even take much to blow up a person or a home.

Heather sucked in a breath, but she didn't look too shocked. She must have considered the danger. That was probably why whoever had left it was still outside somewhere watching the house, waiting until they got close enough to the door to detonate it.

And blow them up.

"We have to go out the back," she said. "With them watching the house..."

She didn't have to spell out her concern. He understood that if the person had a gun, like she was clearly worried they did, she and Trent could get shot coming out the side door. But if they stayed inside, they might get blown up. "We need to move quickly," he warned her.

He hadn't noticed any exits but for the front and side doors. The breakfast nook had that bay window with the bench built into it. To not be seen exiting from the front, they would have to go out one of the windows.

But once they'd just about crab crawled out of the living room, Heather jerked him down the hall, past the bathroom, past the guest room to that door at the end of the hall.

Her bedroom.

He'd wished she'd invited him inside last night. Or just a short while ago. Now they might never have the chance to act on all that passion between them.

Heather rushed around the bed to jerk open blackout drapes that concealed a set of French doors to a small brick patio. "We can go out here…" She glanced around. "Where's Sammy?"

"He went downstairs," Trent said, and he started back out the door. He couldn't leave her pet in the house just in case that was a bomb. He wasn't going to let another life get lost because of him.

"He'll tear you to shreds if you try to bring him outside," she warned him as she pulled him up short and moved to pass him, clearly to get the cat herself.

She wasn't just protective of threatened firefighters but stray cats as well.

"Heather…" He knew, though, that it was no use trying to stop her. So he rushed after her, following her back through the house to the basement.

All the while, his heart pounded fast and heavy with dread that the killer might detonate whatever the hell was in that box. And if he or she did while they were in the basement, the whole damn house could cave in on top of them. "This is too dangerous," he warned her. "We need to get out before that thing goes off."

The basement was clean but unfinished. The washer and dryer, a long table and the furnace and water heater were the only things on the bare concrete floor but for the rack of shelves along one wall and Sammy's covered litter box and food bowls.

Heather headed toward the shelves. First she holstered the weapon she'd strapped over her sweater. Then she shoved aside boxes until something hissed at her. "Come on, baby. We gotta get out of here. You heard the firefighter."

Maybe that was why he hissed. The cat was smart enough to know that this was all Trent's fault.

She moved another box and tried to reach for the cat, but he slipped past her, jumping at Trent. He grabbed at the light bit of fluff and fur, clutching it close. Claws snagged his flannel shirt, so sharp and frantic he could feel them scratching through the fabric. "I got him," he said. "Now let's get the hell out of here."

He ignored the pain of those digging claws as he ran up the steps after Heather and down the hall into her bedroom. He just hoped they made it outside in time. Before the house exploded.

HEATHER'S HEART POUNDED fast and hard like Sammy's had when she'd taken him from Trent's arms and shut him inside the detached garage. Hopefully it was far enough from the house to protect him. After locking the cat into the garage, she'd reported a possible explosive device at her house.

Dispatch had reacted swiftly to the officer-in-distress call and the bomb squad and police units rolled up quickly to the street outside her house. Next to Trent's truck. They'd remained in the backyard, as far from the house as they could get, just in case that person waited outside to shoot them if they knew they'd gotten away from the device.

She thought they wouldn't have been noticed back here, but if that had been the case, wouldn't the arsonist have detonated the bomb?

Wouldn't they have already blown up the home her dad had worked so hard to make beautiful for her? Her heart ached at the thought of the destruction of his craftsmanship and what she had deemed her solitary sanctuary.

But she wasn't solitary anymore.

Trent hung close to her as they awaited news from the bomb squad. He was so close that he had to be able to hear her conversation with Bob Bernard.

"You didn't have to show up," she told the other detective. With his wrinkly suit and messy salt-and-pepper hair, he always reminded her of Columbo. "I got this under control."

The older man snorted. "Yeah, right. You let a suspect stay with you—"

"He's not a suspect. His alibi checked out. He's a victim, and he's here for his protection," she insisted.

Bob snorted again. "And my ex divorced me for bringing my work home with me..."

She could think of a hell of a lot of other reasons that Bob's wife divorced him but none for her marrying the misogynist in the first place.

"But you'll do anything to beat my clearance rate, won't you?" Bob mused.

"Yeah, and it'll take me just a few years to do it, while it took you twenty," she said with a smirk. He really was a pain in the ass.

He glanced at Trent, who was obviously listening to every word and smirked. "Whatever it takes, huh?" Bob asked.

She resisted the urge to blush. "I'm not sleeping with him." But she'd been tempted. Last night and just a short while ago. No way in hell she'd ever admit that to her snarky, sexist coworker, though.

Bob focused on Trent now. "Be careful, Miles. She only cares about her clearance rate."

"At least one of us does," she remarked, although she suspected Bob was stepping up his game now; that had to be why he'd responded to the call at her house. Or maybe he'd just wanted to see her whole world blow up. "And really, you should leave, just in case that really is a bomb stuck in my mail slot. You don't like dangerous cases anymore, Bob," she reminded him. "Just the easy ones. Maybe there's a stolen car you can find somewhere."

He glared at her. "Back in my day, we had respect for our senior detectives."

"Respect isn't something you should just expect," she said. "It's something you should earn." That was why she was working so damn hard to surpass his clearance rate.

The smirk on his face made it clear he knew she was working this hard because of him, just to be better than him. Her stomach churned a bit. That was probably over the fear that her father's hard work and her sanctuary was going to blow up.

But as she'd already suspected, if that box had actually been a bomb, the person who'd stuck it in the slot would have detonated it long ago. Like when she and Trent had been so close to it in the living room.

So she'd traumatized Sammy and called in the bomb squad for nothing, which they confirmed as two of them stepped out the side door. They'd already taken off their helmets, carrying them under their arms.

"Not a bomb," Bob said before they could.

The older one, who was probably as misogynistic as him, responded with a shake of his head and a grimace.

"What was it?" Heather asked the other one, a female bomb squad member.

"A box of matches," the woman replied. "And there was a card wrapped around it, along with some junk mail. We left it in there for the techs to process."

Heather had called Craig, too. He didn't often do field-work, but she'd wanted the best at the scene, especially if there wasn't much left of the scene to inspect.

"Thanks for coming out," Heather said to both of them.

The older man didn't even acknowledge her.

"After the arson fire at my house last night," Trent said, "it would have been stupid for us to touch that thing until we knew what it was."

"Someone blew up your house?" the woman asked, her eyes wide as she stared at his handsome face.

Was he aware of the effect he had on people with his good looks? Or was he so used to their reactions that it didn't affect him anymore?

He shrugged. "We don't know what caused the fire yet," he said. "But it went up fast and is a total loss."

The male bomb squad member turned his attention to Trent now. "You're a firefighter, aren't you?"

Trent nodded. "Yes. With Firehouse 102 on Front."

"There was also a body found in his house last night," Heather told the guy, whose face flushed a little now.

"Who was it?" the woman asked Trent.

"The body hasn't been identified yet," Heather answered for him. She knew it troubled him that someone had died in his house, maybe because of him. She wasn't so sure about that, though, not with the way his crew members had used his house and, more specifically, for what they'd used it.

"The fire was obviously set to delay the identification process and destroy whatever evidence might have been left at the scene. Whoever this is knows what he's doing." Maybe because he or she was also a firefighter. When she'd called Dispatch, she'd also requested someone make contact with Jerome Whittaker's wife.

The male bomb squad guy jerked his head in a quick nod of his own. "Yeah, it was smart to get the hell out of the house and have us check out that box."

Bob snorted, but his face was a little flushed, too, now. She wasn't the idiot he wanted everyone else, including himself, to believe she was. Or maybe he just wanted her to believe that, to doubt herself so she wouldn't be a better detective than he was. Because even though he was a dick, he was good at his job. He just didn't think a female could be as good. But he would find out soon this one could be even better.

Ignoring him, with the hope that he would leave, she focused on the bomb squad members instead. "Thanks for coming out and making sure it was safe."

Sammy would appreciate going back inside the house. She could hear him rattling the door of the garage behind her, just as the front door had rattled when someone had been shoving that stuff into the slot. She wanted to see what it was and make sure her house was secure and all the doors were closed before she brought Sammy back inside.

The older bomb squad guy started down the driveway with Bob, exchanging a few remarks too low for her to catch. The female bomb squad member stared longingly at Trent for a moment before turning to follow the two older men back to their vehicles parked in the street.

Heather headed toward the house, to the side door the bomb squad had left standing open. She rushed inside and up the few stairs into the kitchen. Footsteps pounded the steps behind her, and she glanced back over her shoulder, worried for a moment that Bob had returned to try to take over her case again. But it was Trent.

He didn't look any happier with her than Bob ever did. She wasn't sure why, but before she could question him, Craig called to her from where he stood under the arch doorway to her living room. "You will want to see this, Detective. I've already bagged it, but you can see the box of matches and the Christmas card through the clear plastic." He laid the items on the table next to Trent's forgotten mug. The coffee would have gone cold long ago, like he had. One minute he'd been so hot, pressed up against her in the kitchen, and now...

Heather walked up next to the tall, thin tech. "Thanks for coming out to process the scene for me, Craig."

"Anything for you, Detective," he said, his pale face flushing. Then he glanced at Trent, who stood behind her, peering over her shoulder at the evidence bags.

One contained a brick-sized box of kitchen matches that had been jammed in the slot and was half-crushed now. If it had been a bomb, it would have probably gone off when the perp shoved it inside the slot. The other contained a Christmas card with the same factory-printed message on one side about enjoying the holidays with the ones you loved. The other side had the hand-printed message:

Enjoy the little time you have left, Trent Miles, with your girlfriend. You'll both be going up in smoke soon.

She was glad Bob hadn't insisted on coming inside to check out the scene. Maybe, since it hadn't been a bomb, he'd lost interest. This note definitely would have piqued it again, just as it had obviously piqued Craig's curiosity.

He kept staring at first her and then Trent. "Are you Trent Miles?" he asked.

Trent nodded.

Heather waved a hand from the tech to the firefighter. "Craig, Trent. Trent, Craig." At the moment she couldn't remember the tech's last name. She knew it and used it when she asked for him but was so distracted right now, so curious about how quiet Trent was being.

He should have been relieved it wasn't a bomb. Instead, he seemed pissed off, while she was thrilled it wasn't a bomb and that the perp had made another move.

"My plan is working," she said with a flash of triumph.

"You're just acting like his girlfriend?" Craig asked. "Like undercover?"

Heat rushed through her as she thought of how close she'd actually come to going under the covers with Trent. And how badly part of her still wanted to...

But if she'd been paying attention instead of making out like a teenager on her kitchen counter, she might have caught whoever had put that box and card in her mail slot. She might have closed this case already.

She was lucky it hadn't been a bomb. Or she might not have another chance...

To catch the person.

Not to have sex with Trent. She knew even better now how dangerous that would have been. And maybe not just for their lives, but maybe for her heart as well. She couldn't get too attached to having him around.

But with the way he was looking at her, his topaz eyes dark with anger and that muscle twitching above his tightly clenched jaw, she had a feeling he might not stick around much longer.

Was he furious about the note? About the threat? After how close the person had gotten to them again, maybe he didn't trust her to protect him anymore.

Chapter Ten

He was furious...with himself. He'd been starting to think, to hope, she might care about him. What an idiot he'd been.

Clearly, his was just another case for her to close to beat that old detective's clearance rate. She was competitive and ambitious and determined to best the other detective. It wasn't personal to her. He wasn't personal to her. It was all about her professional career, about furthering it, which reminded him of how his sister had betrayed him and his friends to further her career.

Anger churned inside his stomach that was empty except for the coffee he'd had that morning. His anger was as bitter as that coffee and as sickening. Maybe there was a trace of jealousy roiling around inside him, too. That young tech was obviously besotted with her, since he just about fawned over her like a puppy begging for attention.

She gave Craig some. A smile. Her thanks for his showing up at the scene.

"You really should install some security cameras," Craig said. "If you'd even just had a doorbell cam, you would have seen the person approaching."

She nodded. "I know. I was waiting until my dad finished some more projects around here." She glanced up as a uniformed officer popped into the open door. "Did any of my neighbors have any footage you could use?"

He shook his head. "Nothing was trained on your house. There are a few vehicles that passed, but the camera angles didn't pick up enough to determine even make and model, let alone the license plates."

"Thanks," she said, smiling at both him and the tech as she shifted them back toward that open front door. "I appreciate you responding to the call."

Craig held up the evidence bags. "I'll get back to the lab and process these for prints and trace evidence. Hopefully I'll find something."

"If there's anything to find, you will do it," she said, and the man's thin chest seemed to expand with her praise.

"Shouldn't I stay, make sure that person doesn't return?" the young officer asked.

"I doubt they've ever left," Heather replied.

The officer glanced at Trent, and his hand moved toward his belt and the gun strapped to it.

"Not him," Heather said. "He was with me when that was put in the mail slot, so I don't know who did it. Yet. But I will."

The young officer leaned closer and whispered, "My money's on you, Detective Bolton."

"People are placing bets on us?" Heather asked.

"The whole department," the officer replied.

Heather grinned. "Good. I'll make sure you don't lose your money."

"Maybe I'll double my bet," the officer replied with a grin of his own.

Her grin widened. "And while you don't have to park outside, I'd appreciate you sticking around the area. And if I head out anywhere, I'll let you know."

The officer nodded and backed out the front door, pulling it closed behind him.

Trent drew in a deep breath, trying to calm himself. If he raised his voice at all, the cop would probably rush back in with his weapon drawn. He seemed as besotted as the tech was. As Trent had been until he'd realized what a fool he was being. She was just doing her job, pursuing her goal to the extent that she'd put her own life at risk just to close a case.

He didn't know which one of them was the bigger fool. Him for thinking she might actually be interested in him or her for going to such extremes just to prove her point.

"What the hell is wrong with you?" The question was shouted, but not by him. Heather whirled away from her front window and repeated it, then added, "You're acting all pissed off. Are you disappointed that box of matches wasn't a bomb? Did you want a chance to fight a fire at my house?"

"What the hell is wrong with *you*?" He hurled the question back at her as the fury brimmed over. "You put your life at risk just to win some damn contest!"

She snorted. "I put my life at risk whether there's a contest or not. Kicking Bob Bernard's sexist ass is just a perk for being the best at my job."

"That's all you care about," he said, and a heavy weight settled onto him.

"My job?" she asked, as if she needed clarification, and maybe she did.

He explained, "Being the best at your job. That's all you care about." But she had risked her life for her cat. For the stray that had shown up at her house, kind of like he had last night. But she'd invited him.

"And that's not what you want?" she asked. "Why did you sign up to be a hotshot when you're already a firefighter?

Because you wanted to be the best at what you do. Why is it okay for a man to be ambitious but not a woman?"

"I'm not saying that..." he murmured. But he couldn't say what he really meant, that it stung that all he was to her was a case to close to beat Bob Bernard's clearance rate. His pride was already wounded; if he admitted how disappointed he was that she didn't actually care about him beyond that, he would lose that damaged pride. Of course he was just a case to her; she didn't know him. And he didn't know her.

He thought he was getting to know her. She'd talked about her family. Her home. Her cat. Her life. And it had all sounded so much like his. He'd felt connected to her, like she was a kindred spirit. But she was even more focused on her career than he was on his.

"Maybe you should ask Bob Bernard what you mean," she suggested. "Because right now you sound about as sexist as he does. That it's okay for a man to focus on his career but not for a woman."

"I'm not sexist," he insisted. And he wasn't. "It's not like I think women can't do the same jobs as men."

"And just as good or better?" she interjected.

"I'm not Bob Bernard," he said. "I just don't want to be used in your competition." Like Brittney had used him and Ethan.

She stepped closer to him then, her lips curving into a slight smile. Then she reached out and ran her fingers along the row of buttons down the front of his flannel shirt. "Would you let me use you another way?"

He swallowed a groan, unwilling to utter it. To let her know how damn badly she got to him. How damn badly he wanted her. But right now, knowing that he was in over his head, he just wanted to leave. "I'm not staying here any longer," he said. "I'm getting out of here."

"Good idea," she said.

So she wasn't even going to argue with him. She definitely didn't care about him.

AFTER TRENT WENT down the hall, probably to the guest room, Heather headed outside to retrieve Sammy from the garage and bring him back into the house. She shivered, and it wasn't just because she hadn't grabbed a jacket on her way out. It was because of that sensation.

The one she'd had earlier. She was right when she'd told the uniformed officer that the person hadn't left. They were still out there somewhere, watching her. Watching them…

The plan was working. Even as mad as Trent was, he surely had to see that. This was the fastest way to find out who was after him and stop the person before he or she actually succeeded. She didn't want to catch the suspect just because of her damn clearance rate. She wanted to catch them because she cared about Trent a little more than she'd ever cared about another victim, a little more than she should.

This was getting personal to her, and not just because the person had nearly run her down and now had threatened her, too. It was personal because she didn't want Trent getting hurt.

But he was a fireman and a hotshot. He was going to get hurt. And as a detective, she would probably get hurt, too. It was just the nature of their jobs.

She rushed Sammy through the side door of her house, and he wriggled out of her arms before she could even climb the steps to the kitchen. With another hiss, he streaked down the basement stairs. Either to his litter box or maybe his food and water bowls.

Mostly he probably just wanted to get away from her because he was pissed she'd taken him out of the house he loved as much as she did. A pang struck her heart that she could have nearly lost it. But it was nothing compared to losing people, like that poor woman who'd died in Trent's house, or furry friends like Sammy.

"I love you, too," she called down the stairs after him. Then she started up the couple of steps into the kitchen, and as had happened too often since Trent had come to stay with her, she nearly collided with his chest. He had on a light jacket now, and his duffel bag dangled from his fingers.

"Where are you going?" she asked.

"I told you I was leaving."

"But I thought you just meant you needed to get out for a bit…" She wanted to as well, because if Trent's stalker tried for him again, she didn't want it to be at her house. She didn't want it or Sammy to be a casualty in this war the stalker had waged against the firefighter. A war that Heather was determined to win.

"I can't stay here," Trent said. "This was a mistake."

"Why?"

His jaw dropped down, his mouth opening a bit. "Like you don't know why…"

She groaned. "I hate answers like that, like my sisters always give me when I wonder why they're mad at me. I wouldn't be asking if I knew why."

"That box of matches could have been a bomb," he said.

She resisted the urge to shudder. "Yeah, that's why we called in the bomb squad," she reminded him. "But it wasn't."

"No. It was a threat about burning down your house."

She shrugged. "So? I've received threats before. And that one wasn't even addressed to me. It was addressed to you."

"Yes. That's why I need to leave."

"Because the plan is working?" she asked.

"How the hell is it working? Because we nearly got run down? Because we could have been blown up? We're still no closer to finding out who that woman who died in my house was or who the hell is sending me those crazy Christmas cards."

She bobbed her head in agreement. "I know. While we're waiting for the rest of your list to return the messages I left for them, we should get out for a bit."

He shook his head. "Not we. Just me. I'm getting out of here for good." He started forward, but she stood between him and the stairs leading down to the side door.

"Where are you going?" she asked, tipping her head back to stare up at him. He was close, but she wasn't budging. She wasn't letting him walk out of here alone and put himself in danger.

He stepped back, as if he couldn't stand being close to her, and his broad shoulders slumped a little.

"You have no idea," she surmised. "You know wherever else you stay, you'll be putting the people with you in danger. At the firehouse here and probably even the one in Northern Lakes, and with your family—"

"No. I can't be around them."

She still wanted to call his sister and stepmom, but with as upset as he was right now, she knew not to push. Or he would be even more determined to leave. "You can't be around anyone who doesn't carry a gun and know how to handle a threat like whoever is after you," she said. "You need to stick close to me."

"So that you get killed, too?" he asked, his voice gruff with frustration.

Sticking close to him was dangerous, but for a different reason than he was probably thinking. Heather wanted to leave because she knew if they stayed alone inside her house for the rest of this Saturday, she was going to give in to this attraction. And suspecting now, with his reaction to her career competition, that he probably was a little more sexist than he would admit, she didn't want to get any closer to him than necessary.

"I won't get killed," she said. "I'll call Officer Howard and have him stick close to us in case we need backup." She hoped she would need it, that the perp would act again. She might even have Officer Howard set up a little bit of a trap with her...

Trent narrowed those topaz eyes of his and studied her. "Where are you wanting to go?" he asked.

"You need things," she reminded him, pointing at his duffel bag. "You're going to need more than you have in that bag."

"I'm used to traveling light," he said. "I don't need much."

"Then we'll shop for me," she said. "I need some things. I have to buy a gift for the precinct toy drive, and I should probably get a tree before my sisters show up with one like they did last year. It was so damn big that it scratched the ceiling and the walls up and my dad had to patch and re-paint." He hadn't minded, though, because it had given him a reason to get out of his house.

"So you want to go Christmas shopping right now?" he asked, his forehead furrowed with confusion. "I thought..." He sighed. "That's not what you're really up to. You want this nut to try for us again."

She shrugged. "The more we can lure this perp out to do something, the more opportunities we have to catch him or her and end this." And it would be faster than waiting for

Craig to process that note and box and for him to get through all the security footage around the firehouse.

"Close this case, you mean," he said, his voice gruff with bitterness.

"Isn't that what you want, too?" she asked. "To find out who's threatening and trying to kill you? We need to catch this person before the holidays, so you can spend it with your family and friends without risking their lives."

He released a ragged sigh now. "Damn it. You're right."

Clearly that didn't make him any happier than it ever made Bob Bernard. But Trent had to know the only way he could protect the people he cared about was for her to catch whoever was threatening them. She just had to make damn sure that this person didn't manage to carry out their threats before they were caught. She wasn't worried about her clearance rate right now. She was worried about her life and Trent's.

THE BOMB SQUAD had left. The crime tech van had, too. Even the last police car had driven away. This was a great opportunity to make another move.

Another threat.

To let Trent Miles and the good detective know that their time was running out. There was no way in hell they were living until Christmas.

They'd be lucky if they lived until Sunday.

But it was fun, too, drawing it out a bit. Scaring them...

Letting them know just how close death was. But it wasn't going to come on their terms. It was coming on *his*.

He was the one in charge now. Not the detective and damn well not the hotshot firefighter. They were going to regret messing up his life...when he ended theirs.

Maybe he would wait until evening. Or maybe...

He leaned forward, peering into his side mirror that he'd been using to watch her house. Two figures emerged from the side of the house, walking down the driveway toward Trent's truck. He opened the passenger door and helped her inside like they were really boyfriend and girlfriend.

He wasn't sure if that was real. Either way, he didn't care. They both deserved to die.

While Trent walked around the front of the truck to the driver's side, the detective peered around as if looking for him. As if she knew he was there…

He was far enough away that nobody could see him. Not even them. And even if they did, they wouldn't recognize him. He was wearing a disguise. He hadn't been certain that the detective didn't have security around her house, so he'd donned a long white beard, glasses and a Santa hat and suit. Nobody was going to recognize him…until it was too late. Until they were dead…

Chapter Eleven

Trent wanted to stay angry, but he couldn't. Heather hadn't done anything wrong. She wanted to close a case and, whatever her motivation, it was her job, and she was professional. He was the one who'd wanted it to be personal.

And to him, it was. That was the other reason he couldn't stay mad. She was just too much fun. He was following her directions to a place just north of the city, to a little town square area with competing Christmas tree lots and stores full of holiday decorations.

"I want to find the lot with the saddest, straggliest Christmas trees available," she said. "I should have grabbed one last year that someone threw out after Christmas so that all the needles had fallen off and it had already dried out. That would totally disgust my sisters." She emitted an evil-sounding chuckle.

He laughed. "You're bad."

"Yup." She was totally unrepentant. "They think I am. That I can't take care of my own house."

He could have pointed out that her dad seemed to do it, but he didn't want her pissed off at him like she was with her sisters.

"They are Martha Stewart wannabes who think they are domestic goddesses. I'll show them."

"With a straggly dead tree from last year?" he asked. "Aren't you just going to prove them right?"

She snorted. "I'm showing them that I don't care."

"Seems like a lot of effort to prove that," he remarked with irony. "Kind of like your competition with Bob Bernard. You must care what he thinks or you wouldn't be working so hard to beat him."

"I'm showing him that I belong," she said. "That a woman can do a job just as well as or better than a man."

"But why do you care what he thinks?" he persisted. "For that matter, why do you care what your sisters think?"

She sighed. "I don't know. My two sisters are older than me and have always bossed me around and disapproved of me. I should be like you with your sister and not care what they think. But I haven't gotten there yet."

"I'm not there yet either," he admitted with a heavy sigh of his own. His chest ached over not talking to Brittney. "My sister was just the opposite of yours. She always looked up to me, worshipped me. I could do no wrong in her eyes."

"Your silent treatment is probably killing her, then," she said.

He groaned. "I know. Once we've brought your Charlie Brown Christmas tree back to your house, we can call her." As he'd said before, the two of them would hit it off immediately. They were both driven and ambitious and determined, no matter how much danger they were in or how many people they pissed off. Even him…

Maybe that was why Brittney's betrayal was so hard for him to get over, because she must no longer look up to and idolize him or she wouldn't have gone after his hotshot team just to further her career.

He would have to keep reminding himself that was all

he was to Heather, another case to close so she could further her career.

"We could call her now," Heather suggested.

But he shook his head. "No." He needed to focus on driving per her directions and stay aware of the vehicles on the road around him. Last night his stalker must have followed him back to her place. And he'd thought he'd been careful then. No. If he'd been careful, he wouldn't have gone back to her place.

"He's back there," she said as she glanced out the passenger's window at the mirror.

Trent tightened his hands around the steering wheel and glanced into the rearview mirror. There were a lot of vehicles behind him. "Which one?" he asked.

"I don't know," she said. "I just *know* he's back there."

Trent didn't have to ask how because he knew, too. The short hairs on the nape of his neck rose, along with goose bumps on his skin. He wore a jacket over his flannel shirt, but it was light. More for the weather out West than Michigan this time of year. But his winter clothes had burned in his house. She'd already told the young officer where they were headed, just after she'd told Trent. So he was probably back there somewhere, too, but Trent was still uneasy.

"I have my gun," she said, as if she sensed his uneasiness. She wore her puffy jacket and red scarf again, so he wouldn't have been able to tell if she hadn't told him. But he'd already suspected. While she talked about her family and joked, Heather was still very aware of the danger.

"Are you sure we should go out in public and risk someone else getting hurt like that woman…?"

"That's another reason I picked the place. It's not super congested. We'll be able to spot someone stalking us, and with the backup I already have in place, hopefully we can grab him before anyone gets hurt."

"So this isn't just about pissing off your sisters by finding some ugly tree?"

"Oh, I still want the ugliest tree I can find," she assured him.

He turned onto the street where the buildings were farther apart with fewer people walking around. The decorations that hung from streetlamps and storefronts were worn and a little sad looking, like the tree she wanted. "Maybe we can find you an ugly wreath to match," he suggested.

She clapped her hands together. "That would be perfect. They will be able to see it without even going in the house."

He easily found an open parking spot, a parallel one in front of a dated department store. He would have had to circle the block or find a parking garage with a hefty hourly rate in the more popular area of the city. "Maybe I need to shop here more often," he remarked.

"I do most of my shopping online," she said. "But when I have to get something right away, I can usually find it here." She reached for her door handle before he could open his. While he hurried to catch up with her, she came around the front of the truck before he could. And she'd unzipped her jacket, her gloved hand moving inside it, close to her weapon.

"Do you see him?" he asked. He could feel him, that cold sensation rushing over him, making him shiver.

"Him?" she asked.

He shrugged. "Her. I don't know who it is." But he wished like hell he did, and that he knew the identity of the woman who'd died. He wanted this over, but when it was over…

He would have no reason to see the detective again. No reason but the little sizzle of attraction he felt for her. Hell, it was more than a sizzle. It had threatened to become a wild-fire in her kitchen that morning, and it probably would have consumed him if they hadn't heard that noise.

"I don't see anyone out of the ordinary yet," she said as she reached for his hand, wrapping her gloved one around his.

Even through the leather, he felt a little jolt of awareness, of desire. She tugged him toward the department store. "You need a winter jacket and some gloves, or you're going to freeze when we're tree and wreath shopping."

He let her tug him into the store, mostly because they would probably be safer in it. And he would be warmer. He hadn't expected to find anything he would actually like, but the store had quite a variety of well-made clothing. He found a leather jacket, with a thick sheepskin lining, and gloves. He even picked up a couple of pairs of jeans and some long-sleeved shirts.

Heather urged him to try everything on for her, as if they were some reverse version of *Pretty Woman* with him in the role of prostitute, and then she started humming strip-per music under her breath.

He glared at her even as his lips twitched with the urge to grin, and a laugh bubbled up the back of his throat. His hotshot team treated each other like this, with often very inappropriate humor. She'd fit in well with all of them. A hell of a lot better than his sister had.

But Brittney hadn't been worried about fitting in; she was only concerned with getting the story to launch her career. Heather, if she wound up accompanying him to his hotshot holiday party, was only worried about clearing a case. She probably wouldn't appreciate how cool his team was, and how much he cared about them, despite all the trouble the team had been having. Maybe because of it. In the short time since he'd met her, he and Heather had already been through a lot. Maybe that was why he was so bothered that she didn't care more about him, like he was beginning to care about her.

"Let me pay for this stuff and we can go find your Charlie Brown Christmas tree," he said. "We might have to look in some dumpsters, though."

"I'm up for a dumpster dive if you are," she said with a challenging smile. "I actually planned a little foray into an alley."

Uncertain if she was kidding or plotting, he shook his head. "I'm not going to wind up smelling like garbage just to prove a point. But if you want to…" He shrugged. "That's up to you. You'll just have to ride in the bed of my pickup instead of the cab on the way back to your place. I guess then we don't have to worry about your sad Christmas tree blowing out. You can hang on to it."

He wasn't really worried about her dumpster diving. He was worried about her putting herself in danger just to prove to Bob Bernard that she was a better detective than he was. He didn't want her getting hurt. The thought of that had his stomach churning with dread. It was the only thing inside him now. He headed toward the cash register to pay for his new clothes. Maybe he could convince Heather to eat before tree shopping or dumpster diving, whatever she planned to do.

Hell, what she really planned to do was catch a killer. That was the whole reason they were here, to lure the killer out to try for them again. Despite the warmth of the store, Trent shivered with dread.

Because he suspected her plan was going to work.

But would they survive it?

TRENT WALKED AWAY before Heather could determine if he was joking around or if he thought she was actually serious about getting her tree out of a dumpster. Maybe he was right that she took things a little too far with her sisters. But they were so fun to mess with...

And Bob Bernard. He deserved to be slapped down for being such a sexist idiot. No. She wasn't wrong, and she hated how Trent made her doubt herself.

This was why she didn't have the time or energy for relationships, for actually caring about another person's opinion of her and her actions. Trent had said that she cared too much about what Bernard and her sisters thought, but his opinion bothered her the most right now.

It was good that this relationship was just pretend and temporary. She had to catch whoever was after him as soon as possible so that she didn't start caring any more than she already did about him.

While he stood in line at the register, she could see him in the reflection of the window that she stared out. She could keep an eye on him even while she watched the street. She could feel someone watching her. It wasn't Trent. She could hear the rumble of his deep voice as he responded to the women in line who were trying to flirt with him. He was so damn good-looking that everyone stared at him.

But who was staring at her right now?

Who was out there watching her, waiting for her to step outside?

She saw holiday shoppers. Mostly older couples who'd figured out this was a great area to shop for affordability and convenience without the chaos of the big malls and the shopping areas that were popular because they'd paid for publicity, like the ones Trent's sister promoted in her news stories. Heather had to get him to call Brittney Townsend;

she suspected the reporter was already working the case, too, trying to find out what had happened at her brother's house. Just as she'd tried to find out what had been going on with his hotshot team.

Whatever was going on with them, Trent didn't seem to want to talk about it, and he didn't want to bother them at all if he could help it.

Maybe they could help if whoever had left the pretty holiday cards with those handwritten threatening notes tried again to carry out those threats. Hopefully their shopping trip had drawn him or her out, and Officer Howard was in place for the next phase of the plan. She could have called him to confirm, but that risked scaring off the assailant, if Howard was already in place.

She peered out the window. The afternoon was slipping away, casting shadows all around. A few mothers dragged kids along behind them, away from a Santa ringing a bell. There were more than a few Santa Clauses out there, a couple on each side of the street. Maybe it was a Santa shift change. The door opened and the scent of roasted almonds with cinnamon and nutmeg drifted in on the breeze. Her stomach growled, reminding her that she hadn't eaten.

So much had happened. With Trent...

With this maniac after him, threatening both of them. Maybe it was the cool breeze that had come in through the open door, or maybe it was that stare she could feel on her, but she shivered.

"Where are you?" she whispered with frustration.

"Right here," a deep voice rumbled close to her ear.

She jumped, startled that Trent had sneaked up on her. Some bodyguard she was proving to be for him. Good thing she'd brought in Officer Howard as backup. Maybe that was who she felt watching her. But then she didn't think she would feel so cold, especially in a warm store with her heavy coat on. She'd even zipped it up a bit so that no one would see her holster or the badge she'd tucked inside, underneath her scarf.

She wanted it on in case she needed to draw her weapon, in case she had to defend herself from the person determined to hurt Trent.

She couldn't imagine why someone would, especially when he smiled and leaned closer to her, skimming his lips across her cheek. "Hey, sweetheart, thanks for helping me pick out some new things."

Heat rushed through her from the touch of his mouth, from the closeness of his body and the desire for him that leaped to life again inside her. He was just acting; she was sure of it. Did he think the person was inside the store with them?

She glanced around and noticed a couple of the women who'd been in line with him hovering near them. Their eyes were narrowed, their gazes running up and down her as if determining if she was worthy of him. Heather smiled and linked her arms around his neck. "You're very welcome, honey," she purred back at him.

"You ready to eat now?" he asked. "These nice ladies heard my stomach growling in line and gave me some recommendations for the restaurants in the area."

From the way they glared at Heather, clearly they had wanted to be the ones sharing a meal with him.

"I'm sorry we got so caught up in each other today that we forgot to eat," she said.

One of the women gasped. The other emitted a little sigh and offered Heather a faint smile, full of envy. Heather, resisting the urge to smirk and gloat, returned her smile. "Thanks for the recommendations," she said. "We are starving." Wrapping her hand around Trent's, she tugged him toward the door. Once they were on the street and out of earshot of the women, she said, "I'm supposed to be protecting you from serious threats. Not random women."

He chuckled. "I'm not above taking advantage of this situation." He glanced over his shoulder and whispered, "They're still there." Then he leaned down and brushed his mouth across Heather's.

Her pulse quickened, and her heart lurched as it began to beat frantically. Before she could kiss him back, he lifted his head. She blinked, trying to clear the passion from her gaze. She had to focus. Not on Trent but on their surroundings. She doubted the women were a threat.

But a threat was out there.

"I really am hungry," he said, and his topaz eyes glowed in the fading light.

Was he talking about food?

"Me, too," she said. She wasn't talking just about food, but she could certainly eat. "Where are these places?"

"There's an Italian restaurant on the next street," he said.

They were close because she could smell the seasonings: garlic, oregano, basil and rosemary. Her stomach growled.

"There's also a vegan—"

"Italian," she interjected. "Lasagna or pizza sounds good, or maybe both of them." She was just about salivating. "We can cut through this alley." She pointed to the one behind him, the one where Officer Howard was supposed to be waiting for them. If the assailant had followed them, certainly he wouldn't resist going after them in an alley. She hoped he resisted, though, so that they could eat.

He nodded. "And maybe we can find your Christmas tree in one of the dumpsters."

She shrugged. "I am sure I can find a straggly one on the lot."

The bag he carried bumped against her.

"Do you want to put that in the truck?"

He must have had them take off the tags because he wore the leather jacket. The gloves were shoved in one of the pockets. "No, it's fine. I can carry it."

"You just don't want to go back in case those women are waiting to pounce on you," she teased.

He shuddered. "You're right. Thanks for saving me from them."

The alley was flanked by tall buildings that cast deep shadows around them. The farther they got from the street, the darker it got. And the colder. Goose bumps lifted on Heather's skin. But she wasn't sure if that was from the cold or from the sudden sense of foreboding that struck her.

Had Officer Howard made it into the alley like they'd planned?

She jerked the zipper down on her jacket, but before she could draw her weapon, someone in a blur of red velvet and white fur jumped out of the shadows. Then there was a flash of metal as Santa Claus swung something at them.

Heather had only a second to step in front of Trent before it hit her. Hard. And Santa Claus knocked her out cold.

THE HOLIDAYS WERE HELL. Brittney hated this time of year because she got assigned the worst assignments. She spent most of her time outside waiting for snow to fall so they could get the perfect holiday shot of the big flakes floating down on her as decorations twinkled around her and she blathered on about some great sale and new gift idea and Santa sightings at the mall.

That shot would be coming up next. Right now she was

stuck inside the mall outside a chain bookstore, covering some author's holiday book signing. Had the station forgotten about her scoop? That she was the one who found the Canterbury heir? Maybe if she'd gotten him to do that follow-up interview with her...

But she'd totally forgotten to even ask that morning. She just wanted to find Trent. To talk to him. To make sure he was all right.

And find out what the hell was going on, as she'd asked in her text with the picture of his burned house.

Not for a story but because she loved him and didn't want to lose him. But she worried it was already too late. That she'd already lost her big brother.

Chapter Twelve

Everything happened so damn fast. One minute they were laughing and joking about her saving him from those women. And then she saved him again, from the blow that knocked her out. Was that all it had done? He wanted to check on her, wanted to protect her like she'd protected him.

But he didn't have a gun. He didn't have the pipe that the Santa had swung at her either. All he had was the bag that he whipped at the Santa, smacking him across his bearded face and dark glasses.

When the guy was blinded, Trent grabbed for the pipe, trying to tug it away from him. But Santa was bigger than Trent and damn strong. So strong that he managed to hold on to the pipe with one hand and swing his fist into Trent's face with the other.

The blow hit his jaw and pain radiated throughout his skull. But he dropped the bag, grabbed the pipe with both hands and jerked it from Santa's gloved grasp. The guy swung his gloved fist again, hitting Trent hard, so hard that dark spots fluttered across his vision, threatening to blind him. Threatening to knock him just as unconscious as Heather was.

Unless she wasn't just unconscious.

Fury filled him that this person had hurt her because of

him. Trent swung the pipe at Santa, striking his shoulder. A curse rang out, the beard muffling it, so Trent didn't recognize the voice. Maybe he didn't recognize it because he was about to lose consciousness. To make sure the man left, he swung the pipe again. It swished through the air so fast and hard that it hit the asphalt before he could stop it, the contact jarring his arms and hurting his shoulders.

He had to lift it, had to use it to stop Santa. To protect himself and Heather, if it wasn't already too late. He lifted it, tightened his grip and swung again.

"Hey! Stop! Police!" a voice shouted. Then footsteps pounded against the asphalt.

Trent dropped the pipe, worried that he was going to get shot, that the officer was talking to him. The young man stopped next to him, but his gun was pointed toward the other end of the alley.

"You okay, Mr. Miles?"

Trent nodded, and his head swam again for a bit. "Heather—"

"I'm fine!" she said. "Go! Go after him!" She was sitting up now, leaning against the dumpster, and her gun was in her hand.

The officer hesitated. "I'll call for—"

"Go!" she yelled, and she sounded fine. Strong.

But Trent had seen how hard she'd been struck and how hard she'd fallen. He dropped to his knees beside her. "You need an ambulance," he said, and he reached out to touch her cheek where blood trailed down from her hair.

The gun she held turned toward him. Couldn't she see him? Was she not totally aware of what was going on?

She was conscious now, but with the blow she'd taken, she could have bleeding on the brain. She could still die, and with the way she was pointing that gun at him, so could he.

HEATHER HAD NO idea how long she was out. It felt like hours but must have been just seconds because Trent had still been grappling with Santa over the pipe when she'd regained consciousness. But he'd taken a couple of fist blows to his head. She'd managed to unholster her weapon and draw it, but when she'd tried to aim it at the violent Santa Claus, she hadn't been able to focus.

With the two men fighting, she'd worried that she might shoot Trent instead. So Santa had gotten away, and she was pointing her gun at Trent. The safety was still on, but she jerked the barrel away from him and reholstered her weapon. "Sorry..." she murmured.

She'd screwed up so badly.

Again. She'd been so close to the perp, but due to being distracted over Trent, she hadn't reacted fast enough. She hadn't caught him, and once again, they both could have died. Where the hell had Officer Howard been? Where was he now?

"Are you okay?" she asked Trent, and she reached out, sliding her fingers along his jaw that was beginning to swell. He was a big guy, but the Santa Claus who had attacked them had been even bigger. And the young officer had gone after him alone. She needed to check on him, too.

"I'm fine," Trent said. "You're the one who needs an ambulance."

She needed to get up, to provide backup for her fellow officer. She grabbed at Trent's shoulders, using them to pull herself up. He rose with her, his hands on her waist, holding her steady. Probably holding her up, because her legs felt shaky and weak. Her head felt light, too, and black spots danced in front of her vision. She blinked to clear her eyes and drew in a deep breath. "I have to go after them."

Officer Howard hadn't been where she'd wanted him to

be for her plan, but she didn't want him running off after the assailant, putting himself in danger.

"You can't help him when you need help yourself," Trent pointed out.

She shook her head, and pain reverberated through her skull. The blow hadn't hit her directly, probably because it had been meant for Trent, so when she'd stepped in front of him, it had glanced off the side of her head. "I'm fine."

"You lost consciousness," he said, his deep voice gruff with emotion. "For a second—"

"Yeah, just for a second," she interjected.

"I thought you were dead," he said. "You went down so fast…"

Her hip ached a bit, and now she knew why. She'd hit the asphalt hard. Or maybe it was aching from the night before, when they'd jumped out of the way of that speeding vehicle and had hit the ground.

"You need an MRI," he said.

"I need to make sure that officer is okay," she insisted, that her botched plan hadn't gotten him hurt, too.

Trent pointed toward the end of the alley where the officer who had run after Santa had returned. "He looks fine. Better than you."

She touched her face, feeling the blood on her cheek. It was drying. Whatever wound she had probably wouldn't need stitches. But her own injuries were the least of her concerns.

"You okay?" she asked Officer Howard.

"I'm sorry," he said. "I got stuck behind some kind of parade and didn't make it here in time to hide out in the alley." He gestured toward the end of it. "The parade is still going on out there, where I grabbed some old guy on the street and scared him half to death." He shook his head with self-disgust and frustration.

"Wrong Santa?" Trent asked.

He nodded. "There were too damn many of them running around out there for that parade. I'm so sorry I got held up. I tried calling, but it wouldn't go through."

Maybe that store had some kind of cell signal blocker; some did. Or the assailant had one.

Heather groaned, not with pain but frustration. She'd been wrong that this area wouldn't be busy, that it would be a good place to be able to spot whoever was following them. But the perp was smarter than she was; he'd been ready with that damn Santa suit.

"Are you okay?" the officer asked Heather. "Do you need an ambulance?"

"Yes," Trent answered for her. "She needs to get checked for a concussion."

"No," she said. "I'm fine. I'm mad he got away." Again.

"I'm sorry I didn't get here like we planned and that I lost him," the officer said, his voice gruff with his frustration and guilt. "He got out of the alley so fast and I didn't know which direction he went in the crowd."

He would have been closer to the perp if he hadn't wasted time checking on her. *Damn it!* She couldn't curse him aloud for doing what he'd thought was right. Hell, he was doing a better job than she was.

"You didn't do anything wrong," she assured him. She was the one who'd taken a chance she shouldn't have.

"I'm really sorry, Detective Bolton, that you got hurt." He glanced at Trent. "You, too."

He wasn't nearly as sorry as she was.

To allay his guilt, she smiled at him. "It was my plan, and it was too risky." For all of them...

She'd wanted the perp to try for them again, like he had. But once again, she hadn't been ready like she should have been. While her plan was working in flushing out the perp, she was the one who wasn't following through, who wasn't catching him like she wanted. Like she *needed* to do. Instead of protecting Trent, she was putting him in danger. She never would have forgiven herself if he had died. He hadn't wanted to go along with her plan in the first place and obviously with good reason; he kept getting hurt because of it.

She glanced at Trent then, focusing on the bright bruises on his handsome face. The one on his jaw and the other near his eye were getting darker, swelling more. He needed medical attention, too.

While she didn't need an ambulance, she would make a trip to the ER. Get that MRI, make sure her head was fine. But it hadn't been all that fine even before she'd taken the blow. She kept getting distracted, missing her chances to catch Trent's stalker. If he tried again and she missed, she and Trent might both die.

THIS TIME WASN'T like the parking lot. This time he had no doubt that he'd struck them. That he'd hurt them. He'd even thought he'd killed her for a moment…until she'd come to and pointed that damn gun at him.

She could have killed him, her or that other cop who'd appeared at the end of the alley, distracting her for a second so that he could run. Fortunately, there'd been a crowd on the street, with a lot of other guys in Santa suits. So even though the uniformed cop had pursued him, he'd gotten away. This time.

But so had they.

They were both still alive. But he wasn't going to allow them to stay that way much longer. He had to end this soon. And the next time, he would make damn sure they were dead before he got away.

Chapter Thirteen

Trent wanted to be furious with Heather for putting herself in danger. But he couldn't be angry with her when she was clearly so angry with herself.

At least that was all she was. Well, that and lightly concussed. She'd agreed to go to the ER, though, maybe more for his sake than her own. She'd seemed more concerned about his couple of bruises than what could have been a serious brain injury for her.

While they were waiting for the results of her CT scan, they'd managed to finally eat. But the hospital cafeteria food settled heavily in the bottom of his stomach, along with a sense of dread.

The guy after him wasn't giving up, not until he succeeded. And he'd seen Trent with Heather too many times for her to be safe even if Trent left her house and left her alone. The would-be killer wouldn't leave her alone.

He would know that killing her would make Trent suffer just like he wanted. Trent wasn't even sure how he'd come to care about her so quickly and so much.

Her silence, as he drove toward her house from the hospital, unnerved him. She rarely had nothing to say, at least not since he'd met her. But then she had been focused on solving his case, on finding out who that woman was and who had killed her. So she'd been asking him a lot of questions then.

About his coworkers. About his friends. About his family.

He felt a pang of regret and concern. Brittney had left him more messages and texts. While Heather had been getting her test, he'd texted her back: I'm fine. Don't worry about me. Stay safe.

She'd quickly replied with a: Call me.

When he'd ignored it, she'd called him, but he'd declined accepting it. He couldn't talk to her now without making her worry more. And he couldn't allow her to come anywhere near him, not after what had nearly happened to Heather. Twice.

And that other woman, the woman who hadn't been as lucky. Who the hell was she? And how would they find out?

If only he hadn't let the killer get away...

But those blows had rocked him, threatening his consciousness like Heather had lost hers for those long moments when he'd wondered if she was alive or dead. He glanced across the console at her now, uneasy with her silence.

"Are you okay?" he asked.

"You heard the doctor. I'm fine," she said. "No concerns about swelling or bleeding."

She'd taken that blow for him, stepping in front of him when the Santa had jumped from the shadows. Her first instinct had been to protect him. But that was her job; he had to remember not to take it personally.

"You've been quiet," he remarked.

She sighed and touched her temple. "Got a bit of a headache."

"I'm sorry," he said.

"You're sorry?"

"You got hurt protecting me," he said.

"Some protector I am," she replied. "I was the one who put you in danger. This was a stupid plan. And you were right to question it and me."

"It is working," he had to admit, albeit with concern.

"It's too risky," she said.

He tensed, unsure of where she was going with this. He knew where he was going, though. He turned onto her street and proceeded down it to her house. His spot was still open at the curb, and he pulled into it and reached to shut off the ignition.

But Heather gripped his hand in hers. "Don't," she said. "You're safer if you go stay at a hotel with security, and I'll send the patrol unit that followed us from the hospital with you for protection."

"And who will protect you?" he asked. "You're in just as much, if not more, danger than I am because of how damn well your plan worked."

"I'll have another officer come back here," she said. "They can take your spot at the curb."

"You have a concussion," he reminded her.

She tightened her grasp on his hand and sharply asked, "So you don't think I know what I'm talking about right now?"

"You sure don't sound like yourself," he said. "And what I meant about the concussion was that you need someone to check on you—"

"The doctor said that wasn't a big concern," she interjected.

"Not a *big* concern," he said, repeating her phrasing. "But there could still be complications." The physician had obviously doubted it, though, or he would have tried to keep her for observation.

"I'm fine," she said.

"Really?" he questioned her. "You're giving up on closing this case? You're going to let Bob Bernard's record stand?"

She released a low growl of either anger or frustration. "I'm not giving up," she said. "I will find out who that woman was and who the hell was wearing the Santa suit in the alley."

"Do you think they could be unrelated?" he asked. "Maybe Santa just wanted to mug us?"

"He didn't try to grab my purse. Did he take your wallet?" she asked, one of her dark blond brows arched above her eyes that glowed in the light from the dashboard.

"There wasn't time," he reminded her. "It all happened so fast."

"Too damn fast," she agreed. "But I still should have been ready for it."

"You stepped in front of me," he reminded her. "You took the blow that was meant for me."

"But I let him get away..." Her voice cracked with her frustration.

"Because you were knocked out," he said.

She released his hand then and leaned back against the passenger's door. "Wow..."

"What?"

"I figured you'd be furious with me," she said. "That you'd be acting like the reason I got hurt was because I'm female and that my plan was flaky, like Bob Bernard will say once he hears about this."

"I told you I'm not sexist," he reminded her. One reason he'd been upset about her competition with the older detective was because she'd put herself in danger for it by trying to flush out the killer. The other was that he'd realized he wanted her to care more about him than that competition. "Michaela and Hank would kick my ass if I was."

"Michaela and Hank?" she asked, her brow furrowing beneath her wispy bangs. Then she flinched as if the movement had aggravated the head she'd already said was aching.

"Michaela and Hank, short for Henrietta, are on my hotshot team, and they're badasses. Like you."

"Some badass," she murmured. "I got knocked out cold."

"If you hadn't stepped in front of me, *I* would have been knocked out cold," he said. Or, with the angle at which Santa had swung that pipe, he might have been in worse shape than she was. "And you regained consciousness fast. You're probably more the reason that Santa ran away than the officer catching up to us was."

She released a shaky sigh and the tension eased from her body. He shut off the engine, and she didn't try to stop him, not even when he got out of the truck. She just got out, too, and walked up to the side door with him. Her hand was inside her jacket, probably on her gun. So she was worried.

Like he was...

Their stalker was still out there. No doubt waiting for the chance to try for them again.

HEATHER HAD FULLY intended to call off the plan and force Trent to leave. Ever since the close call in the alley, she'd been kicking herself that she hadn't listened to him earlier. That she hadn't let him leave when he'd wanted to.

But she couldn't know if he would be any safer away from her than he was with her. In fact, she suspected she would try harder than anyone else to keep him safe because he mattered to her. Too much, which was probably why she couldn't focus when she was around him, like she needed to.

She unlocked the side door and stepped inside first, her gun drawn, just in case the stalker had beaten them back and managed to get in and was waiting. But when she flipped on the lights, the only being she found waiting for them was Sammy, sitting on the counter. He wouldn't have been upstairs if there was someone else inside the house.

"You might need to replace your security system with a real one," Trent suggested, pointing at the cat.

"I won't replace him," she said. She reached out for him, and the black cat rubbed against her hand, purring. He'd forgiven her for his trip to the garage earlier. Or he'd forgotten.

She couldn't forget everything that had happened, how many close calls they had had. And if something had happened...

She released a shaky breath of relief that it hadn't. That, except for a few additional bumps and bruises, they were fine. Medically.

Emotionally, she was a mess. Heather couldn't remember ever feeling this unsure of herself.

Big hands gripped her shoulders and turned her around. "Are you okay?" he asked.

She shook her head.

"Is it the concussion?" he asked with concern, cupping her cheek in his palm. "Do you need some ibuprofen?"

"It's not my head," she said. She was worried it might be her heart if she wasn't careful. She certainly hadn't been careful since she'd met firefighter Trent Miles. "I'm fine. I just..."

"What?" he asked.

"I just thought you'd be mad at me," she said. "Mad about what happened..."

"I'm mad at the person who came after us, not you," he said. "And you're already kicking yourself enough. I'm not going to kick you, too. Not when I'd much rather kiss you."

She wanted that, too, so damn badly. When she'd stepped out of Trent's truck, she'd seen the patrol car pulling up to a curb behind them, in front of the neighbor's house. They had protection now.

They were safe from the stalker.

She just wasn't sure if they were safe from each other. "This was just supposed to be a pretend relationship."

"Can't we pretend it's real just for one night?" he asked. "Because if I'd lost you today..." His voice, gruff with emotion, trailed off, as if he couldn't even say aloud what he was thinking.

What she'd been thinking...

They could have died a few times over the past couple of days. Life was short. So maybe it made sense to make the most of it when you could. She reached out and caught his hand in hers and tugged him until they reached her bedroom.

He stopped just inside the door, pulling his hand from hers. "Are you sure?" he asked.

She turned to study him in the soft light from the chandelier that hung over her bed. Even with the bruises and the swelling on his face, he was so damn handsome. And the attraction between them...

It was more intense than anything she'd felt before. She needed to find out what it would be like to be with him in every way.

"Yes," she replied.

"But you're hurt. Your head..."

"I'm fine," she said. Maybe the blow had knocked some sense into her. She'd been so damn worried about being professional, about closing her case, that she'd wanted to resist temptation. If something had happened to them, she would never know what might have been. How much pleasure she might have experienced.

"I am very sure." She unzipped her jacket and tossed it

onto the clawed-up reading chair. Her holster and weapon she put in the drawer beside the bed, within reach, in case she needed it.

She hoped like hell she wouldn't need it. She didn't want any alarm going off or a noise at the door to stop them this time. She pulled her sweater up and over her head, then tossed it onto the chair, too.

Trent's breath audibly caught. He still stood inside the door, as if frozen or unsure. But his eyes, those seriously beautiful topaz eyes, stared intently at her.

She glanced down at the red lace bra she wore and smiled. With the way she dressed on the outside, he probably hadn't expected it. She unsnapped her jeans and dropped them, revealing the red lace panties that matched the bra.

And he grunted like she'd punched him, like Santa had. "You okay?" she asked with a smile.

He shook his head. "No. I'm in pain."

She stepped out of her ankle boots and jeans and tugged off her socks before walking over to him. "Do you need to go back to the hospital?" she asked as she trailed a fingertip down the row of buttons on his flannel shirt.

His leather jacket was unzipped. He shrugged it off now. Then he grabbed the sides of his shirt and pulled it open, sending buttons pinging across the hardwood floor. "I am suddenly very hot," he said.

She touched his bare chest, trailing her fingertips down the rippling muscles of his stomach. She tugged at the button on his jeans, then pulled down the zipper of his fly that strained with his erection.

He sighed as she released him. But when she pushed down his boxers to stroke him, he wrapped his long fingers around her wrist. "We'll be done quickly if you touch me," he warned her. "It's been a while."

Skeptical, she arched a brow. "Really? With the way women throw themselves at you?"

"I've been busy," he said with a sigh.

"Me, too," she said. The last time had been so damn disappointing she decided not to date for a while. But she didn't think there was any way Trent was going to disappoint her.

"So you've let this…" He ran his fingers along the top of the demi cup of her lace bra. "…go to waste?"

She shook her head. "I wear this for me." With as tough as her job was, she liked a reminder of her femininity.

He rubbed his finger along the top of the cup again but touched her skin as much as the bra. Her nipple hardened against the red lace as desire gripped her. Through the bra, he touched her nipple, rubbing his thumb back and forth across it.

She arched her neck and moaned.

He leaned down, sliding his lips along her throat, as he lifted his other hand. He cupped both breasts in his palms and teased the nipples through the lace.

Her legs shook a little as her core began to throb. He was going to make her come with just that touch. A gasp slipped through her lips at the first little jolt of pleasure.

He groaned. "You are so responsive." One of his hands slipped down her body, over her stomach to ease inside her panties. He found her heat, her wetness, as he dipped a finger inside her.

"Oh…" She needed him so badly. She clutched at him, pulling his hips against her, and he stumbled forward, onto her. She fell back onto the bed. They were a tangle of arms and legs and passion. She reached up, finding his mouth with hers. She kissed him deeply, sliding her tongue through his lips, stroking it over his.

He pushed her panties down and kept stroking her with

his fingers, his thumb against the most sensitive part of her body. Then he moved his head down to her breasts, nudging one cup down. He closed his lips over her nipple and gently tugged.

And she came apart, an orgasm gripping her, making her quiver and moan. But still, it wasn't enough. "I want you inside me," she said and found him through his boxers, stroking him.

But he pulled back again and stood up, disappearing for a moment as she lay limply on the bed, staring up at the chandelier. The orgasm had been good but she needed more.

Then he was back, dropping a condom packet next to her head. But he left it there as he moved down her body. He unclasped the bra and pulled it off her, then removed her panties.

He kissed her everywhere. Her lips. Her collarbone. The curve of her shoulder. The side of her breast. Her stomach. Then his lips moved over her core, his tongue flicking and teasing before slipping inside her. And he made love to her with his mouth.

She came fast and furiously, gripping the sheets, trying to hang on as the intensity of another orgasm threatened to overwhelm her again.

Then he grabbed the packet, his hand shaking, tore it open and sheathed himself. Finally he joined their bodies, his erection easing inside her.

He was so damn big that he stretched and filled her. She arched and moved her hips, taking him as deep as she could. Then she locked her arms and legs around him, meeting his thrusts. The tension built inside her again. The friction of his chest against her breasts, of his body driving deep into hers, drove her wild. And she came again, screaming his name.

Then his body tensed, and a guttural sound emerged

from him as he shuddered and joined her in the madness. Or maybe it was the sanity. Because if something had happened to either of them before this, she would have missed out on the most intense pleasure she'd ever felt.

But she couldn't help but worry that, with their lives under threat, it might be followed by the most intense pain.

I'm fine. Don't worry about me. Stay safe.

If he'd sent the text to reassure Brittney, it hadn't worked. She was even more concerned. Something was definitely going on with her big brother, and he didn't want her involved. She'd thought that it was because he hadn't forgiven her for exposing his best friend's big secret. But now she suspected he was protecting her.

Shots had been fired at his house, the body, the fire and then nearly getting run down in the firehouse parking lot.

Someone was after Trent. Maybe he thought anyone close to him was in danger, too. Or maybe she just wanted to believe that so she would stop feeling so guilty about betraying him.

She'd lost his trust. No wonder he didn't want to talk to her. But Trent, being Trent, was protective, so he still cared enough to want to make sure that she stayed safe.

She was more concerned about him and this new girlfriend of his. They were the ones in danger. From whom and why?

Chapter Fourteen

Pain pulled Trent from his sleep, making him groan and grimace. He opened his eyes, struggling to wake up fully, and stared up into that little furry face. Once again he'd awakened with Sammy on his chest, kneading him with those tiny, sharp-clawed paws. Was that who had slept with him last night?

Had he just dreamed what had happened between him and Heather? The mind-blowing sex?

Sammy jumped off him, and now Trent could see the ceiling, the antique chandelier dangling over him. He was in Heather's room, not the guest room. He hadn't dreamed what had happened. And then happened again sometime during the night.

And maybe again this morning.

Or had he dreamed that time?

His body got hard thinking about how damn good she felt. How hot and wet and tight. How her muscles gripped him, stroking him, and her lips and hands…

He groaned with desire, with need, for her now. But when he reached out, he found only tangled sheets. He turned his head to find her side of the bed empty, just a dent in the pillow from where her head had been when it hadn't been on his chest.

The sheets were cold. How long had she been gone?

And where had she gone?

Concern gripped him nearly as much as the desire. Had something happened? Had the stalker come back and managed to get inside this time?

Wouldn't he have heard something?

But with everything they'd been through, and all they'd done to each other last night, he'd been so exhausted that he probably wouldn't have heard a gunshot.

"Heather?" he called out softly.

Something skittered across the hardwood floor near him. He jumped up and stepped on something hard. Swallowing the curse clawing up the back of his throat, he lifted his foot to find one of the buttons from his shirt stuck to it. Sammy chased another one across the floor, and Trent smiled. Then he noticed the chair held only his clothes.

Heather's were gone. Even her puffy coat. And when he opened the top drawer of the bedside table, he didn't find her weapon and holster. She'd gone somewhere and taken her gun with her. Panic squeezed his chest, making it hard to breathe.

What the hell had he slept through?

WHAT THE HELL had she done?

Heather had been awake for a while but felt like she was still in a dream. Was Trent Miles really naked in her bed? Had they done what she thought, what her slightly aching body led her to believe they had?

Had the best sex of her life? And not just once...

The man had satisfied her over and over again. He was like a damn machine. If those women from the checkout line at the department store only knew...

Or maybe they did. Maybe it had been one of them who'd

donned the Santa suit and attacked her. Knowing now what she knew so intimately about Trent, Heather couldn't really blame them. But from the size of her attacker, she didn't believe it had been either of them, so she'd checked police reports in the area for any Santa Claus muggings. She'd also checked with the uniformed officer parked outside to see if she had noticed anyone hanging around the area.

Anyone big and too damn focused on her house. Because she could feel him out there, especially when she stood at the window of that patrol car. Despite her puffy jacket, she shivered with a sudden chill.

He was out there. Watching.

Waiting for her to be stupid enough to give him another chance to kill her and Trent. She was being vigilant now, her holster strapped on, her gaze swiveling around. After she spoke to the officer, who hadn't noticed anyone, she walked back to the house.

The guy was big, so he wasn't invisible. But like yesterday on the street, he had done a damn good job of blending in with his surroundings by wearing the Santa suit. It had also hidden his face so well that she had no idea what he looked like beneath that big white beard and those dark glasses. Had that been so that nobody would describe him if he got caught? Or so that nobody would recognize him?

Was he one of Trent's coworkers? Someone he might have considered a friend? Or was he just some random stalker who had seen articles about Trent and gotten obsessed? But how would he have known the code to Trent's lock? And who was that woman? Not Jerome Whittaker's wife. The young officer at the curb had followed up on that and had worked on the list as well, but of the few additional firefighters Officer Morgan had talked to, none had offered any hints about the dead woman's identity. Maybe if they discovered who she was, they could figure out who *he* was.

He had to be someone close to Trent. Someone who knew him well. Unfortunately, he also knew what he was doing. Like that Santa disguise. Somehow he'd blended into her neighborhood yesterday. Maybe he'd worn a mail uniform, which was why no one had thought it strange that he'd messed with her mail slot.

Heather stood next to Trent's truck and studied the area. It was early morning on a Sunday, so not many people were out and about yet. A woman jogged past. An older couple backed their vehicle out of their driveway, probably heading to church.

So where was he?

Was he inside one of the couple of houses on the street that were empty because their owners had gone away for the holiday? Had he broken in to use the cover of their home to spy on her and Trent?

To watch them and wait for her to give him another opportunity to attack? She wasn't going to give him the satisfaction, not unless she was damn sure she had enough backup that he would not get away again.

Not noticing anything out of the ordinary, she turned and headed back to the house. She unlocked and opened the side door, and as she did, she heard boards creaking with a weight much heavier than Sammy's.

It could have been Trent, but with as deeply as he'd been sleeping when she'd crawled out of bed, she hadn't thought he would be awake yet. Had someone sneaked inside? Maybe through a basement window or the French doors on the primary bedroom?

She shouldn't have left Trent alone, sleeping and vulnerable. But she'd needed to get out of that bed so she wouldn't reach for him again, so she wouldn't wake him up to make love like she had in the night. And earlier that morning...

After everything he'd been through, he'd deserved his rest. And she'd gotten freaked out by how much she'd needed him. She'd never felt that way before, had never wanted anyone that badly, and had certainly never felt so damn much pleasure.

As much as Trent had needed his rest, he also needed protection. If something had happened to him because she'd left...

She drew her weapon and pointed it ahead of her as she slowly ascended those couple of steps to the kitchen.

"Don't shoot," a deep voice murmured, and she turned to find Trent standing in front of her, his hands raised above his head.

"Sorry," she said as she slid her gun back into the holster. "I heard the creaking floorboards, but I thought you would still be sleeping, and I..."

"Am a little jumpy?" he finished for her with a dark brow arched in question.

"Yes, I am," she freely admitted. "Aren't you, after last night?"

"Are you referring to what happened in the alley or what came after?"

"What came after?" she asked, making her eyes wide as if she had no clue, but she couldn't suppress the smile curving her lips.

He chuckled.

"The trip to the ER? That questionable cafeteria dinner?" she asked, feigning confusion.

"Are you criticizing our first date?" he asked.

"If that's your idea of a date, no wonder you haven't been in a relationship for a while," she teased.

He grinned and stepped a little closer to her, staring down at her with desire and mischief glinting in those light brown eyes. "So what's your idea of a good first date?" he asked.

"Oh, fighting off a deranged Santa in an alley probably wouldn't be high on my list, nor would having a bomb squad make sure my house isn't going to blow up."

He sighed. "You're the one who proposed this relationship."

"Pretend relationship," she reminded him and herself. That was all it was supposed to have been.

"That didn't feel very *pretend* last night," he said, and he stepped a little closer, his body brushing up against hers.

A jolt of desire, from the heat of contact, had her stumbling backward. His big hands grasped her upper arms, steadying her. She glanced over her shoulder, realizing she might have tumbled down those couple of stairs to the side door if he hadn't caught her.

"Careful," he said, and he stepped back, bringing her with him, farther into her small kitchen. "After last night, you shouldn't be so jumpy."

Despite acting like she didn't know, she was well aware of what he was talking about, of how many times he'd released the tension in her body, making her feel boneless and completely satiated. Until the desire gripped her again, like now.

That probably made her the most nervous, that no matter how many times they'd made love, she couldn't get enough of him. And she might start hoping this relationship wasn't just pretend.

"Well, I've had a lot of coffee already," she said.

"So you were doing what?" he asked. "Running around the block? Is that where you were when I woke up?"

She shook her head. "No. I was bringing coffee to the officer watching the house."

"As if he wasn't already in love with you," Trent said.

She laughed. "Officer Ashley Morgan? She appreciated the coffee, but I think she's married."

Trent's long body tensed and he dropped his hands from her arms. "Like the woman found dead in my house."

"Yes." A pang of guilt struck her. While she'd been trying to flush out a killer, that woman remained in the morgue. Unclaimed. "We need to find out who she was. I had the missing persons unit forward their list to the coroner, but according to him, none of the missing women matched the size and age of the body of the unidentified woman."

"So no one's reported her missing?"

She shook her head.

"So how do we find out who she was?" Trent asked, and his broad shoulders slumped as if the burden was his.

"I think one of your coworkers knows who she is," she said. "Those guys were using your house for more than sleep." Officer Morgan had just confirmed that Mrs. Whittaker suspected the same thing.

He grimaced. "I really didn't know they were using it that way. I've been gone so much with my hotshot team."

"That's why they used it that way," she said. "For privacy." But just for an affair or for a murder as well? And was that murderer worried Trent might know who he was? Was that the reason for the attempts on his life and hers?

"All of your local crew hasn't called me back yet," she said. She was most interested in the one who'd left the firehouse right before they'd nearly been run down. Whittaker, on the other hand, had an alibi: he'd been with his suspicious wife. "I really need to talk to Barry Coats."

Trent nodded. "I'll check and see if he's scheduled to be on shift right now."

"Yes, I need to talk to him in person," she said. "If he's not on shift, I'll go to his house."

"You? What about us?" he asked. "Aren't you going to stick close to me, for my protection?"

They couldn't have gotten any closer last night. While she'd experienced more pleasure than ever before, it wasn't safe—for either of them—to repeat that.

"Maybe we're safer apart," she said.

"Then you need more police officers to follow us around if we're going different places," he pointed out.

He wasn't wrong. She couldn't leave him unprotected, or herself, any more than she already had.

She sighed.

"And Barry is more likely to tell me the truth than he is you."

She wasn't so sure about that. "I'm a pretty good interviewer," she said. "I can usually manage to get the truth out of a suspect."

"Do you beat them with a rubber hose or use your charm?" he asked with a wicked grin.

Even with the bruises from the fight in the alley, he was so damn handsome. So irresistible.

"Depends on the suspect," she said. "Some of them might like the rubber hose."

He chuckled, a low, naughty chuckle full of amusement and seduction.

Her pulse quickened. She wanted him so badly. But the more they did what they had last night, the more likely she was going to want it to continue.

Forever.

With the danger they were in, not just now, but always with their careers, there was no way they could have forever.

THAT COP CAR hadn't just driven through the neighborhood a few times like it had the day before. No. It was parked right outside her house. Sometimes another patrol car drove up, stopped and both drivers rolled down their windows to talk. They also kept glancing around the area, like Bolton had earlier when she'd brought that officer a cup of coffee.

They looked right past him, not even noticing him inside the vehicle with the tinted rear windows. They'd looked at it a couple of times, but it was clear that no one sat in the driver's seat. He was in the back, staring out the windows from under the pile of blankets that had kept him warm and concealed.

But Bolton must have sensed him there or was smart enough to know he wasn't going to give up. She'd had her hand on her holster. She was scared. Trent Miles, big brave firefighter, must have been scared, too, since he hadn't left his detective girlfriend's side since the fire at his house. Even when they'd gone shopping, they'd stuck close together, so close that she'd taken the blow meant for him. Maybe it was good that she had, or she might have shot him right away. And he wouldn't have the chance to kill Trent. She was going to die, too. They both had to. Soon.

They wouldn't be able to stay inside that house forever. They had jobs; they had to work. To fight fires and investigate crimes, they had to leave that house. And when they did, they would die.

Chapter Fifteen

Trent didn't want to go to the firehouse. And it wasn't just because he didn't want to interrogate members of his local fire crew. He wanted to stay with Heather, in her bed, like last night, enjoying each other and forgetting about everything. About the fact that they were in danger, since someone else had already died.

He felt guilty over his selfishness. But Heather could make him forget about the guilt, too, and leave him with nothing but pleasure. Intense, mind-blowing pleasure. Just as he pushed away from the counter to reach for her, her cell rang.

She pulled it from the pocket of her puffy coat and stared at the screen. "Officer Ashley…" She swiped Accept and put the phone on speaker. "Detective Bolton."

"Detective, there's someone approaching your house right now. Do you want me to stop him?"

Holding the cell in one hand, Heather drew her weapon with the other. Then she rushed past Trent and into her living room, where that big front window looked out over the street and the man walking up to the house, dragging a Christmas tree behind him. The guy wore a Santa hat over his gray hair and a burnt-orange Carhartt jacket, not a full suit like the man from the alley.

"What the hell…" she murmured. "Thanks, Officer, for being vigilant. But I know this Santa Claus. He's my dad."

Trent gasped at the quick jab of panic in his heart. Then he rushed toward the front door, pulling it open to help the older man with the tree.

"What are you doing, Dad?" Heather asked as she followed Trent out. "I thought Mom had projects she wanted you to do for her at home."

The older man stopped and stared at Trent. Ignoring the stare, Trent picked up the tree and maneuvered it carefully through the front door. The scent of pine enveloped him as sap stuck to his hands. He wasn't a fan of real trees, and not just because of the mess, but because people so often let them dry out. And then fires started.

"I…" Her dad glanced back at her. "Your sisters were threatening to get you a tree again this year, and I didn't want them messing up the house like they did last time."

"You've done a beautiful job with all your renovations," Trent praised him.

"Uh…thanks…" Mr. Bolton glanced back at his daughter and arched a brow much the same way she did.

"Dad, this is Trent Miles. He's a…" She glanced at Trent now, her brow furrowing. Then she continued, "…friend. Trent, this is my dad, Charlie Bolton."

"Nice to meet you, sir," he said, holding the tree steady with one hand while extending his other to her father.

"You, too," Charlie said. "You're pretty strong. I could have used your help around here for some of these projects. Wonder why I haven't met you before…"

Trent smiled. Heather obviously took after her dad with the suspicious nature and blunt questions. He liked him.

"Trent is a hotshot firefighter," Heather said.

Charlie chuckled. "She razzes you like that?"

Heather laughed. "No, Dad. A hotshot firefighter is the kind that travels around, putting out wildfires. He's gone a lot."

Trent nodded. "Yes, sir, I just recently returned to the city after a call out West."

"That big one on the news? I saw that," Charlie said. "Some guys died in that."

Trent's shoulders sagged a bit. "Yes, before our team got there." He hadn't lost another friend, fortunately, but he mourned all losses of life, especially that woman who'd died in his house and he didn't even know who she was.

"Dangerous job," Charlie observed with a glance at his daughter, as if he was worried about her getting too attached to him.

Or maybe he was just worried about her, too, because of her dangerous job. One that Trent's case had made even more dangerous.

"Dad, I appreciate you dropping off the tree, but I really don't want to get you in trouble with Mom. Shouldn't you get back to her projects?"

Charlie narrowed his eyes, the same deep green as his daughter's, and stared at her. "Trying to get rid of your old man?"

"Trent and I were just on our way out," she said.

Trent had wanted to delay that, and not just because he didn't want to interrogate his coworkers. He'd wanted to be with her again, to find out what sexy underwear she was wearing today, and experience all that passion and heat. That heat spread to his face as her dad turned his narrow-eyed stare on him, almost as if he knew what had been on

Trent's mind before he'd arrived. Although he hadn't caught them, Trent felt like he had.

"You drink my beer?" her dad asked.

"Dad!" Heather exclaimed. "It's eight o'clock in the morning."

"I didn't touch your beer," Trent assured him. He got drunk enough off the desire he felt for the man's daughter; he sure didn't need any alcohol, especially with some maniac trying to hurt them.

Charlie nodded. "It's fine if you do," he said. "Just make sure you leave me at least one. I'm going to need it with all the work this one's mother—" he pointed at Heather "—has me doing on our place right now."

"Then you should get back to it before she starts looking for you," Heather warned him.

"I'll put this tree in a stand, but you'll have to decorate it," Charlie said.

"I'll help you," Trent said. And he wasn't just putting off the trip to the firehouse now. He was making sure her home wouldn't accidentally burn down. It was up to the police officers watching it to make sure it didn't intentionally burn down like his house had.

Trent rushed around, collected the stand from the basement and grabbed a pitcher of water from the kitchen. When he neared the living room, he overheard father and daughter talking.

"Don't tell Mom about Trent," she said. "She'll tell Hailey and Hannah, and it'll be a whole thing…"

Charlie chuckled. "You don't want your mom and sisters to have a heads-up before they meet him at Christmas? You want to surprise them?"

"I don't want them to meet him," she said.

"So he's not invited to Christmas?" her father asked.

"Dad... I just... We're just friends."

But after what he'd heard, Trent realized he wasn't really even that to her. Despite last night, she had no intention of taking this relationship from pretend to real. She just wanted to clear another case and prove to Bob Bernard that a woman could be a better detective than a man.

Ignoring the hard jab to his heart, Trent forced a smile and joined them in the living room. Maybe her father had realized he'd overheard them, because he gave Trent a look of pity.

Trent forced a smile back at him. He didn't deserve the guy's pity. Heather hadn't done anything wrong; he was the one who hadn't stuck to the plan, who'd started to genuinely care about her. He realized that even if her plan worked and the stalker was caught before he managed to carry out his threats, Trent was still going to get hurt before all this was over.

"How do we play this?" Trent asked as they sat in his truck outside the firehouse. It was the first thing he'd said to her since leaving her place.

She smiled. "This feels like déjà vu. You asked me that the last time we sat in this parking lot."

"Yeah, then we got out and nearly got run over," he said with a slight shudder.

"Right after Barry Coats left the building," she reminded him.

He sighed. "I checked the schedule. He's here now. But I don't understand why he would try to run us down. Or send me those stupid Christmas card threats. We've always gotten along."

"Because you let him use your house," she said. "Maybe he wants to make sure you don't figure out who died in that fire and link it to him. Maybe that's all this is about, covering up a different crime."

Trent shook his head. "I don't know. It feels more personal than that. Those notes feel more personal, like someone really wants me to suffer."

"Could one of your coworkers have it out for you?" she asked. "Could they be harboring a grudge over something?"

He shook his head again. "I don't know. Some guys might think, because the captain and my dad were good friends, that I get preferential treatment. But trying to kill me because of perceived nepotism seems a little extreme."

She shrugged. "You never know what kind of grudges someone else might be holding or secrets they might be keeping," she said.

"No, you don't," he agreed.

"Are you talking about your hotshot friend? The Canterbury heir?"

Or was there something else going on with his hotshot team? In her big news report that had exposed his friend for lying about his identity, Brittney Townsend had also hinted about other accidents and danger that had threatened the lives of everyone on his team.

"Ethan isn't the only person keeping secrets," he said. "I had no idea why my local coworkers were really crashing at my place when I was gone."

While Whittaker had pretty much admitted it, Barry Coats had ignored her messages and not returned any of her calls. She needed answers from him. She just wasn't sure if the best way to get them was as a no-nonsense detective or Trent's pretend girlfriend.

"As for how we play this," she said, "I think we carry on as we did the other night, when we nearly got run over. We were telling the truth about who I am but..."

"Lying about what you are to me," Trent finished for her.

But would they be lying now? After what had happened last night? Or was it all still just *pretend* to Trent?

She wished it was with her. But when he leaned across his truck console and brushed his mouth across hers, her pulse leaped, and her body heated up with the desire he could inspire in her just from breathing.

She wanted more than a kiss, but remembering where they were, she pulled back and touched his swollen and bruised jaw. "Someone watching?" she asked.

She'd felt like there was, ever since leaving her house. Whoever had been there had probably followed them here. Or maybe they were already here. Maybe they'd reported for their shift this morning like Trent had said Barry Coats had after a couple of days off.

"Remember how the lieutenant said he saw us from the kitchen window," he replied. "We don't know who might be up there watching."

Or out there watching?

"Especially since it's lunchtime now," he added.

The truck cab smelled like that Italian restaurant they'd intended to eat at yesterday. Like garlic, oregano and basil, with the added scents of onions and green peppers and sausage. They'd picked up a bunch of pizzas for lunch as an excuse for stopping by the firehouse. Trent had bought them as a thank-you for fighting the fire at his house.

Her stomach growled. But she wasn't sure if she was hungry for the food or for him. If her dad hadn't shown up when he had, she might have been tempted to see if last night had been as incredible as she remembered.

Maybe it was good her dad had shown up, so she didn't get used to Trent Miles sleeping in her bed. Once they figured out who'd died in his house and stopped whoever was after them, their paths would probably never cross again unless her house caught fire. With all the water he'd poured into the tree stand, he was obviously trying to ensure that didn't happen. But what if that other Santa, the one who'd attacked them in the alley, made good on his threat with the box of matches?

"If you're hungry, you're going to want to grab a piece before the guys get a hold of these boxes," Trent warned her.

The piece she wanted to grab wasn't from a pizza, but she just sucked in a breath, smiled and nodded. "Let's do this..." She made certain to get out of the truck first and scan the parking lot.

At least the daylight made it easy to see that the other vehicles in the lot were empty. Nobody was sitting in them waiting to run them down.

Was that person already inside the building?

She carried a few of the boxes while Trent carried the rest. Helping him with the delivery was her reason for dropping in on them. Maybe if they thought she was there for a personal reason rather than professional, they would talk more freely around her.

But she kind of doubted it, especially when all conversation ceased when she and Trent walked into the dining hall off the kitchen on the second floor. A little unsettled by the silent stares, she smiled and quipped, "Pizza delivery."

"We brought this by to thank you guys for helping out at my house fire the other night," Trent explained as he dropped his boxes onto the table.

"Sorry about that, man," one of the guys said. "That was a tough break."

"I just lost material stuff and the house," Trent said. "Somebody else lost their life."

The remark drew Heather's attention and her respect.

He had never once complained about what he'd lost, which would have been a lot more than he'd admitted. Like pictures and mementos of his life, of the parents he'd lost so long ago. Her heart ached as she thought of everything that had gone up in flames with that woman.

"You figure out who that was yet?" The lieutenant asked the question, looking at Heather.

She shook her head. "Not yet. She doesn't match any missing person reports. We have no idea who she is."

"Well, it hasn't been that long yet. Don't you have to wait awhile before a cop will let you file a report about somebody disappearing?" one of the guys asked.

She hadn't met him yet. He looked about her and Trent's age, thirtyish, with blond hair and what looked like a spray tan. From how his uniform stretched over bulging muscles, he spent a lot of time in the gym. He was probably as big and strong as that Santa who'd gotten the jump on them in the alley. She smiled at him. "I'm Heather. Who are you?"

"Don't you mean Detective Bolton?" he shot back at her.

She knew without a doubt who he was even before Trent introduced them.

"Heather, meet Barry Coats," he said.

The guy jumped up from the bench he'd been sitting on at the long table. He tripped over it and stumbled back into the wall. "What the hell are you up to, Miles? Bringing a detective around here to interrogate us? How the hell do you think any of us could have something to do with burning your place down?"

"The first crew on the scene said the door was closed and locked. So were all the windows," the lieutenant said. "No signs of forced entry."

Heather glanced at Stokes, surprised he'd confirmed what the techs had already told her regarding the scene of the crime. "He's right," she said. "So for that person to get inside, she'd either had the key code or somebody with the key code had let her in."

"She?" Barry repeated, and some of the color drained from his face. "I thought the body was badly burned…"

"Not so badly that the coroner wasn't able to determine sex, possible age, in her early thirties, and build, probably about mine. She was also wearing a wedding ring," she said.

Despite his spray tan, Barry suddenly looked very pale. "You're acting like you think I would know, and I don't."

"You've been using Trent's place to hook up with women," she said, as if she had confirmation, when she really only had rumors and speculation. "Like a few of you have been doing." She glanced around the long table where the other guys had fallen silent as they watched and listened to the exchange between her and Barry.

They all looked a little suspicious of him. Except for one guy who looked away from both of them, probably Jerome Whittaker, who had all but admitted to using Trent's place to cheat. Now she had to get the same confession out of Barry.

"So who was in that house that night?" she asked him. "Did you let her inside?"

"I was working," he said. "I didn't get to the scene until everyone else did to fight the fire."

"Did you give her the code to let herself in?"

Now color rushed into his face, flushing it bright red. "No. I…"

"You've been using Trent's place to hook up," she insisted. "Maybe because you're married with kids."

He shook his head. "I'm divorced."

"Just," one of the other guys remarked.

She could imagine why; his wife had caught him cheating.

"The victim was married," Heather said. "We know that.

She was still wearing her rings." Even after she died. "So that's why you were meeting up with her at Trent's place. And now I suspect she's missing…?"

Tears sprang into his eyes and he turned and headed into the kitchen. Before Heather could get around the long table, Trent had already followed him through the doorway into the other room.

"You're not leaving until you answer the detective's questions," Trent told him as Barry headed toward the other door to the hall.

"The detective? So she's not your girlfriend?"

"It's none of your business what she is," Trent said. "Neither of us are married. Neither of us are dead."

"Who is she?" Heather asked. "I need to know her name. I need to notify the family."

He shook his head.

"You don't care about her at all?" Heather asked. "You're going to leave her in the morgue as a Jane Doe?"

A tear trailed down his cheek now. "If that was her, her husband would report her missing, right? Once he can, once enough time has passed?"

"He might not, if he's the one who killed her," Heather pointed out.

He gasped.

"She was shot in the head, Barry," she said. "She didn't just die in that fire."

He shook his head and a few more tears rolled down his cheeks.

"You have nothing to lose by telling me the truth," she pointed out. "You're not married anymore. You have an alibi." Or so he thought, but she'd checked it out. His shift hadn't started that night until after the report of shots fired. And the fire could have been started in the basement or somewhere inside the house where it would have taken a while to burn as hot as it had. Maybe he'd set it up that way to give himself an alibi. "Unless you have something to hide, why won't you tell me her name?"

"If someone, like maybe her husband, killed her, don't you think he'll come after me next?" Barry asked, his voice cracking with fear. Despite his size and dangerous career, the man was a bit of a coward. Unless it was all an act, like those people who got so dramatic in front of the cameras.

She glanced at Trent and an idea occurred to her. "Or maybe he'd come after the guy whose house she was at."

Barry blinked away his tears then and focused on her. "I heard about someone trying to run you guys down in the parking lot."

Heard about it or did it himself?

She couldn't be sure.

"Did her husband ever see the two of you together?" she asked. "Would he know what you looked like?"

He shook his head again. "No. We were real careful. That's why we met at Trent's."

You're going to find out how it feels to lose someone close to you...

That was the message in that card, and it made sense if the guy thought he'd lost his wife to Trent.

"Barry, I need the name now, dammit!" she snapped at him.

And his eyes widened with surprise. "Missy Dobbs. And I haven't heard from her since that night. She's not texting me or calling."

Because she was in the morgue.

"Do you know where she lives?" she asked. "Her husband's name?"

"Roy," he replied. "And she lives—lived in Wyandotte."

He seemed pretty sure she was the dead woman found in Trent's house. Just because he hadn't heard from her or because he'd killed her?

Not wanting him to know she had some doubts, she said, "Thanks, Barry."

He nodded, but more tears trailed down his face. "Do you think he killed her because of me?"

Well, duh...

She didn't say that aloud. "If he killed her, it was because of *him*. Something's wrong with him." Rage over his wife's betrayal. A crime of passion, it was called. After last night, she understood a little better how someone could lose their mind and sense of self in passion.

She'd lost herself for a moment. But she felt like she was coming back now. She had a solid lead to find out the identity of the victim and maybe the killer as well.

Barry rushed from the room, and she let him go. For now. But if the husband had an alibi, she would have to track Barry down again.

"I'm going to call an officer to come pick me up and drive out to Wyandotte with me," she said. Or maybe she'd take Officer Morgan, who'd followed them to the firehouse, and have another officer come to protect Trent.

"I can drive you," he said. "And they can follow us."

She shook her head. "You don't know this guy, and he doesn't know you—"

"But he might be the one who's been trying to kill us," he said.

"Exactly. It's too dangerous for you to come with me."

"I'm with you here," he said. "I was with you in that alley yesterday."

"And look what happened in that alley." She touched his swollen jaw. "You got hurt."

"So did you."

"Then maybe I'll have a couple of officers go with me out there."

"But shouldn't I go? I can explain to this guy that his wife wasn't with me. She was with my coworker."

She ran her fingertips lightly over the bruise below his eyes. "It was your place. He must think you're the guy she was sleeping with, the one he lost her to…"

Trent groaned. "Damn Barry. Damn them all. Damn me. Why do I keep trusting people that I shouldn't?"

She didn't know if he was talking about his coworkers or his sister or maybe even her, too. When he'd heard about the clearance rate competition, he'd acted as if she'd betrayed him just because she wanted to be the best at her job.

"You should go back to my place," she said. "I'll have an officer follow you."

He shook his head. "No. I can stay here."

A chill ran down her spine with a sense of foreboding. "That's not a good idea."

"It sounds like this Dobbs guy is the one behind every-thing."

But they only had one man's word that any of this was the truth. And she didn't trust that man. "You'd be safer at my house," she insisted.

"So would you," he said with a slight smirk.

"I have a job to do," she said.

"A clearance rate to beat," he said.

It wasn't about that anymore. It was about keeping Trent safe. But he probably wouldn't believe her if she told him. Or worse yet, he would ask why, and she'd have to admit that she was starting to care about him. Too much.

He sighed. "I do, too. I've already missed a lot of shifts

here because of being gone on hotshot assignments. I should stick around, help out if something comes in."

"But it's too dangerous."

"This is my job."

"I mean you still shouldn't trust anyone, not until we know for sure who's after you."

He shrugged. "It's gotta be this Dobbs guy."

"You have to be careful until I confirm that," she insisted.

"I won't be alone with any of them, and nobody will try anything in front of the others," he said.

"Okay." There was safety in numbers. She knew that but still had such an uneasy feeling about leaving him.

At least not without a kiss. She wound her arms around his neck and tugged his head until her lips touched his.

Passion caught fire, burning hot and bright between them, making her pulse race and her skin tingle. It didn't matter that they'd had sex over and over last night. She still wanted him. No. She still needed him.

When she pulled back and stepped away, he stared down at her with bright eyes. "Be careful," he told her.

She didn't know if he was referring to her investigation of Roy Dobbs or kissing him. After last night, it was too late for caution.

She was already in danger...of falling for him.

Chapter Sixteen

For the first time Trent understood what he put the people who cared about him through when he went off to a fire. How they worried about him...

Because he was worrying about Heather like that.

He knew that loved ones worried. Brittney had told him; so had Moe. And he'd seen too many other firefighters' and hotshots' marriages fail because of the danger of their jobs and how it put too much of a strain on a relationship.

He'd heard the complaints in the past from the women he'd dated. He'd also seen the rough patch a fellow hotshot's marriage had hit because his wife thought the stress of worrying about him while he was off fighting wildfires had caused her miscarriages.

He'd commiserated with them all, but he hadn't really understood until now. Until he was worrying about someone who was just doing her job. And that was all she was doing...

That was all this was between them. A crime to solve, a case to close.

"You're really dating Detective Bolton?" Tom Johnson asked, his dark eyes narrowed as he joined Trent in the kitchen.

Trent probably could have told him the truth. If Roy

Dobbs was the killer, then she would be closing this case, and she would have no reason to see him ever again. But something held him back. Maybe hope.

Not that the case wouldn't close but that she might want to see him after it had. That they might...

"You really are," Tom remarked. "I thought she might have cooked up some cover to get close to us, thinking we'd talk more."

"Really?" he asked, feigning innocence and covering his surprise that Tom had so easily figured out part of her plan. The other part had been to flush out the killer.

"Yeah. None of us even knew you were seeing anyone," Tom said. "Hell, even your own sister didn't know."

He gasped. "You talked to Brittney?"

Tom grinned and wriggled his eyebrows. "Sure did. She was trying to get close to me."

Trent stiffened with defensiveness of his baby sister. Even though she'd betrayed him, she would always be family, and he would always love her.

Tom chuckled at Trent's obvious reaction. "But she was just playing me, trying to get me to spill."

"So of course you did."

"She was worried about you," Tom said. "Probably more worried when I told her about the parking lot thing and your girlfriend." He chuckled again. "I don't know what worried her more."

Trent groaned. "You told her about Heather?"

"Heather..." Tom repeated in a singsong rhythm, like a kid taunting him on the playground.

He half expected him to spell out the word *kiss*, too.

Tom shook his head. "I didn't name names. Like I said, I didn't know if you were actually together or not. But from the look on your face, I can see that you've got it bad for the lady detective."

Remembering last night and her sexy red lace underwear, Trent groaned again as his body reacted, tightening and aching with desire. "She's so damn gorgeous. And smart and brave and…"

"Damn," Tom remarked. "I never thought it would happen to you, Miles. That you'd fall so hard."

"I…" He wanted to deny it. After all, they hardly knew each other and certainly didn't have the time necessary to nurture a relationship when they were so focused on their careers. No. He hadn't fallen for her. He couldn't.

The blare of an alarm saved him from having to say any more. Not that he had any idea what to say.

"You going to suit up with us?" Tom asked hopefully.

"I'll ask the lieu," he said.

"I'm right here," Ken Stokes said, appearing in the doorway behind Tom, as if he'd been standing there listening to their conversation. Tom hurried past him to get ready for the call. "And yeah, I can use you, especially since Barry took off."

Trent tensed. "Barry took off? When?"

"Right after your *girlfriend* interrogated him," the lieutenant said. Clearly, he wasn't as convinced as Tom that their act was real.

"I should call her," he murmured, mostly to himself. He felt compelled to warn her for some reason.

But warn her about what? Barry had probably just been upset his married girlfriend might have been murdered because of him, and he'd needed some time off, maybe to rethink his life choices.

Just like Trent was tempted to rethink his.

"You in or out?" Stokes asked, his voice sharp. "We gotta go!"

Trent bobbed his head and started after the lieutenant. Heather would be fine. She had her gun, and she was going with other officers.

But he couldn't help but wonder and worry if Barry had said what he had to set her up, to ambush her. And she'd been worried about Trent, that he shouldn't trust his crew. As he suited up and joined them, they all looked at him with suspicion and resentment.

Because of Heather?

Because she'd questioned them?

What were they so worried about her finding out? And how far would they go to cover it up?

He'd figured he was safe, safety in numbers, but what if the numbers were against him?

THE HOUSE WAS in Wyandotte, just as Barry Coats had told her. And the husband's name was Roy Dobbs, and on the deed search, the wife was listed as Melissa. But Heather could see Melissa being shortened to Missy.

She could also see the rest of it.

If the man had followed his wife to her secret meetings with her affair partner, he might have done what Heather had and looked up the owner's name in an online property search. Then, furious that he was losing his wife, he'd left that threatening card for Trent.

But why at the firehouse?

Why not at the house where he'd followed his wife? Maybe he hadn't wanted her to see it? To recognize her husband's handwriting, to be warned that he knew where she was going and who she was meeting. But Roy hadn't really known. He'd just made the assumption it was Trent because Barry had been using Trent's house for his meetings with Missy.

It all made sense.

Maybe a little too conveniently, which was why Heather was suspicious. She didn't trust Barry Coats. The guy had no qualms about cheating and lying, so she had no reason to trust him. She wasn't sure she should have left Trent at the firehouse. She'd requested an officer to stick close to him, but Officer Howard couldn't follow Trent into a burning building. Hopefully they wouldn't get any calls while she was here.

The officer driving her to the suspected victim's house pulled into the driveway of the address Heather had found for Roy and Melissa Dobbs. No other vehicles were present, and the garage door was closed.

"Doesn't look like anyone's home," Officer Ashley Morgan murmured as she looked at the house. The blinds were closed.

"I'm going to check," Heather said.

"I'm going up to the door with you," Ashley said, and she reached for her door handle with one hand and her weapon with the other.

Heather smiled at the officer, seeing a lot of herself in the earnest and determined young woman. "Good," she said. After her loss of judgment with Trent, she didn't entirely trust herself right now.

Or maybe that was her niggling concern that she shouldn't have trusted Barry Coats.

She opened the passenger's door and stepped out onto the driveway. As she glanced at the house, she noticed the blinds opening. Someone was inside, watching them. She reached for her weapon, too.

But then the door opened and a woman stepped onto the

small front stoop. "Hello, Officers," she said. She was in her thirties, about Heather's height and build, and looked very similar to the driver's license picture Heather had pulled up of the woman.

"Missy?"

"Melinda," the woman said.

"I thought it was Melissa," Heather said.

She shook her head. "No. My sister and I look very much alike. But she's a few years younger than I am."

As she stepped closer, Heather could see more lines on this woman's face than had been in her sister's driver's license photo. And beneath Melinda's blue eyes were dark circles.

"Are you here to take the missing person report?" Melinda asked.

"How long has your sister been missing?" Heather asked.

"She and I went Black Friday shopping together, and she was going to stay in the city for dinner and a movie with an old friend from college. I left her and came back home." She gestured with a finger to another house down the street. "I live there."

"But you're here?" Heather asked.

"I'm checking with Roy to see if he's heard from her," Melinda said. "Or if the police finally agreed to take a report." Bright color appeared in her cheeks. "I'm sorry, but it's not like Missy to not at least shoot me a text. And she hasn't even opened any of mine."

"Her husband is home?" Heather asked.

Melinda nodded and tensed. "I know what you're probably thinking, but Roy adores my sister. He wouldn't do anything to her. And he has no idea where she is either." She stepped back. "I'll go get him."

Heather shook her head. "Not yet. I have a few more

questions for you about your sister and who she was really meeting in the city."

Melinda's face flushed again; clearly, she knew about her sister's affair. Since Missy's sister knew, maybe her husband did as well. Melinda pulled the door of the house closed behind her and joined Heather and Ashley on the driveway. She must not have been in the house long, because she was still wearing her jacket. "Roy doesn't know."

"Are you sure?" she asked.

She bobbed her head in a quick nod. "Missy was really good at keeping secrets."

"From everyone but you," Heather guessed.

"We're sisters," she said. "We share everything."

Heather shook her head again. "Not all sisters do." She didn't want hers to know about Trent because they would definitely scare him away. Not that she expected him to stick around once this case was closed. He was very busy with his career, just as she was with hers.

And she needed to focus on that career now. "But your sister told you," she continued. "So what did you know about who she was seeing? Have you met him?"

"No, she wouldn't share him with me," Melinda said, and she glanced down the street, probably at her house. She wore a wedding ring, too. Was she worried that her husband might overhear her?

"What do you know about him?" Heather asked again.

Melinda smiled. "That he's a hunky fireman."

"Do you know his name?" she asked.

"Trent. Trent Miles."

Heather sucked in a breath, feeling like she'd been punched. Had Trent lied to her? Had he been seeing the dead woman?

"You okay?" Ashley asked in a whisper.

Heather nodded. "Yes. Did she show you a picture of him? Or describe him?"

"Big," she said. "Really big. With a tan…"

That could have described either of them, Trent with his natural skin or Barry with his spray tan.

"And blond," Melinda continued. "Like Chris Hemsworth."

Heather released a slight breath of relief. Not that she would have described Barry as looking like Chris Hemsworth, but *he* probably thought he looked like the movie star.

"That's not Trent," Ashley whispered, as if reassuring Heather.

Had she taken her act too far that the uniformed police officers believed it? After last night, she had to admit she had certainly done more than protect a crime victim.

Trent was the victim. Of the attempts on his life and of another betrayal by someone he'd trusted. Barry hadn't just used his house; he'd used his identity as well.

"What do you mean?" Melinda asked. "That's not Trent?" Despite the officer's whisper, she'd heard her. "He lied about his name?"

"The man who admitted to having a relationship with your sister is not really named Trent Miles," Heather said.

"So you've talked to him? You know where she is, then?"

Heather had a horrible feeling that she did.

"Has he told you? Have you seen her? Is she okay?" Melinda asked, her voice rising with a trace of hysteria. "Where the hell is she?"

Missy's sister must have finally figured out why Heather was there. And it wasn't just to take a missing person report.

"Hey, you didn't tell me the police were here," a man said as he stepped out of the house and joined them on the driveway. He was big, like Barry Coats, with pale skin and thinning hair, despite probably being in his thirties.

Ashley reached for her weapon again. Heather's hand was inside her coat, resting on the handle of her Glock.

"Roy Dobbs?" Heather asked.

He nodded.

"I'm Detective Bolton. Would you consent to letting Officer Morgan search your person?"

"What?" he asked.

"Just to make sure you have no weapons on you," she clarified. If this was the man who'd attacked her and Trent in the alley, she wasn't about to let him ambush her again.

He shook his head. "I—I don't have any weapons on me."

"You don't own a gun?" She knew damn well that he did. She had pulled up his permit for the weapon. The coroner was still working on determining the caliber of the gun that had killed the woman, since the bullet had passed through her skull and hadn't been recovered.

"I—I do have one, but I'm not carrying it on me," Roy said.

"What's going on?" Melinda asked. "Why aren't you answering me about my sister? Do you think Roy killed her? Is she dead?" Her voice cracked as a sob erupted out of her, followed by a keening howl, and she dropped onto the driveway on her knees.

"Melinda!" Roy said. He grabbed her arm and tried to get her up as he gazed around, as if worried the neighbors were watching. "Can we go inside?" he asked in a whisper, concerned they were listening, too.

"After you consent to a search," Heather persisted.

He nodded and held out his arms. Officer Morgan frisked him quickly but thoroughly. She stepped away from him and nodded at Heather.

"Okay, we can go inside," she agreed and followed the man and his sister-in-law into the modest ranch house. Roy had his arm around Melinda, half carrying her as she continued to weep.

"Calm down," he told her. "We don't know anything yet."

"They know stuff," Melinda said, and she pulled away from Roy now. Her blue eyes narrowed and she stared at him. "Did you know? Missy didn't think so but…"

He lifted his hands. "Know what? What the hell are you talking about?"

"Her affair," Heather said, and she watched his face carefully.

He sucked in a breath as if she'd punched him. He might have already known and it just still hurt. Or he might have had no idea.

"I thought you were here to take the missing person report," he said, and he lifted his hand to run it over his thin hair. His fingers were shaking.

"They know something," Melinda reminded him, her voice nearly a shriek now. "They must have found her."

"You did?" he asked. "Is she okay? It's not like her to not reply to text messages."

"We don't know if it's her," Heather admitted. "We need to get something with her DNA on it."

Melinda screamed again and started to fall. But when her brother-in-law reached for her, she jerked away from him and stumbled back into Officer Morgan. Ashley caught her and held her up as she sobbed.

"I—I—" Roy stammered and rubbed his hand over his head again.

"I could use her toothbrush or a hairbrush," Heather explained.

"We can't see her?" Roy asked.

He might have been able to handle it, but there was no way her sister would, from the way she was wailing. Maybe she'd already had some inclination Missy was dead.

If Melinda thought that just because Missy hadn't answered her texts, then Heather's sisters would have often thought she was dead. And that was definitely the case with Trent, who kept ignoring his sister's messages.

"Her toothbrush is in here," Roy said, as he started out of the living room, down a short hall.

Heather followed him, her hand on her weapon while the young officer was trying to untangle herself from Melinda, who clung to her now as she kept crying.

"Is she dead?" he asked.

"We have found a body that could be hers," Heather admitted. "We need DNA to confirm."

He sucked in another breath. "That's…" His voice trailed off, emotion choking him. But he betrayed nothing but those nerves as he pushed open a door at the end of the hall.

The bedroom was dark, all the blinds shut like in the rest of the house. Clothes were scattered around the floor and even at the foot of the bed.

"Missy's a little messy," he said.

Some of the clothes were his, so he obviously wasn't any neater. Maybe realizing that, he stooped to pick up some jeans. "The toothbrush is in there." He pointed toward the open door to a small bathroom. "The pink one."

Heather pulled an evidence bag from her pocket and used it to take the brush out of the holder. Then she sealed it inside. "I would also like to see your gun, Mr. Dobbs."

"I have a permit."

"I need to see your gun," she repeated. She would be able to determine if it had been fired recently just by examining it. When she stepped out of the bathroom, with the bagged toothbrush, Roy Dobbs stood in front of her, pointing the barrel of the gun she wanted directly at her.

TOM HAD TEXTED HER, just as he'd promised, when he'd heard from Trent. He's here. At the firehouse.

But by the time she got there, they were all gone. Not just Trent. His truck was actually in the lot now, but the big rigs were gone.

They'd been sent out on a call.

To a fire.

Her pulse quickened with the trepidation she always felt when her brother was fighting a fire. Every time there was the possibility he could get hurt or worse. Like those other hotshots who had died after they'd responded to the recent wildfire out West before Trent and his team had arrived at it.

Trent had lost one of his team members recently, too. And some other ones had nearly died as well. His job was dangerous no matter what.

But now…

After someone had burned down his house with a body inside…

After someone had tried to run him down in this very parking lot…

He was in a lot more danger than he'd ever been in. And once again Brittney worried that she might never see her brother again.

At least not alive…

Chapter Seventeen

If looks could kill…

Trent wouldn't have survived even before they got to the fire as he rode in the back of the rig with his crew. "What the hell, guys?" he asked. "I brought you pizza and you're all looking at me like I tried to poison you. What? You're all on diets I didn't know about?"

"You brought us pizza and a detective who's already been treating us like suspects over what the hell happened at *your* house," Gordy Stutz replied, as if he was speaking for all of them.

And maybe he was.

Tom wasn't glaring at him quite as hard as the others. He almost smirked instead, like he knew something Trent didn't. Hell, they'd all known something he didn't.

"Anybody who had access to my house probably is a suspect," Trent said. "Somebody was killed there, and not because of the fire. And somebody's been trying to kill me. If anyone has a reason to be pissed off, it's me!" And he was, anger surging through him. He'd been hurt and confused since the fire, but the only person he had actually gotten angry with had been Heather.

For just doing her job and having a little fun competing with the chauvinistic detective.

Trent needed to be pissed at the people who had really betrayed him. She hadn't. She hadn't done anything but...

Make him start falling for her. That was on him, just like she'd been once last night. He closed his eyes for a moment, grappling with the heat of that memory. When he opened them, they were pulling up to the fire.

A run-down apartment building was ablaze, burning so fast and hot that he could feel the heat the minute he stepped out of the rig. "Is everyone out?" he asked the lieutenant, who was yelling orders at the crew.

"You need to check, Miles. Place is mostly empty, but a few die-hard tenants have remained, despite the bad conditions."

This reminded him of another fire last year. Another run-down apartment building that was supposed to be mostly empty. He'd checked that one, too, but he'd missed someone on his first time through. When neighbors told him the apartment he'd thought was deserted was occupied, he'd gone back, but not in time to save her.

A pang of guilt struck him, and a moment's panic, too. He had to make damn sure he didn't miss anyone this time. He nodded at the lieutenant and headed toward the fire. He adjusted his helmet, putting on the mask with the oxygen. With as hot as this fire was, he would need it.

This place reminded him of the other building, full of trash and falling down from neglect. Almost as if the fire was putting it out of its misery. He found an older couple, huddling together in one unit, and helped them out through the smoke.

Then he went back inside, making sure to check every apartment. In the one farthest from the fire he saw someone. The person wore a mask and a helmet, too, but through the smoke, it wasn't clear if it was the same as Trent's, the same crew. Other departments had responded to the call.

Trent gestured at the guy, trying to get him to indicate if he'd checked the place. But the guy didn't gesture back. Instead, he swung something that he'd been holding behind him. Like the pipe the Santa had swung in the alley.

This time Heather wasn't there to jump in front of him. Trent stumbled back, trying to duck, but it hit him. Hard, so hard that it knocked off his helmet, sending it skittering across the floor.

The next blow struck him in the legs, knocking them from underneath him, and he dropped to the ground next to his helmet.

Then the pipe swung toward him again...

THE WAY THE gun was pointed at her, the barrel directed at her heart, she didn't have time to draw her weapon. She didn't even dare draw a breath.

But he hadn't pulled the trigger yet. His eyes were glazed over, almost in a trance of some sort, or just so damn tired he didn't know what was going on. Like his sister-in-law, he had dark circles beneath his eyes.

Heather could relate; she was tired, too. Maybe that was why she'd momentarily turned her back on the guy. But after he'd been searched...

Still, she'd known there was a weapon in the house. She should have secured that first before the damn toothbrush.

"Roy, you don't want to pull that trigger," she said, as if she knew. But she really had no idea what the man was capable of doing, especially if he'd killed his own wife.

Roy glanced at the gun as if he wasn't aware that he was holding it, pointing it, but even then he didn't lower it. The barrel was still aimed directly at her.

Officer Morgan noticed that when she stepped into the room, her eyes going wide. She pulled her own weapon, but

Heather gave a slight shake of her head, silently telling the officer to stand down.

For the moment.

She didn't want the guy shot if he truly was so out of it he didn't know what he was doing. She hoped giving him the benefit of the doubt didn't wind up costing her…her life.

"Roy, I got the toothbrush," she said, holding the bag out. "We'll see if the DNA matches. And thank you for getting the gun."

"I… I had it out at the range the other day," he murmured. "I took it out on Black Friday when Missy and her sister were shopping."

So it had been recently fired. Heather wouldn't even have to examine it, but she was going to damn well take it. She took a step closer to him. As she did, Officer Morgan stepped farther into the room.

Then Melinda rushed up behind her. "What the hell are you doing, Roy?"

He moved then, swinging the barrel toward the door, at the young officer and his sister-in-law. Heather rushed forward, locking her hand around his wrist as she threw her weight against him, knocking him to the ground.

Ashley rushed forward, helping her secure the weapon. "I've got it." Then she unhooked her cuffs from her belt and snapped them around his wrists while Heather held him down. "I got him."

"The safety was on," Roy said. "I wasn't going to shoot."

"Don't ever point a weapon at anyone," Heather admonished him. "But especially not a cop."

"You're lucky I didn't shoot you." Ashley added her admonishment.

"I wasn't going to shoot," he murmured again and began

to cry like his sister-in-law, but his sobs were quiet little gasps of breath as tears rolled down his face.

Ashley looked at her. "We're bringing him in?"

She nodded. "He pointed this gun at both of us." And she needed time to determine if his wife was who had been found in Trent's house. Though, she was pretty damn sure it was Missy lying in the morgue. "We're confiscating the weapon and arresting him for threatening us."

"I wouldn't shoot you..." he cried. "I wouldn't..."

"What about Missy?" she asked. "Did you follow your wife to where she was going to meet her lover? Did you shoot her and then set fire to that house?"

Melinda shrieked again. Then she rushed forward and tried to kick him as he lay on the bedroom floor on top of the clothes that were strewn across the carpet. Ashley held her back.

"I didn't do it," Roy said. He was talking to Melinda, though, not her. "I wouldn't hurt Missy. I would never hurt Missy."

Not like she'd hurt him.

If he'd known about the affair...

He'd acted like he hadn't known, but Heather couldn't be certain that wasn't all he was doing: acting. Maybe he'd even intended to shoot her but had known that Officer Morgan would have taken him out.

Was he the one who'd attacked her and Trent in the alley? Who'd tried to run them down? Who'd put that box of matches in the mail slot?

She intended to question him until she got the truth out of him. About everything...

She was tempted to tell him the truth, too, that Trent wasn't his wife's affair partner. But as much as she wanted to take the target off Trent, she couldn't reveal too much to a suspect. She couldn't give him anything he could use in his defense. Fortunately, he hadn't asked for a lawyer yet. But once Ashley read him his rights, he might.

"Let's bring him out to the car and Mirandize him," she said.

He'd seemed reluctant to let his sister-in-law make a scene in front of his neighbors, so he probably wouldn't make one himself. The faster they got him out of the house, the less chance he had of resisting. Even though the guy was handcuffed, he was big. She and Ashley had to both help him up from the floor.

The hallway was too narrow for them to walk beside him, so Ashley walked behind them as Heather steered him away from the bedroom, toward the exit. But before they could get to the front door, a call came through the radio on Officer Morgan's collar.

"Officer, please have Detective Bolton contact Dispatch."

Ashley touched a button on the radio speaker. "She's with me now."

"Have her contact Dispatch."

So whatever they wanted to talk to her about, they didn't want to do it over the radio.

Heather's pulse, which had already been fast after staring down a gun barrel, quickened even more. She helped Ashley get Roy Dobbs secured in the back seat of her patrol car before she pulled out her cell and called Dispatch.

"This is Detective Bolton."

"Hold one moment, please." The line went silent for a long moment.

"Detective?" a male voice asked.

"Yes."

"This is Officer Howard."

The one she'd assigned to stay at the firehouse, to watch Trent and make sure nothing happened to him. And she knew, even before she asked, that something had happened.

"There was a fire," he said. "I followed the rig to it, but I couldn't go inside the apartment complex."

But Trent had. He'd suited up and gone in with the crew he already knew he couldn't trust. She silently cursed. "What happened?"

"He got some people out and went back in, but he didn't come out again—"

"He got trapped in the fire?" Pain gripped her heart, squeezing it tightly. Was he going to wind up like Missy Dobbs had?

Burned beyond recognition?

Tears stung her eyes, so she closed them and prayed.

"I made them go back inside, and they found him."

"Is he alive?" she asked, her heart pounding so furiously with hope now. They'd gotten him out.

He couldn't be dead. Not Trent.

"He's at the hospital now. I don't know his condition."

"Which one?" Heather asked, hoping it was close, that she could get to him.

The officer told her the name, but then sputtered a bit as he tried to tell her something else.

"What is it, Howard?" she asked.

"I don't know…" he murmured. "The lieutenant tried to act like it was an accident. But I don't think it was."

Neither did she.

But if someone had attacked Trent in that fire, it hadn't been Roy Dobbs. She and Officer Morgan and his sister-in-law could alibi him.

So was there someone else out there? Someone else who wanted Trent dead and had maybe succeeded?

AFTER TALKING TO Brittney Townsend the other morning, Ethan had sent a few texts to Trent.

What the hell is going on?

Are you all right?

All he'd gotten in response was a thumbs-up message each time. What the hell did that mean? Was he trying to assure Ethan that everything was fine?

Ethan couldn't believe that, not after Trent had lost his house in an arson fire. And a body had been found inside it.

Thankfully not his.

This time.

But someone was after him.

Someone nearly running him down in the firehouse parking lot hadn't been an accident. None of it had been. His best friend was in danger, and too damn proud and stubborn to ask for help.

So Ethan had asked. He sat now in the office at the firehouse in Northern Lakes, in one of the too-small chairs in front of his boss's desk. Braden Zimmer had made some calls for Ethan, and he'd told him he had news.

Ethan stared across the desk at the hotshot superintendent's grim expression. And he knew it wasn't good news.

Chapter Eighteen

Trent had managed to avoid that last blow. He'd rolled out of the way of the pipe and scrambled to his feet. Ignoring the pain in his legs, he'd run from that apartment unit, and his attacker, back into the smoke-filled hallway. To escape the pipe-wielding maniac, he'd had to leave his helmet and the oxygen behind. With the smoke blinding and choking him, he'd lost his way and eventually his consciousness, falling to the floor in some back hallway.

He could have lost his life, too.

Or had he?

He struggled to open his eyes, and as he did, they burned and watered, like his throat and lungs burned. He definitely wasn't dead, unless he'd gone to hell. But a mask covered his face, pumping more oxygen into him. He blinked against the bright lights and listened to the beeps and the voices. He had made it to the hospital.

He wasn't dead yet…despite someone's efforts to kill him. Who the hell had been in that building?

He'd been wearing a helmet, too. Was he a firefighter? One of Trent's crew?

Heather had been right that he'd needed to be careful. She hadn't trusted any of his coworkers, and apparently neither should he have. He should have gone back to her house and decorated her tree. He could show her sisters that she could damn well be Martha Stewart if she wanted. Or at least he could help her fake it. Just thinking of her made him smile beneath the mask.

"There he is," a deep voice murmured. "Back among the living."

With his eyes still burning, his vision wasn't clear. He could see the uniform. The hat. And he tensed with fear. Had the guy come to finish him off? He tightened his hands into fists. He wasn't going out without a fight. He was mad now, like he'd realized while in the rig that he should have been.

This firehouse crew wasn't like his hotshots. He could trust his hotshot team. Couldn't he?

Or was one of them the saboteur?

He was being more than sabotaged now. Someone was trying to kill him.

"Trent? You okay?"

And he recognized the voice. Manny.

He blinked again and could focus on his boss. His dad's friend. Surely he could trust the fire captain. He tried to move the oxygen mask aside to speak, but Manny caught his wrist.

"Leave that on for now," he said. "You need to get your oxygen levels up."

"They're getting there," a woman in scrubs said as she leaned over the bed. "We need to take you for an MRI, make sure you don't have any internal injuries."

He ached all over from that damn pipe, and not just from today, but from the day before in the alley.

She glanced at the captain. "You have just a few minutes before we take him up," she said. "And then you need to report back to the waiting room that he's stable and doing well. There's about to be a riot out there."

"My men?" Manny asked, his voice hard with disapproval.

She chuckled. "Two women, actually."

Two women?

Heather? Brittney? It had to be; Moe was still on her cruise.

Trent smiled.

"Sounds about right," Manny said. "Women are always fighting to get close to this guy."

"One said she's his sister," the nurse said. "And the other is a detective."

Brittney and Heather.

"Two minutes," she told Manny, and she ducked behind the curtain that was surrounding the bed Trent was lying on.

"Glad you're improving," Manny said. "I told your hotshot superintendent that you would be fine." But from his tone, it was clear he hadn't been as confident of that as he'd led Braden to believe.

Neither had Trent, but the pain in his throat and lungs was easing now and his eyes were clear.

"He and the team were about to descend on Detroit like they were putting out a wildfire, so I had to convince them everything was under control." Manny stepped closer and lowered his voice. "But it isn't, is it? What the hell is going on, Trent? This all started with that damn Christmas card."

You're going to find out what it feels like to lose someone close to you. Soon.

That hadn't been the only one. He'd gotten one at Heather's house, too. Threatening her.

Something niggled at him, something about that apartment fire today. It was so eerily similar to that fire last year. But there had been so many fires over the years, so many casualties, and none of the survivors had the code to his door lock. So, like Heather, he'd suspected it had to be someone closer to him.

"What the hell happened, Trent?" Manny asked. "You lost your helmet and the oxygen, and I know you're too damn good for that to have happened by accident."

Manny's hand had slipped away from his wrist, so Trent tugged his mask down. "Good that you know that."

"Of course I know that."

"I need to talk to…" A cough overtook him, choking off his breath for a moment.

"You need your oxygen back on," Manny said, and he tried to pull the mask back up.

"I need to talk to Heather…"

Manny's forehead creased. "Heather? I thought your sister's name is Brittney."

"The detective," Trent said.

"Well, I'll be damned. You really are seeing her."

He would say he wanted to talk to Heather about the case, but he realized that wasn't the only reason he needed to see her.

He could have died.

And he just *needed* to see her.

"That cop that was at the fire," Manny said, "the one who insisted the lieutenant send people back in to find you, he said something about the detective having a close call. That someone pulled a gun on her…"

While he'd been attacked, Heather had been threatened? Just like Manny, he wondered what the hell was going on.

"I need to see her!" Now more than ever.

"She's fine," Manny assured him. "She knocked the guy down and got his gun."

Trent sucked in a sharp breath, and his lungs expelled it in another hard cough.

Manny slipped the oxygen mask back up. "She's fine," he said again.

Of course she was. She was damn tough.

"I'll go get her," Manny offered. But when he reached for the curtain, the nurse was already pulling it aside.

She'd returned with an orderly. "Time to take you for the MRI," she said.

He tried to protest, but another cough racked him. And he knew he would have to wait to see Heather. To make sure that she was all right…

Because even though she'd taken care of whoever had pulled that gun on her, Trent knew another threat was out there, the guy who'd nearly killed him. He couldn't help but worry that he might be out in the waiting room with Heather and Brittney.

And if he still wanted Trent to feel the pain of losing someone close to him, he could take one of them. Because if Trent lost either of those women, he would be in a hell of a lot of pain.

HEATHER DIDN'T FEEL any safer in this hospital waiting room than she had staring down the barrel of a gun. His local firehouse crew had gathered around, acting all concerned now. But she didn't trust any of them.

If Officer Howard hadn't been there, would they have left Trent in the fire to burn up like Missy Dobbs's body had? Had one of them done that?

She'd arrested the woman's husband, but with charges related to pointing his gun at her. She intended to hold him until she had confirmation of whether or not his wife was in the morgue. But maybe he hadn't killed Missy. Maybe he hadn't even known about her affair. Because if he was her killer, who had gone after Trent again? And why?

It had to be one of them. She glared at them like they'd glared at her and Trent earlier. She was tempted to have them all locked up like she'd locked up Roy Dobbs. If Trent wasn't okay, she would damn well do it.

The only one she could probably trust in this room, besides Officer Howard, was Brittney Townsend. But then she reminded herself that Trent didn't even trust his sister. Not after her betrayal...

And she glared at her, too, her frustration bubbling over. She started toward the information desk again, determined this time to get some damn information. Every time she and Brittney had gone up before, the man at the desk had claimed they were awaiting tests.

Tests for what?

How badly had he been hurt?

And why had she separated from him?

She knew how much danger he was in, how determined someone was to hurt him. But she'd left him. Tears stung her eyes, but she furiously blinked them back. She would not cry. She would not show any sign of pain or weakness in front of these people, suspecting that one of them had probably hurt Trent, had wanted him to suffer.

She was the one suffering now, her heart aching as she awaited news. News that seemed like it was never going to come. Damn it.

Damn them!

"Hey, Detective Bolton—"

She jumped and whirled toward Trent's sister, who held up her hands. "I'm sorry," Brittney said. "Guess you're on edge, too. I overheard the officer saying that you had a gun pulled on you earlier today." She smiled. "I'm unarmed."

"Somehow I'm not reassured," Heather replied. But she was amused. She was also aware that Brittney's smile was as strained as the one Heather gave her. "Since you're on edge, too."

Brittney turned her eyes, the same unique topaz as Trent's, on the information desk. "They won't tell us anything. And it's so damn frustrating."

It was frightening. Not knowing how Trent was...

If he would be okay...

Heather could see that same fear in Brittney, as tears glistened in her eyes. But she blinked, fighting them back, just as Heather was determined to do. Maybe Brittney didn't trust these guys any more than Heather did.

Obviously the reporter had good instincts or she wouldn't have found the scoop she had in Northern Lakes. She wouldn't have found a dead man living under another identity. Jonathan Canterbury hadn't died in a plane crash like everyone had believed he had five years ago. But the man whose identity he'd assumed, a hotshot firefighter named Ethan Sommerly, had.

"You guys have been seeing each other for a while, haven't you?" Brittney asked, and she was intently studying Heather's face, probably seeing that same fear and concern she was feeling over Trent.

"Why do you think that?" She and Trent had not bothered coming up with much of a cover story. Their ruse of a relationship had been to flush out the killer, to make him try for her instead of Brittney or someone else close to him. It had worked because the killer had believed it, so she couldn't tell the truth and risk him overhearing if he was one of the firefighters sitting in the waiting room.

"He's been acting weird for a while," Brittney said, "but

maybe that's just because of everything happening with his hotshot team."

"I think he's acting weird with you because he's mad at you for doing that story on his best friend and his hotshot team," Heather said.

Brittney narrowed her eyes. "You two are close for you to know that. Then you must also know he was acting weird before that, which was why I went to Northern Lakes in the first place. I knew something was going on with his hotshot team and I wanted to find out what, especially when so many of them were getting hurt or worse."

She'd mentioned all that in her story, but the focus had been on the big scoop, on Jonathan Canterbury. What else was going on in Northern Lakes? And had it followed Trent back to Detroit? Her head began to pound as she considered that there could be more suspects, and she already had too many. Roy Dobbs. Barry Coats. Maybe any other of his co-workers who had something to hide...

"What I didn't realize," Brittney continued with a heavy sigh, "was that he was in danger here, too."

"He's a firefighter," Heather said. "He's always in danger on the job."

"I'm not talking about what happened today, and you know it," the reporter said. "I'm talking about what happened at his house. The fire. The dead body. I have sources everywhere, even in your department, Detective. I know the body found in Trent's house had a gunshot wound to the head, and that the fire was deliberately set."

"I can't comment on an ongoing investigation," Heather said, which was her standard reply for reporters.

Brittney snorted derisively. "You shouldn't even be working this investigation, since you're intimately involved with what must be one of the suspects."

"Trent was gone on a call out West." Although technically he had returned. "His alibi checked out. He is definitely not a suspect." But if they had been involved before the fire, she wouldn't have taken the investigation. Brittney wasn't wrong. Because the reporter was so damn smart, Heather wanted to distract her, so she questioned her like a suspect. "What about your alibi, Miss Townsend?"

Brittney laughed. "You think I burned down my brother's house after murdering someone in it? That's ridiculous."

"Besides your mother, you're the only female he knows who had the key code to his house."

Brittney's eyes narrowed with real suspicion now. "You didn't?"

Damn. She was too smart. Distracting her probably wasn't going to work. But the guys were watching them and obviously listening to them, too. So she had to continue the charade. Only it wasn't really a charade anymore.

Heather smiled. "Trent and I meet at my place." Then she glanced around the waiting room at the blatantly eavesdropping firefighters. "Unlike his house, which seemed to have a revolving door on it with people coming and going all the time and using it for all sorts of things, my cat is the only other one around my house."

And her dad and her sisters. But until she knew for certain who was threatening her and Trent, she would make sure they stayed away. Just like she had to somehow get Brittney to stay away.

"I hate to interrupt," an older man said as he walked up to them. He hadn't been at the firehouse earlier today when she and Trent had brought the pizzas, but she remembered him from the scene of the fire. He was the one who'd given him the cards. "But Trent is back from his MRI now and would like to talk to you."

"Me?" Brittney asked, her voice bright with hope.

He shook his head. "No. The detective."

Heather's heart warmed. Then she reminded herself that he probably just wanted to tell her about what had happened. Maybe he'd seen who'd attacked him.

She was torn between hoping that was the case, so this could be over, and fear that if he had seen his attacker, the man would be even more determined to kill him than he already was.

APPARENTLY TRENT MILES had survived. Again. He and that detective were like cats with nine lives. But eventually their luck and their lives were going to run out.

And he was going to make damn sure that happened, just as he'd promised in those cards, soon. Very soon.

Chapter Nineteen

Thanks to his gear, Trent didn't have a concussion or any broken bones. While he had inhaled too much smoke, his oxygen levels had come up and the MRI showed no lung damage, so the doctor thought he would be fine. Still, she was going to send him home with some oxygen.

Not that Trent had a home anymore. But he had Heather's place, that cozy little bungalow with the cat who stood guard over him while he slept. And her...

And all the passion that burned between them, nearly as hot as that fire had. She was so beautiful. Such an incredible lover.

He'd just pulled on his jeans when she ducked around the curtain and stepped inside his cubicle. "What are you doing?" she asked as she rushed up to him. But she stopped just short of reaching for him, and he wished she hadn't. "You shouldn't be trying to leave."

He wanted to close his arms around her, to hold her close. But it was just them in the cubicle. No audience to play up their *fake* relationship. They'd had no audience last night, and that hadn't stopped them from getting as close as two people could get.

Closer than Trent had ever felt to anyone else. With the

rest of his world spinning out of control, he just wanted to grab her and hang on.

"Trent? Are you okay?" she asked.

Realizing he was probably staring at her stupidly, he nodded. "I'm fine. No brain damage."

She smacked his chest lightly with her open palm. "You must have some to be trying to leave AMA."

"I'm not leaving against medical advice," he said. "I'm fine." He picked up the portable oxygen pack. "Just getting sent home with this in case I need it." Thinking of what they'd done the night before, the intensity of the passion and the pleasure, he grinned. "I probably needed this more last night."

She smiled, and her beautiful green eyes sparkled. "You're bad…"

"That's not what you said last night."

"I don't remember either of us doing a lot of talking," she acknowledged.

He grinned as his pulse quickened.

"I thought you just wanted to talk to me now," she said. "That's what that older man told me."

"Older man? Captain Rodriguez. Manny," he said. He'd told him he wanted to tell her something. But first he wanted her to talk. "Are you okay?"

Her forehead creased beneath her wispy bangs. "Yeah. I'm kicking myself for not guarding you myself. I knew there was nobody in that firehouse you could trust—"

"Manny," he said. "I trust him. He and my dad served together. He's a good man."

"One of the few there."

"I hope you include me in that number," he said. That she didn't think he would have knowingly let his house be used the way some of his coworkers had used it. "I asked if you were okay because of what happened. Officer Howard told Manny someone pulled a gun on you."

She shrugged. "He pulled a gun, and it was pointed at me. I'm not sure he intended to threaten me with it."

"But you tackled him anyway," he said with awe. She was so damn tough.

She shrugged. "He was pointing the gun at Officer Morgan and his sister-in-law when I tackled him, but the safety was on. It wasn't as if I jumped in front of a bullet."

"Like you jumped in front of a pipe for me in the alley," he said. "I could have used you in that building."

"What happened?" she asked.

He glanced around the small cubicle area, not certain who could be standing behind the curtain or lying in one of those other beds. "Let's just say it was a lot like the alley."

She gasped and reached out now, lightly stroking his still-swollen jaw. "So I should have Craig looking for another pipe?"

He nodded.

"Was it Santa Claus again?"

"No…" He heaved in a deep breath that had him coughing and sputtering for a moment.

She stepped back and glanced around. "Do you need help? Should I call the doctor?"

He cleared his throat and shook his head. "No. They already signed me out, and they probably need this spot." The ER at this hospital was always busy. He'd brought people here himself. Coworkers. Fire victims.

And he thought again of that victim from a year ago. And the fire that was so similar he'd felt a flash of déjà vu. He needed to tell her about that, too.

"Then let's get you out of here," she said. She helped him finish dressing in the long-sleeved shirt and leather jacket that Manny must have brought him from his locker at the firehouse.

The patient exit from the ER emptied into the waiting room, and as Trent stepped through the doors, everyone jumped up. His coworkers cheered, and his sister rushed forward and hugged him tightly.

"Oh, thank God! Thank God you're all right," she murmured, and when she pulled back, tears shimmered in her eyes.

He wanted to hug her back, but he kept his arms at his sides. After the apartment fire, he didn't trust any of his coworkers. If one of them wanted him to feel the pain of losing someone close to him, they might go after Brittney.

But the one who was actually the closest to him was Heather. She'd insisted on setting herself up as bait to lure out the killer. Unfortunately, it was working too damn well.

"Are you all right?" Brittney asked.

He nodded. "Yeah, I'm fine."

"Come back to Mom's with me," she said. "You can stay there, and I'll take care of you."

"He's coming home with me," Heather said, and she slid her arm around his waist. "I'll take care of him."

Brittney glanced at the detective, then looked back up at him. "Are you ever going to forgive me?" she asked, and her voice cracked with pain.

He relived those long moments he'd been so scared that burned body was hers. He leaned down and whispered, "I'm doing this because I forgive you, because I love you." Then he straightened up and raised his voice. "Leave me alone! What you did is unforgivable. I don't want anything to do with you anymore!"

"You're an ass," Brittney shot back at him. And he didn't

know if she was just playing along or if that was how she really felt.

He didn't talk to any of the crew. Yelling at his sister had strained his already sore throat and drained what was left of his energy. But he did stop to tell Manny, "Thanks for bringing my clothes."

"Your truck is in the lot, too," Manny said. "The keys and the parking voucher, with the location of it, are in your coat pocket. I figured you wouldn't be staying even if the doctor didn't release you. But just because she did, don't think you're coming back to work anytime soon."

"I don't want to," Trent admitted. And he raised his voice so that the other guys standing around could hear him. "I don't want to work with people who don't have my back."

"Are you quitting?" Manny asked.

Trent shook his head. "Not yet." He wanted some time to think about it, some time for Heather to nail whoever was coming after them.

"Good," Manny said, and now he gazed around him. "Give me some time to clean house. I know there have been some issues. Some guys who want the glory of calling themselves a firefighter more than they want to do the job."

There was a bigger issue than that, but Trent suspected Manny knew that, too. He squeezed the guy's shoulder, then headed out of the waiting room with Heather. Once they were in the elevator that brought them down to the parking garage, he asked, "So how are you going to take care of me?"

She winked at him. "You'll see…"

When they stepped out of the elevator into the dimly lit parking structure, she showed him how. She drew her weapon and stayed between him and the shadows. Maybe

she sensed what he did, that deep chill of a cold gaze staring at them.

But how? Had someone slipped out of the waiting room
and beat them down here?

He'd been so angry with his crew that he hadn't paid
much attention to who had been in the waiting room and
who hadn't. Had Barry been there? Or was he here, somewhere, waiting to jump out at them in another disguise with
another makeshift weapon?

With her gun drawn, and her gaze scanning those shadows, Heather was ready for him or whoever the hell else
might be after them.

"You're acting more like a bodyguard than a detective,"
he said.

"I've done my share of protection detail," she said. "And
I won't be caught off guard again."

Was she talking about the alley or earlier today when
Roy Dobbs had pointed that gun at her?

HEATHER HAD VOWED, back at the parking garage, not to get
caught off guard again. By whoever was after them and by
her own damn feelings...

But the minute they stepped inside her house, desire overwhelmed her. He could have died. *She* could have died. And
all she could think of was celebrating that they were alive
with each other.

Her pulse was racing, and she was very aware of her
breathing, like she was panting for air. Like he must have
been panting when he'd lost his helmet and his oxygen.

On the drive home, he'd told her about what had happened
and his eerie sense of déjà vu over the fire reminding him
of a previous one involving a fatality.

This time he was almost the fatality. She'd made some

calls from the truck and discovered that the same company owned both run-down apartment buildings.

Arson for insurance money? The cause of the prior fire had been arson, but no one had been charged with it. But why would the owner or the arsonist be out for revenge against just one of the firefighters? Maybe the victim's family had been. Heather was waiting for more information about her. The name had sounded a little familiar to her, which was weird because the fire hadn't been her case.

"Hmm…" she murmured.

"What's wrong?" Trent asked, and she realized she hadn't spoken since they'd walked into the house.

Maybe because she hadn't trusted herself. Or maybe he'd noticed her erratic breathing. He was breathing heavily, too, but then he had every reason.

"I'm fine," she said, but she had to swallow hard to force down the lie. She wasn't fine. She was still unsettled by how close she'd come to losing him. But he wasn't even really hers to lose. "You should go lie down and get some rest." That would give her some space, so she could get her emotions—her desire—under control.

He walked out of the kitchen but stopped at the arch to the living room. She followed him, glancing into the room at the dark tree.

She sighed. "It looks kind of sad," she said.

"The tree's not the only one," Trent murmured.

"What's wrong? Are you upset about Brittney?"

"Worried about her," he said. "I think she understands now why I'm being such a hard-ass."

"Is it the guys, then? Knowing you can't trust any of your local crew?"

He snorted. "No. That pisses me off."

"Then what's bothering you?"

"You are," he said. "I don't know what room you want me to go to. Back to the guest room or..."

"My room," she said.

"Yeah, I don't know which one to go to," he said.

"My room," she repeated with certainty. She could have lost him or lost her own life today.

He tensed and stared down at her, his eyes gleaming with the same desire that was coursing through her body. "You mean that..."

"At the hospital I said I would take care of you," she reminded him. She reached for his hand, to lead him down the hall like she had the night before. But instead, he reached for her, winding one arm under her legs and the other around her back, and lifted her up against his chest. "Trent!" she protested. "You're hurt!"

"I'm hurting," he agreed. "For you. I need you so damn bad!"

Her heart seemed to swell and warm with his admission. *He's just talking about sex.* That had to be what he meant, all he meant. People with careers like they had didn't have time for anything else.

They really didn't have time for this either, not with someone trying to kill them. But she didn't protest again when he carried her down the hall and through her bedroom door.

He lowered her to the mattress and followed her down. He was breathing hard, maybe from the exertion, maybe from the smoke inhalation. But that didn't stop him from covering her mouth with his, from kissing her passionately.

Heather wrapped her arms around his neck and kissed him back, teasing his lips with the tip of her tongue. He chuckled and deepened the kiss.

She needed him just as badly as he'd said he needed her. So she pulled at his clothes and hers, haphazardly tossing everything onto the floor except for her holster that she put on the table beside the bed. She was going to be careful with their lives even as she risked her heart.

"I wondered all day what you were wearing beneath your clothes," he said, tracing his fingertip along the top of her green lace bra. "Red yesterday. Green today. I should have known."

"Keeping it festive," she said, her breath catching when his finger dipped inside the bra and stroked her skin.

"The green matches your eyes," he said. "Your beautiful eyes..."

She laughed. "You're the one with the beautiful eyes. Such a light brown." Except now, with his pupils dilated with passion, they were nearly all black.

Then she couldn't see his eyes as he lowered his head and ran his lips along the curve of her neck and lower. He moved his hand beneath her back and unclasped her bra. Then his soft hair brushed over her skin, his lips across her nipple. She arched and moaned, wanting more, needing more...

She reached for him, closing her hand around the length of him, stroking up and down.

He groaned and the cords in his neck stood out as he struggled for control. She arched up, kissing his neck, beneath his bruised jaw.

"Heather..." His voice was gruff, his throat probably raw from the smoke. "Heather..."

Knowing what he'd been through, how he could have died, she pushed him onto his back and made love to him with her mouth. Or she tried.

But he wouldn't give in, wouldn't lie back and take the pleasure. His hands moved all over her, down her back, over her naked breasts and then between her legs.

The tension built inside her, then broke, and she cried his name. Then he lifted her and eased inside her. Last night she'd told him about her IUD and that he didn't need to wear a condom since it had been so long for both of them.

"I thought of this…" he murmured. "Of your heat and your wetness and how you moved on top of me…"

She chuckled. "Sure, make me do all the work…"

He chuckled and kissed her, sliding his tongue inside her mouth like he slid in and out of her body, arching his hips, driving deep. His hands cupped her breasts, flicking over her nipples.

That tension built again, so hard and fast that she thought she might break. And then she did…as she came again.

Then he bucked his hips and tensed as if in pain. Or maybe, like for her, the pleasure was so intense that it was almost painful. A groan tore from his throat as he shuddered with his release.

She leaned forward, settling onto his chest, which heaved as he panted for breath. Then he coughed. "I'll get your oxygen," she said, with a flash of guilt that he probably shouldn't have exerted himself like this.

"I'm fine," he said, his voice raspy. "Stay here. I just want to hold you."

That was what she wanted, also, to feel safe and happy and loved. But he couldn't love her yet, if ever; it was just the intensity of their situation. The danger. The rush of adrenaline. Once the killer was caught, they wouldn't have that anymore, and she probably wouldn't have him.

But if they didn't catch the killer and he kept trying to kill them over and over again, eventually he was going to succeed. Then Heather wouldn't have Trent or her own life anymore.

BRITTNEY SHOULD HAVE felt better. Her brother had whispered that he had forgiven her. Then he'd stepped back and shouted at her that he never would.

The situation he was in had to be very dangerous, not just for him, but for whoever was close to him. So were he and Detective Bolton really a thing? Or were they just carrying off some ruse to fool whoever was after Trent? She could ask, but she knew they wouldn't tell her anything. For her protection and maybe for theirs as well.

But she wasn't in danger. Was she?

She had had a strange feeling lately like someone was watching her. She had it now as she walked from her vehicle back into the television station. But since her big scoop, she was getting recognized more. People knew who she was and sometimes they approached her, sometimes they just stared. Like everyone had in the waiting room earlier when Trent had shouted at her.

He hadn't been any happier with any of them, though. Did he think one of his crew could be responsible for what was happening with him?

She'd stuck around the waiting room for a while, listening, talking to them, trying to find out what the hell was going on. But nobody had been willing to say any more than they already had, not even Tom.

Because they wanted to protect Trent or themselves?

Chapter Twenty

A faint buzzing noise pulled Trent from his sleep and Heather from his arms. But he reached out, wanting to hang on to her, wanting to keep her close and safe.

He opened his eyes to see her clearly in the glow of the screen of the cell phone she held. "Detective Bolton…" she murmured softly.

Her long hair was mussed and tangled around her face. Whatever makeup she'd worn, if she ever wore any, was gone, leaving her looking fresh-faced and young. But such intelligence and resolve shone in those green eyes.

"Yes, thank you for rushing the results for me," she said. "I think this is the fastest I've ever had DNA results returned." A smile curved her lips. "You have money bet on me, too?" She chuckled softly. "Any idea if the gun I turned in to evidence could have been the murder weapon?" She expelled a soft breath. "You need the slug and then could declare it a definite match? Okay, I'll go over the scene again. Thanks." The light went off as she ended the call, plunging her bedroom back into darkness.

He waited for her to settle back against him, her head on his chest like she'd been moments ago. But instead she pulled away from him, and cool air rushed over him as the covers lifted up. "Where are you going?" he asked.

"Back to your house," she said.

"My bed won't be as comfortable as yours," he said jokingly, but there was really nothing funny about her going there.

She chuckled, though. "I'm hoping to find something around your bed," she said.

"The bullet that killed that woman? It was Missy Dobbs, Barry Coats's married lover?"

"Yes, it was. The coroner confirmed the DNA from her toothbrush matched the DNA he managed to get off the body."

He expelled a ragged sigh of relief. At least now they knew who she was; she wasn't just a Jane Doe anymore.

"I'm sorry the call woke you up," she said. "You need your rest."

"So do you," he said. But he flipped on the lights and got out of bed, too. "I don't suppose you'll just send the techs back out on their own?"

"I'll have Craig meet me," she said.

"It's late," he pointed out. "And dangerous." Not that that would stop her.

"So was going into a burning building with people you can't trust," she said. "I trust my people."

"Your people worship you," he said. "And they all have money on you beating Detective Bernard's clearance rate."

She laughed. "That's a great incentive for them not to kill me."

"I really don't know for sure that it was someone I work with who attacked me in the fire," he said. "Anybody could have gotten a helmet like that online."

"True," she agreed. "But someone attacked you in that building. And I had Roy Dobbs in custody."

"So he's probably not the one who killed his wife and

threatened us." It would have been so much better if it had been. Then they would be safe and Trent would be able to trust his coworkers again.

Her teeth nibbled at her bottom lip that looked a little swollen already. "I don't know. He had some story about going to the shooting range on Black Friday."

"You don't think he did?" Trent asked.

"I don't know what to think anymore." She was staring at him now, her teeth sinking into her lip once more.

"Are you talking about Roy Dobbs or me?"

She smiled. "I don't know…except that if we have a chance to close at least one case, we need to do that as soon as possible. If you don't want to stay here comfy with Sammy, you can come along."

He'd expected more of a fight from her, but maybe she'd realized that it was probably safer, at least for him, if they stuck together.

HEATHER HAD WANTED to keep Trent close to keep him safe. But she hadn't thought about how he might feel to see his house reduced to blackened joists and ashes. The ashes blew around on the cold breeze, looking like snowflakes in the first light of dawn.

With so many new leads to follow and a suspect in custody to interrogate, she hadn't meant to fall asleep after they'd made love. But she'd been so exhausted and so damn comfortable in his arms. Maybe leaving Roy Dobbs in a cell while they confirmed if the body belonged to his wife was a good thing and would make it easier for Heather to crack him if he'd killed his wife.

She wouldn't know until she found the bullet that had passed through Missy Dobbs's skull. "We need to go inside and start looking," she said as she looked up and down the street, checking out the vehicles parked along it and looking for Craig's crime scene van. She was also trying to determine if someone else was out there other than the uniformed officer who had followed them there. The police cruiser was parked at the curb right behind Trent's truck, Officer Popma leaning against the side of it.

Morgan's and Howard's shifts had ended. But she wished one of them would have worked overtime to cover their protection duty. They'd proved themselves to her, and she trusted them. She didn't know this officer. He'd barely acknowledged her and had given Trent a dismissive glance, reminding her of that strange rivalry between police officers and firefighters.

She had enough rivalry within the detective squad. She didn't want anyone else as a rival, especially not Trent. It was bad enough that someone was after them. She wanted to beat that rival even more than she wanted to beat Bob Bernard.

"I don't want to wait for Craig much longer," she said. She only had so much time she could hold Roy before they had to arraign him. She could get him for threatening an officer, but he could argue that she'd asked for the gun and he'd just been handing it to her, albeit barrel first. And when the others had walked into the room, he hadn't realized he'd been pointing it when he'd turned toward them. Even a half-assed public defender would be able to get him bail, if not the charges thrown out. She needed more to hold him. Like a bullet from his gun, if he was the one who'd shot his wife.

Barry Coats could have done it. Maybe Missy had decided to end their fling, and he'd lost his temper over her rejection and killed her. Who the hell knew?

Without a confession or evidence, she had nothing to prove either man had killed her. Yet.

Trent switched on one of the big flashlights he'd had in his truck. She turned on the one he'd handed her. "You have to be careful in there," he said. "The fire burned hot. That and all the water used to put it out weakened the structure. You have to test every place you step before you put all your weight on it." He groaned. "Maybe I should just go in there alone."

"I'll be fine," she assured him. "And I have the evidence bags."

"You could hand me an evidence bag," he pointed out, his sexy mouth curved into a slight grin. He was so damn good-looking even with the bruises he'd gotten in the alley. He had new ones from the attack in the apartment building. But those were mostly on his legs, where the blow had knocked him to the ground.

He was lucky he'd gotten away from his attacker. But she wasn't sure he'd gotten far enough. She glanced around the area, feeling the chill again that had nothing to do with the early morning breeze scattering the ashes around.

"Craig's still not here," Trent remarked.

She hadn't been looking for Craig.

"I'll let you know when the tech gets here," the officer told her. Clearly, he had no intention of going inside the burned house with them. Officer Morgan and Officer Howard would have tried or at least offered to help search.

Maybe that was why she felt so uneasy right now; she wasn't entirely sure she could trust this guy to protect them. "Make sure you keep an eye out," she cautioned Officer Popma.

"I told you I'd let you know when the tech gets here," he said, his voice sharp with annoyance.

Now she was pissed. "I want you to keep an eye out for

whoever the hell has been trying to kill me and Mr. Miles," she sharply replied.

The officer shook his head as if disgusted. "I know how to do my job."

Heather bit her bottom lip like she had earlier with Trent. But this time she did it to hold back the insult she wanted to hurl at the cop. At least he was here; he was better than nobody at all. Maybe just his presence would keep their attacker from coming at them again. She ducked under the crime scene tape and started toward the house, Trent close behind her.

He sighed. "Now you know how I felt earlier today."

"Guess he has his money on Bernard," she replied.

Trent chuckled. "If that's the case, then we might be in trouble. He might decide to take you out himself since he has to know that's the only way to stop you from winning."

Pride and pleasure warmed her, chasing away that chill she kept feeling. While she appreciated his confidence in her, she had to remind him, "I thought you disapproved of my competition with him."

"That was my pride talking," he said.

She furrowed her forehead. "What? You think if I prove to one guy that I'm better than he is at his job that I prove it to all guys?"

"No," he said. "I wanted you to want to clear my case for *me*, not for a contest."

She sucked in a breath with sudden understanding. "Trent, of course that's why I want to clear it." Had she come across like she didn't even care about victims? "Do you think I'm not concerned about justice, just bragging rights?"

He shook his head. "I know you better now." And in his eyes that suddenly went hot, she could see the memories of just how well, how intimately, he knew her.

Flustered, she moved to start around him into the house.

But he caught her arm and held her back. "I know this house better than you do," he said. "So let me lead the way. If something can hold my weight, it'll be able to hold yours no problem."

Her body heated as she remembered how easily he'd held her earlier, when he'd carried her down the hall to her bedroom. Then after, all through the night, he'd held her against him, his heart beating strong and steady beneath her head.

She blinked, trying to clear those images, that feeling from her mind and her body. She had to focus, not just to find that bullet, but to keep them alive. She couldn't trust Officer Popma to be as vigilant as Officer Morgan and Officer Howard had been.

She drew in a deep breath, then coughed and sputtered over the smoke she'd inhaled from those swirling ashes. "How do you do this?" she muttered.

"Usually I have a helmet and oxygen on…"

When someone hadn't knocked it off.

She shone the flashlight beam through the holes in the walls that must have once been windows. She couldn't see anyone hiding inside, like that person had been hiding in the unit in the apartment building, lying in wait to attack Trent as if he'd known he was one of the firefighters who cleared the buildings, who made sure everyone got out safely.

He hadn't managed that last year. At the fire in the building owned by the same company that had lost another building just now…to another arson fire. Was Trent right? Were those fires related to what was happening to him? To all these attempts on his life and the fire that had taken his home? But he'd admitted that there had been other people he hadn't been able to save over the years, not just that person.

"Is this hard?" she asked. "To come back here?"

He moved his flashlight beam across the floor. "It's dangerous. Not hard."

"It doesn't bother you that you've lost your home? All your possessions?" she asked.

"Missy Dobbs lost her life," he said. "That bothers me a lot more than this."

She nodded. "I get that. Human life is far more important than material things, but…"

"But what?" he asked.

She shrugged. "I guess I'm a material girl," she admitted. "It would have bothered me to lose my house, my things…" Her cat. She'd been so scared when she'd thought that box of matches was a bomb.

"You care because it's all your dad's hard work," he said. "If it was just what this place had been to me, a place to sleep between jobs, then you wouldn't have cared either."

He was right. A house had been the same thing to her, until Dad had started personalizing the place. Making it so comfortable, making it her home. But the past few days it felt even more like home with Trent staying there with her.

But he wasn't staying forever. He might not even stay in Detroit. If he left his local firehouse, he might become a full-time hotshot. If there was such a thing…

"It's safe here," he said, "just stay to the left."

She hadn't even realized he'd stepped inside; she wasn't any better protection than Officer Popma.

She started after Trent, concentrating on stepping where he had. But even then the wood gave slightly beneath her, feeling spongy from the water it had absorbed. It was slippery, too, from the water having frozen in the cold, like her breath and the snowflakes that started to flit around with those wind-scattered ashes.

"The bedroom was here," he said. He grimaced in the faint light of dawn. "All the bedrooms were on this end."

"Which is probably why the other guys stopped coming here," she said. They hadn't wanted to be part of the affair. "Some of them really were just using the place as you intended, to sleep."

"Maybe Tom," he agreed, then sighed. "Or he was just coming here hoping to run into Brittney."

She glanced around, half expecting that maybe his sister had followed them. Brittney probably wasn't going to listen to her brother's warning to back off.

But when she glanced over her shoulder and through the gaping holes in the structure, she didn't even see the officer standing on the street where he'd been moments ago. "Hey!" she yelled. "Officer Popma! Officer Popma!"

Where the hell had their protection gone?

She started back across the floor. But she didn't pay enough attention to where Trent had told her it was safe to step. And the floor gave way beneath her just as shots rang out.

HE SQUEEZED THE trigger and fired. He had a gun now. And not just any gun that he could have scored easily enough on the street. He had a police officer's gun, the police officer knocked out cold on the other side of his car, where Detective Bolton couldn't see him.

He couldn't see her now either. Had he hit her?

It would be the ultimate irony if this police officer's gun killed Detective Bolton. She was all about law and order, with no understanding for people who got in bad situations, people who just wanted to do the best they could.

Since she thought that only bad people made mistakes, she would learn that good people made mistakes, too. Mistakes that could cost people their lives, and she was going to pay for her mistake with her life, just like Trent Miles was going to do. He was still visible, a tall, dark shadow in the ruins of what had once been his house.

And standing there, on the other side of the vehicle, concealed in the shadows like the prone officer, he fired again and watched Trent Miles fall just like the detective had.

Chapter Twenty-One

Panic gripped Trent. He didn't know if Heather had been shot or if the floor had given way beneath her. He rushed to where she'd disappeared and fell through, too, just as more bullets shot past him.

Wood grabbed at his clothes, tearing them. Or maybe a bullet had done that, and then his knees struck concrete and debris. And a curse slipped through his lips.

"Shh…" Heather whispered out of the darkness. Her flashlight was either broken or switched off.

"Are you okay?" he whispered back.

"Yes… You?"

"Yes…" But they wouldn't be if the shooter came into the house to make sure they were dead.

He fell silent, like she had, and strained his ears to listen. Finally, tires squealed, metal crunched, and then a voice called out. "Detective Bolton?"

"Craig!" she called back. "We're in here…" She flipped on the flashlight and shone her beam around the debris that had fallen through the floor like they had. The light reflected back from the short concrete walls.

"We're in the crawl space," Trent said.

"Is Officer Popma all right?" she called out again.

"He's down, but he's breathing!" Craig called back. "I

already called it in when the van almost hit me. Are you two really all right?"

Sirens wailed in the distance, growing louder as backup and hopefully an ambulance headed toward them. They would be safe now. The shooter wouldn't risk coming back.

"I'll help you up," Trent said, reaching for Heather, but she'd moved her flashlight beam back across the floor, and something metal glinted back at them.

"There it is!" she exclaimed. "The bullet…" She pulled out one of those bags and collected the evidence, no doubt to give to Craig.

Craig extended his hand through the hole in the floor, helping them up from the crawl space. Once they were safely out of the precarious structure, he also gave them a description of the shooter's vehicle. A commercial van with dark tinted windows. He hadn't been able to see the plate, though. And he hadn't gotten a look at the driver.

IT HAD BEEN a few days since they were at Trent's house and the van hadn't been found yet. Trent glanced in his rearview mirror to see if it was following them now as they headed up the highway toward Northern Lakes, just a few hours north of Detroit. They could have driven up the day of the Christmas party and made it in time, but they'd decided to drive up the night before.

Maybe a change of scenery would bring them some clarification. Trent tried for some now. "So the bullet that you found in the crawl space, that was the one that killed Missy Dobbs?"

Craig had confirmed it the day before, but Trent still didn't understand everything. Fires made much more sense to him than people.

"And it was from Roy's gun," she said.

"Did he confess?"

She'd spent some time over the past few days interrogating the man. She sighed. "He just cries."

"Do you think he did it?"

"He admitted he had his gun that day," she reminded him. "If he'd said that it had disappeared, then I might have believed that someone else had used it."

"But Roy was locked up when someone shot at us," he said. "And he wasn't the one who attacked me in the apartment complex."

She sighed again. "I know."

"So what does this mean, Detective?"

"That there could be more than one person after you," she suggested.

He groaned at the thought.

"Maybe Roy followed his wife to your house, killed her and set it on fire, but he didn't send you those cards. Maybe he didn't even know it was your house."

"So the two things are totally unrelated? Missy Dobbs didn't die because of me? Because her husband thought she was cheating with me?"

She groaned now. "I forgot to tell you that part of it."

"Part of what?"

"Barry used your name. According to Missy's sister, Melinda, she thought Missy was having an affair with Trent Miles. Apparently, Missy thought that, too."

Trent's temper flared that Barry had used him that way, betrayed him that way. Even if the man hadn't attacked him and Heather, Trent would never trust Barry Coats again. "Thanks to my coworker, Roy might have also thought his wife was having an affair with Trent Miles."

"But he couldn't have gone after you in that apartment fire or that morning at your house."

"So someone else has it out for me?" He always tried to do the right thing, like his dad had, like Manny, and his hotshot team. At least most of his hotshot team…

"I checked out that company this week, the one that owned both those apartment complexes," she said. "There were complaints against them. Even a lawsuit filed over that fire at the first complex. Wrongful death."

Trent grimaced. "The place was a mess. A definite fire hazard and health hazard. I hope they lost that lawsuit."

"They won," she said. "They used the fire department as the reason the woman died, that they should have gotten her out in time."

He groaned, his stomach churning with the guilt he always felt over that. "She'd already been overcome with smoke and had collapsed beside her bed. With the ceiling tiles that had fallen on her, I missed her the first time. When neighbors asked about her, I went back in, but I was too late. If only I'd found her earlier…"

Heather reached across the console and squeezed his arm. "Don't torture yourself this way, Trent. You did what you could, what anyone else on your team would have done."

He released a shaky sigh. "I don't know about that."

"Your team nearly missed you in that apartment fire," she reminded him. "But that might not have been an accident."

"My hotshot team would have found her. They're really good firefighters," he said. "The best I've ever worked with, all of them."

"You really love them," she said.

"Yeah…"

She squeezed his arm again. "What is it? What's going on with them?"

"I wish I knew," he said. "Someone has been messing

with some of the equipment. Some hotshots have gotten hurt and it could have been worse. Way worse."

"I know one guy died—"

"That was a murder. His wife did it."

"Like Roy probably killed his wife," she said.

"There were other things that other people were responsible for. Then there are incidents for which everyone denied responsibility," he said.

"Doesn't mean they didn't do it," she said. "Just like Roy Dobbs. He might be saying he didn't do it, but that doesn't mean he's telling the truth."

"But you don't know," he said.

"I think he's lying, but if I'm wrong and he is telling the truth, then Barry is probably the one responsible for her death and the attempts on our lives," she said.

"Why?"

"He stole your identity," she said. "There's something not right with the guy."

"If Missy's husband found out she had a lover, he wanted the guy to think it was me, not him," he pointed out.

"Yeah, and there's that…"

"Barry will have a reason to come after me now," Trent said. "Manny told me that he fired him."

"He's trying to get you to come back," she said. "Will you? Or will you become a full-time hotshot?"

He glanced across at her, wondering about her tone and the sudden tightness of her face. She seemed worried about his answer. As if she didn't want him to leave Detroit…

She looked away from him, gazing out the window at the pine trees on either side of the road. "It is pretty…"

Even though they were just a few hours farther north, it had snowed more up here, the pine boughs covered and glittering with white, the road coated with it. His truck was four-wheel drive, so the tires gripped, despite the snow. But he also drove slower, making sure to keep the truck under control.

He noticed the vehicle behind them was coming up fast, too fast for conditions. When it slammed into his back bumper, he realized it was a commercial van, like the one that Craig had seen at his house, the one the shooter had driven away in after stealing Officer Popma's gun.

Their attacker had followed them from Detroit all the way to Northern Lakes. They were just outside the village limits now, coming up on a sharp curve around one of the many inland lakes in the area.

But the van struck them again, on the curve, and the truck spun out of control, off the road, toward the snow-covered surface of the lake that couldn't be fully frozen yet, not enough to hold the weight of the truck. They were going to crash through it into the icy water.

THE IMPACT KNOCKED the breath from Heather's lungs, the seat belt squeezing her chest, rubbing against her throat, nearly strangling her. She had to fight against it, had to fight to breathe.

What the hell had happened? Where were they?

She couldn't see anything. Even the dashboard lights had gone dark. She couldn't see Trent. But she thrashed her arms out across the console, trying to feel him.

She only felt the sudden jolt of icy water. And she realized what had happened: the truck had gone into a lake, had gone through the ice…

And if she didn't find a way to get the seat belt loose, she would go down as deep as the lake was. And even if she could get out, she would freeze before she could swim to the surface.

And Trent…

Where the hell was Trent?

Would he die with her? Or was he already dead from the crash?

"THEY SHOULD HAVE been here by now," Ethan said. He sat in the corner booth in the Filling Station bar, studying the door on the other side of the scarred wood floor with peanut shells strewn across its surface. Trent should have come through that door before now. "Where the hell is he?"

"You don't know something happened," Rory VanDam said, but he didn't sound all that convinced himself. He was the one sitting closest to Ethan in the booth that overflowed with hotshots and their significant others.

Tammy sat on the other end of the booth, next to her friends, the dark-haired twins Serena and Courtney Beaumont. But she caught his gaze across the table and offered him a reassuring smile. Despite her efforts to ease his concerns about his best friend, Ethan couldn't stop worrying.

"I told you what his sister said," Ethan reminded Rory. While he was as bonded to the man as a brother, he and Rory looked different. Ethan had dark hair and a beard, that was neatly trimmed now, while Rory had a blond buzz cut and a cleanly shaven face.

Rory grimaced at the mention of the reporter. She'd exposed Ethan's secret about the plane crash that had ended his life as Jonathan Canterbury IV and rebirthed him as Ethan Sommerly. But he wasn't the only one who'd been in that crash and was keeping a secret about it.

"You can't trust that reporter," Rory said.

She wasn't the only one they couldn't trust, and they weren't the only ones with secrets. Someone else was keeping a secret, harboring an agenda or a grudge that had compelled him or her to sabotage their equipment, to cause those accidents that could have been so much worse, that could have taken lives, like Dirk Brown's wife had taken his.

"She's probably up to something, trying to get you to talk to her," Rory said with suspicion.

"Braden talked to Trent's captain at the firehouse in Detroit," Ethan said. "Even more stuff happened than Brittney told me." He didn't know if she knew; she hadn't called him again after that first call.

And Trent had only sent him text messages. Those stupid thumbs-up emoji things and then three hours ago: On our way now.

"They should have been here by now," he insisted.

"Maybe his girlfriend made him stop at the outlet mall or something," Carl Kozak, sitting on the other side of Ethan, suggested. He was the oldest of the hotshots. Maybe that was why he shaved his head, to hide his gray hair. But he was probably in as good or better shape than a lot of them. Except Trent.

A former Marine like their team member and local paramedic, Owen James, and like his dad, Trent was fit and muscular. He was strong. Whoever was trying to kill him wasn't going to find it an easy job.

The door opened, and Ethan expelled a breath of relief. But it wasn't Trent who walked in. It was Braden, and he was running. "A truck went in Half Moon Lake!" he shouted.

And Ethan knew why Trent hadn't made it to the bar yet. It was his truck that had gone through the ice, his truck sinking deep in the icy water.

He jumped up and ran out with his crew, but no matter how fast they got to the lake, it was probably going to be too late. Trent would have already frozen to death.

Chapter Twenty-Two

"You forget how to drive on snow like all the other people from downstate?" Ethan asked, jabbing his elbow into Trent's side as he joined him near the pool table in the back room of the Filling Station. The bar had closed for their Christmas party.

In response to the physical and verbal jab, Trent glared at his friend. "Downstate?" He snorted. "Like you're from Northern Lakes."

"People say *downstate* in other states, too," Ethan said. And they probably did where he was really from, out East. "And at least I know how to drive on snow."

"I do, too," Trent said. "As long as nobody's trying to drive me off the road."

"Really?" Trick McRooney asked. "When we showed up, we didn't see any sign of another vehicle, just your truck blowing bubbles as it sank to the bottom." The red-haired firefighter had joined their team when Dirk died, and everybody had resented him for taking the place of their dead friend and because they'd figured he only got the job because he was the superintendent's brother-in-law.

Braden hadn't hired him because he was his brother-in-law but so that Trick could give him an unbiased opinion on the team and figure out who the saboteur was. But

Trick had fallen hard for Hank, so he was no longer unbiased or resented.

Trent looked at him now. "Yeah, you guys took your sweet time showing up at the scene. Had to finish your beers first?" he teased.

"Had to finish a game of pool," Owen James said. "You know how long Kozak takes to sink the eight ball. He's gotta study every angle."

"Damn good thing I got myself and Heather out before the truck went under…" He would never forget those long moments he'd had to hack through her seat belt with his knife, that he'd had to break her window to get them both out. As it was, they probably would have frozen to death if they hadn't gone in the shallow side of the lake and managed to get onto some ice that had held their weight.

But their clothes had been so wet, freezing to their bodies when Owen had shown up in his paramedic rig along with the rest of the crew in a fire truck. They'd spent the night in the hospital, getting warmed up, making sure they didn't succumb to frostbite. His face was chafed, and hers, too.

She stood across the room talking to Braden's wife, Sam McRooney-Zimmer. Heather was a lot like Sam, who was an arson investigator. They were both beautiful women dominating a male-dominated field.

Heather's face looked only flushed and not frozen like his still felt. Although when she met his gaze across the room, heat rushed through him again. He didn't even realize he'd crossed the peanut-strewn floor of the Filling Station until he suddenly stood beside her. He'd just been drawn across the room toward her, and his arm was around her waist, pulling her close against him.

Ethan, Owen and Trick had followed him. "So you've just gone undercover as his girlfriend, right, just to protect his weak ass," Ethan teased. "You couldn't actually be interested in him."

"Ignore him," Trent said of his best friend. "He's just jealous. When Braden got rid of his rule against hotshots dating, Ethan thought I was going to ask him out. It was a whole awkward thing…"

Heather laughed so hard tears sparkled in her eyes. She got them. Got their sometimes very politically incorrect camaraderie. And for some reason, he was so relieved, since he wanted her to like his friends. His real friends.

He wanted his relationship with Heather to be real and not just what Ethan had correctly joked about her being, his undercover girlfriend.

"Look at him, though," Trick said. "He's such a homely guy. No woman could really want to go out with him."

Hank walked up and wrapped her arm around Trick's broad shoulders. "Yup, he's about as ugly as you are," she told her fiancé. A diamond on her ring finger reflected the twinkling Christmas lights Charlie Tillerman had strung around the bar he owned.

"Hey, I'm way better looking," Trick insisted. "I don't have those bruises all over my face."

"Did you have to beat him up to get him to behave?" Hank asked Heather.

Heather shook her head. "No, Santa is the one who kicked his ass. Guess he was on the naughty list."

Everybody laughed, accepting her easily into their circle. She fit with her wicked sense of humor and sarcasm and wit.

"That makes sense," Ethan said. "Is that why you burned your house down, Trent? So Santa wouldn't come down your fireplace to finish the job?"

"I think he did it so he could move into my place," Heather said.

They all knew he hadn't burned down his place and that someone had run them off the road. And everyone in town was on the lookout for that commercial van with the dark windows. But this was the way they handled stress and fear, mercilessly teasing each other.

Heather had instinctively understood that, just as she understood his bond with these people. She leaned against his side, her arm winding around his waist.

"Now, that makes sense," Ethan said.

"Yeah, smarter than blowing up your beard or your truck," Trent teased. Neither of those explosions had been Ethan's fault or accidents. His brother-in-law had been trying to eliminate the heir to the Canterbury fortune.

Tammy walked up to join Ethan, who wound both arms around her. "I don't know," he said. "If I hadn't blown off that beard, I wouldn't have had a reason to come to this one's salon."

"You looked like a Sasquatch before you burned off your beard and hair," Trent said. "That was a reason to go to her salon."

"And he's pretty much never left," Tammy said. "So be careful, Heather. Trent might never leave either." She winked.

Heather laughed, but it sounded a little uneasy now. Maybe she was worried about him never leaving.

Tammy wasn't worried about Ethan staying. She snuggled into him just like he snuggled against her. Ethan was happier than Trent could ever remember seeing him. Too bad all the hotshots weren't. Rory was hiding in the shadows of the bar for some reason. And Michaela kept ducking in and out of the bathroom as if she was sick or hiding from someone. And Trent...

He couldn't get over how close he'd come to dying. Again. How close he'd come to losing Heather. Again.

He tightened his arm around her. "You guys all need to stop trying to scare her off," he said.

"If you driving her into the lake hasn't scared her off, I don't think anything will," Owen said with a chuckle.

If only that were true...

She had been scared in the truck, panicking as she'd fought the seat belt. And when they'd gotten onto the ice, she'd clung to him for more than warmth.

He let out a shaky breath as he remembered it all. And his friends moved closer. "Stay up here," Ethan said. "We've got your back. We'll make sure nobody kicks your ass but us."

Now tears stung Trent's eyes, but he blinked furiously. "It would take all of you together to take me," he joked back.

"Or just Santa Claus," Owen quipped.

Heather laughed. But she eased away from him.

With everyone else crowding around, he couldn't snake her back against his side. Then suddenly she was just gone, disappearing into the crowd in the bar. No matter where he looked, he didn't see her.

Where the hell had she gone?

TRENT SHOULD STAY here in Northern Lakes with his hotshot team. As much as they teased him, they loved him even more. As Ethan Sommerly or Jonathan Canterbury had said, they all had his back. They would keep him safer than she had.

He was the one who'd saved her the night before, getting her out of that truck and out of the icy water. She would have died for certain if he hadn't been there. If he hadn't cut her loose and stopped her from sinking to the bottom of the lake, where she would have drowned and froze.

She shivered now as she stepped out of the bar and the cold air and snow hit her in the face. She just needed a minute. A minute to catch her breath. A minute to stop acting like she and Trent were more than they were.

That they were in love like so many of those other couples in the room. She was losing him, just as she'd nearly lost her life in that lake.

She was losing him because how could he go back to the firehouse where he couldn't trust the rest of the crew to get him out of a burning apartment? But these guys and women...

Every one of them would have jumped into that freezing lake for him, would have given up their lives to save his. Or died with him...

That was a team. No. That was a family.

An even closer family than his biological one, than her biological one. He would be safer here with them than he would be in Detroit.

But the killer was here. Even though everyone had been looking for that van and hadn't found it, she didn't believe like they did that he'd left town. That he'd run them off the road and driven away, back to Detroit.

He was here. Somewhere...

Then she shivered, and not just from the cold or the falling snowflakes. She shivered because she sensed that stare on her, that stare she'd felt so often at her house and at Trent's that early morning.

Then she saw him as he stepped out of the shadows and pointed a gun at her, the gun he'd taken off Officer Popma. She narrowed her eyes, studying his face more than that gun pointed at her. He was so big, tall and muscular. But with his rosy cheeks and freckled face and red hair, he looked like a kid. A kid she'd arrested for robbing a gas station. Over a year ago...

"Were you after me this whole time?" she asked. Had this had nothing to do with Trent at all?

Had she put Trent in more danger when she'd brought him home with her than if she'd just let him go to a hotel? She'd screwed up so damn badly.

But she could make it up to Trent right now, if she could get the kid away from the bar, away from Trent and his friends. She didn't want them to hear the gunshot and rush out and get shot as well.

She didn't want anyone else getting hurt because of her, but most especially not Trent.

BILLY HADN'T BOTHERED with a disguise this time. He didn't care if she saw him now. He didn't care if anyone saw him. This was the day. The year anniversary of when he'd lost his grandmother. The only person who'd ever loved him.

He couldn't let them live a year longer than she had. He couldn't let them live a minute longer.

"We need to get out of here before someone sees you, Billy," she said.

She had recognized him, just like he'd feared she would. But he'd also had his doubts that she would even remember him. How the hell many people had she arrested over the years, over the year since she'd arrested him?

He wasn't the only one in juvie who'd wanted to get revenge on her, who'd wanted to kill her. He really wanted to kill her. But not just her...

"You were supposed to die so many times," he murmured with frustration. When the truck had gone into the lake, he'd been so sure that it was over. That they were dead. He'd driven off but not far.

They'd survived too many times for him to trust that they were really dead this time. So he'd hung around the hospital and watched, and sure enough, an ambulance had raced up to the ER, lights flashing. And they'd been in the back. They'd even walked themselves into the ER.

They'd survived again.

"Come on, Billy," she said. "Where's your van? Take me wherever you want to take me, wherever you want to go to kill me."

He snorted. "Like you're going to go without a fight."

"I will," she promised. "You don't have to hurt anyone else like you hurt that officer and Trent. You don't have to hurt anyone else. Just me."

Now he laughed. "You think this is just about you? God, you're full of yourself, Detective Bolton. This isn't just about you. I wanted to kill Trent Miles even more than I wanted to kill you. He was the one who didn't get her out. Who let her die. I almost forgot about you until I saw you with him on the news, standing outside his burning house."

"Did you set his house on fire and kill that woman?" she asked.

He snorted. "I wouldn't have sent his card to the firehouse if I knew where he lived. Hell, if I knew where he lived, he would have been dead a long time ago." But he couldn't be sure about that. Was it Bolton who'd kept Miles alive or just plain dumb luck?

Dumb luck might have been what had had him watching the news that night. He never watched the damn news.

"When I saw you with him, it all made so much sense. If you hadn't put me in juvie, I would have been there that night. I would have done what he was too stupid to do. I would have saved my grandma. I wouldn't have let her die like Trent Miles did. Some hero he is."

"What?" she asked, as if she didn't know. "Your grandma died?"

Tears rushed to his eyes, but he blinked them away and focused on her, on pointing that gun directly at her heart. "And now you're both going to die, just like Grandma did."

This time he could not fail. He had to do this for her. She was the only one who'd ever been there for him, who had ever cared about him. And he had to repay her for her love with his loyalty and with Detective Bolton's and Trent Miles's lives.

Chapter Twenty-Three

Charlie had let him know Heather had stepped outside. "She probably just needs some air," he'd said. "You guys can be a lot." But he hadn't looked at the guys then. He'd glanced across the bar to where Michaela leaned against the wall outside the restroom.

Trent felt a flicker of concern for Michaela. Maybe she was sick. But he had a sick feeling of his own, a sick feeling that something was wrong with Heather. So he hadn't rushed out the door after her. Instead, he'd just pushed it open a little, and he'd heard the voices.

He'd heard every word Billy and Heather said.

And he'd realized what she was trying to do. She was trying to protect him at the risk of her own life. No. At the certainty of her death. Billy was determined to kill her. But he was even more determined to kill him. Probably so determined that he might charge into the bar with the gun drawn.

And innocent people, his friends, might get hurt as well. Maybe if he could distract Billy, Heather could get her gun…if she was even wearing it beneath her sweater.

"We need to get Trent Miles out here now," Billy said, his voice getting louder as if he was moving closer to the door.

"You can't go in there," she said. "Someone will try to stop you."

"Then I'll shoot them, too."

Just like Trent had feared. He pushed the door fully open and stepped out, his hands raised above his head. "I'm here, Billy," he said.

While Billy whirled toward him, he expected Heather to pull her gun. But instead she moved closer to them, stepping between them like she was his damn bodyguard. "Billy, your grandma wouldn't want you to do this," she said.

Billy glared at her, waving his gun at her. "Don't you dare talk about my grandma! You didn't know her!"

"The hell I didn't," she shot back at him, her voice sharp. "I didn't know she died." Her voice cracked a little. "But I knew her. Your grandma was fierce. I talked to her a lot over your arrest for robbing that gas station."

"She probably yelled at you," Billy said. "She always protected me."

Heather shook her head. "She couldn't anymore. She told me that you got into a bad crowd and you stopped listening to her. She didn't know what to do. And when I offered to reduce the charges, she told me she would kick my ass if I did that. That I was her last chance to get you on the straight and narrow again. She wanted you to go to jail, Billy."

"You liar!" he shouted. "You liar!"

"You didn't ignore her? Stay out past your curfew? Stop going to school?"

He cursed now, and tears started to roll down his face.

"She wanted her sweet boy back, she told me," Heather said. "She wanted her Billy Boy back, and so she asked me to put you in juvie so that you would never commit another crime. So that you'd get your life back."

"And she died…"

Heather started crying now, tears trailing down her face. "I'm sorry. I didn't know that was her. The lawsuit you filed used different names for both of you than what was in my case files."

"Grandma always called herself by her maiden name, but she was legally still married to my grandpa, who took off a while ago. And sometimes I used her name and sometimes I used that married one," Billy explained.

That must have been why Heather hadn't made the connection when she'd looked up that prior apartment building fire.

"She was such a beautiful person," Heather said. "I'm so sorry for your loss."

"That was his fault!" Billy shouted, and he swung the gun toward Trent now. "He didn't get her out. He failed her!"

"No, Billy, that was an accident. He couldn't see her because of all the trash in that building—"

"But the owner's lawyer said it was his fault."

"The owner didn't want to pay you," she said. "He didn't want to lose any money. That's why he didn't take care of those buildings."

"I took care of that one for him," Billy said. "I burned it down, and Miles was supposed to burn up in it, just like he let Grandma burn."

Trent felt like crying now. "I am so sorry, Billy. I didn't see her. I didn't know she was in there, and when I went back and found her…" His voice trembled as tears threatened. "She was already gone."

"How come she didn't get another chance, like you both do?" he asked, his voice cracking. "Why won't either of you die?"

"Because of your grandma," Heather said. "Because she wanted you to be her good Billy Boy again. She didn't want you to be a thief, and she certainly wouldn't want you to be a killer, Billy."

A sob broke out of the kid, and his big body began to shake. "I just want her with me again."

"Killing us won't bring her back," Heather said. Then she actually laughed. "Although, from what I remember of her, she probably would come back to kick your ass for trying to hurt us, for trying to hurt anyone."

Billy's wide shoulders shook, but he wasn't crying now. He laughed with Heather. "She would. She really would kick my ass." Then the sobs overtook him again. "I'm so sorry. I screwed up. I screwed up so bad."

"No," Heather said as she took the gun easily from the kid's grasp. Then she closed her arms around him, holding him while he cried. "We'll fix this, Billy. You didn't kill anyone. We'll figure this out. We'll get you some help, like Grandma did."

"She was the only one who helped me."

"Not anymore," Heather said. "Not anymore…"

Standing there, watching her hug and console and reassure the kid who'd tried again and again to kill them, Trent lost something, too. He lost his heart. To Heather…

TRENT HADN'T RETURNED with her and Billy to Detroit. He'd stayed up in Northern Lakes with his hotshot team. He was probably furious with her, furious with the way she intended to deal with Billy.

She didn't want to put him in prison. Or even back in juvie, if she could have. He was old enough to be tried as an adult. She didn't want him prosecuted, though. She intended to get him real help, psychological help. Because his grandma had been right. He was capable of being her Billy Boy again. If only Heather hadn't gotten so damn caught up in her competition with Bernard, she would have followed up with him after his release, would have remembered his damn name and alias. Maybe she would have checked up on his grandma, too. This was her fault that Billy had spiraled, more so than it had ever been Trent's.

Trent's friends and his sister probably realized that they had been right, that she and he weren't really involved. Since the case was closed, they didn't even have to pretend they were.

So he hadn't come back. Over a week had passed since she'd seen him last. She'd spent most of that in the office, finishing up her paperwork, clearing those cases. Missy's murder. The arson at Trent's. She'd finally gotten Roy to confess to both. And Billy...

Billy had done so many things. He'd attacked them in the alley. While hanging around the firehouse, he'd stolen some gear and had attacked Trent in the apartment fire. He'd shot at them at Trent's house and struck their truck by the lake. He'd admitted to all of them on the condition that he be treated at a psychological facility. So Heather had cleared a lot of cases.

And everybody who'd bet on her had won a lot of money. Even Bob Bernard. He'd grinned and shaken her hand when he'd congratulated her. "My money was always on you, Bolton. You are a damn good detective. Better than I ever was."

She had his respect. Apparently she'd had it all along. But the victory wasn't as sweet as she'd thought it would be. Hopefully the cookies that Bob and his grandson had baked for her would be sweet.

She turned her vehicle onto her street, lifting her foot from the accelerator, dreading going home to that empty house again. Well, empty but for Sammy. But he was snubbing her, sleeping in the guest room instead of with her.

She hated sleeping alone now.

But it wasn't Sammy she missed in her bed. It was Trent. Hell, she just missed Trent everywhere. And she dreaded going to that dark, quiet house. Maybe she should have taken up some of the people on their offers to buy her drinks to celebrate her victory. But she hadn't felt much like celebrating.

She just wanted to go home, but she wasn't sure she was pulling into the right driveway, because the house wasn't dark. The front window was aglow with multicolored, twinkling lights. Her sisters must have gotten the new code out of Dad and decorated her damn tree.

She'd kind of liked it standing there, bare and stark and dark, looking as empty and lonely as she'd felt. It didn't look like that anymore. It looked bright and happy.

She was going to take all the codes out now so that not even Dad could get in. But at the moment, she just wanted to get in and tear down that tree. Maybe she'd torch it in the backyard. Maybe she would start such a big fire that the hotshot crew would get called in...

Sighing at her own drama, she climbed the stairs to the kitchen, dropped the tin of Christmas cookies on the counter and rushed into the living room. But when she started toward the tree, she hit something and fell, sprawling onto a long, hard body.

"You can't let this tree dry out," Trent admonished her as he scooted out from under it with an empty pitcher.

"I was just thinking about burning it up," she said, her heart pounding fast and hard at his presence.

"Why?" he asked, staring up at it. "Don't you like how I decorated it?"

"You decorated it?"

"Yeah. Think your sisters will approve?"

"I don't give a damn what my sisters think," she said. But

she could imagine, and she had to laugh and admit, "They won't think you're any Martha Stewart either."

"Only Martha Stewart is," he said.

"True."

"So did you win your bet?" he asked.

"I didn't place a bet," she admitted. "But Bob Bernard did."

"How'd he feel losing his money?"

"He didn't," she said.

"But with all the cases you closed…"

She smiled. "He bet on me."

"Wow…"

"Yeah." She'd been so wrong about him. Who else had she been wrong about? Trent? Was he not mad at her for how she'd dealt with Billy?

"So why were you going to burn up the tree?" he asked.

"To get a certain hotshot to come home," she admitted.

"Home?" he asked, his eyes twinkling like the lights on the tree. He leaned closer and brushed his mouth across hers.

"Yes," she said. "You can stay here, if you're going to stay in Detroit."

"I am," he said. "For now…"

"Just for the holidays?" she asked. Of course, he would probably want to spend those with his sister, now that he knew he wouldn't be putting her in danger anymore. But if he stayed with Heather, at least she would have a hotshot hero for the holidays.

"Until I get called up for a wildfire or a hotshot meeting, or you get sick of me," he said. "How long can you handle me staying with you, Heather?"

She wrapped her arms around his neck and leaned closer, moving her lips over his before she pulled back and asked, "How about forever?"

He grinned. "Sounds good to me."

"You look good to me," she said. "Like the perfect present under my Christmas tree." And just like all her presents, Heather couldn't wait until Christmas to unwrap him. She undressed him as he undressed her, and they made love under that tree.

A long while later, boneless with pleasure, panting for breath, they lay staring up at the tree. "Merry Christmas to me," she murmured with satisfaction.

"Merry Christmas to me," Trent repeated, and he leaned over to kiss her again. "This is real, right? No more pretend?"

"Who was pretending?" she asked with a smile. "But if you wanted this to be real, where have you been?" Her smile slid away. "I thought you were mad at me for not being harder on Billy."

"That was the minute I knew without a doubt that I love you and it wasn't just because you kept saving my ass."

"You kept saving mine, too," she said. "You are definitely my hotshot hero. I could have died in that lake."

He shuddered against her. "I came too close to losing you too many times."

"So why did you stay away?" She tensed. "Did something happen in Northern Lakes? More sabotage?"

He shrugged. "I don't know. Maybe it was an accident."

"I can investigate—"

He kissed her. "Still working on that clearance rate?"

"Still working on keeping you safe, and I don't want anything to happen to your friends either," she said.

"That's another reason I love you," he said. "You fit right in with my family."

"My family will love you, too," she assured him.

"What about you?"

She realized she hadn't said the words yet. "I love you, Trent Miles. I wouldn't want you here forever if I didn't know that I will love you forever. And, despite our dangerous jobs, we will have forever."

"We will," he agreed. "We'll also make time for each other. Make each other a priority."

"Yes…" Nobody else was slipping through the cracks of her busy life like she'd let Billy and his grandmother slip. She would make certain of that.

"Merry Christmas to both of us," he said and kissed her again.

Then something suddenly rustled in the branches of the pine and the decorated tree tipped forward, falling onto them. Sammy jumped and scrambled away, claws scratching the hardwood in his haste to escape the mess he'd made.

"You okay?" Trent asked from beneath the branches and lights and bulbs that covered them. "Are you hurt? Cut anywhere?"

"No. He's why I buy shatterproof decorations. But we're going to have some fun getting off the pine sap."

"Yes, we are going to have some fun."

She knew they would, no matter what life threw at them. They would face it together with a sense of humor and a forever love.

* * * * *

COMING SOON!

We really hope you enjoyed reading this book.
If you're looking for more romance
be sure to head to the shops when
new books are available on

Thursday 7th
December

To see which titles are coming soon, please visit
millsandboon.co.uk/nextmonth

MILLS & BOON